BOOK ONE IN THE GOI

THE GODS OF MEN

BARBARA KLOSS

The Gods of Men

by Barbara Kloss

Edited by Laura Josephsen

Cover Design by Damonza

www.barbarakloss.com

To Jenny, Briana, and Carly, for without whom this would've been a very different (and awful) story.

the Five Provinces

THE WILDS
Tül Bahn
Skanden
Craven
Riverwood
White Rock
HIDDENSEA
THE CROSSING
THE FINGERS
THE RIM
DAVROS
Stovichshold
CORINTH
Sanvik
Skyhold
BREVERA
GRAY'S TEETH
BLACKWOOD
Rodinshold
ISTRAA
BARAGA MOUNTAINS
Trier
SOLVELOR
THE OTHERLANDS
N

PROLOGUE

Imari stood upon the palace rooftop, the tip of her toes peeking over the stone ledge. Hot desert wind ripped through her thin clothing, and her loose pants swelled like two small sails. She blinked, and her teeth ground on grit. There'd been a good bit of sand with that gust.

She'd always loved the view from this side of the desert palace. A huge orange sun floated over the Baraga Mountains like a great balloon, the sky around it the colors of Ricón's fires. Her oldest brother called it magic fire, but Imari knew that magic didn't exist within the Five Provinces. Their ancestors had seen to that. Besides, she'd seen the powder he'd put in the flames.

A heavy blanket of bruised and swollen clouds marked the endless desert lands due south: Ziyan, her people called it, though the rest of the Five Provinces called it the Forgotten Wastes. There, the sky remained forever volatile and angry. Even though Ziyan's edge lay a few days' ride from the palace, she'd never been allowed anywhere near.

Imari had heard the stories of wanderers who'd braved the endless sea of sand, searching for treasures that'd been left behind by a forgotten people. Those wanderers never returned.

Vana, her kunari, said the wanderers found refuge in an oasis deep within the sands and simply did not want to return. Ricón said the sands ate them alive. Imari believed Ricón. Ricón was the only one who didn't treat her like she was nine years old. Which she was.

"Surina Imari…?"

It was Vana, which meant it was time to perform.

"Sano kei," Imari said, climbing down from the rooftop.

Vana stepped around the potted palm just as Imari jumped from the parapet and landed upon the hot, dusty tiles below.

Vana frowned, dangling Imari's sandals like two pieces of incriminating evidence. "Surina, you know how Sar Branón feels about your climbing all over the palace like a chimp."

Imari smiled. "Yes, that's why I always make sure to do it when he's not watching."

Vana rolled her dark eyes to the setting sun and motioned for Imari to come to her. Imari crossed the veranda, but Vana grabbed her arm as she passed. Vana tried desperately to tame Imari's loose braid, then licked her thumb and rubbed at a spot on Imari's jaw. With a helpless sigh, Vana handed over the sandals and shoved Imari at the open archway.

Imari slipped her sandals onto her feet, then stepped into the great dining hall where her papa's guests were gathered. Her papa, the sar of Istraa, entertained his rois often, but tonight marked an important dinner. The divide between the Five Provinces' two most powerful territories—Corinth and Brevera—grew increasingly hostile, as in the days of the rebellion from her papa's youth, and her papa feared for their border. This dinner was his plea to the rois of Istraa's various districts, asking for their assistance in fortifying the northern boundary, which separated Istraa from the other Provinces.

Of course, her papa hadn't told her this. It'd been Ricón. He really was the only one who ever told her anything. And if he hadn't told her this news, she wouldn't have agreed to perform tonight.

It wasn't that she didn't like performing—she did. But the past few days, playing made her feel strange. Her fingers would tingle, and it didn't stop there. The tingling would travel down her arms and into her chest, where it would build and build and push against her lungs until she couldn't breathe. She thought it some sort of illness, and she would've said as much to her papa had she not known the importance of this dinner.

Perhaps Ricón shouldn't always tell her everything.

Plates of seasonal fruits and spiced tea had been set out—a final course to enjoy while Imari performed. Good, then perhaps no one would notice if she faltered.

Anja, the sura of Trier and her papa's wife, waited beside the stool set at the front of the room, tapping her long finger impatiently upon the seat. Her heavily painted eyes narrowed as they raked over Imari, and then darted accusatively to Vana. Imari didn't look to see Vana's expression, but she imagined it well enough.

Anja handed Imari the little bone flute and leaned in close, as if to bestow an encouraging kiss. "I hope you take your playing this evening more seriously than you take your appearance," she whispered instead.

Imari glanced down and her cheeks warmed with embarrassment. She wanted Anja to like her. She really did. It wasn't that Anja was mean to her. Anja had just never understood Imari. On top of that, Imari was a constant reminder to Sura Anja of her papa's unfaithfulness. It was as if Anja couldn't look upon Imari without seeing the vile temptress herself. Whoever she was. Imari didn't know. No one spoke of it. Not even Ricón.

Anja's gaze slid over her once more, as if to say "the *sieta* are punishing me for some past ill," before returning to the table.

Vana stood near one of the large columns, providing no solace.

Imari climbed on the stool and let both feet rest upon the support. She couldn't reach the travertine floor, anyway. She spotted her brother Kai first, sitting between two rois from the western ridge. Kai's onyx hair was tied back in a long ponytail that looked neater and tighter than anything Imari had ever managed, and he wore a bronze sash over his white tunic, marking him as a sur of Trier. He was much too deep in conversation with the two rois to catch her eye. There were many other prominent men and women—most she recognized, some she did not—and then she spotted Ricón, sitting beside their papa.

Ricón kept his black hair long and free but neatly combed. Like Kai, he wore the traditional bronze sash over his tunic, though his bore an embroidered black stripe at the shoulder, marking him as the oldest sur and Trier's heir. He spoke to an elderly gentleman with braided black and silver hair, but, feeling Imari's attention, he glanced up and met her gaze. His lips turned in a slow grin, which spread wider and wider as he took in her appearance.

Her papa glanced over at her then, with joy at first. She saw the moment her appearance registered, and rather than watch his disappointment flourish, she turned her attention back to her flute. She angled her legs, lifted the instrument to her lips, took a deep breath, closed her eyes, and played.

This particular piece wasn't her choice, but her papa had requested it. It was the ballad of Istraa, telling the story of the war with Ziyan, formerly known as Sol Velor. Imari didn't know all the details of that battle, but she'd been forced to memorize the important parts, thanks to Vana's scrupulous tutoring. A little over a century ago, that war had almost destroyed the Five Provinces, because it was spearheaded by Azir Mubarék, leader of the Liagé—a title given to those few Sol Velorians who'd been born with supernatural power, called the Shah. According to the histories, vague as they were, Azir Mubarék had grown consumed with his power, and so the world united to stop him, thank the spirits above.

The ballad, however, was much too bombastic for Imari's tastes, but her papa's guests seemed to appreciate it. When she finished, they all stood and applauded. Ricón's was loudest, and his broad smile said just how much he knew she hated the piece.

The guests settled in, which meant the remainder of the musical menu was in her control. She played on. She chose other favorites of Istraa, moving fluidly from one piece to the next, but when she slid into the fourth piece, *Soul a mon Sieta*, she hesitated.

One note sustained, soft. Uncertain and wavering.

It was as if the flute didn't want to play *Soul a mon Sieta*. As if it had awoken, latched on to that note with all its might, and now that it had hold, it wasn't letting go. Not only would it not let go, it wanted to direct the next note.

Imari was quickly running out of air for her E flat. She ended the note and dropped into an A sharp.

The note breathed, swelling as if opening its lungs for the first time. Something stirred inside of her. She thought it mere improvisation—instinct. She had no idea how wrong she was.

She followed that instinct through a pentatonic scale, dancing with flourishes and augments. Losing herself in the notes, the melody, drifting with the sound as it filled the empty spaces, slipping out the door and onto the rooftops of the palace she'd climbed only moments ago. But this time she jumped off, soaring through the air, weightless, heading straight toward the Baraga Mountains. No, not the Baraga Mountains.

Ziyan.

A gale scooped her up, whipping and tossing her, clawing her deeper and deeper into forbidden wastelands. Melodies screamed out of her flute for the voice she did not have. Her fingers flew faster and faster, notes rose and fell like the tides of the great dunes, and with one final gust, she was thrown from the sky, dropping and spinning to the ground in a whirl of sound.

Spinning and falling in a melody of dizzying madness, and then...

Silence.

Imari gasped and pulled the flute from her lips, her body drenched in sweat. Her arms tingled, a pressure throbbed in her chest, and the symbols etched upon her flute glowed a pale white, fading even as she watched.

She looked up. She wasn't in Ziyan. She was at the palace, seated upon her stool. She put a hand to her chest, trying to calm herself, and then she saw the dinner party.

Each and every one of them had slumped over their plates; some had faces in food—even Ricón lay with his chin drowning in cream, his hand still wrapped around his goblet. An entire court... sound asleep.

At least, she hoped they merely slept.

Trembling, Imari slipped from the stool. The air sizzled and hummed strangely, and her arms and legs tingled with energy as she padded over to Vana. Her kunari had slumped down the column she'd been leaning against, her head bent forward, chin resting upon her generous bosom.

"Vana!" Imari whispered, tucking her flute beneath one arm and using her other to feel around Vana's face.

Vana didn't move.

With growing horror, Imari pressed her ear to Vana's heart.

There was a slow beat. But it beat.

And Imari knew: She had done this. She had lulled everyone in this room into a deep sleep, with music.

No, with *the Shah*.

Her pulse drummed in her ears. If her papa's guests realized what she'd done—what she had the ability to do—and if word got out...

Metal clanked on the table. Imari's gaze whipped back. A few of the guests stirred. Ricón slowly lifted his head, one hand pressed to his forehead as if he suffered from an immense headache. His gaze whirled and landed on Imari.

"*Go*," he mouthed, but the fear in his gaze terrified her.

She got to her feet and ran out the side doors of the dining hall, and she stopped short.

Her little sister, Sorai, lay on the floor wedged against the door. No doubt listening in on the performance. Sorai loved hearing Imari play, and she'd thrown quite the tantrum when her mama had forbidden her from attending this dinner. It looked like she'd come anyway. Imari could hear Anja now, scolding her for teaching the littlest princess of Trier bad habits.

The music had affected Sorai even out here. Imari glanced around. The dark and narrow hall lay empty. Still, it wouldn't do for Sorai to be caught like this.

"*Mi a'drala*," Imari whispered, bending down beside her sister to wake her.

Sorai didn't move.

It was then Imari noticed Sorai wasn't breathing.

The flute slid out from beneath Imari's arm and clattered to the floor, but Imari barely heard it. She pressed her ear to her little sister's chest.

Only silence greeted her.

And Imari ran.

1

Ten Years Later

Sable lit the small candle, and her nose wrinkled. The butcher's cellar reeked of rust.

Storage crates vomited chicken feet on the floor, shelving bowed beneath the weight of too many brining jars, and bird carcasses dangled from the ceiling in macabre decoration, dripping remnants of life all over everything. Garlands of meat casing draped like beaded curtains, and Sable almost missed the enormous workbench, buried beneath a tangle of bloodied cleavers, meathooks, and feathers. Overall, Velik's cellar was a bloody mess. Not that she'd expected any different.

If I were Velik, where would I store bones? Her gaze snagged on a hutch.

Sable slipped around the table, careful not to knock into anything, which was no small feat, considering, and opened the top drawer. Inside, she found wads of cloth and rope, but no bones. She opened the next drawer, and the next, and frowned. They had to be there somewhere. She'd watched him carry some in just this afternoon.

And then, beneath the smothered table, she spotted a huge bucket of animal fat, with the pale end of a femur sticking out of it.

Not where I'd keep them, but I'm not Velik, thank the wards.

Sable crouched beside the table, set down her candle, and grabbed the femur and a greasy hip joint. She tucked them into the pouch secured at her belt, slipped her hand back through the fat, and she'd just found a boar's foot when the latch on the cellar door clicked.

Sable cursed, snuffed out her candle, and bolted beneath the stairs. The cellar door creaked open, and lantern light split the shadows.

"I know you're down there," Velik growled. Heavy boots thumped down the wooden stairs. Through the slats, Sable caught the glint of a meat cleaver in his hand.

He stopped at the foot of the stairs. "Come out, come out," he taunted, setting his lantern on the table. "The longer you wait, the more painful I'll make it." He bent lower to search beneath the table.

Sable seized the opportunity. She chucked the boar's foot at the lantern. Bone struck, glass shattered, and the lantern crashed to the floor, plunging the cellar in darkness. Sable leapt onto the staircase, bounding up two steps at a time, then shoved through the door and out into the fresh, wintry night air.

Behind her, Velik exploded through the cellar door. "Come back here, you bastard!" Velik yelled, charging after her.

Sable grabbed hold of a neighboring fence post, used it to pin her momentum, and made a hard left. A dozen more yards, and she'd be under the cover of the village center, where she could lose Velik. She hurdled over another fence.

"Skanden won't hide you forever!" Velik shouted, thundering after her.

Sable's boots pounded the frozen earth, and her arms pumped, propelling her faster. The lights of Skanden's main square flickered ahead, but Velik was still too close. Whatever happened, she absolutely could not give away her destination.

Making a last minute and possibly very stupid decision, she dodged right, sprinting through the lower residences. This side of town had a climbable section of wall. She used it sometimes when she wanted to avoid the guards at the main gate. She'd just never used it at night. No one in their right mind went beyond the village walls after dusk. She decided not to dwell on that fact.

She bolted past the last house, wiped her greasy hands on her pants, then scrambled up storage barrels and jumped to the handholds in the palisade, compliments of a resident woodpecker. She pulled herself up, hoisted one leg over the tip of the wall, then the other, careful not to kick over the stone wards secured with nails and thin strips of leather, and jumped down on the other side, landing in a low crouch. There, she stopped to listen.

On the other side of the wall, wood crashed and exploded. Sable pinched her lips together and studied the trees, wary. She'd wandered the forest's edge often enough to pick herbs, but always during the day. She knew it well, but night brought a very different forest. Now, the dark pines loomed like giant sentinels, hiding the evil festering within.

A grunt sounded above her, and she glanced up as one of Velik's boots poked over the top of the wall. With a curse, Sable shoved herself to her feet and bolted into the forest.

"Come back here, you filthy little maggot!" Velik yelled.

By the wards, he made it sound so tempting...

Low branches slapped her legs and hands, stinging her face. With each stride, her unease intensified. She shouldn't be there. She should turn around before the forest took her as it'd taken so many others. As a healer, she knew firsthand what this forest could do to a man's body, and his mind. She stole a glance back, but Velik followed stubbornly on.

Sable cursed again. She couldn't let him catch her, but she

also couldn't run much deeper into the woods. With quick decision, she skidded around a boulder, bolted for the low branches of a huge pine she'd gathered sap from just this morning, and started climbing. Hand over hand, scrambling up the fat tree trunk, careful not to make too much noise as she tucked herself away in its branches.

Velik's hulking silhouette lumbered around the boulder, and Sable held her breath. Velik stopped at the base of her tree and looked around.

One second.

Two.

Her lungs burst, but she didn't dare breathe. She needed him to go, because they both needed to get the burning wards out of there.

At last, Sable heard him growl in frustration. She peered through the branches to see him retreating toward the village. She loosed a relieved breath but hid in the boughs until she was certain Velik had gone before climbing down. Her boots had just grazed the hard earth when she heard whispers.

They slipped in on a breeze, the hush of many, muffled and obscured, but faded as quickly as they'd come.

Sable froze, still gripping the lowest branch. Her gaze swept the shadows, but the forest lay quiet. The trees wouldn't help. They never did. They prided themselves in keeping secrets, but she couldn't fault them for that. They'd also kept her own. She was starting for the village when an unnatural stillness fell over everything.

Sable stopped in her tracks, eyes pinned on the roiling darkness, and the back of her neck tingled.

Something was here.

The air grew teeth, pierced her bones, and the rotten stench of decay soiled the air—so pungent, Sable stifled a gag.

"*I...ma...ri...*"

The name drifted from the past, haunting and inhuman, and a chill ran through Sable from head to toe.

She bolted.

Her boots crunched over dead leaves and fallen twigs, but she ran on, trusting her memory to guide her back to the village.

"Imari..." the shadows repeated, closer this time. The wind raked icy claws down her back. *"You... cannot hide..."*

Pure terror pushed her faster than she'd ever run before, and finally she reached the wall. She scrambled up the small divots in the wood, and her hands slipped twice, trembling. She cursed and gripped again, climbing higher and higher, hoisting her legs over the wall and between the stone wards before dropping down on the other side. She staggered to her feet and glanced back.

The wall blocked most of her view of the forest beyond, though she could still make out the forest's spired silhouettes against a starlit sky. The warded stones cresting the wall slept. She waited a breath, then took a few steps back, trying to see farther beyond the wall. Just to be sure.

Nothing.

Sable exhaled and wiped sweaty palms on her pants. Whatever it was, at least it wasn't foolish enough to test Skanden's centuries-old enchantments. She'd started turning back to the village when a spark of light caught her eye.

It'd come from one of the warded stones.

Pale blue light pulsed from the ward directly before her. Sable stilled. With each passing second, its overlapping circular etchings burned brighter and brighter, slowly waking. A second stone sparked to life, its etched lines and angles burning bright, just like the first.

Skanden's warded stones ran the perimeter of the wall, spaced at regular intervals. They all looked the same: oval in shape, smooth and pressed into a disc, with wards etched upon both faces. Ward enchantment was a lost art, but villages like Skanden, nestled deep within the heart of The Wilds, relied upon that old art to protect themselves from the dangerous remnants of the Shah that still existed in these parts. Most dangerous creatures stayed away from the villages, but every so often, something wandered close enough to wake a ward. But never, in all of Sable's ten years living in this place, had she seen one glow so brightly, let alone two at once.

A third pulsed to life.

Sable was searching the darkness beyond, trying to find the source, when a shadow stretched forward in a tendril of smoke. It leaked from the night like ink, and reached for one of the stones. Sable prayed to no one in particular that those wards would hold.

The strange smoke stretched closer and closer, dancing around each ward, teasing and testing. The wards burned bright and insistent as the darkness poked and prodded and touched.

Sable knew she should run—that she should get far away from whatever this was—but she had to know if the wards would hold. If the wards didn't hold, no amount of running would save her from this. That, she felt deep in her bones. It'd said her name. Her *true* name. How it'd known, she had no idea, but if it'd found her here, it would find her anywhere.

The smoke slid forward like a serpent and enveloped one of the glowing stones. The stone hissed and flickered like a candle struggling in the wind, and the ward light vanished.

A heavy weight settled deep in Sable's gut.

Maker's mercy.

The smoke slid to the next stone, and the next, putting each out in turn. A finger snuffing out flames.

Sable took slow steps back, watching in horror as the smoke slid past the dark wards and leaked over the wall. Closer and closer, its serpentine finger stretching across the ground, reaching for her.

One of the stones sparked. A sphere of blinding blue light exploded out of it, blasting through Sable, and she shut her eyes against the brightness. A keening wail shattered the quiet, followed by a sizzling hiss, and then...

Silence.

Sable opened her eyes. The world muted to night once more, though one stone pulsed brightly atop the wall. A beacon, a warning. No signs remained of the otherworldly darkness, and the shadows were left to themselves again.

2

Sable sagged back against the crate and heaved cold air.

Bless the early settlers who'd constructed those wards in the first place.

After casting one last, untrusting glance at the forest beyond the wall, Sable tugged on her cowl, glanced around to make sure no one was watching, and went on her way. She slipped through the sleepy town like a spirit, keeping to the shadows, for the shadows inside Skanden's walls had long been a comfort. In them, she hid from the scornful glances, the judgment. In them, she existed outside of society—a thing living on the fringes, and as long as she didn't wander outside of them, the people (mostly) left her alone. But she found no comfort in the shadows this night.

The terrifying voice from the forest haunted her thoughts, persistent as a stain. Her skin crawled with memory, and more than once, she caught herself glancing over her shoulder to be sure.

What was it? The question swirled in her mind. Never, in all her years here, had she encountered anything like it, and she'd encountered her share of frights. How had it found her, and why? And...

How had it known her name?

Her thoughts followed her all the way to the rear wall of the small apartments where the Smets lived. All of the buildings in Skanden boasted thick scars of time and season, like the people who lived here, but this building carried more scars than most. It was an original, built when Skanden was first erected, and like a stubborn old man, it clung defiantly to this world, ignoring its own slow deterioration.

Sable jumped and grabbed hold of the wooden supports jutting out from the framework, using them to pull herself up and scale the rear wall, deftly navigating her way toward the open window. She gripped the windowsill and pulled herself up enough to peek inside. The narrow corridor lay quiet, and a lantern burned at the far end, casting gauzy light upon the crumbling brick and plaster walls. She hoisted herself through the window, landed softly inside, then made her way to the Smets' door and rapped three soft times.

A floorboard creaked inside the house, the door cracked open, and Kat Smet's heart-shaped face appeared. At the sight of Sable, her eyes lit up, and she glanced furtively down the hall, checking to make sure no one spied them before ushering Sable inside.

The Smets didn't have much, not even when it came to warmth. The rising heat from the lower levels did nothing to chase away the cold in their small apartment. Neither did the landlord. A pane was still missing from their one window, and a few buckets sat upon the floor, positioned to collect rainwater from a leaking rooftop. Soon, the rain would turn into snow.

Sable followed Kat to the corner where little Jedd lay on his cot, sleeping beneath a pile of old blankets. Jedd had turned ten last week. They hadn't been able to celebrate because he'd come down with this terrible cough and fever that refused to let him go, and now it ate away at his mind.

Jedd moaned and tossed his head from side to side, his forehead wet and deathly pale. It made Sable's chest hurt, seeing him reduced to this.

Mikael looked up as she crossed the room. His hair was disheveled, and strain pulled at the corners of his eyes. He looked like a man about to lose his only son. Because that's exactly what he was.

Sometimes Sable wished someone loved her that fiercely.

"You've been watching his fever?" she asked, kneeling beside Jedd.

"Aye," Mikael said, wringing his hands. "And Kat's been rubbing the leander oil on his chest every day, like you said."

Sable pressed her palm to Jedd's forehead. By the wards, he was still hot as embers.

She pushed the hair from his forehead and began to sing. She didn't sing words, just notes, as they poured form her soul, unbidden. Mikael and Kat watched, curious and then hopeful as Jedd's breathing calmed, and the rise and fall of his chest matched the rhythm of Sable's lilting melody. As the last few notes left her lips, Jedd's body relaxed into a deep slumber.

There. He was peaceful, at least.

Sable pulled her hand away and adjusted Jedd's covers, and when she turned back to Kat and Mikael, Kat's eyes welled with tears.

"Here's bread, marrow, and root vegetables," Sable said, pulling the pouch from her belt and handing it to Mikael. The bread and vegetables were from her own pantry, but she preferred letting Mikael believe they *all* were.

Mikael untied the strings, opened the pouch, and inhaled deeply. Sable didn't doubt it'd been days since they'd eaten a decent meal. She knew her gifts were hard for Mikael to accept, but any bit of pride he'd once held had vanished when his son fell ill.

Mikael had been a farmer in Brevera—one of the Five Provinces' southern provinces—before losing everything in a fire, and soon after, he fell into crippling debt. He, his wife, and son had migrated north, all the way to Skanden, hoping to find a way to start over, but The Wilds' landscape was ruthless, and its citizens —mostly criminals and outcasts from the Five Provinces—were arguably more so. After one full year, Mikael still hadn't found enough work to provide for his family, and being that food was a scarcity in this climate, people didn't often share. Sable gave everything she could to those who needed it, but it was never enough.

"I brought this, too," Sable said, pulling out a cloth satchel from inside her cloak.

Mikael took it with a question in his eyes.

"Derriweed."

His expression fell open. "Sable, we can't... you know I would've given my old farm for this, but I could never—"

"Take it," she insisted, putting her hand over his. "He needs it, and I won't risk his life over a few crowns. I can get more derriweed."

Emotion welled in Mikael's eyes. "I... I don't know how to thank you."

"I just hope it helps him," Sable said, glancing back at Jedd with concern. "There's enough derriweed for four days. Crush the leaves and mix a pinch with hot water three times a day. Now repeat what I said."

"Crush the leaves," Kat replied in a voice trembling with hope. "Mix a pinch with hot water. Three times a day."

Sable nodded. "Make sure he drinks all of it."

Mikael placed a hand on Sable's arm. One of his fingertips was bubbled and bruised from frostbite. That'd happened right before she'd stolen a pair of leather gloves for him to wear. Those, too, had come from Velik.

"I will," he said. "Maker bless you, child."

Sable didn't believe in the Maker, or any gods, for that matter. If they existed, they certainly weren't in the habit of blessing *her*. She didn't know how Mikael still believed in them either, not after everything he and his family had been through.

"I'll come by to check on him in a few days," she said. She cast one last glance at Jedd and quietly escorted herself out, back through the window and down the wall.

Sable took her time walking back to the little hut she shared with Tolya at the opposite end of the village. She kept an eye out for Velik, just in case. Velik had yet to discover she'd been the one stealing from him, but it would look suspicious if he spotted her out at this hour.

A thin web of mist wove through the dark and empty streets. The town slept, though the windows of The Honest Thief still pulsed and flickered with warm light. Ivar owned the only tavern within thirty miles in all directions, so it usually lay awake well into the morning. The front door creaked open and Benioff, the smithy, stumbled out of it, tripping over his feet on his way down the steps. Ake and Polich followed after, hoisted a drunken Benioff between them, and sang a bawdy song as they carried him off. They'd forgotten to close the door, and lute music escaped, echoing across the street.

Sable pressed her lips together and glanced down the dark path leading home. She should go. She'd already been out late enough. Still, the notes persisted, floating around her, eerie and beautiful and seductive. It was always so, with music. Like a tether she couldn't break.

Sable had just forced her feet to move in the opposite direction when the musician slipped into a new piece—one from Istraa.

Unable to help herself, Sable stopped and closed her eyes. It was like listening to a memory. Notes rattled at uneven intervals, climbing and falling through a lurid sky, the golden sands ablaze, and the world smelled of heat and fire. The music swelled against a percussive beat, and suddenly, she saw her brother Ricón, laughing and dancing inside the palace hall. She saw her brother Kai, too, and her papa and Sura Anja, wrapped elegantly in fabric the purple of a desert sunrise. Sable called out to them, though she had no voice. Like a breeze, she floated in the keyhole arches above, weaving around columns until her family's forms faded, and Ricón's laughter echoed into nothingness.

"Little late for a walk, don't you think?"

Sable snapped her eyes open as a silhouette peeled itself from the shadows. Velik. She ground her teeth, furious with herself. She'd known better.

Velik stopped a few feet before her. His eyes narrowed with suspicion, along with something else Sable didn't care to examine too closely. Instinct told her to run, but she stood strong and unyielding. Only guilty people ran.

"I could say the same," she said dryly.

He took a threatening step closer. "I'm looking for a thief."

"You're in luck. Skanden's full of them."

His eyes hardened, and he took another step. "And one of them is stealing from *me*. Just now, in fact." He stood so close, Sable had to crane her head to gaze up at his boxy face. "You wouldn't happen to know anything about that now, would you, *Scablicker*?"

Her eyes narrowed. "If I notice any suspicious behavior, I'll be sure to let you know."

"Like a Scablicker wench walking the streets—*alone*—in the middle of the night?"

Before Sable could respond, he wrapped an arm around her waist and yanked her forward, pulling her body against his.

"Velik!" She shoved against him, but he was too strong, too solid. "Let go!"

His one arm held firm while his other searched. "Where is it?" he snarled.

"I don't know what you're talking about!"

His free hand felt beneath her cloak, grabbing her waist, her backside. And... her backside.

"Stop it!" she growled, squirming and reaching for the knife she kept in the shaft of her boot. Her fingertips had just grazed the hilt when a new voice called, "Velik...?"

It was Brinn, the tavern maid and Ivar's granddaughter. Brinn still wore her apron, and her blonde hair was fastened in a tight coil at the nape of her neck, though a few wisps curled about her temples.

Velik shoved Sable off. Sable stumbled forward and barely caught her footing.

Brinn approached with hesitant steps, her gaze sliding from Velik to Sable and back to Velik again. "What are you doing?" she asked.

"Making sure the Istraan isn't causing any trouble," Velik said, glaring at Sable.

Sable smiled, all teeth. "I'm flattered you think I could."

His lips curled, and his hand flinched into a fist, but he wouldn't strike. Not in front of Brinn. "I'm watching you, Scablicker."

"Clearly," Sable replied curtly. She cast one quick glance at a confused Brinn, then continued on her way.

Scablicker.

The derogatory term for those accused of protecting Sol Velorian refugees—Scabs.

Istraa had a history of protecting the refugees, and since Sable was easily identified as Istraan, with her coppery skin and onyx hair, she was rewarded with unfair prices by local merchants and, as in Velik's case, an outright refusal to sell to her. Their treatment was what had turned her to thieving in the first place.

And, when she was being honest, it also felt good to get back at them in this small way.

The little hut was dark as she approached. She snuck through the back door and closed it behind her, careful not to wake Tolya, and she'd just hung her cloak on the hook beside the door when a lantern sprung to life.

Sable winced inwardly.

"Where have you been?" Tolya asked in a tone that suggested she knew very well where Sable had been.

With a deep breath, Sable turned to face her.

Tolya sat at the small table near the hearth, the lantern burning brightly beside her. White ringlets sprang out from beneath the wool blanket she'd wrapped around herself, but despite Tolya's old age, those pale eyes were bright and clear and glaring at Sable with all the wrath and judgment of the Silent's High Priest.

"The derriweed is gone," Tolya said, slow and even, daring Sable to deny it.

Which, Sable knew from experience, was futile. "I know. I took it."

"Why."

Because Jedd would've died without it. Because she couldn't bear to watch Mikael and Kat suffer. Because she *had* to pay for the wrong she'd done all those years ago. "Someone needed it," she said.

Tolya slammed a fist on the table, and Sable jumped. The lantern rattled.

"*Stupid* girl! *We* need it!" Tolya growled. "Herbs are our only currency in this godforsaken land, and you just gave away your inheritance!"

Sable steeled herself. She'd known Tolya would be furious, and part of her hated herself for deceiving Tolya like this, but she hadn't expected Tolya to say what she'd said, about Sable inheriting the business, and it humbled her.

"By the wards! What am I going to do with you?" Tolya rubbed her temples. The blanket slid from her head, freeing her wild mess of curls. Tolya dropped her hands and looked hard at Sable. "I will never recover that. Never. Do you understand, girl?"

Sable held Tolya's gaze and nodded once. She didn't apologize. She wouldn't tell Tolya she was sorry when she knew that, if given the chance to go back in time, she'd do it all over again.

Tolya seemed to sense this as her eyes roved over Sable and then fixed somewhere above Sable's ear. "Why are there pine needles in your hair?"

Sable reached up and patted her head. Sure enough, she pulled two sticky balsam ends from her hair. Thank the wards Velik hadn't spotted them beneath her cowl. Tolya eyed Sable as she walked to the sleeping hearth and tossed them on the ash.

"You can't keep this up," Tolya said in a quiet voice. "This thieving."

"We live in a town of thieves," Sable snapped.

"We don't steal from each other."

"It's not like I'm endangering anyone," Sable said with exasperation. "I only take the excess. They hardly notice." Which was true. The only one who seemed to notice was Velik, the stingy boor.

Tolya placed a hand on Sable's arm, surprising her. Tolya had always been like a slab of granite. Cold, hard, and forever. It was how she'd survived—alone—in a place like this for so many decades, well before Sable had arrived, trembling in fear and self-loathing, on her doorstep.

"You think I don't understand, but I do," Tolya said suddenly, quietly. "It's a cruel world we live in, and each of us tries to survive in the way we know how. A way that seems right to us." Tolya hesitated, and her eyes softened. "But eventually you'll get caught, Sable. This thieving, even for reasons that seem right to you, is still against the laws of this land, and it will get you killed, or worse. And I swore to the almighty Maker that I'd protect you for as long as He put breath in my old lungs. Promise me... promise me you'll stop."

Sable wanted to say that Ricón had promised to protect her too. But he, like everyone else, had let her go. He, like everyone else, had abandoned her to these cursed lands.

Tolya's gaze didn't relent, as if she'd heard everything Sable hadn't said. Uncomfortable, Sable glanced down at the old and withered hand gripping her arm. It wasn't a hand that'd touched her often, but it was the only hand that'd kept her warm and fed, and it'd provided a roof over her head for these past ten years.

And Sable jeopardized that. Over and over again.

"I'll stop."

Tolya searched her, looking for a fray in the oath.

"I promise," Sable said. She meant it.

Satisfied, Tolya squeezed Sable's arm, removed her hand, and grabbed the lantern. "I've stayed up long enough waiting for your skinny legs to return, and now I'm going to bed," Tolya said with her usual deriding gusto. It made Sable grin.

"Wipe that smirk off your face, girl."

Sable clamped her lips down.

Tolya hobbled back to her room and disappeared behind the curtain.

Sable lingered a moment in the darkness. A gust of wind pushed against the small hut, and the walls groaned. She glanced at the beaded curtain leading to her room. With quiet steps, she ducked through the narrow doorway and through the beads, then lit the small candle upon her nightstand. She set the candle on the floor, carefully lifted her nightstand and set it aside, so as not to make a sound, then knelt and tugged a floorboard free. A rectangular wooden black box stared back at her. She reached in, opened the lid, and raised the painted black flute to the soft candlelight.

At her touch, its etched glyphs pulsed silvery white, as if they'd been carved from moonlight. The flute had been a gift from Ricón on her fifth birthday. She'd been so enchanted by a flutist's performance at a bazaar that she'd failed to join her guard at the designated time, inciting quite the uproar as the sar's entire guard searched for his missing daughter. It'd earned her one month's confinement to her chambers, but it'd also earned her this exquisite bone flute, thanks to an ever observant brother.

Her next exhale trembled through tight lips.

The glyphs hadn't glowed in the beginning, but ever since that horrific night, they'd illuminated at her touch. She didn't know what it meant, and she didn't want to know. In fact, she'd tried getting rid of it. Four separate times. The first being the day *it* happened, when she'd left it behind on the travertine tiles. But when she was halfway to The Wilds, it'd suddenly reappeared in the pocket of her cloak. She'd wondered if someone had slipped it there without her notice, but when she'd chucked it into a river, only to find it in her pocket the next day—completely dry and unharmed—she grew suspicious. Again, she tried ridding herself of the cursed weapon when she'd passed over The Crossing by throwing it into the gorge. That time, however, her chest squeezed tighter and tighter the farther the flute fell, and by the time she reached the other side of the bridge, the flute had nestled itself into her cloak again. Her chest hadn't relaxed till evening.

The fourth time had been her last, because when she'd tossed the flute into Benioff's forge, her body responded as though she'd tossed herself into the flames instead. After that, she'd decided it was easier to just hide the cursed thing. She might not be able to rid herself of the past, but she could certainly bury it beneath her feet.

Sable shut her eyes and sighed. She might've buried it, but it was still there. The plank of wood she always avoided, the spot in the floor her gaze subconsciously marked, checking grooves and woodgrain, making sure the board hadn't been tampered with.

Always fearing someone would notice and discover her horrible truth.

It was so easy to blame the flute. She'd found solace in it, initially. It was a Liagé weapon that had, unfortunately, found its way into her eager hands—*she* was innocent. For a little while, she even believed that. But as time matured, and guilt weighed heavier, she was forced to recognize that it was *her hands* that'd held the flute. It was *her breath* that had given it voice, and for that, she would never forgive herself.

She would never forgive herself for being the reason her little sister, Sorai, no longer lived.

A gust of wind rattled her window. Sable opened her eyes and stilled. The curtains weren't shut completely, and through the exposed panes, she thought she'd sensed someone there.

Curious, and a little bit anxious, she set the flute back in its box and crept to her window. The small herb garden beyond lay dark, the world quiet, save the howling wind. An owl launched from the fence post and was swallowed by the night. Sable waited a moment, watching the shadows.

It must've been the wind, she thought with a frown, then tugged her curtains closed completely.

Sable returned to the hole in the floor, crouching beside it. The glyphs had faded.

"I can't blame you for my actions anymore," she whispered.

She closed the lid on her past and set everything back in its proper place, then changed her clothing and climbed into bed. Tolya was right. She needed to stop using the past to excuse her present before it got her killed.

HE WATCHED her from the shadows.

She was a curious thing, small and slight and inconspicuous.

Not forgettable, exactly, but not at all what he'd imagined. However, he was not one to question the Maker's will.

She cradled the flute in her hands as though it were a gift from the heavens—too precious, too sacred for human touch—though he did not think she knew what it was. *He* did.

Her eyes snapped open and fastened on the window. No, on *him*.

He ducked away in surprise. The girl shouldn't have been able to see him, sense him. He checked himself; his power hummed true. But she set the flute down and crept toward the window.

It was time for him to go. He'd watched her long enough, and he'd gotten what he'd come for anyway. In a twist of wool, he switched forms and launched into the night. Sleep would have to come later, because he had a very important message to deliver.

He'd finally found her.

"Sorcery is death.

Like a temptress, it seduces with honeyed lips, beguiling man into its bed only to slaughter him in his sleep. For sorcery, a man's existence is nothing more than a temporary diversion, sacrificed for mere amusement in homage to its implacable god.

Let us not forget the mighty Sol Velorians. Let us not forget how, though their kingdom stretched from the Vendaran Desert to the Western Lands, and though their prophets—the Liagé—had been given unnatural power, still they hungered for more. They hungered for us. *And by the gods' great mercy, the Five Provinces staved off that hunger by defeating them.*

But we did not defeat sorcery itself.

It lives on in the darkest corners of our world, hiding from us. Its followers persist like weeds, encroaching upon our boundaries, sprouting inside our homeland, slowly spreading chaos and corruption. They must be plucked swiftly, lest the Sol Velorians rise again."

— Excerpt from the teachings of Gasta, Temple Head Inquisitor, the month of Aryn's Light, year three and thirty A. R.

3

Twenty-six Scabs.

It was the largest group Jeric had scouted yet. It still amazed him how many Scabs existed from a war that'd happened nearly one hundred and fifty years ago. He tried his best to hunt them, kill them, enslave them. They couldn't be allowed freedom, not after what their people had done. Not after what their survivors did *still.* A supposed religion of peace, and their sorcery had nearly annihilated the continent. If one ever forgot how dangerous power of that magnitude could be, a quick glance at the Forgotten Wastes proved an effective reminder. An entire land... destroyed, at the hands of their Liagé. Their so-called *blessed* for the sorcery they wielded. Sorcery wasn't a rutting blessing. It was a curse upon the land, and Jeric refused to let that *peaceful* culture thrive on *his* watch.

But no matter how many Scabs Jeric caught or killed, there were always more, as if the earth kept spitting their dead from the ground just to keep him busy. Recently, small groups of them had been coordinating attacks, demolishing bridges and intercepting important trade routes, slowly cutting of their resources along Corinth's southwestern border, where it touched the city of Highvale—trying to weaken Corinth. Godsdamned demon-worshippers.

And here were twenty-six of them.

He and his pack could take on twenty-six.

Jeric gave Braddok the signal. Braddok flashed a wicked grin and vanished around a rock. Which said a good deal about the rock, since Braddok was the size of a mountain. Jeric waited, crouched behind a tree, his sword, Lorath, in hand. A bird called from above.

Jeric grinned to himself. Gerald must've been practicing. He'd sounded less like a dying mouse and more like an eastern red-tailed finch.

Gerald made the call a second time. Jeric signaled the three men beside him. As one, they leapt out from the trees and bolted straight for the Scabs. Bolts zinged above. One Scab cried out and collapsed. Another fell right behind the first. Gerald was up there alone, but he didn't miss. He never did.

The remaining Scabs drew weapons and sprinted forward, engaging Jeric and his pack. Jeric hacked through the first few while his men fought hard behind him. These Scabs were better fighters than most. Jeric actually broke a sweat.

"Wolf!" Braddok yelled. "Get down!"

Jeric dropped in a plank. A bolt whizzed overhead, followed by a wet *snick*. A voice cried out, and a Scab collapsed in a heap beside Jeric, a bolt sticking out between his eyes. Jeric gave a curt nod to the trees, exchanged a glance with Braddok, leapt to his feet, and kept fighting.

Braddok swung his hatchet, sending three Scabs flying backwards into a tent. Jeric sprinted for them as the tent collapsed, and they were dead within a minute. Jeric turned and wiped his brow. Scabs lay everywhere, broken and bleeding. A worthy sacrifice to the gods. Lorath, the god of justice for whom he'd named his sword, should be pleased.

Braddok was finishing off the last two when Jeric said, "I need one alive!"

"Pliss!" begged one in a thick Scárib accent—the language shared by Istraans and Scabs. "I swear to gott..." A red line spread across his throat, and his words gurgled and died as he slumped to the ground. Braddok wiped his dagger clean on the dead Scab's thick, black ponytail.

Chez and Stanis shoved the last remaining Scab down upon her knees.

A woman.

Jeric sheathed his sword and strode over to her.

She glared up at him, all defiance. "Cowart," she hissed and spat on the ground. "That's why you slaughter us. Because you are cowarts. All of you. You are terrifite of our gott, of everything we repres—"

Jeric punched her square in the jaw.

The Scab reeled, but Chez and Stanis held her firmly on her knees. She flexed her jaw and spat blood at Jeric's boots. Jeric squeezed her jaw and jerked it up. Her face strained against the pull.

"You'll cooperate," Jeric said darkly, "or what we did to your friends will seem a mercy. Understand?"

She grunted against the pain in her jaw, her eyes burning with hatred.

"Are there more of you?" Jeric asked.

She didn't answer.

Jeric squeezed harder.

She winced. "No."

Jeric searched her angular eyes. *Scab* eyes. Dark and deceptive, like the sorcerers they worshiped. But he didn't think she was lying.

"What are you doing here?" Jeric demanded.

"We are heading to the Baraga Mountains..."

Jeric jerked her chin hard. "You've been heading *east* for the past two days. I've been tracking you. So, I'll ask again. What are you doing here?"

The Scab seethed but didn't answer.

Jeric slapped her face with his free hand.

Water filled her eyes, she blinked, and an angry red handprint blushed her cheek.

"Is Kormand leading you? Has he promised amnesty if you did his dirty work?" Jeric snapped.

She didn't answer.

He slapped her again, harder this time.

She glared back at him, eyes narrowed. "And whose tirty work are you toing, *Wolf*?"

Jeric gripped her chin so hard she squeezed her eyes shut and a tear leaked out. "All you godsdamn Scabs are the same. Arrogant. Self-righteous. Rutting pains in my ass. We'll see how far that gets you at the Temple."

The Scab's eyes opened wide with fear.

Jeric released her jaw. She slumped forward, and just as she began relaxing her neck and shoulders, Jeric kicked her in the stomach. This time, Chez and Stanis let go. She sprawled on the ground, clutching her stomach as she gasped for breath.

"Bind her," Jeric ordered his pack, glaring down at the woman. "You should've answered my question, Scab. My inquisitors aren't nearly as merciful as I am."

"GODS, GERALD, SLOW DOWN," Chez said. "Some of us haven't eaten!"

Gerald, who'd been helping himself to a third scoop of the tasteless slop, dropped the ladle back in the kettle and stepped aside with a grunt.

Chez picked up the ladle and eyed Gerald's long and willowy frame. "Where do you put it, man?"

"I still think he's got parasites," Stanis said, glancing up from his bowl. He wiped dribble from his lips. "You been sleeping with Scabs, Gerald?"

Chez snorted. Gerald rolled his eyes.

The Scab prisoner glared at them from where she sat at the campfire, bound and gagged.

Stanis noticed. "You got a problem, Scab?"

The Scab turned her head back to the fire.

Stanis set down his bowl, strode to the prisoner, and kicked her in the side. The force sent her onto her back, and she grunted into her gag. He was moving to kick her again when Braddok said, "Enough."

Stanis glanced back.

Braddok shook his head. "You know how the inquisitors like them healthy."

Stanis glared down at the woman, restrained by the truth of Braddok's words. "Rutting Scab." He spat on her face instead. She winced, his spittle slid down her cheek, and he stalked back to his bowl.

Braddok glanced over at Jeric, who sat a few yards away studying the goods they'd uncovered. Braddok filled another bowl and approached Jeric.

"You should eat something," Braddok said, setting the bowl on the ground beside Jeric, who surveyed the items they'd acquired. A few crude blades made of black metal, two hundred crowns, a map of Corinth, and a small vial of gods knew what.

"Baraga Mountains my arse." Braddok grunted. "What's in the vial?"

"It's not ale," Jeric replied wryly.

Braddok sniggered, picked up the vial, uncorked, and took a whiff. "Gods above..." He coughed. "My scat smells better."

"I find that hard to believe," Jeric mused.

Braddok pressed down the cork and returned the vial to

Jeric's small collection before picking up one of the blades. "Huh. This isn't skal..."

"No," Jeric said and glanced up at Braddok. "It's not."

Braddok tested it between his teeth. Studied it again. "Looks like a piece of night sky." Braddok eyed Jeric. "You have an idea."

Jeric frowned at the map and tapped his thumb against the scrawled waves of the Yellow Sea. "I think it's nightglass. I've never seen it, but the material was named because it looks like a shard of night sky." And this particular metal did, as though the gods had carved out a piece of the universe and given it to man as a weapon, stars and all.

Braddok frowned back at the blade. "I've never heard of it. Where's it from?"

"The Wilds."

Braddok looked sharply at Jeric. "What in the five hells would Wilds' fugitives be doing down here?"

It was a good question. People didn't often venture down from The Wilds. The reasons that generally took them to The Wilds in the first place usually prevented a safe return to the provinces.

"I don't know," Jeric replied distractedly, "but I'll wager they're not particularly concerned with a shipment of skal ore headed for Rodinshold."

Jarl Rodin governed Corinth's southwestern edge, where it touched Brevera. According to a messenger, his last two shipments of skal arms and weaponry had been intercepted by Scab raiders. He had no proof, only conjecture, but nevertheless, he demanded more resources to replace that which had been lost. However, skal arms weren't so easily replaced. Peace was a brittle thing in these uncertain times, and all of Corinth's jarls demanded more reinforcements. Skyhold's skalsmiths worked day and night filling orders, in addition to stocking the king's own, and Rodin was not the sort of man who liked to be kept waiting. He also had a very inflated view of his own importance.

"You think Rodin is making it up?" Braddok asked.

"Doubtful."

"Could be his way of getting more than his ration." Braddok shrugged.

"He's not that smart."

Braddok waggled his brow in agreement. "Then who's stealing it?"

"Scabs, probably."

Braddok frowned. "Wolf, you're not making much sense."

"Neither does this map," Jeric said, studying a marking near The Fingers. It denoted the city of Dunsten, but it'd been called by a different name, in the Scárib tongue. Jeric had studied Scárib for the sole purpose of knowing his enemy, and he thought he knew it well enough. He'd studied the Istraan dialect, which differed somewhat, but not so much that he couldn't piece together Scab variations. But this word, standing isolated and out of context, held no meaning for him, and it seemed important. "Do you know this word?"

Braddok crouched beside him, leathers creaking and groaning as he did so. "No rutting clue."

"Look here. Reichen is also wrong." Jeric pointed to a marking designating the city of Reichen, which had been replaced by another Scab word. "And here." He pointed to a location along the Fallow River, which had also been replaced with a Scárib phrase.

"Maybe they made a mistake," Braddok suggested. "Didn't know the names, so they made up their own."

Jeric stopped tapping his finger, and his gaze narrowed on their prisoner. "Maybe." He wanted to ask her, but that wasn't his role in this sport. He did the tracking and hunting, then tossed his catch to the inquisitors for dissection.

Still…

"So?" Braddok asked in a voice too quiet for the others to hear. "Once we return, you still planning to meet with Hersir?"

Jeric jerked his dagger from the ground, where he'd stabbed

the map's edge to hold it in place against the wind. Hersir was head of Corinth's Strykers—a group often referred to by the people as the gods' private assassins. Strykers were sanctioned by the gods, their purpose strictly to defend Corinth's crown and borders. It also happened to be Jeric's one and only chance at severing the chain that bound him to his older brother's whims. Not even Corinth's king could defy the gods' laws where Strykers were concerned.

"Hersir," Jeric answered quietly, rolling up the map. "The ordination is set to happen three evenings from now."

"What if your brother returns before we do?" Braddok asked.

"He won't..." Jeric's voice trailed, and he tilted his ear to the trees. His gaze shot to the shadows, narrowing, and he jumped to his feet, leaving the map on the ground.

Braddok started to stand, but at a gesture from Jeric, he held back. Jeric ran his tongue over his teeth, crept through their contraband, and slipped deeper into the trees, silent as a ghost. He soon spotted what had caught his attention.

A man crouched in the trees, slowly approaching their camp.

Jeric was on him in two strides, holding a dagger to his throat. The man let out an undignified squeak.

"Hands out," Jeric growled.

The young man's arms spread wide. "I didn't mean—"

Jeric shoved him forward.

"I swear, I'm—"

Jeric shoved him again, harder this time, and the man toppled into their camp. Chez and Stanis's laughter died as the man fell to the ground before them. They jumped to their feet, weapons drawn, and Chez pinned the intruder down, while Gerald shoved his face in the dirt with his boot.

"Please!" the intruder said frantically, arms splayed in surrender. "I'm a messenger from Skyhold!"

Jeric studied the man. Curly, straw-colored hair. Average height and build. Pinched, annoying voice.

"I don't know you," Jeric cut back.

"My name's Farvyn."

Gerald pushed his boot harder against Farvyn's face.

"Please! I'm new! I swear to the gods... I mean no harm," he added to Jeric's amusement. "I've a message for the prince!"

Jeric stilled. He and Braddok exchanged a glance.

"Who told you to look for him here?" Jeric demanded.

"The Head Inquisitor!" Farvyn continued with desperation, happy to pin suspicion on anyone other than himself. "He said to search these parts, so I did, and then I saw your fire. I swear to the gods. It's extremely urgent that I find the prince... please..."

Jeric frowned, then tipped his chin at Gerald. Gerald lifted his boot, and Braddok grabbed Farvyn by the collar, jerking him to a stand. Farvyn, thus permitted sight, gaped at Braddok's hulking mass and, for the first time, looked at Jeric. His eyes widened with realization, and he dropped to his knee. "Prince Jeric... I didn't realize. Please forgive—"

"Silence," Jeric snapped.

Farvyn shut his mouth.

Jeric stared hard at Farvyn, who shifted feebly upon his knee. "You give far too much information without verifying your audience. What if we'd been part of a Breveran scouting party?"

Farvyn's expression faltered, humbled and embarrassed. "I'm sorry, Your Grace. It won't happen again."

"No, it won't." Jeric's eyes narrowed on the messenger, letting him feel the weight of his disapproval. "Well? Out with it."

Farvyn cleared his throat, shifted again. "His Highness, Prince Hagan, has returned, and he requires your presence at Skyhold immediately."

Jeric met Braddok's knowing gaze. His brother rarely sent for him while he was on a hunt. But even more pressing was the fact that Hagan had returned.

Jeric ground his teeth together. *Godsdamnit.*

4

The city of Reichen was one of Corinth's most treasured, situated under Jarl Stovich's jurisdiction. It provided most of Corinth's grain, for it possessed what most of Corinth did not: sweeping fields of fertile soil. This month, instead of grain, Commander Anaton had received a note from Jarl Stovich, requesting his presence immediately.

And so the commander had gone. Jarl Stovich wasn't one for dramatics.

Commander Anaton met Jarl Stovich at Bieler's Watch—a guard post just outside of Reichen—and the two rode together to the village. Stovich's and the commander's personal guard followed close behind.

"It's better you see it in person," Stovich had said, when Anaton had asked.

Anaton hadn't missed the distress in Stovich's eyes.

They crested a rise, and before Stovich said a word, Anaton knew something was wrong.

Reichen sat at the center of a valley usually bustling with life, from noise of harvest, Scab workers in the fields, and the calls of cattle and sheep. Today, it was silent. The fields stretched uninhabited, plows abandoned in the grasses, and the buildings beyond sat dark.

Anaton looked at Stovich. "What happened here?"

Stovich stared ahead, his expression grim. "Come. I'll show you."

The men cut through empty fields, and a bitter wind nipped at them, warning them away. Finally, Stovich stopped, and the men dismounted. Reichen was a ghost town, its streets empty, its chimneys cold. A sign creaked on rusted hinges, setting Anaton on edge.

Stovich jerked his head for Anaton to follow, and their heavy boots plunked up the wooden steps of the dining hall. Stovich pushed through the doors and into a dark chamber. Rodents scurried. Plates of half-eaten food and mugs of ale littered the tables, swarming with flies. As if everyone had simply vanished mid-meal.

Anaton wiped his forefinger along the table, pulling away dust. Maggots wormed in a lump of old potatoes. "You found it like this?"

"Yes," Stovich replied. "When Leon didn't report, I sent a few men." His eyes trailed the room. The walls groaned against the wind. "This way."

Anaton peeled his gaze from the hall and followed Stovich through a back door. There he stopped.

Ahead stood the temple of Sela, the goddess of field and harvest, and upon the steps was a pile of bodies.

"Lina's mercy..." Anaton said.

He smelled it then, the rot, the decay. He was no stranger to death. He'd seen it countless times; he was Corinth's military commander.

He had never seen this.

An entire town of men and women and children—dead. He approached slowly and noticed the strange ashy color of their skin and the web of black veins staining it. Like ceramic, fractured. Horror distorted their faces, twisting their features, and their eyes had been ripped from their sockets, leaving crusted black pits behind.

By the gods.

One of Anaton's guards gagged.

"They're all Corinthian," Anaton noted quietly.

"Yes," Stovich replied.

Anaton stopped a few paces away, surveying the carnage, hardly able to bear the stench. "Where are the slaves?"

Stovich shook his head. "We don't know. We couldn't find tracks of an exodus. It's like they just... vanished."

Anaton studied a little gray hand, still pudgy with childhood, and his stomach turned over. "Burn the bodies."

Stovich eyed him. "Do you know who could've done this?"

Anaton's gaze swept the abandoned town and the empty fields, and a dark cloud of trepidation settled over him. "I have no idea."

SABLE SPRINTED THROUGH THE FOREST, but no matter where she turned, she couldn't find the village wall. The trees kept rearranging themselves, drawing her toward their heart.

Toward death.

Darkness swirled and thickened, blotting out the world, and an ice-cold grip squeezed her arm.

Sable bolted upright, heart pounding, and her eyes opened to a dark room. *Her* room. Fumbling, she lit the candle upon her nightstand, then pushed up her sleeve. Three red lines stretched around her forearm, fading even as she studied them. She trailed her thumb over the marks. It'd been like this every night for a week—since her encounter in the forest.

Frustrated, she threw back her blankets and slipped out of bed. If her mind was determined to keep her awake, she might as well make the most of it. She snatched her candle and padded to the kitchen, ducking beneath lines of hanging herbs to sit at the table. She reached overhead and grabbed a bundle of dried euctis, careful not to disturb the flower heads, and, by candlelight, she crushed the heads over a colander, picking out the old petals and chaff from the tiny black seeds. The process relaxed her in a strange sort of way, the monotony of it. Her practiced hands moved quickly and carefully, and it wasn't long before she'd moved through the entire bundle.

Sable picked up the next and hesitated, admiring the clover-shaped leaves that stained her fingers with sweetness. Euctis always reminded her of her uki, Gamla Khan, who'd served as Trier's *alma*—healer—since before she'd been born.

Sable held the little dried leaves to her nose and inhaled deeply. Euctis was Gamla's favorite, and he'd grown pots and pots of it at his bedside. He'd claimed it grew better there, where beetles and grasshoppers couldn't feast upon it. Sable had managed to keep hers alive in The Wilds' harsh climate, but it never thrived. Not like it had in the confines of Gamla's chambers.

"You can plant seeds in other lands, give them plenty of water and sunshine, and hide them from pests, but if the gods designed them for sun and heat, they will not *thrive* in any other," he had said. So often, when he spoke, she'd wondered at which point he'd stopped talking about plants and started referring to people. They'd been interchangeable to him. And now, as she sat there, thinking on her own displacement, she wondered if he'd seen the future.

Sable pressed the dried stem between her fingers. She wished she hadn't taken him for granted.

She wished a lot of things.

Tolya's coughing rattled through the thin curtain separating her room from the kitchen.

Sable stopped humming and glanced up from her work. Tolya's cough had become a savage thing these past few days.

After a particularly long fit, Sable set down the euctis, tiptoed to Tolya's room, and listened from behind the curtain.

"I know you're there, girl," Tolya called out. "Go back to bed." And then she started coughing again.

Sable returned to the kitchen, snatched some freshly dried lavender from the line above, grabbed a pinch of poppy seeds from the shelves, and made an herbal tea, which she carried to Tolya.

"You never listen," Tolya rasped.

"That's not true. I listen very well, when you're rational." Sable set the tea and candle upon Tolya's nightstand.

Tolya glared at the ceiling while grumbling things Sable couldn't decipher but easily guessed.

"Drink it," Sable said firmly. "You have to get over this. Belfast is in two weeks, and we still have deliveries to make."

Tolya grunted and, begrudgingly, propped herself against her pillow and took the mug with unsteady hands. "You could go on without me."

Sable didn't respond.

Tolya peered at Sable over the mug. "You'll have to eventually, girl." Cough. "I won't be around forever."

"And I'd appreciate it if you didn't expedite that fact."

Tolya took a sip of the tea and closed her eyes as though her lids were too heavy to hold open. Sable's concern intensified.

"Go on, girl," the woman said, though the gusto was gone.

Sable pinched her lips together, grabbed the candle, and left. She waited outside Tolya's room a moment, and once she was satisfied the poppy had done its job, she returned to her room and went to bed.

Tolya didn't get out of bed the next morning.

"Tolya," Sable said, bleary-eyed, setting bread beside the old woman's bed.

Tolya didn't stir. Her skin looked papery white, and her eyes sat too deep inside bruised sockets.

"Tolya," Sable repeated, louder this time, and she gently shook the old woman's shoulder.

Tolya moaned, and her eyes roamed behind closed lids.

Sable pressed the back of her hand to Tolya's forehead and frowned. Her skin blazed. Tea wouldn't be enough. Tolya needed something strong, and she'd need something even stronger to wash it down.

"I'll do the morning rounds and stop by Ivar's on my way back," Sable said.

Tolya moaned a reply.

"I'll be back."

Sable returned to the kitchen, where she gathered the usual tinctures and wrapped them carefully in cloth, which she further identified with small flowers. She snatched her fur-lined cloak from the bench, grabbed the bundled cloths and a few coins from the drawer, and stepped out into the brisk morning.

The air smelled cold, spiced with the peppery scent of burning wood, and her breath rose from her lips in a thick cloud. It was the bud before the bloom, the prologue of season, and Sable wondered if, perhaps, winter would come early this year.

By the wards, she hoped not.

A breeze blew past, and the windchimes on their porch danced, singing a soft and hopeful broken chord. Sable tugged her heavy cowl over her head and went on her way.

The muted light of dawn dappled the treetops, gently coaxing the sleepy town awake, and a haze of chimney smoke made everything gauzy and gray. Sable kept to the long morning shadows, moving lightly upon her feet as she placed packages on appropriate porches. A few chickens squawked, pecking at the dirt, and somewhere a rooster crowed. She spotted a sober

Benioff on his porch, bent over his forge and squeezing the bellows over hot coals. For many of them, the weeks preceding Belfast—The Wilds' final harvest—were difficult, everyone scrambling to finish last-minute preparations before the first snowfall. Once snow arrived in Skanden, it stayed till spring, and there would be no leaving town until then.

Benioff hammered steel, and as Sable passed, the percussive beat synched with her steps until she turned down the narrow road leading to Ivar's. The mottled windows of The Honest Thief were dark this morning, but smoke rose from the chimney, and the sweet scent of baked bread teased the air. She stepped through the front door and into a quiet dining hall. A fire yawned in the large hearth, and seated alone at a table, tearing into a steaming roll, was Velik.

Velik glanced over, his dark eyes narrowed.

She hadn't seen him since that night, and now, looking at him, she suddenly remembered the way he'd touched her.

Velik tipped his head a fraction, eyes never leaving hers. There was challenge to the gesture, a warning and a promise. As if he'd read her thoughts and relished in the fear they'd incited.

Sable graced him with a glare of her own before making her way to the counter, where Ivar busied himself wiping and stocking shelves. He noticed Sable and set the rag down.

"Mornin'," he said with a slight nod, though his eyes drifted to Velik.

She couldn't fault him for it. Associating with her was bad for business, and Velik—the town's sole butcher—possessed highly coveted clout.

"Good morning," Sable replied politely, but not too friendly. She set the five coins on the counter. "Do you have any of that elderberry mead? It's for Tolya."

"You're in luck. Bottled a fresh brew yesterday. I'll be right back," he said, casting Velik a perfunctory glance before ducking through the back door.

A log crackled in the hearth, and Velik slurped his ale louder than necessary. Sable tapped her thumbs upon the countertop, ignoring him.

"Haven't seen you in a while," Velik said lowly, suggestively.

Sable ignored him.

"I'm talking to you, Scablicker."

Sable stopped tapping and glanced over her shoulder, eyes narrowed on Velik. "What do you want, Velik?"

His lips curled as he chewed on his roll, slow and steady. "I'm not sure yet."

Sable opened her mouth to give a sharp retort, but Ivar reappeared. He looked slowly from Velik to Sable, and Velik smiled, leaned back in his chair, and folded his arms while he chewed, tauntingly.

Ivar's brow wrinkled, and he set an amber bottle on the countertop. "Here ya are."

Sable took it. "Thanks."

"Give my compliments to the old woman." He winked.

"I always do." Sable gave a small grin and left, feeling Velik's eyes on her back every step of the way.

VELIK WATCHED the Scablicker leave and caught Ivar's keen gaze before returning to his roll. He was about to take another bite when the door opened, and a scrawny boy rushed in. The boy spotted Velik and motioned for Velik to follow him.

Velik wiped his mouth and stood, sending the bench screeching across the wooden floorboards. "Thanks, old man. Say hello to Brinn." Velik winked.

Ivar's eyes narrowed.

Velik had a little arrangement with Brinn, Ivar's granddaughter. He gave them a good deal on meats, they gave him a good deal on meals and ale. Of course, he only gave Brinn the scraps and fatty cuts, but she wasn't smart enough to know better. She didn't fill his heart, but she filled his stomach, and he found that the two balanced each other out. It also helped that she never shied away from his touch.

Velik followed the boy out the door and into the shadows of an empty path.

"What's taken you so long?" Velik snarled, once he was certain no one was near.

"This is the first time she's left the house since you asked me to spy on her!" the boy defended.

Velik's gaze darted furtively, just to be sure no one looked on. "Well? Find anything?"

The boy pulled something from his pocket: a painted black bone.

Velik cuffed the boy on the head. "How's a painted bone supposed to prove anything?"

"It's not just a bone," the boy stammered, ducking back as if anticipating another hit. "It's a flute."

Velik raised a hand to cuff the boy again, but the boy jumped back and hissed, "It's covered in Liagé glyphs!"

Velik froze. He tilted his head to the side, studying the flute. What he'd initially dismissed as faint swirls were, in fact, glyphs —the old language of Scab sorcerers. Liagé, the Scabs called them. He didn't know the language, but he recognized it. Anyone from The Wilds could. They were the same symbols etched onto their wards.

"Give me that." He jerked the flute from the boy. "Where'd you find it?"

The boy rubbed his head. "In her room."

"Where was the old woman?"

"Sleeping. She didn't hear me. I looked for the things you mentioned, but I couldn't find them."

That meant scat. The Scablicker could've easily given the items away, but it made proving her guilt difficult.

"The flute was hidden in the floor," the boy added.

Velik's gaze shot to the boy.

"Beneath a floorboard," the boy continued. "I noticed one sticking up from the others, so I tried it, and it pulled free. Found that in a box."

Velik tucked the flute inside his cloak.

The boy stuck out a dirty hand.

Velik dropped a crown in his palm.

The boy frowned at the crown, then up at Velik. "That's not what you promised."

"You didn't deliver what I asked. You're lucky I'm giving you scat."

The boy's brow hardened as he curled his fingers around the crown and shoved it in his pocket.

"Now, git," Velik snarled.

The boy ducked and vanished down the alley.

Velik discreetly withdrew the flute and glanced over it again. He had no idea what it meant, but considering the markings, and where the Scablicker had kept it, she hadn't meant for anyone to find it.

What are you hiding, Scablicker?

Velik slipped the flute back inside his cloak. He would bring this to Ventus. Ventus would know what it meant, and he and his Silent would be here soon—for Belfast.

5

Jeric hesitated at the door.

Gods, he didn't have time for this, but if he didn't make time, suspicion would follow. He couldn't afford to be followed by suspicion. Not now.

He pressed down the front of his doublet, took a deep breath, opened the door, and strode inside.

His older brother, Prince Hagan Marsellius Tommad Angevin, heir to Corinth's throne, stood in a small group, speaking in hushed tones. If Hagan's height and broad, soft bulk didn't set him apart from the others, his flaming red hair finished the job. That, he'd inherited from their father, as well as the steel gray eyes that could cut a man down where he stood.

Jeric had inherited their father's height, but his constant training kept him muscular and lean, and his burnished brass hair, dark blue eyes, and high cheekbones had come from their late mother. Hagan used to tease him for being too pretty but stopped once they'd hit puberty and he'd realized all the women were starting to agree with him.

The men in Hagan's present company were all members of their father's council—save Commander Anaton—all pining to be the future king's lapdog. Hagan's lap was a cramped place to be. Which was why Jeric typically avoided it.

Jeric was halfway to them when Hagan finally glanced up.

Hagan's smile was synthetic, Jeric's wolfish. His older brother might hold a special place of disdain in his heart for him, but Hagan still needed Jeric to cover up his messes, and Hagan knew it. Which, consequently, contributed to that disdain. On both sides.

"Ah, there you are," Hagan said, all bombast and good cheer. "I was beginning to think you were avoiding me."

"I was," Jeric said as they embraced. "Lina's mercy, you reek."

Hagan laughed. A few of the council decided to laugh too.

Jeric never understood how Hagan could bear having so many heads up his rear.

"Excuse us, gentlemen," Hagan dismissed the others.

The council members gave quick bows to both princes and retreated. Commander Anaton exchanged a weighted glance with Hagan, who said sharply, "We'll discuss later."

The commander nodded and tipped his head respectfully to Jeric. "Good to see you've returned, Prince Jeric," he said, then exited the door, leaving the two brothers alone.

"Discuss *what* later?" Jeric asked.

Hagan pulled his gaze from the door and fixed his attention on Jeric. "Nothing of importance to a Wolf." He smiled, all teeth, but Jeric could see that whatever the commander wanted to discuss rattled his brother.

"So...?" Hagan strode around his desk, closing the discussion, and unstoppered a decanter full of akavit—a Corinthian spirit and, unfortunately, an Angevin family staple. Jeric liked strong drink, but this tasted like scat and burned like a forge. "How have things been in my absence?"

"Boring as hells." Jeric thumbed through the various drawings and schematics strewn upon Hagan's desk—one of which was the map he'd found. Curiously, Reichen had been circled. "You leave and take all the scandal with you."

Hagan poured himself a drink. "Well, if I'd known how much you thrived on my scandal, I would've asked you to come along."

"Gods, no. I'd rather be thrown to the Wastes than endure another voyage on that oversized chamber pot."

Hagan eyed him. "It's not so terrible if you stay above deck."

"And it's really not so terrible if you stay off of it altogether."

Jeric had taken one sea voyage in his life, and he'd sworn to the gods it would be his last. He'd spent two weeks below deck retching, and then—when he'd had nothing left to retch—he'd vomited bile and blood. It'd gotten so bad, the physician on board had expressed concerned for Jeric's survival. Jeric had survived. He never could decide if Hagan was happy about that or not.

"Come on, it couldn't have been *that* boring," Hagan said, pouring a second glass of the tawny liquid for Jeric, though he knew Jeric loathed the stuff. "Anaton says you and your Wolf pack hunted down and destroyed five rebel groups while I was away. *And* you brought me three prisoners."

Jeric sat down in the leather chair, draping one long leg over its arm. He never fit in any of these rutting chairs. "Have you learned anything?"

Hagan slid one glass to Jeric. He didn't meet Jeric's gaze. "No."

Jeric studied his brother, not bothering to reach for the glass. "What about the map?"

"Simple mistakes."

Jeric slid his leg down to the floor and leaned forward. "You're telling me that I just risked my neck—my men's necks—acquiring those Scabs, and your inquisitors couldn't find one rutting clue about who's behind the raids?"

"Risk your neck?" Hagan gave Jeric a flat look. "Please. I thought you said you were bored."

Sometimes Jeric really wanted to punch Hagan in his smug, square face.

Hagan gave him a tight smile. “Why don’t you take a drink, Jeric. You look like you need one.”

Jeric eyed his glass. “I don’t know how you stand it.”

“I wouldn’t expect you to. It’s a king’s drink.”

Jeric saw the goading in Hagan’s eyes—the challenge in those steely grays. Jeric wouldn’t bite. Instead, he glanced down at the papers on Hagan’s desk. “What did you do with the other artifacts we found?”

“They’re with Rasmin under evaluation.”

Rasmin was Skyhold’s Head Inquisitor, feared by the public almost as much as the Wolf himself. All matters pertaining to Scab affiliation ultimately went through him and had done so since the beginning of even their father’s reign.

Jeric watched Hagan. “Do you trust Rasmin?”

Hagan met his gaze. “Father does.”

Not the question he’d asked, but he knew that face. It was the same face their father made. Pressing the issue would only make Hagan more resolute in his secrecy. Both Hagan and their father liked holding power, and holding it closely. It was a treasure they entrusted to no other.

“Speaking of Father, have you visited him yet?” Jeric asked.

His question had the intended effect, and Jeric drew a great amount of pleasure watching the muscle in Hagan’s thick neck tighten.

“Briefly. He didn’t speak much.”

“One can hardly blame him. He’s dying, and you’re gallivanting about the coast.”

Hagan frowned. “It’s called diplomacy, Jeric.”

Jeric flashed his teeth. “Is that what we’re calling it?”

Hagan’s eyes shone with warning.

Jeric picked up his glass. “Cheers.”

Hagan picked up his own glass and tilted it toward Jeric’s. “Cheers.”

“To…?”

A triumphant spark lit Hagan's eyes. "To reclaiming Sanvik."

Reclaiming Sanvik.

The statement shouldn't have surprised Jeric. It'd been their father's dream as well. Before the war with Sol Velor, Sanvik had belonged to Corinth. It was a trading mecca, situated along a delta that touched Brevera, Corinth, and Davros before dumping into the sea. But Corinth had suffered great losses during that war, and Corinth had returned to their former capital only to find that Brevera had claimed it for themselves. Ever since, the people of Corinth—including their father and his father before him—had dreamed of a day when they could take it back. It was their right, according to the gods. But none had voiced this desire as assuredly as Hagan had just then. Which meant Hagan *had* learned something, and he was lying about it.

They clanked glasses, and both men drained the contents. The alcohol burned down Jeric's chest. He repressed a cough as he set his empty glass down on the table with a hollow *thunk*.

Hagan graced him with a condescending grin. "As much as I've missed your company, brother, there is something very important that I need to discuss with you, which is why I sent Farvyn."

Jeric watched his brother carefully. Hagan had been absent almost two months. It was impossible he could've discovered...

"It concerns Father," Hagan said.

Jeric masked his relief.

Hagan crossed over to the window and gazed through the murky panes. The sky beyond was dark. The days grew shorter and shorter as winter approached.

"Clearly, our healers are proving ineffective," he continued. "It's been four months, and Father's still sick. He hasn't worsened, but neither has he improved. One of my rats discovered someone who might be able to help."

Jeric hadn't expected this turn of conversation. Leather creaked as he leaned back, stretching his legs and crossing his ankles, trying to make himself comfortable in the too small chair. "I thought you'd already bled Corinth dry for healers."

"She's not in Corinth."

Jeric eyed Hagan, wondering what he had up his deep, dark sleeves.

Hagan looked steadily back at him. "She's in The Wilds."

Jeric waited, his expression neutral, though his senses went on high alert. It was the same feeling he got in battle when he knew he was about to be cornered.

Hagan continued. "She's originally from Istraa, but she's living in Skanden now. Apparently, she trained under Gamla Khan. You remember—"

"I know who he is," Jeric cut him off.

Gamla Khan was a legend in the healing arts, but they hadn't sent for Gamla Khan because Gamla Khan was a prominent citizen of Trier, the capital of Istraa, and unceasingly faithful to his brother, the sar. The last thing they needed was for Sar Branón and the rest of the Five Provinces—Brevera, in particular—knowing the weakened state of Corinth and its even weaker king. They were vulnerable enough as it was.

"And your *rat* knows this how?" Jeric asked. Hagan had rats everywhere, but this news seemed a bit extreme.

Hagan shrugged and looked back to the window. "Some... reconnaissance in The Wilds."

"Your rat's lucky to be alive."

"You always underestimate my rats."

"And therefore they always exceed my expectations."

Hagan allowed a small smile, then returned to the table. "I want you to find her and bring her here."

Silence.

Jeric waited for Hagan to say he was joking, but Hagan did not.

Jeric bent forward, elbows on his knees. "You want me to travel to Skanden—deep into the heart of The Wilds—to find a woman your rat thinks *might* be able to help Father when Corinth's *masters* have failed?"

"Yes."

A pause. "How much did you drink while you were away?"

Hagan's gaze sharpened. "This isn't funny, Jeric."

"Do you hear me laughing?"

Hagan looked back to the window.

"Gods, Hagan, this is madness!" Jeric threw his hands as he leaned back in the chair. "Even if this healer exists, it's foolish enough traveling through The Wilds with*out* a prisoner in tow."

"I never said take her prisoner," Hagan said evenly, suggestively, and maybe even a little bitterly. "Women love you. They always have. Once she sees you, I'm sure she'll be begging to come along. She'll be begging you for a lot of things."

His compliment was a rose covered in thorns.

"No Istraan woman will come willingly with *me*, Hagan. You know that."

"Then don't tell her who you are. These are details I trust Corinth's deadliest assassin is capable of figuring out for himself."

Jeric's eyes narrowed. "Why not have one of your lapdogs go after her?"

"Oddly enough, *Wolf*, you're the only dog I trust with this. Don't worry for Corinth. Anaton has agreed to send more guards to the roads and passes while you're away, and if you're quick, you might even beat first snowfall."

Jeric stared at his brother. Hagan never took no for an answer, but Jeric would not do this. Not that he didn't want his father healed—he did—but they were on the brink of war with Brevera, and the risk of this preposterous mission far outweighed the possible gain. No, not gain. Dream. That's what it was. A flicker and a hope that, for some reason, Hagan was set upon, and risking Jeric's life to retrieve.

"No," Jeric said. "Find someone else. The journey alone

would take the better part of a month, and considering Father's state—"

"Please, Jeric. You don't actually expect me to believe that Father's health is your real concern." Hagan's tone cut like cold steel, but his gaze cut even sharper.

Jeric stilled. Looking into his older brother's face, he knew that Hagan knew. Somehow, while he'd been a hundred miles away, indulging in drunkenness and debauchery, he'd discovered Jeric's plans.

Godsdamn those rats of his.

"I'm not an idiot," Hagan said. "I know you've convinced Hersir to let you join the Strykers. I know you intended to take your vow tonight, and I have every right to have him tried for treason."

Jeric leaned forward. "Don't you dare. This is my doing, Hagan. Not his. *Mine*."

Hagan gripped the edge of his desk and leaned toward Jeric in a not-so-subtle display of domination. "And I say no. I need you here, in my court."

"You talk like you're already Corinth's king," Jeric said through clenched teeth.

"I will be soon, and my opinion will not change on the matter."

Jeric squeezed his hands into fists.

Godsdamn birth order, too.

"But..." Hagan continued. "If you go to Skanden for me and bring back the healer, Hersir may keep his station, *and* his life. I might even permit you to continue on this"—he batted a demeaning hand—"sanctimonious path of yours."

This was exactly why Jeric had sought to join the Strykers in the first place—to have some semblance of self. To have something separate from Hagan that didn't require him being subject to Hagan's every foolish whim. Becoming a Stryker, he'd still be a servant of Corinth, but he'd serve the gods directly. As soon as he took the oath, Hagan couldn't touch him. The laws of the gods wouldn't allow it. Not even for a king.

And he was *so close*.

Jeric uncurled his fists and draped them over his knees, giving himself a moment to calm down—think. He'd already given away too much, and the key to dealing with Hagan was to never let him know your weaknesses, because Hagan would invariably use them against you. Jeric had discovered that the hard way, as a boy. He was being sorely reminded of it now.

But he would not let Hersir suffer for this.

Jeric grabbed his empty glass and tilted it toward Hagan, who promptly refilled it. Jeric swallowed it in one gulp, slammed the glass on the table, and wiped his mouth. Gods, he hated the stuff, but the burning in his chest helped mute the burning in his blood.

"*If* I'm going to do this," Jeric said at last, "I need more information. Her name, age, what she looks like..."

"Her name is Sable, and she's nearing twenty, I believe. She shouldn't be too difficult to find. She's Istraan. I believe the rest is *your* specialty, *Wolf*."

Jeric grunted.

"It's not like I'm telling you to search all of Istraa," Hagan said. "*You* only have to search one little town."

"One little town in the five hells," Jeric growled. He couldn't believe this. Hagan had trapped him into doing his dirty work. Again. Only this time, he was sending him all the way to The Wilds. He couldn't help but feel that Hagan was trying to push him out of the picture. Permanently.

"This mission is futile," Jeric said.

"That's why I'm sending you."

It could've been a compliment or an insult.

The brothers stared each other down.

Jeric relented. Not by choice. His birth order demanded it.

He was about to ask something else when a light knock sounded on the door.

Hagan stood. "Come in," he said, as if he'd expected the interruption.

Though Jeric still had a flood of protestations, he'd just been dismissed. Two guards entered, holding a slave girl between them. The girl looked to be in her late adolescence, and her coppery skin, angular dark eyes, and black hair declared her a Scab. Her eyes fixed on the floor as if everyone around her might vanish if she simply didn't see them standing there.

Hagan often had women brought to his chambers. If there was one thing Hagan liked as much as power, it was women. That, too, he'd inherited from their father, but worse. Jeric had never understood Hagan's need. Plenty of women wanted to sleep with the future king, paunchy though he was, so it wasn't as if he lacked the attention. But for some reason, he still had this need to take from the unwilling, to dominate, and he preferred the Scab slave girls. Perhaps it made him feel powerful, instilling fear in the daughters of a land that had almost ruled them all. But these girls weren't a threat. Any Scab girl living in this castle had been captured and enslaved, or born in the mines and deemed too pretty to stay there.

Hagan was already distracted, his gaze devouring the girl as he waved for his guards to leave. They did.

"Don't you get enough attention from you courtiers?" Jeric remarked dryly.

"I suggest you keep your opinions to yourself before I change my mind about our little bargain." Hagan leveled his gaze on Jeric.

Jeric stood and strode for the door.

"And Jeric...?"

Jeric glanced back. Hagan grabbed the Scab girl's hand and pulled her toward a small door off to the side. Jeric knew a small bed lay inside.

"Gather your pack," Hagan said, opening the door. "Be discreet. You're leaving tonight."

Hagan pulled the Scab girl through and closed the door before Jeric could argue. Jeric cursed and strode out of the room, wondering why he—the Wolf of Corinth—was once again walking away from Hagan with his rutting tail between his legs.

6

Jeric watched his father sleep, though this man no longer looked like his father. The body was too thin, too frail, the skin ashen. The sight unnerved him. Not that he was about to lose his father, but that his father—someone he'd thought invincible—could be reduced to *this*. A behemoth of a man, whose girth parted crowds, whose voice shook mountains. The giant of Corinth—of all the Five Provinces and beyond—they had called him. King Tommad Coristus Marcel Angevin the third had been a god in the flesh, and surely it would take a god to bring him down. Not a disease. It was too... ordinary.

His father's chest rattled with a cough. It was a vicious sound that bubbled up from sick lungs, and when it stopped, pink-tinged saliva trickled out of the corners of his mouth. Jeric grabbed the cloth from the king's chest and dabbed at his lips.

Jeric wasn't a stranger to death. He'd lost many men on various assignments over the years, and he'd always taken their losses in stride, as he'd been trained. Still, this was his father, and Jeric expected to be grieved, but all he felt was disappointment—that this god was a mere mortal after all.

It was nothing at all like the pain he'd felt losing his mother.

Jeric sensed another presence and glanced back. Astrid, his younger sister, stepped into the doorway. Between the three siblings, Jeric shared the most physical similarities with his sister. They'd both inherited their mother's lean build, fair complexion, and sharp facial structure; however, Astrid's chin tapered femininely in contrast to Jeric's square and very Angevin jaw.

"I thought I'd find you here," Astrid said quietly, stepping into the room. She stopped behind him and gazed at the man they both endured. At least in this, they shared common ground. "Hagan said you'd returned."

He wondered if Hagan had also mentioned Jeric's new assignment. He almost asked, but he held back.

"I looked for you earlier," Jeric said, which was partially true. He'd kept an eye out for his sister, but he hadn't specifically searched for her.

"I've been at the temple."

Astrid had always been the most devout of them. He didn't doubt that, had she not been born a woman, she would've joined the priesthood long ago.

"I understand you returned with three prisoners," Astrid said.

Jeric stood. "Yes, and we're still no closer to finding the person behind the raids."

Astrid glanced sideways at him. "I thought you'd determined it was Kormand."

Jeric watched the king's chest rise and fall. "He is the most obvious choice."

Which was exactly why Jeric wasn't so certain, and he grew less certain with each Scab tribe he and his pack encountered. He knew Kormand—Brevera's king. He knew how Kormand worked, and these little attacks were far too neat and tidy—too methodical. Kormand was like a bear. He reacted. If he meant to fight Corinth, he wouldn't chip away at Corinth's armor piece by piece. He'd stand at full height, show his teeth, and roar.

Astrid studied him. "You don't think it's him."

Jeric didn't answer.

"Who, then?" Astrid challenged.

"I don't know," Jeric said at last. "But it's in Hagan's hands for the time being."

Surprise flickered across her face. "Another assignment?"

Hagan hadn't told her.

Jeric pressed his lips together. "I should get going."

"When are you leaving?" Astrid asked. She knew better than to ask *where*, though the word dangled at the end of her tongue.

"Tonight."

She frowned. "But you just returned."

Jeric flashed a bitter smile and glanced back at their father. "Pray for me, next time you're at the temple. The gods seem to favor your voice."

A strange look crossed Astrid's face.

Jeric snatched his cloak from the chair and left Astrid standing over their father, the king.

JERIC FOUND Braddok tossing one back at the Holey Barrel.

"Hand it over, sweet cheeks." Braddok taunted a dwarf of a man. To be fair, most men looked dwarvish compared to Braddok.

The dwarf—Björn, one of the regulars—grumbled and slapped a silver crown in Braddok's outstretched palm. Braddok's smile gloated all over the place. It looked like Björn's fist was about to gloat all over the place. Jeric empathized. Most people wanted to punch Braddok at one point or another, but Braddok's sheer size usually deterred them.

A few noticed the prince and bowed out of his way. The hostess, however, smiled.

Braddok spotted Jeric, and his grin spread. Jeric jerked his chin toward their usual booth, tucked away in a shadowed corner.

"Sorry, ladies..." Braddok said to the surrounding men, sliding the crown into his pocket. "The Wolf calls." Braddok picked up Björn's glass and downed it. Björn looked murderous, especially when Braddok winked at him.

Jeric had known Braddok since they were in swaddling clothes. Braddok's father had been Corinth's military commander before Anaton had assumed the role. He'd died in battle during the Scab uprising when Braddok was only four, and being that Braddok's mother had died in childbirth, Jeric's late mother had taken him in. Once Braddok had come of age, he'd joined the king's guard. He'd always taken his duties seriously, but he never forgot to take his free time seriously, too. Which was why he'd never followed his late father's footsteps as commander, and also why he and Jeric still got along so well.

Braddok slid into the bench opposite Jeric, and the whole thing creaked and shifted from his weight. The hostess followed them with a tray and handed a drink to Braddok. She started handing one to Jeric, but he waved a dismissive hand.

Braddok eyed Jeric suspiciously as the hostess sauntered off.

"I'm guessing I'll be needing the whole pitcher after you finish telling me whatever it is you have to say." Braddok took a slow sip.

Jeric folded his hands on the table and leaned forward. "We're leaving tonight."

"We just got back yesterday!"

Jeric raised a brow. "And here you are bullying a dwarf. Clearly, I'm not keeping you busy enough."

Braddok smirked. "All right. Where are we going?" He took a long draught.

Jeric glanced askance, making sure no one hovered near as he whispered, "Skanden."

Braddok spit out his drink, some of which landed on Jeric's chin. Jeric wiped it clean with the back of his hand.

Braddok leaned forward. "Why in the five hells? This have to do with those Scabs we killed?"

"A healer."

Braddok held Jeric's gaze a long moment as if waiting for the real answer. When he realized that Jeric had, in fact, given him the real answer, he leaned back in the bench. The booth moved as he shifted, and his breath whistled through his big teeth. "Hagan?"

It almost hurt Jeric to say, "Yes."

Braddok sighed heavily. "And you told him no rutting way?"

"He knew about the vow."

Braddok looked on at Jeric, then dragged a hand over his face. "Gods, he's even worse than your father. No offense."

Jeric waved it off with a flick of his hand.

"This timing is scat," Braddok said.

Jeric didn't disagree.

"All right, Wolf." Braddok scratched the ruddy stubble on his chin. "You want the whole pack?"

Jeric looked steadily at Braddok. "You. Gerald."

When Jeric didn't say more, Braddok raised both brows in a silent *that's it*?

"*Or* I go alone."

"Like hells you will." Braddok snorted and folded his arms. "I'd just feel better with more of us. It's The godsdamned Wilds we're talking about."

"I know, but we can't be spotted. Discretion is top priority."

Braddok eyed Jeric, and a crease formed between his brow. "So? Who is he?"

"*She*," Jeric corrected.

Braddok arched a brow. "You sure this is about your father?"

Jeric flashed his canines.

Braddok grunted and gulped down the contents of his mug. "How'd he hear about this one?"

Jeric leaned back in the bench, one arm stretched along the table. "One of his rats." His gaze trailed the room. "Her name's Sable. She's Istraan. Apparently, she studied under Gamla Khan."

"Huh. So it's *not* just another female conquest."

"Maybe." Jeric doubted this mission was strictly about their father, but he didn't believe it was about Hagan's libido either.

"This is gonna be challenging with a prisoner," Braddok said.

"That's why we need to convince her to come willingly."

"Yeah, good luck with that," Braddok scoffed. "Pretty as you are, no Scablicker's gonna follow a *Wolf* anywhere."

"Who said she'll know who I am?"

Braddok stared at Jeric. "You plannin' to sweet talk a Scablicker, Wolf? A hundred crowns says you'll last two minutes."

"Oh, come on, Brad." Jeric smiled, all teeth. "Have a little faith."

"In the beginning, there was light. And where the light did not touch, darkness existed. But the darkness grew restless, wanting also what the light commanded."

— Excerpt from Il Tonté, As recorded in the First Verses by Juvia, Liagé First High Sceptor.

7

Sable was plucking the last of the lavender from the garden when Ventus and his Silent rode into town. Townsfolk stepped out of their homes and gathered along the street. Children stopped running, chastised by eager and fearful parents, all of them drawn toward the pulsing trot like sandflies to blood.

Behind her, the windchimes sang a single, fearful note. Sable gathered her shears and lavender, and hurried to her porch to watch.

Clip-clop.

Clip-clop.

Through a break in the buildings, Sable spotted the guards first, adorned in leathers and thick furs, with nightglass swords at their waists. They rode enormous black stoliks—a rare breed of horses native to these parts, prized for their ability to traverse the heavy snow. Sable counted seven guards in total, which surprised her. Usually, Ventus brought two, not that he required them for protection. His guards served as little more than glorified slaves upon whom he bestowed menial tasks. His *real* guard was the Silent.

The guards passed, and a Silent came into view, draped in heavy black robes and wearing two wicked nightglass swords crossed upon its back. Its chin was just visible beneath a drawn cowl, though every inch of pale skin was covered in swirling patterns of ink. Some said they were old sorcery markings, but others claimed they were a crude tally of kills. Sable didn't know which was true, but they'd killed enough for the latter to be possible. Ten times over.

Ventus had never brought more than one Silent with him. Today, there were two.

And then she spotted Ventus, The Wilds' High Priest.

Fog clung to his robes like spirits, and the world fell unnaturally quiet. Ventus was like a creature from another world, fated to an existence here, his punishment a human form. All of nature recoiled in his presence, cowering before the thing that should not be but was, impossibly. And rolling behind him, bobbing and creaking as his stolik powered it forward, was Ventus's infamous wagon of nightglass.

It was the one mineral that could effectively kill some of The Wilds' cursed, like shades, and, conveniently, only Ventus and his Silent had access to it. Where they gathered it, and how it'd come to be in their sole possession, no one knew. Ventus bestowed nightglass in exchange for tithes, claiming the Maker entrusted nightglass to *him* to give to the people as he saw fit.

Sable didn't understand how people like Tolya and Mikael could follow the same god as a creature like Ventus. She'd asked Tolya about it once. Tolya's only response was that man often claimed god's will to disguise his own, and she'd urged Sable to get to know the Maker for herself and make up her own mind. Regardless of Tolya's particular view and urges, Sable didn't want to know the sort of god whose servants evangelized through fear and brutality. Unfortunately, she still had to deal with that god's servants.

Tolya had always given the tithe when Ventus came to town.

"My tithe is for the Maker," Tolya had said. "Not that creature who claims to follow him. Nevertheless, I am accountable for my part." But Tolya hadn't risen from bed in two weeks.

Ventus had almost passed out of view when the wagon creaked to a halt. The wind stirred, and Ventus's cowl slowly turned in Sable's direction.

The windchimes silenced. Sable ducked behind the post of their front porch and held her breath until the clip-clopping resumed. With a slow exhale, she slipped inside, shut the door, and loosed a tight breath.

By the wards, this timing was awful.

Sable set the lavender and shears on the table and stepped into Tolya's room.

It smelled sour this morning.

Sable walked to the window. "Good morning," she said softly, though Tolya didn't respond. The window's hinges creaked as she pushed it open. "Ventus is here."

Still no response.

Sable sat on the edge of the bed, gazing at the old woman. Tolya might've been a nasty herb to swallow at times, but she was all Sable had. She brushed a lank strand from Tolya's forehead.

Tolya had trained her well enough to assume the role of healer over Skanden and all of The Wilds, but despite Tolya's intentions, Sable doubted the people would accept her. A *Scablicker*. Many of them only tolerated her for fear of the old woman. They needed their healer, and they'd respected Tolya, but what would happen to Sable once Tolya passed on? The Wilds still needed a healer, but would that be enough? She thought of Velik. No, it wouldn't—not for some.

The only safe place for an Istraan was in Istraa, and though her heart yearned for the desert, she could not go back there.

By early evening, when Sable decided she couldn't put off tithing any longer, she grabbed the amount she and Tolya had set aside, put on her cloak, and headed toward the small temple in the dark. A heavy fog had settled in Skanden, turning everything damp and dreary and cold. Even the lantern flames shivered inside their glass cages. Sable hurried to the town's square, keeping to the shadows. She hadn't gone far when she noticed the small crowd gathering at the edge of the square.

Sable ducked into an alleyway and climbed a two-story wall, careful not to draw notice. Her hand slipped a couple of times, because the fog made everything slick, but she eventually made it to the rooftop and crept to the ledge.

In the mist, the temple looked like a tear in the world, its doors a gateway to hell. A glow pulsed from the square, where one of Ventus's guards held a torch, and shadows danced upon the crowd. Ventus stood before them, his two Silent flanking him, and at Ventus's feet sat a low basin. A device used to collect blood.

Sable crouched on the roof's ledge, watching as three guards dragged a man forth.

Mikael.

She cursed and gripped the roof's edge, scanning the crowd for Kat and Jedd, but she couldn't find them. Jedd had lived, miraculously. Kat had sent a note, because Sable hadn't dared check on him after what'd happened with Velik.

The guards shoved Mikael before the bowl. One of the Silent stepped forward, a wicked nightglass sword gleaming in hand. The crowd was quiet, the square silent as a tomb.

Ventus stood before Mikael. "Any last words?" He didn't speak very loudly, but the power of his voice filled the square.

Mikael did not answer.

"This is the third year in a row you've insulted the Maker with your refusal to tithe," Ventus said. "Your life is forfeit."

Third? How had she not known this?

Ventus's cowl turned toward his Silent.

The night held its breath.

In a glimmer so swift, the sword came down, severing Mikael's head from his body.

Sable flinched and looked away, but she could not stop seeing. Over and over, Mikael bent over the bowl, the streak of nightglass. The blood. She gripped the ledge so hard, wood splintered her palm.

She hated the gods.

She hated what men did in their name.

And, most of all, she hated that she was powerless to stop them.

Sable looked back to see the guards dragging Mikael's body away. The head, however, had been left in the basin.

She forced herself to look. She owed Mikael that, at the very least.

Ventus pulled a nightglass dagger from his robes, dragged the edge over his palm, and sliced it open. He squeezed his hand into a fist, and blood dripped onto Mikael's head. He then pushed up his sleeve, revealing a pale arm covered in black glyphs. Using Mikael's blood, Ventus painted along his own forearm, lips moving as he did so. His writing pulsed white, and Mikael's head caught fire. Unnatural white flame licked at the fog, and the crowd stepped back with a gasp.

Fury boiled through her, and a great gust of wind ripped through the courtyard with so much force, it almost snuffed out Ventus's fire. Ventus's cowl tilted up and turned toward where Sable crouched upon the rooftop.

Startled, she slunk back, deeper into the roof's shadows.

And waited.

Finally, Ventus turned, his Silent followed behind, and the three of them disappeared into the temple. The heavy doors closed, and Ventus's guards took position in the square.

Sable waited until the crowd had mostly dispersed, then wiped her hands on her cloak and climbed down from the rooftop. Her boots landed softly, and she crouched until she was certain no one had spotted her before crossing into the courtyard.

Beside the basin, she paused, gazing down at the white flames that would burn the duration of Belfast, long after Mikael's bones turned to ash. "I'm so, so sorry," Sable whispered through clenched teeth.

Sorry wasn't enough. It was never enough.

She glared at the temple, hating every piece of it and wishing she could burn it to the ground, then strode past the guards. Their eyes followed, but they made no move to stop her.

She had a tithe to give.

And really, what was *she* against Ventus and his Silent?

The door opened silently as she pushed it in. The chamber beyond was dark, softened slightly by wall sconces and a candelabra standing near the far wall, where Ventus was kneeling in prayer before a statue. The statue had been chiseled from the same black material as the basin outside, sculpted in the shape of a world resting on a man's back while four giant, vulture-like birds raked at it, their enormous wings spread wide. It depicted the Maker and how he carried the world forward, rescuing it from adversity. But Sable saw only claws tearing at the world, making it bleed and leaving deep scars behind.

Ventus lifted his head, but he didn't turn.

Sable.

The word pierced her thoughts, clear and powerful. Sable expected it, but the intrusion always startled her. Ventus's strange power was understood as being one-directional: he could speak into a person's mind, but he couldn't draw someone's thoughts back to him. Sable kept her thoughts clear regardless. She wouldn't take chances.

"Master Ventus," Sable said sharply, taking a step forward. She couldn't see his Silent, but she sensed them there like spiders in the shadows, weaving silk around her and trapping her inside. "I've brought our tithe."

Ventus stood and turned to face her, and Sable suppressed a shudder. The light cast haunting shadows upon his pale face, deepening the hollows of his cheeks and the pits of his eyes. He looked like some sick perversion of humanity.

Where is Tolya?

"She's not feeling well." Sable took another step, pulled the pouch from her cloak, and dropped it unceremoniously in the small offering bowl. It landed with a tinny thud and a jangle.

Ventus watched her, silent.

She turned to go.

You and I aren't so different, healer.

Sable paused and glanced back.

He took a small step forward. Inhuman black eyes shone from the depths of his cowl.

We both tend to our gardens, culling the weak and the dying so that the strong may thrive.

"Is that how you justify it?" she snapped. She should have left it, but the image of Mikael was too fresh in her mind.

Ventus studied her. *Weak trees do not yield strong fruit, healer. I trust you know this.*

Sable didn't trust herself to speak further, so she said nothing. She didn't trust herself to think, so she thought of lavender. Of letting it dry and harvesting seeds. Of next year's sowing, how much space she would give them and where they would grow best.

The silence stretched. Ventus's spiders crawled in the shadows around her, weaving their sticky web, and the light flickered and dimmed.

Sable thought of her euctis, how it survived stubbornly in a climate it was not designed for. How it would survive next year too, because that's what it did. It survived. Year after year.

At last, Ventus pulled a nightglass dagger from the depths of his robe and set it on the small table standing between them.

You have the Maker's blessing. You may go.

Sable took the blade, shoved it in her belt, and forced her steps steady as she left, slamming the door behind her.

8

Nine days had passed since Jeric, Braddok, and Gerald had left Skyhold. The first six of those days had been spent riding through Corinth and skirting Davros' eastern edge, then sneaking past The Fingers before finally reaching the infamous bridge that linked The Wilds to the Five Provinces. Built even before the time of Azir Mubárek, The Crossing spanned impossibly high over the Rotte Strait, connecting two crests of a magnificent gorge, as if mankind had defied the gods by connecting two landmasses the gods had intended to keep separate.

Today's masons couldn't replicate such architecture, nor fathom it, and somehow it'd successfully prevented creatures of the ancient world from meandering into the Five Provinces.

It was also a godsdamn frightening bridge to cross. Jeric wasn't afraid of heights, but that bridge challenged even his constitution.

After crossing the bridge, they navigated The Wilds' savage landscape for three days, riding along a narrow thread of dark earth that wove through the forest like an artery. Skanden wasn't far from The Crossing, but they'd been advised to travel strictly by daylight, and this far north, the sun didn't hover long. Jeric would've ignored the advice, but on that first night, which they'd spent in a small town called White Rock, they'd heard the distant and unearthly howls. One, in particular, had made Jeric's skin crawl.

"Shades," the innkeeper had called them when he'd inquired the next morning, whispering as if pure mention of the creatures might make them appear.

"Shades?" Jeric had repeated.

The innkeeper had nodded. "Used to be men, but then the shadows claimed them. Now they're hunters of men. They only come out at night. That's when they see best. Just make sure you're behind a village wall by sundown, and you'll be fine. The wards keep 'em away."

Jeric was skeptical of the tale, and the wards, for that matter, but he was a tactical man. One didn't challenge a predator when the environment suited its strengths; therefore, he'd leave the night to the nocturnal.

However, the days weren't exactly bright. The trees stood taller than anything Jeric had ever seen in the Blackwood, effectively blotting out the sun, and an eerie fog settled over everything. He'd traveled through fog plenty of times. In Corinth, the clouds nestled often in the valley at Skyhold's feet, trapped there by the sharp rise of mountains at its back. Once, the fog had grown so thick, he'd ridden all the way from Skyhold to Flen with only his intuition to guide him. Fog had never bothered him before.

It bothered him here.

This fog had eyes—a consciousness—but every time he looked, he found nothing but shifts of vapor, twists of gray. Tricks, he told himself, but he couldn't shake his unease.

"I gotta take a piss," Braddok said.

Jeric brought Saskia, his horse, to a halt. Her ears twitched, and he gently rubbed the space between them. These woods made her restless too.

Braddok walked his horse a little farther ahead and stopped.

"*Again*?" Gerald stopped his horse beside Jeric. "Maybe this healer should check *you* out. Something's wrong with your pecker."

"Oh, there's nothing wrong with that. Trust me." Braddok winked. "But if she wants to check... by all means."

Gerald snorted. "She could be hideous."

"Nothin' a few pints can't fix. Besides, we can't all be as picky as our Wolf. Give this healer a few pints, she might even take care of *your* pecker."

Gerald rolled his eyes, and Braddok dismounted with a chuckle, turning away from them to handle his business. Gerald looked to Jeric for solace but found none. Jeric watched only the fog, his senses tuned to the world around them.

"You know," Braddok said over his shoulder, "I'm beginning to think that blacksmith in White Rock pulled one on us. Three days in these woods, and we've seen nothing but fog."

"I wouldn't be so eager to meet anything else," Jeric said quietly.

"I'm not." Braddok climbed back into the saddle and urged his horse forward. "I'd just like to see how this nightglass works."

"Assuming it works," Gerald said, following after.

"Always a skeptic," Braddok chided.

"A *realist*."

"A rutting pain in my arse."

Jeric gently rubbed Saskia's neck to comfort her, then nudged her after his men.

"It's a shame we didn't keep the nightglass from those Scabs," Braddok said, admiring the nightglass dagger he'd pulled from his belt. "Didn't have this craftsmanship, but it would've saved us a pretty crown."

"Hagan can afford it," Gerald said.

Braddok glanced back at Gerald as if he were an idiot. "Yeah, and we could've spent those crowns on something—"

A howl echoed in the distance.

Saskia tugged against the reins, and Jeric steadied her with a gentle hand.

Braddok sat upright, slipping the dagger back in its sheath. "Some kind of wolf?"

"Hopefully," Jeric said, studying the fog. It swirled and deepened, creating soft shadows and fluid silhouettes, teasing his eyes. Night was almost here.

"Shouldn't we have reached Skanden by now?" Gerald asked.

They should have, but it was difficult to gauge distance in this fog, and Jeric didn't know the landscape.

Suddenly, Saskia bobbed her head against the reins. Her ears twitched, and her left ear pinned on the trees. Jeric sat forward, his senses prickling with premonition. It was the stillness before battle, when earth and trees and sky held their breath. It was the pause before fate pulled and power shifted, when present became past, and future stretched into the present. It was when the gods set destinies in motion.

"Wolf?" Braddok glanced back at him.

Gerald watched him too, silent as he reached for his bow.

"Run," Jeric snarled, gripping the reins tight. "*Now.*"

His men didn't hesitate. Jeric galloped after, glancing back just as a dark shape melted from the fog and started bounding down the road after them.

Its shape was distantly human, its proportions too long, too awkward. It sprinted on all fours with incredible speed, and the fog clung to it, shadows shifting and obscuring its lines. Jeric had never seen anything like it before.

A shade. It had to be.

Gerald fired a bolt behind him. The bolt struck the shade's shoulder and bounced off.

"Did you use nightglass?" Jeric yelled.

Gerald cursed and dug in his quiver. Another shade melted from the shadows, right behind Braddok.

"Brad, behind you!" Jeric called out.

The shade, which was easily the size of Braddok's horse, caught pace with Braddok and swiped. Braddok jerked his horse away just in time. Jeric ripped the nightglass dagger from his wrist strap and threw. The shade reared back for another swipe, but Jeric's blade struck true, right in the back of its head. The shade yelped, staggered, and skidded face first in the dirt. It didn't get up again.

Jeric relaxed a little. The nightglass worked. He suddenly wished they'd filled their saddlebags with it.

The first shade barreled after them with a deep and menacing snarl.

"Come on, you rutting demon," Braddok growled, throwing his own nightglass dagger.

The shade leapt into the air—higher than any normal creature could jump—and the blade whizzed beneath. The creature landed fluidly upon all fours, its pace uninterrupted as it sprinted after them. Jeric grabbed his second—and last—nightglass blade from his belt and threw it at the shade. It dodged to the side, skidded across the ground, and launched itself at Braddok's heels.

Jeric cursed. He was out of nightglass. Braddok scrambled for another weapon.

"Gerald, get your head out of your quiver!" Jeric yelled.

But even as Jeric spoke, an arrow whirred. The shade yipped and collapsed to the ground in a violent fit of convulsions.

"The tips were stuck!" Gerald defended.

"I told you that you shoved too many godsdamn arrows in that quiver!" Braddok yelled back.

Howls echoed from all directions, dissonant and cruel.

"Where is that rutting town?" Braddok shouted.

Yips sounded behind them, and three more shades peeled

from the shadows, bounding after them with impossible speed.

Godsdamn you, Hagan.

Jeric was about to order Gerald to hand him the bow and run on ahead with Braddok when one of the shades stopped, right in the middle of the road. It tilted its nose to the air as if catching a scent, then crouched low in a snarl.

It wasn't snarling at them.

Jeric's gaze darted to the trees. Beneath him, Saskia snorted, pulling against the reins. The other two shades stopped behind the first, and, like fearful pups, they whimpered as they bounded off into the shadows.

"What in the—" Gerald started.

"*Quiet.*" Jeric cut him off.

The forest fell unnaturally still, their thundering tread too loud in the eerie silence.

"Can you see anything?" Braddok asked, sidling closer to Jeric.

Saskia whinnied, and her nostrils flared. A split second later, Jeric caught whiff of a new scent. Something spoiled, something rotten.

"Do you smell that?" Jeric asked.

Braddok looked wildly around.

And then, like a sign from the gods, Jeric spotted lights ahead. "Skanden," he said like a prayer.

The three of them pushed harder. The tree line broke, and they galloped across a small clearing toward Skanden's main gate. Jeric glanced back, half expecting the shadows to chase after them. To his relief, they did not, and the stench vanished.

"Remind me to thank your brother when we get home," Braddok growled.

If I don't kill him first, Jeric thought.

Four silhouettes moved atop the palisade wall, looking on as they approached. Jeric pulled Saskia to a halt before the gate, and his men stopped, flanking him.

The silhouettes didn't move.

"Open the gate!" Jeric said.

The wind howled. Two of the silhouettes bent together, obviously discussing how to handle Jeric's command. Jeric exchanged a wary glance with Braddok and steadied Saskia, who shifted uneasily beneath him. One of the guards bent over and crossed his arms atop the wall to better appraise Jeric and his men.

"You're cuttin' it close." The guard's eyes narrowed with scrutiny. "*Provincial.*"

"It's Jos." Jeric gave a sharp tilt of his head. "Braddok. Gerald." Jeric nodded to each in turn. "We've come from Southbridge," he said, careful to enunciate his Rs, to hide his true nationality. This was the story they'd decided upon and had executed ever since passing over The Crossing. People in these parts didn't like Corinthians, since Corinthian jurisdiction was largely to blame for their exile here, and the fewer conclusions drawn about Jeric and his pack, the better. "We've business with one of your merchants here. Now, if you'd be so kind as to open the gate." Jeric flashed his teeth. "Your woods are a godsdamn nightmare."

One of the silhouettes chuckled.

The guard eyed Jeric and his pack, slowly chewing on whatever plant was in his mouth. He wasn't in a hurry, and he was taking every opportunity to let Jeric and his men know who was in charge. Finally, the guard signaled another. Wood ground against wood, and the gate slowly hinged inward.

"You cause any trouble, I'll throw you to the shades," the guard called down to them.

Jeric held his wolfish smile. "I wouldn't dream of it." He nudged Saskia forward, and his men followed quickly behind.

Within the hour, Jeric, Braddok, and Gerald sat around a booth at The Honest Thief, sharing a platter of cured fish, soured cabbage, and warm bread. The food was better than Jeric had expected from a town buried so deeply in the world, and the sweet mead tempted even his refined palate. An old troubadour plucked a lute in the far corner, playing pieces Jeric had never heard.

They'd arrived just in time for Belfast—The Wilds' annual harvest, so they'd been told. Jeric and his men were lucky to get a table, let alone a room. But luck, Jeric knew, could always be insured if one simply had enough coin. Which they did.

Even now, more guests wandered in, but every table was accounted for, leaving them with no other choice but to stand at the bar where Ivar worked, pouring mead and chatting with the locals. He seemed a friendly enough old man—the sort who'd seen a lot of terrible things over the course of his life and now found happiness in simply being alive.

A handful of men sat at a nearby table, playing Ruin—a popular card game in The Fingers—and casting bets. A fire blazed in the large hearth, giving too much warmth to a stuffy hall, and the general murmur made everything seem normal.

Almost.

A table in the far corner snagged Jeric's attention. Five men sat around it, speaking only to each other, regarding the crowd with minimal interest. They wore leathers and wools finer than anyone else's in the room, and the crowd ignored them in the way people ignore things that make them uncomfortable.

"More mead?" asked the hostess, interrupting Jeric's thoughts.

The hostess wasn't much younger than him. She had an attractive face and pleasing curves, which she evinced with a dress too small for her shapely frame, and a light blush stained her cheeks as she regarded him.

"Who are they?" Jeric asked quietly, jerking a chin toward the table in the corner.

Her gaze flickered there and back, and she refilled Braddok's empty glass. "Where you from...?" She left her question open for him to fill in the details.

"Jos." He inclined his head. "We're from Southbridge."

"Brinn," she said with a smile. "Your friends?"

Braddok set down his mug and cleared his throat with a smile. "Braddok. But you can call me whatever you like." He winked.

She chuckled with good humor, which, Jeric mused, was an important skill living in such an isolated town.

"Gerald." Gerald tipped his head at the hostess, his expression one of self-pity.

She grinned. "You three've come all the way from Southbridge?" She took their silence for confirmation, then looked at Jeric. "We don't get many visitors from so far south. How long have you been on the road?"

Jeric regarded her a moment before answering, "A long time."

Brinn's gaze faltered, and her blush deepened. "Those are Ventus's guard." Seeing that the name meant nothing to him, she leaned closer to Jeric and continued in a low voice, "Ventus and his Silent run these parts. Those are his guards."

Jeric frowned. "This... Ventus and his Silent. They're here?"

Brinn's gaze shifted to the guards, uncomfortable. "Yes, but I'd rather not talk about it here. Lots of ears, you know. If you like, I can meet you after closing... answer any questions you might have." Her gaze found Jeric's, and he didn't think answering questions was all she had in mind.

In the corner of his eye, Braddok leaned back in his chair and folded his arms with a warning look.

Across the room, a grizzly-looking man watched them, his expression dark.

"No need," Jeric said.

Disappointment flickered in her eyes, but she hid it quickly. "Of course. Just let me know if there's anything else I can do for you."

She started to leave.

"There is one more thing..." Jeric added.

She turned back.

"Is there a healer in town?"

The question took her off guard. She tucked a curl behind her ear and absently pressed down her apron. Nervous habits.

"Brad, here, has been suffering from a nasty case of the runs for the past few days," Jeric continued, gesturing toward Braddok, ignoring the withering look Braddok gave him in return. Gerald laughed and coughed into his mug to cover it up. "I think he caught something from a stream."

Brinn looked pityingly at Braddok. "Oh, you poor thing. Some of those streams can clear you right out."

Braddok looked only at Jeric as he gave a slow nod.

"We have a healer..." Brinn hesitated. "She lives on the other side of town. Make a left past the courtyard, head down a small path, and Tolya's house is the one at the end with the herb garden. You can't miss it."

"Tolya," Jeric repeated, two distinct syllables.

"She's ancient," Brinn continued, misreading him, "but she can heal anything. Best go first thing in the morning. There's a lot of people here for the harvest, and she'll be busy once they all sober up."

Jeric nodded curtly and turned away. She lingered for an awkward moment, smiled at the other two, then scurried off to tend other tables. It was only then that the man across the room turned his gaze away.

Braddok chucked a hunk of bread at Jeric. It hit Jeric's shoulder and bounced to the floor. Jeric looked up, met Braddok's annoyed gaze, and flashed his teeth, all innocence.

Braddok snorted. "You're such a bastard."

Jeric picked up his mug and toasted the air.

"Well...?" Gerald asked.

Jeric took a slow sip. Gerald wanted to know the plan, now that they'd learned the town's healer was *not* named Sable.

Jeric glanced to the men in the corner, drumming his fingers, his frustration leaking out of him in firm taps. "We pay Tolya a visit tomorrow. And then we rutting go home."

9

Sable held the spoon to Tolya's cracked lips, but the woman didn't stir. Sable dropped the spoon in the bowl, set it upon the nightstand, and stood. It was time to make morning rounds, and she wanted it done before Skanden's seasonal guests woke from their mead-induced slumber. It wouldn't be long before they began stumbling through her door, desperate for anything to ease the pain of last night's indiscretion.

She laid a hand gently against Tolya's forehead. "I'll be back."

She didn't get a reply, but she hadn't expected one.

"Hello?" called a deep male voice from the entryway.

Sable froze. She hadn't heard anyone enter. It wasn't a voice she recognized, either, but Belfast was in two days. Many travelers had arrived already. Still, she hadn't expected anyone to be awake at this hour.

Sable ducked out of Tolya's room, and there, before the curtain, she stopped short.

A man, tall and broad-shouldered, stood near the kitchen table, surveying her precious collection of drying herbs. His black leather boots were dirtied, but not boasting the holes and patches the locals flaunted, and though he wore a plain black cloak, the wool looked expensive, tailored perfectly to accommodate his lean height and muscular build. His hair was a soft brown, threaded with brass undoubtedly polished by hours spent in the sun, and he'd pulled it back in a tidy knot, showcasing a muscular neck and strong jawline. He was angled away from her, so she couldn't see his face, but she didn't think she'd ever seen him before.

He ducked closer to the herbs, curious and completely unaware of Sable's presence as he reached for the drying buds of nightshade.

"I wouldn't touch that if I were you," Sable said from the shadows.

He stilled, fingertips hovering midair. His face turned, and a pair of sharp, intelligent blue eyes landed on her.

No, she'd never seen him before. She would've remembered. A person didn't forget a face like his. Beautiful in its severity, imperial in its strength, with eyes so clear, so piercing, they cut through every defense in one swift glance.

Sable steeled herself. She'd have to be careful around this one.

Outside, the windchimes stirred.

"That's nightshade." She gestured toward the buds he'd been about to touch. "And unless you intend to spend the harvest unconscious on my floor, I suggest you keep your hands to yourself."

The blue in his eyes shifted like monsoon clouds. Dark and powerful. His gaze flickered to the nightshade, and then he lowered his hand.

"You're here early," she said.

He turned to face her. Looking at him fully, he was a lot to take in.

"Have I come at a bad time?" he asked. He had a voice like a cello, deep and warm and resonant, but she couldn't place his accent.

"No." Sable stepped out of the shadows and into the room as if to claim it back from him. "Where are you from?"

A beat. "Southbridge. The Lower Quarters."

Ah, that was it. His accent was harsher than she would've expected, but then she hadn't been to Southbridge since she was a child. The wealthiest lived in the Lower Quarters, and looking at him, she wasn't surprised. Southbridge itself was a merchant's dream, located on the Breveran and Corinthian border, situated along the Fallow River, which also grazed Istraa, though Istraans generally avoided it for fear of King Tommad.

Now, everyone feared his son, the Wolf.

Sable eyed him. "You're a long way from home, Provincial."

The blue in his eyes darkened. "I know." His head tilted a fraction. "The hostess at the inn said I'd find Tolya here."

"Yes, but Tolya's not seeing anyone today. It's just me."

His eyes sharpened. "Brinn didn't mention you."

"She wouldn't." Sable chuckled lowly. She made her way to the table but stopped opposite him, keeping the table as a barrier between them.

He took a small step along the table's edge to look at her around the hanging herbs. "And you are...?"

"Extremely busy." She slipped the appropriate flowers into the cloth satchels she'd prepared. "I don't really have time to stand here and chat, so unless there's something you need..."

He placed a hand on the satchel she'd been arranging, stopping her.

She stilled and glanced up.

His expression was inscrutable, but a powerful current swelled within the blue. Satisfied he had her full attention, he released the satchel. "My father is dying," he said quietly. "We've done everything we can and... I'm desperate."

Sable studied him, then leaned back against the table, arms folded. That explained his sobriety, at least. He hadn't come for Belfast. "Describe his symptoms."

A crease formed between his brow, and he glanced about the room as if to pluck words from the shelves. "We can't wake him. He cries out at times. Most of it's unintelligible, but... sleep seems to torment him." His words tugged on that last point, as if he were uncertain how much to share, or maybe he still hadn't decided what to believe for himself.

"Torment how?" Sable asked.

"Nightmares." It was a guess. "It's like he's trapped inside of his mind."

Sable tapped her fingers, thinking. His description of his father's illness mirrored Tolya's. "Will he eat?"

"A little. We've managed to feed him broth."

"And you've ruled out poison?"

"Yes."

"How long has he been like this?"

He pressed his lips together. "Three months, two weeks, and... four days."

Sable stopped tapping her fingers. This was much worse than Tolya.

He smiled, all lips. "As I said, I'm desperate. Desperate enough to come *here*."

Sable had lived amongst thieves long enough to know a liar from an honest man, and while she didn't doubt his father's condition, she didn't believe he was being completely honest with her. And it was by those hidden details she hesitated, wondering at them, heightened by the twinge of unease she felt in his presence. It was the same sort of unease she experienced those rare times she'd been caught in the woods at dusk.

"What makes you think *I* can help?" she asked, watching him.

"Why do *any* Provincials come here for healing?" His question was rhetorical, his tone patronizing.

It was true: people from the Five Provinces sometimes journeyed here in search of resources found only in The Wilds, but they rarely traveled this deep. Before she could reply, he reached into the folds of his cloak and produced a fist-sized pouch, which he tossed upon the table. It landed between them with a jangle.

"Five hundred crowns."

Her gaze shot up.

His eyes challenged.

"Word of caution," she said. "That's a lot of coin to be carrying around thieves."

He took another step, placing himself directly before her. He smelled of the forest after a thunderstorm, spiced with threads of woodsmoke.

"And you'll receive another five hundred crowns once we reach Southbridge," he said.

Maker's Mercy. One thousand crowns!

How had he acquired such a sum? She might've assumed this was a lie too, but looking at him, she knew he was good for it. It would take her ten years to earn a sum like that. She could pay Tolya back for the derriweed *and* buy a new life with what remained—a life far away from the bitter cold and Velik and Ventus and his Silent. But she couldn't leave Tolya. If she left Skanden now, there'd be no returning until spring, and Tolya needed her. And there was also the fact that he'd be taking her to the mouth of the Wolf's den.

"I... can't," she said, oddly unsure of the words as they tumbled out of her mouth.

His eyes narrowed. "Can't."

The word dropped with distaste and inexperience, demanding a reason.

She glanced away from him and gathered the herb satchels into a neat pile. "I *won't* abandon the people of Skanden."

I won't abandon Tolya.

"I'm not asking you to abandon them," he said in a voice now frayed with irritation. "I need your services for a short time, and then you can return to *this*." He batted a dismissive hand at the room, as if he couldn't possibly fathom what could propel anyone to want to live here.

His superiority irked her.

Sable glared at him. "I *am* sorry about your father," she said sharply, "but I will not sacrifice every person in this village for the life of *one* man. I don't care who he is."

His teeth flashed. "Then it's fortunate there are two of you."

His persistence became her certainty.

"My answer is no," she said firmly. "I'll send you with herbs, but I'm not leaving."

Her words were met with a dark and brittle silence, and his eyes stormed. Finally, he slid the coin pouch off the counter, tucked it away into the folds of his cloak, and backed away, taking the scent of forest and woodsmoke with him. The storm quieted, but the clouds brooded.

"I'll stop by in the morning, before I leave," he said. "I hope you change your mind, healer."

It sounded like a threat.

Sable didn't respond.

He strode for the door, but when he opened it, Sable called out, "Who are you?"

He paused in the threshold and turned his head just enough to make his strong profile visible. "Jos." He tugged on his cowl and stepped out into the rain, and the door closed behind him.

Silence settled, expanded. Even the windchimes had ceased their song.

Sable let out a long exhale and sagged down upon the bench, thinking on how a name didn't answer anything at all.

JERIC STRODE BRISKLY DOWN the path, his breath rising in a cloud before him. This wouldn't be as simple as he'd hoped.

Instead of turning right, toward the square, he turned left and headed deeper into town. The streets were empty this morning, and the fog had settled as if it had battened down to stay. Jeric strode on regardless, his boots splashing through puddles as he took it all in—the cold air, the cramped buildings, the narrow streets—drawing a mental map of the town's layout, marking every vantage point and every potential hiding place.

The townsfolk began to stir, and the few he passed made a wide berth around him, as people usually did. They didn't know him, but Jeric believed man was designed with survival instincts, and his disposition naturally warned others away. Still, he found it oddly refreshing walking in a place where he was unknown. Where people didn't want or manipulate him.

Where people didn't do exactly as he asked.

He kicked a brazier out of the way, and its tinny echo pinged through the quiet street. A chicken squawked and waddled away.

The healer wasn't at all what he'd expected. In a world where most cowered before him, he might've applauded her strong constitution had that constitution not interfered with his objectives.

"So...?" Braddok asked when Jeric finally returned to their room. He washed down a bite of honeyed cakes with mead.

Jeric tossed his damp cloak over a chair and swiped a small cake from Gerald's plate before heading to the window.

"I was gonna eat that," Gerald murmured.

Jeric ignored him, took a seat at the window, and propped one boot on the bench while stretching his other leg across the floor. He took a bite of the hot cake and watched the village beyond the window.

Gerald mumbled something unflattering about princes, and Braddok chuckled.

"Did you find any nightglass?" Jeric asked.

"Yeah," Braddok said. "Turns out, it's supplied by that Ventus and his Silent."

This piqued Jeric's interest. He turned the cake in his hand.

"So they're nightglass dealers... who also happen to rule The Wilds."

"They're technically priests, but they serve more as executioners, according to the smithy." Braddok's chair creaked as he leaned back. "And Ventus is their high priest, I guess you'd call him. They live in a temple northeast, but they're here for the harvest."

Jeric's gaze trailed a child who scurried through the streets like a thief on the run. He probably was just that. "And how does the nightglass factor in?"

"The smithy said Ventus comes around a couple times a year and gives nightglass in exchange for tithes to the Maker."

The Maker. God of the Sol Velor and, apparently, this high priest.

"How convenient," Jeric mused.

"Isn't it?" Braddok agreed.

"These Silent... are they a concern?"

"Dunno. The smithy seemed nervous saying much more than that, so I did some investigating."

Jeric waited.

"They just beheaded a man in the village square for not paying his tithes."

"That seems a little extreme," Jeric said, taking another bite of his cake.

"I went to the square to see if I could get a look at them myself," Braddok continued. "One of them stepped outside. Couldn't see scat through the fog, but he just stood there on the steps, like some demon guarding his master."

Jeric frowned.

"Creepy bastard," Braddok added with a dramatic shudder. "I could swear he knew I was there and stepped outside just to warn me off."

"I think you've been drinking too much mead," Gerald said, stabbing a berry on his plate.

Jeric eyed Gerald. "And where were *you* during this reconnaissance?"

"Tending to the horses."

"And your rutting belly," Braddok drawled.

Gerald grinned and shoveled a bite into his mouth.

"You purchased more nightglass?" Jeric asked.

Braddok nodded. "Got more arrows for the princess"—he nodded at Gerald, who grunted—"and a nightglass blade for each of us. Cost you a shiny crown, but I didn't think you'd mind." He beamed, showing off his big teeth.

"It's only coming out of your salary," Jeric replied.

"You can't afford me, anyway."

Jeric smirked. "Nor can I be rid of you."

Braddok chuckled, took a swig, then wiped his mouth. "Still haven't answered my question, Wolf."

Jeric draped an arm over his knee with a sigh. "She's here."

A beat.

Braddok cleared his throat.

Gerald groaned.

"Pay up, pay up," Braddok gloated, flapping his open palm.

Jeric glanced over as Gerald dropped a few coins into Braddok's outstretched hand.

"What's this about?" Jeric asked.

"Gerald and I had ourselves a little bet," Braddok said, palming the coins. "I didn't think you'd be able to convince the girl to come. Being nice to Scablickers isn't in your nature."

"Such little faith." Jeric feigned offense. "For the record, I *was* nice. You would've been impressed."

Braddok raised a challenging brow. "Then where is she?" And then, as an eager aside, he asked, "She as pretty as you?"

"Gods, Brad..." Gerald moaned.

"Oh, get off your self-righteous—"

"I gave her until tomorrow morning to think it over," Jeric said.

Braddok's expression sobered, then pinched with confusion. Even Gerald looked up from his plate. Berry stained his lips.

"Why'd you do that?" Braddok asked.

Jeric tilted his head back against the wall and absently flexed his fingers. "Because she said no."

A pause.

Braddok tipped his head back and laughed.

"Wait." Gerald looked from Braddok to Jeric. "You were nice to her and she *still* said no? You gave her the story and everything?"

Jeric looked back at the window. "Everything." He turned the one word into four.

Braddok's laugh became one of resignation, and he sighed, elbows on his knees. "Gods." He dragged a hand over his face. "We're going to be dragging her Istraan arse through the rutting forest, aren't we?"

Jeric watched a rivulet slide down the murky pane. "Yes, I'm afraid we are."

10

The Temple of Aryn was a masterpiece of stonework, composed entirely of refined skal ore. For hundreds of years, its glossy black pillars and impossibly high dome sat like a god-sized jewel upon the earth, the city of Skyhold its lustrous band. It was the prize of Corinth, the heart of its people. A place of worship, a place of judgment. It was Rasmin's home, and he despised it.

A low sun touched the horizon, gilding Skyhold's storefronts as Rasmin strode through the cramped streets. People stepped out of his way, with reverence as much as fear. Positions like his were necessary, but not liked. Inquisitors were the swords of the gods, exacting justice in their name. No one regarded a sword without thinking of blood; no one regarded an inquisitor without thinking of death.

He passed an alley where three little boys played, throwing stones at squares, hopping through a rough course they'd drawn. Sol Velorian children—dark eyes and skin and hair, clothes in tatters. Commander Anaton was tasked with their collection. His men swept the streets for both purebred and bastards, then the commander distributed them where Corinth had need. Lately, however, the commander's attentions had been spread far too thin, and proof of that strain kept materializing upon Skyhold's streets. Rasmin had almost passed by the alley but stopped short when the boys began chanting a rhyme, in their language.

"We are legion,
Legion is We,
One... two... three...
Soon we'll be free."

RASMIN KNEW ALL the Sol Velorian verses. He had never heard this.

The boy hopped to the end of the squares and turned around. His dark eyes found Rasmin. The boy froze, the other two glanced up, and all three scurried like mice, darting out of sight, leaving their stones behind.

Rasmin's eyes narrowed, and he walked on to the temple, turning the rhyme over and over in his head. Perhaps it was nothing. The mere whim of a child's wild imagination.

Perhaps it was not.

On either side of the magnificent doors stood Corinthian guards, each accoutered in black plates—armor forged of refined skal, a staple of Corinth, coveted throughout the Five Provinces for its lightness, durability, and strength. Rasmin was almost at the doors when a figure he knew well slipped out of them.

"Princess Astrid," he said, somewhat startled but not surprised. She visited the temple regularly.

She glanced up. Her grin came delayed. "Head Inquisitor."

Out of the three Angevin children, Princess Astrid was, without question, the gods' most devout. Prince Hagan served Corinth with shrewdness, Prince Jeric with might, but the princess served it by prayer. The past few months had brought her to the temple more often than not.

Rasmin tipped his head respectfully. Princess Astrid adjusted her cowl and hurried on her way. For a moment, Rasmin watched her go, and then he strode past the guards and through the temple's enormous double doors.

The temple was quiet this afternoon, its circular auditorium mostly empty, save a handful of scattered citizens, all kneeling with heads bent in prayer. Candles burned upon the depressed stage, located at the center of the auditorium, where a collection of flowers and coins lay in offering. More candles lined the temple's upper rim, casting light upon the statues of Corinth's gods.

The gods had been chiseled from the purist marble, carried down from the tops of the Gray Teeth Mountains, each figure standing roughly three times the height of man. The white marble gave a sharp contrast to the temple's glossy black interior—a reminder that though the people might add colorful interpretation to the law, the gods worked in black and white.

Rasmin's eyes lingered on the statue of Aryn, master of the gods, ruler of the skies and all that spread beneath them. The one for whom this temple had been named. Aryn's form had been chiseled to human perfection, boasting a strength and proportion men admired and envied. In Aryn's right hand was the sun, and in his left was a scepter which he'd stabbed into the earth, claiming it and everything in it as his.

Rasmin's gaze drifted to the statue left of Aryn's: Lorath, the god of justice. In contrast to Aryn's broad and boastful figure, Lorath's strength was hidden beneath heavy robes with only a chin and mouth visible. Watchful. Deadly. He held a sword, pointed straight down, his cowl bent over the hilt as if blessing the blade for its higher purpose. Rasmin found their resemblances to Corinth's two princes uncanny.

He strode onward, winding beneath the arched hall that

wrapped around the perimeter and headed for a door tucked in back. One of his inquisitors stood guard, pale hands clasped before him, head bowed. Upon sensing Rasmin, he glanced up.

The inquisitor's face was a face that frightened many, with his snow-white skin and three vertical scars cording each cheek. One scar for each of the six god-given laws every inquisitor had sworn to uphold.

"Head Inquisitor." The inquisitor bowed his head.

"She is ready?" Rasmin asked quietly.

The inquisitor nodded once.

Rasmin pushed through the door, striding down a winding stairwell and into the bowels of the temple. It was here that another people had built a temple dedicated to a god they called Asorai—the Maker. It was here the Sol Velorians had honored and worshiped the Maker until the Five Provinces had driven them out. It was here they had spent countless hours in prayer before Corinth had destroyed their temple, erecting its own upon the remains.

It was here he and his inquisitors did their work.

Rasmin found an irony in it all, to be using what remained of a god's temple to torture and interrogate his followers.

Iron, must, and blood clung heavily to the air, and even after all these years, Rasmin hadn't numbed to the smell. The torchlit tunnel ran beneath the temple of Aryn like an artery, lined with the skulls and bones of the dead. It branched off into smaller capillaries, each ending in what had once been rooms of prayer and teaching. Now, they were interrogation chambers.

Rasmin wound through the familiar network, passing more inquisitors as he headed for where they kept Prince Jeric's prisoner. Two inquisitors stood guard before the door, stepping aside as Rasmin approached. One handed Rasmin a scroll. Rasmin took it, slipped the tie free, and unwound the paper. He scanned the writing, rolled it up tight, and slipped it inside his robe.

"I'll take it from here," he said.

The inquisitors stepped around Rasmin, and Rasmin watched their silhouettes retreat down the narrow corridor before he turned back to the door. It was a single slab of thick oak reinforced with five skal bolts and a bar. This Sol Velorian wasn't Liagé; he didn't need old Liagé doors to hold her. One by one, Rasmin turned the bolts, slid the bar free, then grabbed the torch from the wall beside him, pushed the door open, and stepped into the chamber.

The metallic scent of blood struck him at once, and the torch illuminated a Sol Velorian woman fastened to a stretching table in the center of the room, arms and legs spread. Her black hair had been brutally hacked off, one lid was swollen shut—most likely covering an empty socket. Blood coated that side of her face, and an assortment of cuts and slashes and welts decorated her naked body.

Rasmin closed the door and set his torch in the hook in the wall. The stone chamber was small—they all were—but then, these rooms hadn't been intended for this.

Rasmin stopped beside the table and gazed down at the woman. He wondered, as he had so often wondered, how a people with so much fight and resilience could have been vanquished all those years ago. But pride was a dangerous flaw, for it refused to see the cracks in its foundation, and it was upon those cracks that kingdoms imploded.

"You are keeping secrets from me," Rasmin said.

She did not answer. He hadn't expected her to.

"I read your report," Rasmin continued. "After everything you've been through, the only additional information my inquisitors extracted was a handful of very colorful curses."

Still, she said nothing.

"So prepared to die for your cause," Rasmin said, edging his way along the table, feet to head. "I admire that. It shows dedication. Loyalty. Invaluable traits in a person. Rare, I might add. Your son is very fortunate to have such a mother."

Her breath hitched. It was the faintest sound, but he'd been listening for it.

Rasmin leaned closer to her. "Do you know how I became Head Inquisitor, Taviána?"

Fear marked her stillness now.

"Because not one man or woman has escaped my walls without first telling me their secrets." Rasmin wrapped a hand around her wrist, and she flinched, expecting pain.

He did not give it. That wasn't his way.

"Let us first pray to Aryn that he illuminates the truth," he said as he always did. He flexed his fingers around her wrist and cleared his mind.

A flash.

Laughter echoed. A child. Sun blinded, sands gleamed.

Too far into the past.

Rasmin pulled back. The fates swirled, a tunnel of color blurred.

Another flash.

Dark shapes seeped over fields of wheat—the fields of Reichen. He had been there many times. The shapes wove through village fences, slipped through walls, and then...

Screaming.

A man walking the street collapsed, his face a twist of horror.

The scene changed into trees. Thick as spires. Sunlight mottled their thick canopy. Swaying, dizzying.

Whispering.

The landscape blurred, brown and green and black, and a lake came into focus. The scene halted on a silhouette, crouched, fingers digging into the earth. The cowl turned back. Teeth bared within. A hiss cut through his ears.

Rasmin's lungs cramped, and his breath strangled. He let go of the prisoner and turned away.

He remembered the commander's report of Reichen. The

carnage of a kind Rasmin had not seen in a very long time, and yet no Sol Velorian slaves had been found amidst that carnage.

Here was one. She had seen it.

The wolf prince had unwittingly intercepted Reichen's Sol Velorian fugitives, and this woman was their sole surviver. Jeric and his pack had slaughtered the rest. The lake, Rasmin had visited—recently, in fact. It was a location he'd determined from the map Prince Jeric had retrieved. There'd been no marking, but he'd known the altered words scratched upon the cities. Together, they'd described an uninhabited location deep within the Blackwood. He'd investigated it shortly after, but his search had turned up nothing. Clearly, he'd missed something.

"Im e'Liagé."

The voice was so soft, so fragile, Rasmin almost hadn't heard it.

You're Liagé.

He glanced down to find the woman glaring up at him with her one eye.

She had felt his Sight.

"Im e'Liagé!" she growled, insistent.

Rasmin turned to face her completely.

"Vou'za im var qué e'fíen jarén?" she cried out passionately.

How can you do this to your own people?

"Vou'za im—"

Her words bubbled and died, and a red smile stretched across her throat. Rasmin wiped his bloodied knife clean and returned it to the folds of his cloak with a frown. He hadn't intended to kill her, but death was the only friend he trusted with secrets. Especially a secret such as his.

A KNOCK SOUNDED on Velik's door.

"Hang on!" Velik yelled. He wiped bloodied hands on his

apron, lifted it over his head, and hung it on the meat hook in the kitchen. The company he expected wouldn't require his services as a butcher. He hurried to the front door and opened it to the cold rain. His eyes met Brinn's blues.

Not who he'd been expecting.

She smiled at him. "Papa wanted a few extra things to make sure we don't run out of supplies. You know how busy it gets." A pause. Her smile turned into one of annoyance. "Well? Are you going to let me in?"

"You know I'd never turn you away," he lied, flashing a smile, and held the door open as he stepped aside.

Her gaze lingered on him as she brushed past, and the scent of woodsmoke clung to her cloak. His eyes flickered briefly past her to the street. He didn't see any sign of them. Where were they?

"What do you need?" Velik asked, closing the door behind her.

With her back to him, she lowered her cowl, freeing her tidy bun. She reached into her cloak and produced a list written in Ivar's shaky hand. Brinn couldn't write, or read.

Velik stood right behind her, then dipped his head and trailed his nose against her ear. "I'll take this," he whispered against her skin.

Her breath caught, and her lids fluttered.

He smiled, snatched the paper from her hands, and disappeared to the pantry to grab the items listed. Once he'd gathered everything, careful not to grab his best cuts, he shoved the items in a small sack and met Brinn in the hall.

"Saw you making eyes at that newcomer," Velik said darkly, approaching.

Brinn stood a little taller. "I don't know what you're talking about."

"You know good and well what I'm talking about. You were flirting with him. The pretty one."

Brinn took a step back but bumped into the wall. "I was not. You were there. You saw me. I didn't treat him any differently than I treat everyone else."

He dropped the sack on the floor beside her, grabbed her wrists, and pinned her to the wall. "You know I don't like it when you flirt."

"Velik, I really should—"

He kissed her mouth hard, silencing her, and wedged his thigh between her legs. A soft moan escaped her mouth. She hadn't been to see him in over a month, and he was ravenous. He pressed his body to hers. She moaned louder and arched herself into him.

Suddenly, the woman in his arms wasn't Brinn. It was the Scablicker. They were *her* wrists in his hands, *her* mouth against his, *her* body arched into his.

His blood ran hot. He pressed his mouth harder against Brinn's—so hard, Brinn cried out—but his lips held firm. Silencing her will, her fight. It was always a fight with her, but it was a fight he would win, just as he always did. She might flirt with other men, but she was his. He'd remind her of it.

Knock-knock-knock.

The pair froze, breaths quick and heaving.

Velik cursed. "One minute!"

He stepped away from the wall so fast, Brinn dropped to the floor. She glared up at him as she crawled back to her feet, and she was adjusting her neckline when Velik glanced back.

"Fix your hair," he barked.

Brinn made a face and tugged on her cowl instead. Velik frowned, then opened the door.

Ah, finally.

Ventus stood on the other side, heavy cowl drawn, and he'd brought one of his Silent.

"Good afternoon, Master Ventus," Velik said. "Thank you for coming."

Ventus stood too still, too quiet. His pointed chin tipped sharply to the side. "Shall I come back later?"

Though Velik couldn't see his eyes, he had the distinct impression Ventus was looking past him, at Brinn, who stood exactly where he'd left her.

Velik glanced over his shoulder at Brinn. "No need. We're done here."

Brinn's jaw set. She was angry, but he didn't care. He had more important matters to tend to. Besides, she'd come back. She always did.

She picked up the sack of items he'd gathered, then strode to the door, tipping her head to Ventus as she passed. "Good day, Master Ventus." And without another glance at Velik, she hurried out the door and into the drizzling rain.

"Come in," Velik said, stepping aside.

Ventus lingered a moment, regarding Velik from the depths of his hood, then strode past him. He smelled of the spices they burned inside the temple. The Silent followed.

Velik closed the door after them. "Thanks for coming like I asked."

Ventus stood with his back to him, quiet. He looked out of place in Velik's simple home. Or, rather, he made Velik's home look simple.

"Uh... have a seat." Velik gestured to the two chairs he'd placed before the warm wood stove.

Ventus didn't move.

Velik scratched his neck. "I'll, uh... go get it." He charged up the stairs and returned with the item in hand.

Neither Ventus nor the Silent had moved.

"I found this on the Istraan." Velik held out the flute.

Ventus turned to face Velik, and at sight of the flute, he fell impossibly still. The stillness seeped out of him, soaking into the floorboards, the furniture, through space and through time, holding it all suspended. Then, as if releasing time's invisible binds, he held out a hand.

Velik set the flute in Ventus's palm, but Ventus hissed and flinched away. The flute clattered upon the floor.

Confused, Velik started to pick it up, but Ventus held out an arm, stopping him. Velik watched curiously as Ventus tugged the end of his sleeve completely over his hand, using the fabric as a barrier while he picked up the object. He brought it close, studying it in silence.

At last, Ventus said, "*You* found this?"

Velik hesitated. "I paid Lucan to search her room."

"Why."

"She's been stealing from me," Velik said. "I wanted proof, so I sent the boy to find it, but I'm starting to think she gives away everything she steals. Lucan found that in her room, hidden beneath a floorboard."

Ventus paused long enough for Velik to repeat the words in his mind, and upon hearing them the second time, they sounded ridiculous to him. He wondered if he'd been too hasty in calling Ventus here.

"He found… a flute."

Velik flushed. "Yes, but did you notice the inscriptions?" He pointed to the silvery swirls. "Looks like Liagé writing to me. What's she doing with one of their artifacts?" His voice dropped. "What if she's Liagé? I hear there's a Wolf in Corinth who pays a lot of coin for that kind of information. Thought you'd want to know. Think what a sum like that could do for The Wilds."

And what standing he *would receive for being the harbinger of such information*, Velik thought, suppressing a smile.

"Have you mentioned this to anyone other than Lucan?" Ventus asked.

"No. I didn't dare."

Ventus's cowl tilted to the side. "Not even your whore?"

"Never." Velik smiled tightly. "A woman who's loose with her skirts is just as loose with her lips."

Ventus stood quiet. "Good."

There was a flash of movement, and a sharp and sudden pain exploded in Velik's chest. He glanced down. A bright red stain seeped through a hole in his tunic, over his heart. There, a bitter cold bloomed and flooded his veins. He staggered back once, twice, then bumped into the wall he'd pinned Brinn against just moments ago.

Ventus looked lazily on as his Silent wiped the bloodied nightglass blade clean upon its robes. Velik slid down the wall, his body like ice, each heartbeat too loud and slowing with every pulse. He opened his mouth to speak, but only blood gurgled out of it, and the last thing he saw were two black robes exiting his front door.

11

Sable's cheek slid out of her palm, her head dropped, and the sudden motion startled her awake. The open apothecary book stared up at her, its words and diagrams blurring in and out of focus, and the little flame of her candle struggled in a deep pool of wax. Maker's mercy, what time was it?

Yawning and bleary-eyed, she leaned back and stretched her arms overhead, popping her spine in two places. She should've gone to bed hours ago, but her mind wouldn't join her there. It kept wandering back to the Provincial named Jos.

Because an offer like that would never come her way again.

She hadn't realized how badly she'd wanted to get out of The Wilds until Jos had dropped the opportunity upon her table. It taunted her now as it did then, like a mirage in the sands.

To distract herself, she'd plopped down at the kitchen table with a stack of Tolya's medicinal books, hoping to find a remedy she might have overlooked—something that could pull Tolya from whatever ailed her—but she'd found nothing. With a wince and a yawn, Sable grabbed the candle, got up from the bench, and made her way to Tolya's bedside.

"What should I do, Tolya?" Sable asked, setting the candle

upon Tolya's nightstand. She knew Tolya wouldn't answer, but it felt good talking to her all the same. "You've trained me to follow in your footsteps. I see that now, and I want to make you proud. But… the people still don't accept me. You know they don't. And… I miss the sun." She allowed herself this small confession. At last, Sable sighed, and she was reaching for her candle when Tolya grabbed her arm, startling her.

"Sable… " Tolya rasped.

It was the first time Tolya had spoken in three weeks.

"*Tolya*…?" Sable clamped a hand over Tolya's, holding it there. "Tolya, can you hear me?"

Tolya's breathing quickened. Her eyes slid back and forth behind closed lids, agitated.

"Tolya, I'm here," Sable urged. "Talk to me."

"You're… not safe here. You must… find Tallyn…"

"Tallyn?" She'd never heard the name before. He certainly wasn't on their regular circuit. "Who's—"

"Find him… he will help—" Tolya's eyes snapped wide open, wild with fear. "*Go*!"

Suddenly, Sable was in Trier. A heavy sun poured orange light through open archways, a stiff desert wind pushed white draperies into sails, and an entire court slept. Ricón's eyes found hers, wide with fear. His lips mouthing for her to *go*.

Go.

"They… know what you are." Tolya's voice brought Sable back to the present. "I'm… sorry. I tried to—" Tolya gasped painfully and arched her back

Sable grabbed Tolya's wrists as if she could physically pin Tolya to this world. "Tell me how to fix you! Tolya, please!"

Tolya strained, back bowed, and with a final cry, she slumped onto the bed, motionless, eyes unseeing.

One second.

Two.

Sable's heart stopped. "Tolya." She tugged Tolya's wrists.

Tolya did not respond.

Sable grabbed Tolya's shoulders and shook hard. "Tolya! Don't leave me like this. Don't..."

Sable gritted her teeth.

Abandon me too.

But Tolya didn't hear. Tolya was gone.

Sable turned her head away and shut her eyes, her hands squeezed into fists. She'd known this day would come, but she hadn't known just how much it would hurt.

"Why?" she hissed at the silence. "Why must you take everything away from me?"

She clenched her teeth harder, swallowing the pain, the anger. Willing it to pass. She dragged a fist across her cheek and the windchimes rang a solid, augmented chord. It shattered the quiet, sounding alarm.

Sable froze, fist at her cheek, her grief momentarily forgotten.

And the latch on the front door softly clicked.

Someone was there.

They know what you are.

Sable blew out the candle just as the front door creaked open.

Quick and quiet, Sable snatched the nightglass blade from Tolya's nightstand and slipped into the shadows of Tolya's doorway, listening. The night was a silent witness, the whispering rain an adversary to her ears.

Was it Jos? Had he come back to take her? Certainly he wasn't stupid enough to leave Skanden at night. Or had Velik come back to finish what he'd started?

No, Sable didn't believe either of them would come to her like this. And Tolya had warned of *they*. Not *him*.

There is no use in hiding.

Ventus's voice cut through her thoughts, but this time his words were more than an intrusion. With them came pain—a horrible, wrenching pain—as if he'd gripped both halves of her skull and was slowly ripping it apart. Sable lurched forward, gritting her teeth to keep from crying out.

I'd wondered about you, he continued, and Sable put a hand against the wall to steady herself. *I'd sensed it, though I could not be sure. You see, the Shah leaves traces. Like a stain, visible only to those with the right... perspective, no matter how faded the mark.* A pause. *Someone has spent a great deal of energy erasing yours.*

Sable crept toward Tolya's bedroom window, knife trembling in her hand. She didn't know what Ventus was talking about, but she wasn't going to wait around and find out.

It's unfortunate they forgot to erase your flute.

This caught her off guard. Her step faltered, her eyes fixed on the dark wall separating her room from Tolya's, as if she could see her flute through the boards.

Where it was supposed to be.

An exquisite object. I wonder if you truly understand what it is. Surely, if you did, you wouldn't keep such an artifact lying around for butchers to find. I sense you're smarter than that.

She stumbled forward, barely catching herself on the end of Tolya's bed, but the dagger slipped from her hands and clattered to the floor. Desperate, she scrambled after it, patting down the shadows in search of her nightglass blade. She'd just grazed the cool metal when another shock wracked her skull, knocking her flat on her back. With a moan, she rolled onto her side, her head throbbing so painfully she thought she might be sick.

Outside, the chimes rang in chaos.

She staggered upon all fours and crawled to the window, her head spinning as she gripped the windowsill and pulled herself up. One hard shove and the window hinged open.

Sable.

The word dripped with condescension.

You can't hide from me, sulaziér. Not anymore.

A new pain pierced Sable's skull, one so sharp and so great,

Sable cried out as her legs buckled. The chimes silenced, and darkness enveloped her.

TWO GUARDS WALKED down a dark street, carrying a slender body between them. Their captive's head slumped forward, unconscious, her boots dragging through the puddles speckling the wet cobblestones, and her wet hair clung to her face like a mask. Ventus trailed close behind, dark eyes fixed on the girl, and a wicked smile curled his thin lips.

So consumed he was in his sudden good fortune that he didn't sense the figure watching from a distance. He didn't notice the figure jump from its perch, falling in a drip of shadow before landing silently on the street below. He didn't see it melt into the darkness of the cantilevered facades, then follow steadily after them.

They reached the butcher's house, or what *had been* the butcher's house. The windows remained dark, the house quiet as a tomb.

The guards started for the door.

"No. The wagon," Ventus said quietly.

They found the wagon nestled in the shadows at the back of the house. Ventus followed behind and tugged back the tarp, showering them with icy beads of rainwater. The wagon usually carried nightglass. Tonight, it carried the butcher's dead body, his whore, and the boy who'd discovered the artifact.

The guards waited.

"Careful," Ventus said.

The bodies left only a slip of empty space in the wagon's bed, and the guards took great care sliding the girl into it. The girl didn't stir. She wouldn't, not for some time. Ventus had made sure of it.

"Take the old healer to the temple square, where my Silent

will prepare her body for public burial," Ventus said quietly. "Tomorrow, you will tell the people that I'm holding the Istraan responsible for her death and multiple accounts of thievery. She must be dealt with. Do not mention the others yet." Ventus gestured to the butcher. "I'll leave for Tül Bahn at first light but will return before the Maker's light burns out. I will... inform them at that time that their butcher will not be returning."

"Yes, Master Ventus," one replied, and both took their leave.

Ventus waited at the wagon, reminding himself that she was real, that she was his. At last, he dropped the cover, patted the edge affectionately, and strode into the dark house, closing the door behind him.

Across the street, a wolf watched. There, he lingered a moment more and then slipped away as if he never was.

12

Sable's hip slammed against a hard surface, and she jolted awake. Wood groaned a screeching song while her body rocked. The world was dark, the air chilled. She tried to sit, but her ankles and wrists had been bound. Her gaze whirled as her eyes adjusted, and she soon realized she lay in the bed of a covered and moving wagon. She focused on the rhythmic trot of horses, counting ten in total. Maybe eleven. And then she spotted the body beside her.

She flinched away with a gasp, but Velik didn't move, didn't react. His features were frozen in surprise, his dark eyes open wide forever. Dead.

And he wasn't alone.

Brinn lay on top of him, neck arched painfully back, sliced open and stained black with old blood. Sable's heart pounded harder, and then she noticed the young boy wedged beside them. Lucan was his name. She'd caught him stealing camphus from their herb garden a few times, but, having done her own fair share of thieving, she'd never stopped him.

You wouldn't keep such an artifact lying around for butchers to find, Ventus's words echoed.

A sudden rush of adrenaline drew Sable's hazy world into sharp focus. She was in Ventus's wagon, which meant she was most likely on her way to his temple at Tül Bahn, along with Velik, Brinn, and Lucan's dead bodies. Because—somehow—they had found her flute, and they'd paid for it with their lives.

Maker's Mercy. She had to get out of there.

She arched her back away from the wagon's wall, pressing herself against Velik's dead body. She squeezed her eyes shut, turning her face away as the stench assaulted her—the ale, the rot, the mildew and blood. Some of Brinn's hair tickled her cheek, and Sable cringed, holding her breath and revulsion as she strained to reach beneath the cuff of her boot, where her small knife should have been. It wasn't.

Sable cursed just as the wagon creaked to an abrupt halt.

"...move it," a man's voice was saying.

More voices murmured from the front of the wagon, leather creaked, and a pair of boots landed with a thud.

A bird whistled nearby. Sable whipped her head toward the sound, eyes narrowed. She knew the birds of this forest well, and she'd never heard that particular intonation before. The intervals were too long, the notes too purposeful.

The air pulsed, followed by a wet *snick*. Someone cried out.

"Secure the wagon!" another voice yelled.

All around her, leather shuffled and metal scraped. Carefully, so as not to draw attention to the wagon, Sable scooted nearer the slats, where she spotted a small hole. She peered out, but a guard blocked her view.

"Watch the trees!" someone yelled.

The silence breathed with anticipation, horses snorted, and Sable wondered who was stupid enough to intercept Ventus and his lethal entourage.

"Excuse me, ladies," boomed a big and unfamiliar voice from up ahead, "but you might wanna watch the road, too."

Shouting erupted all around her.

Sable craned her neck, frustrated by her blindness and her bindings, and something flat and glossy caught her eye.

Nightglass.

It wasn't more than a forgotten shard, probably meant for an arrowhead, but it would work. With renewed hope, she inched herself forward and grabbed the shard. She moved fast but carefully, slicing her wrists free. She ripped the gag from her mouth, untied her ankles, and lifted the tarp's edge just enough to peer out.

A felled tree blocked the road ahead—the reason the wagon had stopped in the first place.

And then she spotted a mountain of a man with reddish hair and a beard to match, swinging a hatchet into one of Ventus's guards, while another cloaked figure—equally tall, but leaner—was caught in a whirlwind battle with a Silent. The lean figure ducked, his cowl fell back, and a knot of bronze hair gleamed.

Jos.

By the wards. What was *he* doing here, and where in the world had he learned to fight like *that*?

The tarp pulled back completely, and Ventus loomed over her. He noted her unbound wrists and ankles, and his dark eyes narrowed to slits.

You will come with me.

She winced from the sudden intrusion and scrambled away, but pain seared her skull like a hot iron, knocking her flat. Ventus leapt into the wagon's bed and clamped a firm hand around her wrist.

"Let me go!" she yelled as he dragged her out of the back of the wagon, his grip like a steadily winding chain.

He led her to an unmanned horse waiting at the side of the road. Its rider—one of Ventus's guards—lay sprawled on the ground with an arrow through his skull.

Mount, his voice snarled in her head.

With a burst of resolve, Sable reared her head back, right into

Ventus's nose. He growled, his grip loosened, and the stabbing in her head faded. Sable seized the opportunity. She dove beneath the horse and rolled back to her feet, but her temples wrenched again. Spots danced before her eyes, and she collapsed on all fours, heaving.

You will not escape me, sulaziér.

That word. What did it mean?

Sable clenched her teeth against the pain, curled her hands into fists, and crawled away from him. Bursts of heat shocked her skull like lightning, and Sable fell to her side, her insides on fire.

A man's dying scream cut through the blaze—the sound of life being cruelly stripped away—and it'd come from the trees. It had to be one of Jos's men. A Silent must've found him.

"I'll go!" yelled the mountain with red hair. He climbed the embankment, but Sable knew he was too late.

Jos staggered before the remaining Silent, blood dripping from his temple, his expression murderous. He spat on the ground, then charged the Silent with a fury Sable had only guessed at before. To see it in full was terrifying.

I said mount! Ventus's voice snarled in her mind, twisting and squeezing it into a pulp.

"What... do you *want*?" Sable growled as a wailing filled the air.

It was the sound of a dozen strings, screeching dissonant intervals in the highest pitch, suddenly cut short. The Silent's head bounced to the ground and rolled to a stop at Ventus's feet.

Never, in all her ten years of living here, had she seen anyone kill a Silent.

Jos wiped blood from his forehead only to smear it with more blood. He was covered in it. Sable didn't know how much of it was his.

"Call back your Silent," Jos said through his teeth. His blue eyes looked black.

Ventus cocked his head to the side.

Jos's next step faltered, and he steadied himself against the wagon. "I said—" He gasped, his features twisted with pain, and his bloodied sword clattered to the ground.

Ventus had lifted his hold on Sable to focus on Jos.

Jos yelled through his teeth, hands curled into fists.

She could run, but even if she got away, Ventus would never stop hunting her. Proof of that lay dead in his wagon. Making a sudden decision, Sable pulled the nightglass shard from her sleeve and crept forward, her steps falling with practiced silence. Ventus didn't notice. He only had eyes for the man who'd killed his Silent, and his vengeance would not be swift. He would make Jos suffer.

Ventus's vengeance would be her redemption.

Jos doubled over and fell to his knees, fists pressed to his temples as if he could physically push Ventus's power out of his skull. Ventus took a step toward him, reveling in Jos's agony, and Sable jammed the nightglass shard into the bend of his neck, where an artery pulsed.

Ventus jerked and staggered; Jos collapsed with a gasp. Ventus whirled on Sable, eyes livid, black teeth bared. He reached for her, but his body flinched. He hiccuped in surprise, slumped to his knees, and fell face-first to the ground. A hilt protruded from his back. Sable looked up and met Jos's severe gaze. Held it.

"What are you doing here?" she yelled at him.

"You're… welcome," he hissed, rolling his shoulder, then clenched his teeth. "I need to find my men."

Sable surveyed the carnage around them, the broken bodies, the blood. She'd worked with death—witnessed brutality of the worst kind—but she'd never seen so much at once. Jos and his men had taken on seven guards, two Silent, and Ventus. And *won*.

She looked back at him, eyes narrowed. "Who *are* you?"

"Now's not the time to chat, healer." He grabbed the reins of a nearby horse. "Get in the saddle."

He expected her to go with him.

"I'm not going anywhere with you."

His eyes darkened, violent and storming. "I just saved your life."

"And you have my eternal thanks." She turned away from him, plucked a couple of daggers off of Ventus's fallen guards, and shoved them in her belt. She approached Ventus and considered searching him for her flute but decided against it. The last thing she needed right now was for this lethal Provincial to witness some Liagé artifact illuminating at her touch. Besides, history had proven that if it meant to find a way back to her, it would. Without her help.

"Get on the godsdamn horse."

Sable pulled the dagger from Ventus's back, then faced Jos. "I see that I didn't make myself clear. When I say I'm not..." Her voice trailed as Ventus's hand twitched.

She gaped at him. It wasn't possible. She'd severed his carotid artery... but even as she stared, the skin at his neck was knitting itself together, and his fingers began drawing symbols on the ground, in blood.

"What in the five hells...?" Jos said behind her.

Trees rustled above, bending toward each other, whispering secrets, and a shadow fell over everything. Jos's horse whinnied, ears twitching, and she jerked against the reins.

Ventus began to chant.

Sable punched him in the face, silencing him. He smiled up at her with bloodied teeth. Before Sable could wonder, the crimson symbols flashed white. Energy pulsed in a shockwave of power, a wall of wind barreled through the trees, and all fell still.

"The horse," Jos said quietly, pulling a knife from somewhere on his bruised and battered body.

This time, Sable didn't argue. She started backing steadily toward him, and a click sounded nearby. A yip echoed opposite. And then a black form melted from the shadows of a tree.

A shade.

Here, in broad daylight.

It crouched upon all fours, swaying back and forth, back and forth, its head cocked to the side with animal curiosity, yellowed eyes fixed on them. Its slitted nostrils flared as it sniffed at them, and its black lips curled with a deep and rumbling snarl.

"I thought they only hunted at night," Jos said behind her.

"I did too," she said.

Another shade materialized from the shadows, beside the first. And another, and another, blocking the road while more lined the crest of the escarpment.

Sable had never seen so many at once.

Her gaze met Jos's. Wordless understanding passed between them, and in a whip of motion, Jos leapt into the saddle and clasped thick fingers around Sable's readied hand. She jumped, letting him swing her onto the horse's rear, and Sable had barely secured her arms before he kicked them into a full gallop. Shades snarled and bounded after them.

The shades on the ledge leapt down, tearing up clumps of earth as they sprinted. Jos urged their horse faster when a handful of shades appeared ahead, blocking the road.

Their horse skidded to a halt and reared.

Jos cursed.

Sable just tried to hold on.

Their horse landed on all fours again and bolted into the trees.

Jos regained some control, deftly maneuvering through the thick trees, but the horse couldn't run fast enough. Not while carrying the weight of two bodies. Shades flanked them on both sides, pressing in closer and closer.

"Do you have nightglass?" Sable yelled.

"My belt," he yelled back.

Sable felt around his waist and jerked the nightglass dagger free right as a shade closed in. It swiped, but Sable hacked off its hand.

It shrieked and fell back, but another sidled up to replace the first. Jos positioned himself to kick it away.

"Careful!" Sable yelled. "Their claws are poisonous!"

Jos hesitated, and Sable threw the nightglass. It landed in the shade's shoulder, and the shade staggered and fell back.

"That was my last nightglass blade!" Jos yelled.

"Then run faster!"

"This is as fast as it gets, healer!"

The shades were gaining on them.

Sable scanned the landscape. The Kjürda snaked through this part of the woods. If only they could find it...

The sound of rushing water whispered through the trees, and Sable felt a surge of hope. A song of salvation.

"There!" Sable pointed.

Jos veered their horse in the direction she pointed. In a sudden burst, a shade pushed closer, all saw-like teeth and snarls, but Sable knocked it away with the sole of her boot, careful to avoid its claws.

"Get ready to jump!" Sable said.

The trees broke, and a narrow canyon stretched before them.

The shades closed in.

Sable grabbed Jos's arm. Their horse skidded to a halt, and they leapt from the saddle. Sable landed with a stagger, but Jos landed on his feet and pulled her forward, and the two of them charged the cliff.

One shade leapt, claws open and greedy.

They jumped.

Nails sliced air; a snarl raged in defeat.

The moment froze. Jos and Sable hung in the air, silhouettes suspended between gray sky and rapids. They dropped like arrows, boots piercing the frothy surface of the Kjürda, and ice-cold water swallowed them whole.

13

Prince Hagan leaned his head back against the bathtub while a Scab girl rubbed soap into his hair. Her fingers moved to his temples, and he let out a soft moan. His headaches had intensified ever since Jeric had left. So had the tension in court.

Since the horror at Reichen, the city of Dunsten had met a similar fate. Per the commander's report, Scab slaves were nowhere to be found, and the bodies of the townsfolk had been left in a heap at the foot of their temple. Corpses with skin like ash, stained by a web of black veins, eyes missing. Rumors of the atrocity circulated throughout Corinth, and the jarls were quickly losing faith in King Tommad's ability to protect them from the enemies within their own borders.

As much as Hagan was loath to admit it, Jeric's presence at Skyhold held the vultures at bay. He was the silent threat, the swift blade in the dark, the thread that pulled the delicate scales in perfect balance. He was the promise fulfilled, the secret weapon, the one who secured the Angevin reign. Without him, the jarls squawked and bit and raked their sharp talons, each vying for the largest piece of the king's withering body. And how it withered.

Rasmin had better be right about the girl, Hagan thought. Because he didn't know how else to combat the power this mysterious army wielded—a power Rasmin believed to be led by a Liagé.

The Scab wrung water over his hair, rinsing it clean, and then stepped away.

Hagan lazily opened his eyes and watched her retrieve one of the towels. She was a new servant. Murcare, who oversaw the skal mines and their laborers, had pulled her from one of the mines, thinking Hagan might find… use for her. She was a pretty thing. Large, dark eyes and full lips. Her shape was soft and slender with dawning adolescence, yet supple where it mattered most. She returned with the towel, but Hagan reached up and wrapped his fingers around her wrist.

She stilled at his touch, and the pulse in her wrist quickened.

"Undress," he said.

Her gaze dropped to the floor, and she swallowed.

He squeezed her wrist harder. "I don't like to be kept waiting, Scab."

With her free hand, she fumbled with the ties of her dress. Hagan released her wrist and watched hungrily as she slipped out of her clothing. Jeric didn't understand his appetite for the Scab girls; Hagan didn't understand why Jeric didn't have one. Scab girls were like wild horses. Hard bodies and iron wills. Difficult to break. Each time, Hagan felt a sense of triumph he was certain Jeric would relish, if only he tried.

The girl crossed her arms over her young breasts.

"Don't cover yourself," Hagan commanded.

Her arms fell awkwardly to her sides. His eyes raked over her, and his body responded. Not for the first time, he thought the gods had given a disproportionate amount of the world's beauty to the Sol Velorian women.

"Look at me," he said.

Her dark eyes lifted to his. Through the tears, he saw the iron will. The flame of defiance—a flame that only aroused him further.

"Join me," he said, motioning to the tub.

She didn't move.

His eyes narrowed. "I won't ask you again."

She stepped closer, trembling, then stepped into the tub. He grabbed her arm to steady and guide her into his lap, her back to his chest. She sat rigid, her eyes shut tight as he pulled the clip from her hair. He combed his fingers through her thick mane, then grabbed a handful and pulled it back, exposing her neck. A tear leaked down her jaw and dropped into the bathwater.

"I won't hurt you," he said, licking the salt from her cheek. "In fact, I believe that, in time, you'll come to find it rather... enjoyable."

Her breath quivered. "*Fava...*" she pleaded in her native tongue. "*A'noi.*" Please. Don't.

A sharp knock sounded on the door.

Hagan ignored it.

The door flung open.

Hagan growled and looked up as Astrid breezed into the washroom. Astrid never visited him like this, alone. She regarded the girl with disdain and regarded him with something far worse.

"Get out," Astrid snapped, snatching a towel and tossing it at the girl.

The girl barely caught the towel before it hit her in the face.

Hagan grabbed the girl's arm, holding her firmly in place. "You don't give the orders here."

Astrid's expression darkened. "You know I wouldn't come here *willingly* if it wasn't important."

Hagan studied his sister, then batted a dismissive hand at the girl. "Go."

The girl hurried out of the tub, wrapped herself in the towel, and scurried out of the room.

"Honestly, Hagan," Astrid said scathingly. "Brevera is attacking our roads, our *allies* have knives at our throats, and you're in here bathing a Scab. If you're not careful, one of these days, you might discover your Scab is really Liagé in disguise, and she'll kill you in your bed."

He would've argued that Rasmin sifted through every Scab, searching for the Liagé among them, but considering the recent events happening in Reichen and Dunsten, he was beginning to lose faith in the Head Inquisitor's abilities. Instead, he leaned back and stretched his arms along the rim of the tub. A cord of silvery skin stretched from his elbow to his wrist—a scar, a reminder.

"I'm not really in the mood for your admonishment this morning," he said, eyeing her. "Say your piece and leave."

Her eyes flashed. She turned to the window.

The silence stretched.

"Father's gone," she said at last.

The words were a hot iron to his skin.

He bolted upright. Water sloshed in the tub. "Just now?"

"Yes."

Hagan clenched his fists. Godsdamnit. He needed more time. He needed Jeric.

"Were you there when it happened?" he asked.

Astrid didn't answer immediately. "Yes. His heart stopped. I… think he finally gave up fighting." Her shoulders lifted with breath before she turned to face him. He couldn't read the expression that greeted him, but Astrid was a master at masking emotion.

He was largely to blame for that.

"Who else knows?" he asked.

"Tolov and Bern." She paused. "And Jarl Rodin."

Hagan struck the tub with his fist and cursed. "How does Rodin know?"

"*Apparently*, he'd gone for a walk and found himself near the king's chambers."

"That pandering, opportunistic..." Hagan raked a hand through his wet hair. "Half of Corinth will know by nightfall."

Astrid smiled, all lips. "Then I suppose we're lucky *you're* here to quell all fears."

Hagan studied Astrid. As usual, there seemed to be another meaning hidden in the package of her words. One he couldn't extract.

Astrid picked up a fresh towel and draped it over the tub. "The jarls will expect a statement. Especially Stovich. He's still waiting for your answer concerning the event at Reichen."

Hagan took the towel, stood, and to his amusement, Astrid looked away to give him privacy. He stepped out of the tub and wrapped the towel around his waist. Perhaps he should start training with Jeric. The towels were fitting tighter and tighter. "The jarls don't want a statement. They want my blood."

Astrid didn't disagree. "It's a pity Jeric isn't here."

Hagan ignored the slight and made his way to the vanity, dabbing a few drops of cologne upon his neck.

"You never said where you sent him."

He caught Astrid's gaze in the mirror. "No, I never did."

"Where is he?" she asked, her tone neutral, though the emotion in her eyes betrayed her.

Hagan turned around and approached her, step after slow step. The pulse in her temple quickened, making him smile.

"Astrid, Astrid, Astrid..." Once he was close enough, he reached out and rested a palm against her cheek.

Her breath hitched.

"Let me worry about Jeric and this kingdom," he said quietly, slipping his hand into her hair, grabbing a fistful. Tugging on it.

Astrid stood still as granite, though her throat moved as she swallowed.

"You, out of anyone, should know that I *always* protect what is mine," he said.

"Let go of me, Hagan," she said lowly, though the edges of her voice trembled with old fear.

"You're still my favorite," he whispered.

Her eyes seared through him, hating and powerless, but she didn't move, didn't speak. He rubbed his thumb over her cheek once more before releasing her hair.

Astrid stormed past him and left, slamming the door after her.

Hagan watched her exit, then sighed and glanced to the window. "Godsdamnit, Jeric," he growled at the silence. "Where are you?"

THE WATER of the Kjürda was so cold it burned. Sable opened her mouth to breathe, but only water rushed in. She opened her eyes to see, but there was no sky. Her hand broke the river's surface. Encouraged, she kicked her legs, but the cold made them leaden, and the current pulled her under again. A rock smashed her elbow; another slammed her hip. Pain registered, though dimly. She needed air.

Just when she thought her lungs might burst, her head surfaced. She inhaled sharply, drawing water with air, and coughed on them both. She kicked her legs as hard as she could, holding herself above water while trees and sky blurred, and the river carried her onward, roaring louder than before.

The waterfall.

Frantic, she clawed for the bank, fighting the current with stiff and frozen fingers, but then she caught sight of a cloak. It bunched amidst the froth and boulders, bubbling with the current.

Jos.

She hesitated. He was trapped in the current, and if she didn't help him, he'd die. He might be dead already. Sable glanced at the bank, cursed, then took a deep breath and started swimming for him.

Water rushed over her head, pulling her under again, but she persisted until finally, she caught the edge of his cloak and gripped it tight. The current dunked her again, but she held firm, his cloak her anchor. She tugged on it, straining against the water, the cold, and the rocks. With a final jerk, it tore free. His motionless body came with it.

She wedged her arms through the pits of his, then lay on her back and kicked hard. Water spilled over her face, into her mouth, and the hungry river dragged them under again. This time, she couldn't pull them up.

Sable fumbled at his cloak with cold and clumsy fingers, grabbed hold of his neck ties, and ripped them open. The current stole the cloak away, and Sable kicked again, breaking the surface with a loud gasp, right before his weight dragged her under again.

The Kjürda swallowed Sable's curse, and she kicked with everything she had left. His scabbard dug into her thigh, her legs cramped, her fingers ached, and just when she couldn't kick anymore, her back scraped against rock.

They'd reached the shore.

She staggered out of the frigid water, sopping wet and shivering as she dragged Jos onto the bank and rolled him onto his back. The knot in his hair had come undone, and his hair stuck to his face like a mask. She pushed it aside. The river had washed away most of the blood, but a gash marred his brow. His skin was whiter than snow lilies, and blue tinged his lips. He wasn't breathing.

Sable knelt beside him, pressed her palms to his heart, and pushed, again and again.

He didn't stir.

"Come on," she growled, shoving him harder, trying to force rhythm into his sleeping heart. Suddenly, Jos lurched with consciousness, and Sable backed away. Water gurgled from his lips, and then he rolled on his side and vomited.

He spat the last of it on the ground and dragged a hand over his lips. "Gods*damn*it."

Sable breathed hot air on her trembling hands. Her white fingertips were swiftly turning purple, and snow began falling around them.

"Did they... follow?" Jos's words shivered as he gazed past her to the opposing bank.

"No," Sable said. "They c-c-can't swim, but we need to get moving." They needed to get dry. They needed to get *warm*. Sable knew from experience that this sort of cold was the cleverest of thieves. It confused and it paralyzed, then slipped in and stole your existence.

Jos staggered to his feet and checked his sword, which had, miraculously, survived. His hands shook uncontrollably, and he shoved them into the pits of his arms. "My men are still out there."

"We can't go back."

"I won't leave them out here to die." Not even the cold could steal the bite from his words.

"We need to worry about *us* right now, Jos. We need to get *warm*."

Jos pressed his fists to his temples and shut his eyes. His body shuddered with cold. "Where's the n-n-nearest town?"

"Um..." Sable squeezed her eyes shut, forcing herself to focus. It was increasingly difficult to think.

They couldn't go back to Skanden, and she didn't dare cross back over the river right now. They needed to head deeper into the woods, away from the main roads. She opened her eyes. "Craven. A half day's walk from the f-f-falls. Southeast."

Jos growled in frustration. Shivers racked his body, ice crusted his brow and lashes, and clumps of his hair had frozen. Sable noticed clumps of her hair had frozen too.

"Godsdamnit," he hissed, rubbing his arms, dusting off the newly fallen snow. "We need a fire."

"We c-c-can't."

"We can't wait for Craven."

"If you start a fire, they'll f-f-find us," she snapped.

His eyes blazed. "How do you want to die, healer?"

Sable glared back. "Not facing a dozen shades."

Jos gritted his teeth and looked to the landscape. Then, with sudden decision, he grabbed her arm and pulled her after him, toward the roaring waterfall.

"What are you doing?" she demanded.

"Saving our godsdamn lives."

He didn't elaborate, and Sable's teeth chattered too much to make him.

They stumbled along the river's edge, using each other for added support. Walking did nothing to warm Sable's frozen limbs. She was far beyond that. They reached the top of the waterfall, and Jos stopped. Water careened over a granite shelf, plunging into the swirling mist below, and Sable realized his plan.

The mist, combined with snowfall, might just hide the smoke of a small fire. And they needed a fire. *Now*.

"There." Jos pointed to a crop of boulders nestled near the falls, a little farther down. "Get branches… needles… anything—"

"I know," she cut back.

They broke apart, collecting fallen branches and pine needles. Sable carried her meager findings to the designated location, stumbling like a drunkard all the way. Her toes felt like rocks inside her soggy boots, and she couldn't curl her fingers.

She spotted Jos approaching with a small pile, each step a similar battle. He dumped his findings in the small niche between rocks, removed his scabbard and tossed it below, then slid down after them. Sable followed. The space was tight—just a crack between boulders—but it shielded them from sight and spray and snowfall. She hoped it would be enough.

Jos reached into his boot and pulled a small dagger from the shaft. His clumsy fingers fumbled with the hilt, but he eventually twisted the pommel free, revealing a small wad of wool inside. He dumped the wad into his palm, but his hands shook so violently, the wad slipped to the ground, and a slab of flint tumbled out of it. With a curse, he picked it up, then stacked a handful of smaller branches. He tried striking flint to steel, but his hands trembled and the flint slipped from his grasp again.

He growled in frustration, too cold even to curse.

Sable scooted closer and held out a quivering hand. His expression warred, but he relented, handing her his dagger, hilt first.

She took the dagger, picked up the flint, and managed a spark on the third try. She blew on the spark, careful not to overwhelm it, and, thankfully, the needles caught. They blackened and curled as the flames ate them up, then licked at the wood. She handed him back his dagger, which he took in silence, and then he grabbed some of the larger branches and propped them over their entry like a canopy. She stood to help him, both of them shaking violently, and when they finished, their gazes met. Held.

Mutual understanding passed between them.

He glanced down and started unfastening the ties of his tunic.

Sable had never been naked in front of anyone before, not since she was a little girl, and she'd certainly never imagined her first time being like this—for survival in its most rudimentary form. But any insecurities she'd expected to feel had dissolved in the frigid waters of the Kjürda. She turned away from him and started peeling off her shirt. It stuck to her like a second layer of skin, but slowly, in the cramped and hidden spaces of the rocks, they shed layer after wet layer, stripping themselves of their pride, their dignity, leaving only two humans—one man and one woman—united in a desperation to live.

Jos lay before the fire, on his side, leaving a slip of space for her. Sable didn't look at him as she lay down beside him. Their bodies were stiff at first, awkward and uncomfortable, and then the urgent need for warmth triumphed all else. He wrapped a trembling arm around her and pulled her shivering body against his, skin to skin.

The closeness shocked her at first. The pure vulnerability of it, the brush of his breath against her neck, his damp skin flush with hers. The solidness of him. But as his body heat slowly seeped into her skin, quieting the cold, her shock turned into gratitude. That if she were to die this day, at least she wouldn't die alone.

14

Around a bed where only dead lay, the priests of Aryn worked tirelessly. They tried giving color where there was none, attempting to fill voids rent by disease and starvation, but they could not make this body what it once was. The gods had taken his life, his glory, and his power and left only a withered shell. It was in times like this, when Hagan observed the dead, that he considered the afterlife. That he thought of what made man *man*. It was not the body. For one only had to look at this corpse to see that what was there was there no more —the thing that'd made his father *human*.

The priests of Aryn spied their new king standing at the edge of the great chamber in the shadows of the stone archway. In an elegant display of synchronization, they bowed their heads and moved around the platform, joining in single file as they exited a passage at the back of the chamber, leaving Hagan alone with his father.

What *had been* his father.

Hagan approached.

The Room of Sanctification had always made him uncomfortable. It was too dark, chilled with a cold that seeped from the very stones, and the air smelled stale and metallic despite the steadily burning incense. Rows of arched niches decorated the walls like windows made of stone, and dozens of candles burned upon their mantels, but the flames did little to light the domed chamber. Shadows crowded the room, as if every soul that'd ever passed through these walls had stayed, seeking solace in multitudes.

Hagan stopped before his father's body.

King Tommad Coristus Marcel Angevin the third: a man worshiped by the people, revered for his valor and strength. Hagan took in the deep lines of his face, the ashen skin sagging over bones made too prominent from malnutrition. He regarded the late King Tommad's thin lips, settled together, never to open again. In his mind, a voice boomed—a voice that'd once commanded lines of men. A voice that'd given Hagan an immense source of pride.

But that was a long, long time ago.

"You gave up," Hagan said, quiet, so that his voice wouldn't echo. His hand curled into a fist upon the platform, beside his father's body. "You gave up, and you left me a disaster." He did not hide the bite from his words. He could not. It was an anger that'd festered for years, and now that his thoughts were free to be voiced, he couldn't stop them. "You could've at least *tried* to be the man you were, but you grew lazy. Weak. And now my throne is rotted from your godsdamned negligence." His nostrils flared. "It would've been better had you died with mother."

A sound stopped him short.

He pulled his fist from the platform and glanced back at his robed intruder. "Rasmin," he said sharply.

Rasmin stepped into the room. Candlelight danced upon his ancient face. "Am I... interrupting?"

"Interrupting what? There is nothing to be said here." Hagan frowned at the body beside him.

"Every man needs time for grieving."

"My grieving happened a long time ago," Hagan said, more to himself, then turned completely to face Rasmin, who respectfully bowed his head.

"I've drafted the invitations," Rasmin said. "The messengers will ride first thing tomorrow morning, assuming the weather holds."

They were invitations for the Day of Reckoning—a provincial holiday, celebrated by Corinthians as the day Corinth defeated Azir Mubarék, his Liagé, and all of the Sol Velor nearly one hundred and fifty years ago. It was, however, a bittersweet day, for it was also the day that Brevera had taken Sanvik, Corinth's original capital. His father hadn't given much attention to the holiday, and Hagan planned to remedy that. It would symbolize his reign.

"But...?" Hagan prodded.

Rasmin cleared his throat. "I have... concerns, your grace."

Hagan waited.

"The jarls haven't been together in many years," Rasmin continued quietly. "We already suspect Stovich works against you. I don't think it wise to host everyone here, at Skyhold, until we know whose allegiance lies where."

"And what better way to discover their true allegiance than by asking them in person," Hagan said, taking a step forward. "I *will* have them here, Head Inquisitor. We will feast as we have never feasted. I will remind them what it means to be Corinthian. And I will remind them who is king."

Rasmin's black eyes glittered. "Whatever your grand display, your grace, the fact remains that we have traitors in our midst. Hosting them here—inside the walls of your home—puts *you* at risk, and I can't be everywhere at once."

"Then perhaps you shouldn't have sent my brother on some godsdamned fool's errand."

Rasmin's eyes narrowed. "I could not know that King Tommad would pass so soon."

"Nor could you know that he would *live*," Hagan said lowly.

"As Head Inquisitor, these are potentialities I've entrusted to *your* care, though I'm beginning to wonder if I've misplaced that trust."

Rasmin's lips tempted downward. It was the closest example of a frown he ever made. "The reasons I believe in the girl stretch beyond the state of your late father's health. You know this."

"Yes, because *her power* will help persuade my jarls," Hagan answered with a sneer. Then his expression tightened, and he made a fist. "Persuasion won't matter if I lose my throne. You know what Jeric is for this family." Hagan hated admitting Jeric's indispensability, but fury unbridled his tongue and pulled out the truth. "I wonder at your sensibilities in sending him away, knowing the tenuity of our circumstances."

"I did not intend to put you in danger, Your Grace. I only—"

"Then you will bring him back," Hagan demanded. "Immediately."

Rasmin didn't answer right away. "But his mission—"

"*I don't care*"—Hagan cut him off—"about his mission. I don't care about the power you claim this girl has. *We don't have time* for your fantastical theories. My father is gone, and some underground *legion* of men is terrorizing my villages."

Rasmin stilled.

Hagan smiled, all teeth. "Oh, yes, I've heard of this rebel group—this legion. You might be surprised what I coax from my slaves in the privacy of my chambers." He cocked his head. "Though I'm a little disappointed I didn't hear it from you first."

Rasmin regarded him, his face stone. "I haven't yet gathered enough evidence to form a conclusion. I, too, have heard rumors of a legion of rebels, but we still don't know who, or what, they are, considering how we found those unfortunate people at the two villages within Stovichshold."

"Does it matter?" Hagan seethed. "I have an enemy within my borders, slaughtering *my* people. The jarls already doubt my ability to protect Corinth... *How in the gods* have my *best* men failed to locate entire *legion*?" Hagan slammed his fist into a candelabra. It crashed to the floor with a clang, candles toppled and rolled, and flames sputtered out.

"I am… working on that, Your Grace," Rasmin said at last.

"And you will bring me the weapon Corinth understands. You will bring me the Wolf. I need his rutting nose. Let him sniff out this legion, since he's, apparently, the *only* one in this gods-damned kingdom who knows how to hunt."

Rasmin's cool expression did not waver. "Your Grace, retrieving the Wolf now would expose him, and his mission, to—"

"Your Grace," a new voice interrupted.

Commander Anaton stood in the archway and bent sharply at the waist.

Hagan wondered how much the commander had heard, but he never would've interrupted if something weren't terribly wrong.

Commander Anaton stood straight, boots together, but unease chipped at his granite eyes.

"What is it, Commander?" Hagan asked.

Commander Anaton's gaze settled on Rasmin, and then he said, "It's better that you see for yourself, Head Inquisitor."

HAGAN STOOD in the temple courtyard, staring down at the body.

An inquisitor lay there, embedded in stone as if he'd fallen from the heavens. Fissures cracked the stones around his body, and his arms and legs twisted unnaturally. Around him, scrawled in a perfect ring of blood, were symbols. It was the language of the Liagé—those few Sol Velorians born with unnatural power. Hagan didn't know it, couldn't read it—not many could—but he recognized the shapes from their histories. Lines crossed inside the circle, beneath the body, as if the gods had drawn a target on the ground and thrown the inquisitor at it.

"I secured the courtyard immediately," Commander Anaton said quietly, his expression grim.

Hagan spotted guards stationed at every channel leading into this courtyard. Even now, townsfolk passed by, their path diverted, though they strained to see whatever sight they'd been forbidden. Hagan was glad for the commander's prudence. His throne was brittle enough; if the people caught glimpse of this, it might shatter what remained.

Rasmin crouched at the circle's edge and gazed upon his inquisitor's face. His eyes strained. "Iza."

Iza was one of Corinth's oldest inquisitors. Hagan had heard him teach a number of times, and out of all inquisitors, Iza hated Liagé the most. He had a particular talent for prolonging death, and his methods of torture were often studied and taught for their unique cruelty.

Rasmin's gaze moved over Iza's body. The Head Inquisitor looked troubled, and Hagan understood why.

Moonlight made Iza's white skin almost luminous, though his scarred face was marred by a strange web of black veins. Iza's eyes were missing, as though they'd been ripped from their sockets, leaving only grotesque black pits behind.

"Lina's Mercy…" Hagan gasped.

Rasmin met his gaze, his expression grim.

"Did anyone see this happen?" Hagan asked the commander.

"None that we've questioned, Your Grace," the commander replied. "Two of my men heard a scream and found him, but the square was empty when they arrived. A handful of citizens were inside the temple, praying. We have them in custody, but I don't believe they're responsible for this."

"No, they did not do this." Rasmin stood, dusting his hands. His voice was unusually heavy.

Hagan and Commander Anaton looked to the Head Inquisitor.

"You speak as if already you know who did," Hagan said, eyes narrowed.

Rasmin gazed at Iza's body, at the bloodied inscriptions under and around it. "I've seen many manifestations of Liagé power, but this..." He looked to the commander. "He bears the same appearance as those you found in Reichen, yes?"

"Yes," the commander confirmed. "But we didn't find any Liagé writing."

A guard jogged over and spoke quietly to the commander.

"Have you seen this before?" Hagan asked Rasmin.

"No."

Something in Rasmin's voice made Hagan uneasy. "But you know what it is."

"I know we're dealing with an enemy far more powerful than anything I've encountered within the temple."

"Do you think this enemy is working with the rebel legion?" Hagan asked.

Rasmin hesitated. "It seems likely."

Suddenly, the air pulsed cold. It ripped through Hagan's robes and his hair, and all the lights in the courtyard flickered out, bathing them in darkness. Something snarled. It was a vicious sound, gurgling and animal, and in the next instant, Iza was on his feet, clamping inhumanly strong hands around Hagan's throat.

Hagan squeaked in horror as his breath sputtered out, his throat constricted by Iza's hands. He grabbed at Iza's wrists, but Iza's grip was rock solid.

"Jenui che'Ziyan, mol daré," Iza hissed, but it wasn't his voice. This came from another world, grinding like a rusted hinge in the night, and his breath stank of rot. "Jenui che'Ziyan, mol—"

Silver flashed.

Iza's words died. His head slid from his shoulders and

bounced to the cobblestones. Hagan clawed Iza's hands from his neck, and Iza's headless body crumpled to the stones. An inky black vapor seeped from Iza's severed neck. It twisted violently with a keening wail, then dissipated, diluting into a silent night.

Hagan staggered back with a curse and dragged the back of his hand across his sweaty brow.

Rasmin stood over Iza's headless body, Hagan's sword in his hands. The blood on the blade glistened black. Hagan couldn't tell if it was the color of Iza's blood or because of the moonlight.

Rasmin knelt beside the dead inquisitor, then touched his forehead and his heart in blessing. "May Lina's grace rest upon you." Rasmin wiped the blade on Iza's robes, then stood and held the sword out to Hagan with a look that said *will you listen now?*

Hagan ground his teeth and took the sword. "What was he saying?"

Rasmin's gaze drifted to Iza. "Free the Sol Velor. Or die."

"There is no hiding from the Maker when he calls, for He made the universe, and everything in it, and the universe will deliver you to Him when He has need, to serve His great purpose."

— Excerpt from Il Tonté, As recorded in the Fourth Verses by Vesuin, lesser prophet of the Sol Velor.

15

Sable stood at the edge of a butte, gazing out over the desert sands. A great wall of indigo clouds obscured the horizon, churning and swelling like the sea, casting shadow over the golden waves. A cold wind ripped through her, and with it came the scent of rain. Thunder shook the ground beneath her feet, but Sable did not fear. She gazed confidently on while the storm transformed this barren wasteland of brown into a pride of terrifying color.

Lightning speared; rain fell. It came in a torrent, blurring the world in a canvas of gray, soaking Sable's thin silks within seconds. Her hair stuck to her face and neck, and she hooded her eyes with her hand as the ground shuddered with thunder.

Be strong and courageous, Imari Masai.

The voice came from everywhere, from outside and within. It wasn't a voice Sable had ever heard before, and every string inside of her rang out as though called—a harmonic responding to a fundamental tone. It beckoned her in a way nothing else had. It plucked at her soul.

Do not fear the path ahead, it said. *I will be with you.*

The rain relented. A bolt of lightning struck, scorching the sands.

You're in danger. You must wake.

Thunder exploded, deafening.

Wake, child.

Sable's eyes snapped open to glowing embers. A warm and muscular arm draped over her, holding her against an even warmer body, and the slow and steady rhythm of breathing brushed her ear.

Jos.

Maker's Mercy. They'd survived.

She blinked away the fog, wondering at the dream's meaning, but then Jos shifted against her, and her thoughts turned away from the dream and toward the fact that she lay naked with a man. It hadn't bothered her before, while trembling at death's precarious edge, but she no longer walked that edge.

Careful, so as not to wake him, she slipped out of his arms and leaned over to grab her shirt. It was still damp, but not sopping, and she pushed her arms through the sleeves and pulled it over her head. A few of the buttons snagged on her hair, but she managed them free, then pulled on her pants and gazed at the canopy above, where lines of daylight shone.

You're in danger...

Anxious, she climbed to her knees and gently pushed one of the branches aside. Bright light made her wince, and without Jos's warmth, the wintry air shocked her. She scanned their surroundings, blinking back the unfiltered light, but the forest lay quiet, empty. A few inches of snow had fallen, dressing the pines in white, throwing a soft blanket over everything. It'd probably just saved their lives.

Still, the voice was right. They needed to get moving. Sable didn't know how much time remained before sunset, and even if the shades had moved on, they'd return in full force at dusk.

"See anything?" Jos asked, startling her.

She glanced down at him, then promptly looked back outside. Sable was no stranger to the human body, but after the unexpected closeness they'd shared, his nakedness made her blush.

"Snow," she answered, clearing her throat. "It covered our tracks."

A beat. "We're fortunate."

"I know."

Without another word, Jos picked his clothes off the ground, and Sable reached for her boots. They were still wet, but not soggy, and she tugged them on, feeling suddenly... awkward. She'd never been so vulnerable with anyone, and there was something strange about being near death with another person. It knit pieces of her soul with his whether she meant it to or not. She wondered if Jos felt it too, and when he reached for his boots, carefully avoiding contact with her (which wasn't easily done in their cramped space), Sable thought he probably *did* feel it, and this brought her some consolation.

"Any signs of shades?" Jos asked, lacing his boots. His motions were swift, and his chin-length hair shielded his face.

"Not that I can see," Sable replied.

"They won't cross the river?"

"They shouldn't."

He glanced up at her, perturbed. "Shouldn't, or *won't*?"

She glared back at him. "They *shouldn't* be out during the day, but apparently they're not following normal behavioral patterns. I don't see them now, so whatever Ventus did to make them come out, it didn't magically turn them into swimmers."

He regarded her, his expression flat.

"But there *are* bridges," she continued. "So depending on how determined they are, they could still track us. Anyway, it won't matter which side of the river we're on once the sun sets. They'll come from all directions."

His nostrils flared with a sharp inhale, and he glanced away.

He pulled back his hair as if to tie it, but then he remembered he'd lost his tie, and, with a flicker of irritation, he let go. His hair fell about his face again. Despite the tangles, he had nice hair, Sable noticed. Warm brown, streaked with sunlight.

"At some point *we'll* need to cross," he said.

Yes, they would. Sable wondered if she was okay with his use of *we*. She still didn't know what she was going to do, not that she'd had time to consider a plan, but one thing was certain: She couldn't stay in The Wilds. Tolya was gone; there was nothing left for her here.

Thinking of Tolya made her chest squeeze.

Regardless of her future plans, she *could* use Jos's skill on her side—at least until they reached the border. Ventus might still be alive, and if he was, he'd be hunting her. And Jos had already proven himself a remarkable fighter. In fact, she'd never seen his equal. Jos's proposal could be her way out—a way to start over. Southbridge was closer to Corinth than she liked, but she didn't exactly have any other options. Not that she'd tell Jos that.

"How far is Craven from White Rock?" Jos asked.

"Two days on horseback. Why?"

He rolled his shoulder, testing it. "White Rock is our rendezvous."

He was referring to his men.

"Jos..."

"*We* survived," he said sharply. "There's a chance they did too. Don't underestimate my men."

"Don't underestimate these woods."

His lips pressed together, and then he climbed to his knees and squinted at the gray sky mottled by trees. Sable could tell he was having a difficult time determining the hour. It was always so, in these woods, as if the trees played tricks with the light to trap its victims inside.

"You said a half day's walk to Craven?" he asked.

"Yes, and we should hurry," Sable said. "I don't know how long we've been here."

Jos's gaze swept left to right. Methodical, calculating. "Three hours. Maybe four."

She wondered how he knew that with such certainty. "When did you intercept me?"

"An hour after sunrise."

She thought about this. "Then we have roughly four hours of daylight to travel a distance that usually takes five *without* snow."

Their gazes met. Unspoken urgency passed between them, and Sable stomped on the embers. They sizzled and hissed, and Jos pushed the remaining branches aside, dusting them both with snowflakes.

"Anything else I should know before we go?" Jos asked.

Sable stood. "Yes, your tunic's on backward."

He glanced down at his tunic, which was, in fact, on backward. He looked back at her, eyes flecked with irritation. She didn't know why this satisfied her, but it did. She winked at him, pressed her palms to the opposing rocks, and hoisted herself through, clambering out of their hideaway and into the cold. She stood, wiped her hands on her pants, and glanced around. The forest lay quiet as though in a deep slumber, the waterfall an artery pumping life into a frozen world, its mist one long exhale.

"Which way?" Jos asked beside her, his breath leaving his lips in a cloud.

He'd turned his tunic back around.

"We follow the Kjürda until it veers west." She nodded in the direction they needed to go. "And then we head the other way, along a feeder."

He looked to the opposite side of the river. "You lead. Stick to the bank. We can't leave tracks."

She gave him a withering look that very clearly said *I'm not an idiot*, then trudged on ahead. Jos followed close behind. The cold persisted, but it wasn't debilitating like before, and Sable found that the pits of her arms were toasty enough to keep her fingers from going numb. Though she did struggle to pluck some berries for them to eat, because her fingers couldn't grip very well. After a few frustrating attempts, Jos just cut the clusters free.

Sable found an unexpected comfort in Jos's steady presence, and if it weren't for the situation, she might have felt a peacefulness in it all. The hum of moving water, the stillness of the forest, and the soft palette of slates. As a child, she'd loved the snow and romanticized it. How it transformed a wild land into a dreamscape of white, smoothing rough patches, burying its scars. How it morphed hard surfaces into something soft and forgiving. How it dusted her black hair like diamonds. But that was before she'd known cold. That was before she'd known how it burned.

She thought of Tolya. Recent events had made it impossible to dwell on what had transpired. Sable thought of Tolya's warning, and the timing and circumstances. Not once had Tolya eluded to knowing where Sable had come from or who she truly was.

"I take people as they are," Tolya had always said. "Not who they've been or who they want to be. The past and future are for the Maker. The present is for *us*."

Why the old woman had taken *her* in, Sable couldn't answer. It seemed fortuitous that Sable had shown an aptitude for the healing arts, but neither of them had had any way of knowing that the day Sable had arrived. Tolya hadn't asked questions. She'd simply wrapped Sable in an overly large cloak and ushered her inside. It was one of the rare times Tolya had shown gentleness in all of Sable's years knowing her.

Wind whistled through the pines, and Sable remembered her flute. It hadn't reappeared, and, unlike every other time she'd tried ridding herself of it, she didn't feel pain from its absence. Maybe it was finally gone for good. She hoped so, because if it appeared out of thin air and started glowing in her hands, she'd have a hard time explaining that one to Jos.

"Sable."

Sable stopped and glanced back to find Jos studying her. She had the feeling it wasn't the first time he'd called her name.

And then she remembered she'd never given him her name. "I never told you my name."

He arched a dark brow. "If you meant to live a life of anonymity, perhaps you shouldn't be one of two healers in a small village." His gaze slid pointedly to the river, which, Sable realized, was bending west as a wide stream fed into it. This was their marker to change course, and she hadn't noticed.

"Right." Sable cleared her throat, then turned east and started walking along the feeder stream.

A few seconds later, Jos followed.

They'd gone a few paces when he asked, "What is that song you keep humming?"

She suddenly realized she'd been humming and stopped herself. "Just... something I made up." Which was true, even if those melodic creations were unintentional.

A beat. "What did Ventus want with you, anyway?" he asked.

She glanced at him over her shoulder. She couldn't tell if he genuinely didn't know the truth, or if he was indirectly trying to trap her into confirming what he already suspected.

"How'd you know where to find me if you don't already know the answer to that?" she asked sharply.

Jos looked steadily back. "I watched Ventus's guards dump you in the back of a wagon in the middle of the night. I could be wrong"—he arched a brow, his tone dry—"but I didn't think they'd be too eager to tell me why."

Sable's eyes narrowed. "So you followed me."

"Unintentionally," he said, still holding her gaze. "I was out for a walk when your windchimes started ringing. *Despite* the lack of wind. So I investigated. It seems to have worked in your favor."

"My favor, or *yours*?"

He cocked his head to the side, studying her. "Are you always this suspicious?"

"Yes." She looked back to the trees and kept walking.

Jos followed a second later. "So?" he said behind her. "What did you do to get yourself kidnapped by that creature?"

"It's not really your business."

"Neither was saving your life."

Sable smacked a branch. Snow fell, dusting her arm. "Tell me where you learned to fight, and I'll tell you."

"It doesn't work that way, healer."

"It does if you want my answer, Provincial."

Jos was quiet for so long, she assumed he'd given up.

"I was three," he said suddenly.

Sable glanced back at him, surprised by his answer and that he'd answered. "*Three*? When you started training with a sword?"

"Yes." The word came out strained at the edges.

She regarded him. "Either your parents are exceedingly ambitious, or they didn't love you very much."

His eyes brightened. "Both."

Sable couldn't tell if he was teasing or serious.

"I've had many instructors over the years," Jos continued, looking to the trees as the wind stirred his hair. "The rest, I learned on my own. My parents were fortunate I developed a certain… aptitude for it."

"*Aptitude*?" She laughed. "You killed half a dozen men, two Silent, and Ventus. That's not—"

"Your turn," he said, cutting her off. He'd allowed her a small peek into his life, and he'd firmly shut the door.

"All right," she said, stepping over a fallen branch. "I stole from the butcher, and I was caught."

It was the story she'd decided on, the one with just enough truth to keep him from digging deeper, but the bloated pause that followed suggested she wouldn't get away so easily.

"Ventus kidnapped you. In the middle of the night. For

stealing meat." Jos laid down each word like a tile, each exaggerated pause a gaping hole in the floor.

"Bones, actually."

"Couldn't you just pay for them?"

"Huh. Why didn't I think of that?" she remarked dryly.

Jos's eyes narrowed, his interest piqued. "The butcher wouldn't sell to you, would he?"

Sable clapped twice, slow and deliberate. "Bravo, Provincial."

"But why risk it?" he asked. "You had your needs met. The necessities, at least. You certainly didn't need the crowns," he said with sarcasm, alluding to the offer he'd made that she'd refused.

She should've left it alone right there, but she couldn't. "Some things are worth more than crowns."

"Then you can't count high enough."

She stopped and glared back at him. He flashed his teeth. She walked on.

"Ah, I see," he said with revelation. "You stole for someone else, didn't you?"

Sable pressed her lips together and walked faster. Jos increased his pace only slightly, but his long legs carried him farther. Closer to her.

"That makes more sense," he continued, answering himself. He wasn't really asking her, anyway. He was thinking out loud, chasing a trail. Grasping at details and gathering prints. "It probably felt good to get back at the butcher, but you don't strike me as the sort to risk your life for petty vindication. But… if *another* life was in jeopardy… someone you cared about—"

"That's enough," Sable said firmly.

But he didn't stop. "That's why you refused to leave this rutting hells hole, despite the small fortune I offered you. Because there's someone you don't want to leave behind. It can't be the old healer. The butcher would've helped *her*. So was it a lover? Was he the one in the wagon with—"

Sable whirled on him in a twist of fury, and he startled to a stop. "I said, *that's*—"

Her words were cut off by a snarl, and a figure slunk out from behind the trunk of a large pine.

It was a... young man, or what was left of him. It crouched upon all fours, its gangly shape rocking back and forth in the snow as if it couldn't hold still. As if it were dying to release the insanity wound up inside. Snow and ice caked its bloodied frame, its light hair fell in frozen chunks, and its clothing hung in tatters. Translucent skin stretched over sharp bones, and dark bruises pillowed its wild eyes—one blue and one a startling shade of yellow—but the most unsettling of all was the blackness. It stained half of its pale face like spilled ink, slowly wrapping it in a cocoon of darkness. A cocoon—Sable knew—it would emerge from as a shade.

A changling. *It* was what happened when shade poison went untreated.

Its teeth bared in a crimson snarl, and blood stained its mouth and chin—a bold splash of color amidst the gray. It had eaten recently.

Sable opened her mouth to warn Jos, when he said, "*Gerald...*?"

Sable froze. She looked from the changling to Jos, who'd lowered his sword.

By the wards.

This changling had been one of his men.

The changling cocked its head to the side. It was an animal movement, sensing with its ears rather than its mind, and then it sniffed the air like a dog.

"Gods, what's happened to you?" Jos took a step toward him, confused and bewildered.

"Jos, wait," Sable said sharply, her attention fixed on the changling. "Remember how I warned you about shade poison?

Well, *this* is why. If their poison infects you, you become one of them."

The changling rocked back and forth, and its yellow eye narrowed as a deep snarl rolled through its body.

Despite Sable's warning, Jos started forward.

Sable grabbed his sleeve and pulled him back. "*Don't*," she said. "Your friend is gone. You have to kill it."

"Like hells..." Jos jerked his arm free and pushed on.

"Jos... stop! *Listen to me*!"

Jos did not stop, and the changling pounced in a snarl of arms and teeth.

Jos dodged out of the way, whirled around, and whacked the changling over the head with the flat of his sword. The changling staggered in the snow, snarling and furious.

"Gerald, godsdamnit! Stop this!" Jos demanded.

"He can't, Jos! He's gone!"

The changling whirled and attacked again, faster than before. Jos shoved it off, but barely, impeded by fidelity to his friend.

"You have to kill it!" Sable yelled.

The changling flung Jos back with a strength no normal man possessed. Jos flew through the air and landed in the snow, flat on his back. His sword landed near Sable's feet.

"Gerald... *fight it*, godsdamnit," Jos growled. All covered in snow, he staggered to his feet as the changling approached him. "You're stronger than this!"

"He can't fight it!" Sable yelled. "The only way to save him is to kill him!"

The changling snarled and pounced. Jos wasn't fast enough, and the creature landed directly on top of him.

Sable snatched Jos's sword from the snow, bolted forward, and plunged it into the changling's back, directly behind its heart. The changling jerked, whimpered, and sagged on top of Jos. It hadn't converted fully; steel proved effective. Or whatever Jos's sword was made of. It was black like nightglass, but without the stars.

Jos rolled the changling off of him, climbed to his feet, and glanced down at his man, bleeding and dead in the snow. His gaze shot to Sable, and she took an involuntary step back.

Looking into his eyes, Sable realized he hadn't truly believed his men were gone until this moment—until he'd seen what Gerald had become. His faith in his mens' abilities had been a light holding the darkness at bay. That light was gone, and the dangerous edge Sable had caught glimpse of before now consumed him. He was fire, uncontained.

"That was *my man* you just killed," he said through his teeth.

"He was already gone, Jos," she snapped. "If I hadn't done it, you would've ended up just like him."

In a motion too quick, Jos grabbed her collar and jerked her up as if she weighed nothing. Her collar dug into her neck, and she dropped his sword, clasping his wrists to pull them away, but his grip was unshakeable.

"*How dare you.*" He shook her hard. He was a storm, violent and raging, and Sable was trapped inside of it. "His life was *mine*, and you—a common, rutting thief—thought it was *your* right to take it. His life was worth *ten thousand* of yours, you godsdamned Scablicker."

She glared straight back. "Finally, some honesty. I wish I would've known that *before* I dragged you out of the Kjürda."

The blue in his eyes shifted, deepened and swirled. Jos and Sable glared at each other, breaths mixed in a hot cloud of fury. The moment teetered on a knife's edge. Jos's jaw clenched, unclenched, his instinct demanding retribution. If he acted on that instinct, Sable wouldn't be able to stop him, but she'd make sure his perfect face bore the scars of it for the rest of his life.

And then—abruptly, surprisingly—he let go.

Sable dropped in the snow.

Jos stepped around her, picked up a fallen pine cone, and

chucked it into the woods with a yell. The pine cone whizzed through the trees, collided with a trunk, and exploded. For a moment, Jos stood there with impossible stillness, a permanent fixture in the forest, and then he dropped to his knees beside his friend, curled his hands into fists upon his knees, and bowed his head in a posture of defeat.

Sable was too angry to feel pity. She was trudging away from him when a sharp intake of air made her glance back. Jos lifted the edge of his tunic, and there, carved into his side, were three bright red lines.

Sable cursed.

Jos's gaze met hers and narrowed, and he looked back at his friend, letting his tunic slide back in place.

"He got you, didn't he?" she asked, striding toward him. She shouldn't care. It served him right.

He climbed to his feet, and Sable reached for his tunic, but he blocked her with his arm. She slapped his wrist. He looked more surprised than angry, and she grabbed his tunic anyway. The cuts were deep and rimmed black—a blackness that was already seeping into the surrounding skin.

"We need to hurry," she said, dropping his tunic. "Someone in Craven will have an antidote."

"There's a *cure*?" he asked darkly, his expression even darker.

"Only for the initial infection," she cut back. "Once it spreads to your heart, there's nothing I can do."

A muscle feathered in his neck. "How long will that take?"

"An hour." Probably less.

He looked like he might argue, then swallowed as if forcing down a particularly large lump of pain.

She could leave him. She owed him nothing. She'd already saved his life in the river—they were square, as far as she was concerned. She looked ahead, in the direction of Craven. If she hurried, she might make it before nightfall, but if Jos changed before she reached the wards...

Jos sucked a breath through his teeth. His hand curled into a fist, and he pressed it to a tree for support. Shade poison worked fast, and Jos was no exception.

Sable cursed beneath her breath. "Lean on me."

"Give me a minute."

"We don't have a minute."

His jaw clenched, and his features strained. He dropped his fist from the tree, took a step, and his knee gave out. He cursed in a strange accent, but Sable caught him as he fell, his verbal slip forgotten. His weight almost pulled her down, but she wrapped one arm around him and managed to hold them both upright. She took note of the sword at his waist. If they didn't reach Craven in time, she'd have to kill him.

Together, they hobbled along the stream's bank. It wasn't long before his steps tumbled and his breathing panted. The exertion quickened his pulse, spreading the poison faster, but they couldn't slow. Night was too close.

Jos slipped against her, and she cursed, adjusting her grip, and then through the woods, riding the back of a breeze, she heard a voice.

"I...mar...i."

Maker's Mercy, not now...

It was the voice from before, the horror that'd followed her to Skanden's walls.

Sable held tight to Jos, but he didn't react to the voice. The back of her neck tickled with premonition and fear, and she urged Jos forward. He fought to keep pace; his breathing rasped and his boots dragged. All of a sudden, Jos stopped, anchoring Sable in place. His face turned sharply away and his nostrils flared.

"What's that smell?" he asked.

A few seconds later, she smelled it too—the rot, the stench of decay. It was the same putrid scent as before, but there were no wards protecting them now.

"Come on," she demanded, dragging him onward.

"Something's following us."

It was both statement and question.

"It's nothing we can fight," she said, urging him faster. "Not without wards."

He didn't say more. Sable thought he probably couldn't, even if he wanted to, and then suddenly, he tensed against her. "It's here."

A shadow fell over the forest. The air turned ice cold, and an unnatural stillness descended over everything.

And Sable was afraid.

"I need you to run, Jos," she said.

He didn't need prompting.

She let go of his waist and grabbed his hand, half expecting him to pull away.

He didn't. He gripped her hand tight, and together they sprinted. They splashed through water, bounding over rocks and fallen branches, their joined hands giving them balance. All around them, the shadows whispered. Jos squeezed her hand hard. He'd heard those. The whispers persisted, fading in and out, reaching for them.

Jos slipped and Sable jerked him up. She tripped over a branch, and he pulled her forward. The darkness swelled all around them, closing in like a slow-moving tide. It lapped at their heels, but they didn't slow, didn't stop. Sable's lungs burned with cold and exhaustion, but adrenaline pushed her harder. She had no idea how Jos managed their pace.

"*You... cannot... hide from me.*"

The voice cut through the whispers, clear and distinct. It was pain personified, a song of cruelty and wickedness. It curled and caressed, seeping into Sable's mind like poison, and the shadows became too dark to see. Jos squeezed her hand, but his sweat made it difficult to grip, and Sable realized that, in their frantic desperation, they'd lost the stream.

She spun around, and her boot caught. Her hand slipped from Jos's. The world spun as she fell, sliding and tumbling, round and round and round until—finally—she landed face-down in snow.

She planted her hands in the cold and pushed herself up, but Jos was nowhere to be seen. The world smeared into silhouettes, outlined by soft white, like shadows in reverse.

She felt it before she saw it.

Inky darkness coiled at the edge of her vision, oozing over the blanket of white as if the night itself were bleeding across the snow. Instinctively, she stepped back. Her boot sank in the snow.

"What do you want?" she demanded. Her voice showed little of the terror pounding inside of her.

The darkness leaked closer, spreading wide, stretching in a slow arc around her.

"*Your soul, little sulaziér.*"

It spoke slowly, certainly, stretching outside of time. As if it had always existed, as if it would always exist.

Sulaziér.

First Ventus. Now... *this.*

"You've got the wrong person," she hissed, taking another step back. "I don't know what that is."

The darkness pressed closer. A tide of whispers rose and fell, and Sable felt cold.

So.

Cold.

It bit through her clothes, sinking teeth into her bones.

"*It...*" The darkness rolled up before her, coalescing into a pillar of smoke. Two points of white light blinked open, like eyes. "*... is you.*"

It came at her in a rush, colder than the waters of the Kjürda, and poured into her mouth as she screamed.

16

Rasmin patted the map in his pocket, though he did not need it. He knew this forest well, for he'd once spent his days wandering beneath its ancient boughs in quiet reflection, as did so many others. Those days were but a memory now, this forest abandoned to their ghosts and the romantic fancies of storytellers.

He inhaled deeply.

The Blackwood had a distinct smell, one he'd know with his eyes closed. The balsam, the moss, the ripe earth. The dampness that clung to the edge of rot, held at bay by the cold, for the air was a prisoner here, bound between walls of earth and pine.

It had not always been so, but like any abandoned thing, time slowly buried it, made it dark and turned it wild.

Rasmin reached out and pressed his hand to a tree. The trees had once been his friends—a silent audience for his prayers. He didn't think they'd hear him now.

He'd made himself their enemy.

With a sigh, he pulled his hand away and approached the pond. The water lay still and dark, like a piece of polished skal. Moss-covered roots snarled along its banks, gnarled and twisted as they dipped into the black water like snakes. He reached the pond's rim and crouched before it, his boots depressing the mossy earth.

"You are keeping secrets from me," he said quietly, watching the still waters.

What had it seen? Or, more importantly, *whom*?

Rasmin frowned, stood, and just as he was beginning to turn, he felt a pull from deeper within the woods, in the direction of a place he had not visited in a very long time.

Wary, he followed the pull, letting it draw him beyond the lake, deeper into the woods, where a natural escarpment stretched for miles in either direction. That, too, had not always been there. The back of his mind tingled, and his eyes narrowed on the place where a curtain of ivy swayed as if pushed by a breeze.

He approached, then pressed a hand to the patch that'd moved, and he pushed it aside. A small tunnel lay beyond, a natural crack in rock. Pale green light shone ahead. He ducked inside and let the curtain fall behind him.

The tunnel was narrow and small, but it'd been designed so that only those who knew where it was could find it. Still, Rasmin barely squeezed through a few tighter places, eventually emerging on the other side where a small clearing lay, surrounded by a natural rock wall that hid it from the world.

Rasmin stopped in his tracks.

At the center of the clearing, a dozen paces away, stood the tree where they had buried *him*.

Azir Mubarék. The one who had almost destroyed this world with the help of his Liagé all those years ago.

The tree had split down the center, each half folded open like the pages of a book. An unnatural blackness coated the bark, spilling onto the ground like pitch, and a foulness clung to the air. Something sour, something spoiled.

Something dark.

Rasmin had seen this kind of power before, a long, long time ago. With growing trepidation, he walked forward and stopped at the edge, boots grazing the black. Slowly, he pressed his fingertips into the stained earth.

A cloaked figure, fingers clawing the earth. A flash of light, a blood-piercing scream.

Ink leaked from the tree.

And then...

Fire.

His fingertips seared, and he pulled them away with a gasp. Where he'd touched the power, his skin burned red. It'd taken a dozen Liagé to bind Azir inside the earth, and even then, they'd struggled. He remembered. He'd been one of them.

And someone had set Azir's spirit free.

Only a necromancer had this kind of power—a zindev, the Liagé called it—someone with power over the dead. The same type of power, he suspected, had been used at Reichen and Dunston. The same type of power used on Iza, his inquisitor. And it was of a strength Rasmin had never seen.

He'd wondered how many men were in the legion that'd been attacking Corinth's villages, but now he wondered if the legion was composed of men at all.

A breeze whispered, and the treetops creaked and groaned. Rasmin looked up. In a whirl of his cloak, he Changed and took flight, exploding through the trees and into a gray sky.

A SHOCKWAVE of white ripped through Sable. Something screamed. The sound was inhuman, a shrieking chord of madness and pain and nightmares. The world fell silent, the light vanished, and the stench faded to a memory.

Panting, Sable lowered her arm.

The thing was gone, and a strange silvery light pulsed behind her.

Wards.

They glowed from a free-standing pillar, the symbol pulsing from stone like a beating heart, humming faintly with power. It was then she noticed the ruins, illuminated by the soft wardlight. A ring of broken pillars, save the one, encircled her, situated as if they'd once supported a ceiling between them. There was no ceiling now, only open sky. She had no idea what it'd been intended for, or why it was here, in the middle of nowhere, and her luck at stumbling into it was such that she thought she might start believing in the gods.

She remembered Jos.

By the light of the wards and snow, Sable scrambled up the snowy embankment, following the tracks she'd left from her tumble. Her fingers were numb with cold, and she slipped a few times before clambering over the edge. There, she stopped short, heart pounding.

An inky silhouette stood a few paces away, its back to her, but even in the night, she knew what it was. A Silent.

Were the gods determined to destroy her?

The Silent crouched and bent over a body. *Jos's* body.

Sable hesitated, uncertain of what she should do. She could slip away. She'd already done more for Jos than he deserved, but she remembered how Ventus had controlled the shades. What if this Silent permitted Jos to change, only to use Jos's remarkable senses to find her?

Or...

She could kill the Silent. Jos had already proven they *could* be killed, and this Silent hadn't spotted her yet. She had the benefit of surprise, *and* she had one of Jos's daggers. She'd snagged it off of his belt when she'd been supporting him.

Sable slipped the blade free and crept toward them.

"I know you're there."

The Silent's deep voice stopped her halfway to her goal. "You can talk," she said, stunned. It wasn't her best response, but in all her time living in The Wilds, not once had she heard a Silent actually speak. After all, it was how they'd earned their name.

"And here I heard you were clever," the Silent said. "There's still time for him, but we must hurry. Come. Help me with him."

A dozen questions pushed for voice, all of them in a tangle. "You want to *help* us."

The Silent placed a hand on Jos's forehead. "Yes. Unlike the others, I don't work for Ventus."

"You expect me to believe that?"

"I don't see that you have much choice." The Silent pulled his hand back and his cowl turned to her. She couldn't see the face within the shadows, but she didn't need to. She knew what it looked like.

"Every moment you stand there is a moment lost to darkness," the Silent continued. "I can't carry him on my own. Neither can you. And he'll come for you if he turns. You know this, healer."

Sable hesitated, weighing her options, and then distant howls echoed in the night. Shades. Many of them.

Jos let out a soft moan, his body suddenly restless as if responding to their call. Sable shoved the dagger in her belt, rushed forward, and grabbed Jos's boots. Together, she and the Silent carried Jos's body through the snow and trees. The howling persisted, but, curiously, it never drew nearer. The Silent didn't seem concerned. He walked steadily on, a splotch of ink in the night.

"You don't fear them?" she asked.

"I don't believe in fear. To fear a thing only gives it power over you."

"It also keeps you alive."

"A man imprisoned is also alive. But that does not mean he lives."

One particular howl pierced the air, and Jos kicked so hard that Sable dropped his boots. The Silent waited while she picked them up, and they trudged on. Soon, through the trees, golden light flickered from a candle standing in a window with a small house attached. The Silent directed them up a narrow pathway, flattened somewhat by previous footprints. They staggered up a short stair and through the front door, and a blast of warmth enveloped her, smelling of woodsmoke and spices.

"By the stove," the Silent said.

Together, they set Jos on the floor before the woodstove. She snagged a pillow from a nearby chair to prop up Jos's head. His sword she unhooked from his belt and lay on the floor beside him.

"I'll be right back," the Silent said, retreating through a small doorway.

Sable stared after him a moment, then glanced about the small yet tidy room. What sort of cruel joke were the gods playing on her?

With a sigh, Sable knelt beside Jos. His pale skin was a waxy yellow, his sharp features hollow, and his body twitched erratically. As a healer, she'd seen sickness take many forms. She'd seen it cut down the strongest of men. It didn't discriminate. Mortality made men equals.

She pulled Jos's lids open. Bloodshot eyes rolled restlessly, and she lifted his shirt. A black, tar-like substance filled the three gashes, and the stain webbed all the way to his heart. Disappointment pricked her. Jos would not recover from this.

She sat back on her heels, slipped the dagger from her belt, and set it on the floor just as the Silent returned. The low light caught his face, and Sable stifled a gasp.

Pink and bubbly scar tissue disfigured one side of his face, and the lids on that eye had melted together. If he noticed Sable staring, he didn't say. He rounded the chair and uncorked a vial of blue liquid, and the smell of camphor filled the room. Lastrava oil. Tolya had tucked away a small vial of it. It had taken her five years to brew.

"Who *are* you?" Sable asked.

"My name's Tallyn."

The name gave her pause. Was *he* the one Tolya had told her to seek out?

The Silent—Tallyn—knelt beside Jos and held up the vial.

"You should save that," she said, gesturing at the wound. "He's too far gone."

Tallyn dumped the contents over the cuts anyway. The cuts foamed white, and Jos arched his back with a hiss.

"I'll need you to hold him down," Tallyn said, pulling a smaller ampoule from his robes. Only a few drops glistened inside, tinted like nightglass. Sable had never seen it before.

"What is that?" she asked.

His one black eye fixed on her, ancient and fathomless. "It's what makes shades shades. It can also unmake them, if administered at the right time." Sable wondered at his words when he said, "Hurry. Our window is closing."

She climbed onto Jos, squeezed his legs between hers, and gripped his shoulders tight. Tallyn tilted the vial over the wound. Drops fell.

One.

Jos screamed, his neck arched.

Two.

He bucked. Sable squeezed her thighs to hold him steady.

Three.

His body shuddered; his eyes snapped open. Pinpricked pupils fixed on Sable, and his teeth bared with a snarl. Insanity writhed inside of him, clawing for release.

"Fight it, Jos," she demanded, feeling the sudden need to say his name. Remind him of who he was. "Do you hear me? *Fight it.*"

Sable squeezed him harder, digging her nails into his shoulders, eyes locked on his. Refusing to look away. Refusing to let him go. The seconds passed, teetering on the edge of insanity. The light in his eyes dimmed, and corruption clouded the blue.

Jos was losing.

Suddenly, he was Mikael. He was Tolya. He was every life Sable hadn't saved, every person she had failed—one more cruel reminder of the life *she* had unwittingly stolen.

"Damnit, Jos," Sable growled. "You didn't come all this way to quit now! Fight *back*!" She slapped him hard across his face.

He blinked, and the moment froze: the snarl, his body, the battle.

The blue in his eyes swirled with confusion, his head slumped to the side, and his eyes closed to unconsciousness.

17

Sable made one last stitch, tied the knot, and cut the string with Jos's dagger.

"He's fortunate in you," Tallyn said, rounding the chair.

She doubted Jos would agree.

Tallyn watched her as she picked up the rag and wrung it over Jos's neatly stitched wounds. She'd made thirty-five stitches in total, over the deepest parts. It helped her some, focusing on a simple task, using her hands in a way that was familiar to her, when the rest of her world had turned to chaos. Black and red flecks flushed onto the towel Sable had laid beneath him. The stain on Jos's skin had receded, but the cuts remained black, like three lines of ink.

"How long will he sleep?" she asked.

"That depends on him," Tallyn replied. "Days. Weeks, perhaps. It's been a long time since I've reversed the effects. Even so, I haven't done it often."

"And I've never done it with someone so far gone. Where did you get the cure?"

He didn't answer immediately. "It was given to me by someone who no longer lives. I've been saving it for the right occasion."

"Did Tolya give it to you?"

He searched her, and sadness squeezed his eye. "So she *is* gone."

Sable glanced away. "Yes."

Silence settled, expanded, and then he said, "Tolya didn't give me this antidote." He held something out to her. "Here. Take it. It'll help."

In his hands was a mug that smelled wondrously of peppermint, cinnamon, and leander. Sable grabbed it and took a slow sip. The tea warmed her from the inside out, and the leander tingled on her tongue. Already, her muscles began to unknot themselves. "Tolya never mentioned you," she said quietly. "Not until... just before."

Tallyn sat in the chair. "She wouldn't. She was a great keeper of secrets."

Sable couldn't argue that. Tolya had been a vault.

"She used to visit often," he continued, "giving me salves for my scars. They still burn. But after you arrived, she visited less. She wasn't comfortable leaving you alone."

Sable allowed herself to look at him then—really look at him—and he angled his face to let her see the breadth of his affliction. Scar tissue shone grotesquely in the candlelight, completely disfiguring one side of his face, making him look otherworldly. She could only imagine the pain they'd caused. The scars didn't stop at his neck, either, and she wondered how much of his body suffered this same fate.

"How did it happen?" she asked quietly.

He reached out his hand. Like his face, it was bubbly and pink, but swaths of it were smooth, like brush strokes of normal skin. In those places, the skin was painted in glyphs.

Her eyes narrowed on his hand, on him. "You don't serve Ventus?"

"Take it," he said, urging his hand closer. "I'll show you."

"Show me what?"

"The truth."

She eyed him, holding her tea close.

"I am on your side, Sable," he said in earnest. "I can show you the past. That way, you may draw your own conclusions."

"You mean... share your memories?" She didn't know much about the power Ventus possessed, but Ventus had been able to push words into her mind. It wasn't too farfetched, she imagined, for someone to push images.

Tallyn merely turned over his hand.

Habit made her leery, but Tolya had trusted him, whoever he was. And if he'd meant her harm, he would've capitalized on that by now. Sable set down her mug and took his hand. His fingers were surprisingly warm as they wrapped around hers.

Her world flashed.

Her body squeezed, as if the world were collapsing all around her, but before she could cry out, the pressure vanished. She gasped for breath and staggered forward, coming to the quick realization that she was no longer in Tallyn's room.

On second thought, this power was *very* different from Ventus's.

She was standing in a great domed chamber. There were no windows, only decorative alcoves filled with burning candles, but their flames did little to chase away the shadows. At the center of the chamber sat a stone altar with a naked body stretched upon it. Robed men hunched over the body, holding little black knives and carving glyphs into the pasty white skin. Frantic, Sable looked for some place to hide.

"It's all right," Tallyn said, startling her.

He appeared beside her, and she pressed a hand to her chest to still her leaping heart.

"They can't see us," he said. "Go on. Look."

She looked back at the robed figures, who didn't seem to notice their audience. They worked steadily on, dipping blades in bowls of black ink before carving glyphs upon the dead body.

Sable could not fathom this kind of power.

"What is this place?" she whispered, fearing she might still be overheard.

"A memory." Tallyn nodded for her to go on ahead.

She hesitated, and then a robed figure walked *through* her from behind. She jumped, surprised, but the newcomer walked on and approached the table. This figure was a head taller than the rest, his shoulders broad, and he walked with a surety of purpose. The kind only leaders bore, as if he were used to the world shifting beneath his feet.

"That's Azir Mubarék," Tallyn said behind her, nodding gravely at the newcomer.

A chill breathed over Sable's skin.

Azir Mubarék.

It wasn't a name spoken often, because the man signified a time of desperation and fear the world would rather forget. It'd been a time when the Five Provinces had been one land with different religions, each with individual identities and gods. But one man had challenged all of that: Azir Mubarék—High Sceptor of the Liagé, ruler of the Sol Velor, Asorai's supposed chosen and destroyer of gods. He and his followers had brought war to what was now known as the Provinces, wanting to establish their god and their ways above all others, and they had executed anyone who opposed him.

And there he was.

Strangely, Sable found herself expecting... more.

"How... is this possible?" Sable asked, looking down at her hand, touching it, but it was substantial.

"Through the Shah."

The Shah. A power possessed only by Sol Velorian prophets, given them by their Maker.

"You're Liagé?" Sable asked.

"Not… exactly," he replied. "I'm Sol Velorian, but I wasn't born with Liagé power. You see, under Azir's rule, the Liagé dwindled beyond repair. He pushed them too far, too fast, and many of them perished. He grew desperate, as men do, fearing the Maker had failed him, and that desperation drove him to create his own miracles. To seek *other* ways to strengthen his movement—one of which was creating us."

Sable glanced back at the body upon the altar. Azir stood over it, analyzing the markings his Liagé had drawn. He picked up a pale hand, then spoke to the man in front. She couldn't hear his words, but his deep voice rumbled.

"We were created *by man. Man* gave us power," Tallyn explained, "but it's not as pure or as strong as those Liagé-born. You can't turn a mouse into a hawk. You can splice and paint and enchant, dress it with all the feathers in the world, but to its core it remains a mouse, and now it's confused. It needs meat, but it wants only crumbs. It must fly, but it doesn't know how. And so it is with the Shah. When we were created, we could tap into its power, but we didn't know how to properly use it or control it. Our bodies weren't designed to process the energy required, and, over time, the Shah changed us to make our bodies better suited for *it*. But in doing so, it dissolved whatever it was that made us human."

Sable moved forward, eyes trained on the sight before her. Azir stepped around the table, thus exposing the dead man's face, and Sable froze.

The man lying on the table, the one the Liagé had been carving into, was Ventus.

She looked at Tallyn for answers, but the pain in his eyes held her back. In them, she knew he'd seen more tragedy than one human life could bear.

"I don't know the Sol Velorian man Ventus was before," Tallyn said at last. "I only know the creature they created. But in those days, we were not *silent.* We were prophets, tasked with spreading the Sol Velorian faith to the Provinces. Through speech. Through violence, if necessary. Azir didn't care how. He only cared that it was done."

"Wait." Sable looked from Ventus back to Tallyn. "This is... *your* memory?"

"Yes."

Which meant... "You're almost one hundred and fifty years old," she said, astounded.

"One hundred and forty three," he confirmed, to her amazement. "I was the first creation. It was Azir's intention that I lead his alta-Liagé, or so they called us." He gazed at the sight ahead in quiet reflection. "Come. Let me show you something else."

Before Sable could ask, her lungs squeezed tight, and the dome blurred. The world spun to a sudden halt, and Sable toppled right into Tallyn. She gathered her balance, let go of him, and looked around.

They stood in a forest she recognized immediately as The Wilds. Ahead of them, in a small clearing, stood another Tallyn, though his face was unblemished, and he spoke heatedly to another.

"This isn't the way," the unscarred Tallyn was saying.

The second figure turned his back to Tallyn and started walking away. It was Ventus, and he looked just as frightening then as Sable knew him now.

"When Azir died," the present Tallyn said beside her, "those of us who had evaded capture fled here, to The Wilds. After what Azir had done, the Provinces did not trust the Sol Velor, as you well know, and they trusted the Liagé—especially us alta-Liagé—less, even those who'd turned against Azir to help defeat him. Ventus was the strongest of us, and without Azir, the other prophets elected him as our leader." A pause. "Follow me." He started for the younger Tallyn and Ventus, who were walking away.

Sable followed.

"Ventus!" a younger Tallyn called after Ventus.

Ventus whirled on him in a fury, and the younger Tallyn held back.

"You've always been weak," Ventus hissed. "That's why you're *second* here. Remember that."

"This isn't weakness," the younger Tallyn snapped. "This is *wrong*. Those creatures are an abomination—"

"Those *creatures* are going to protect us," Ventus hissed. "Azir is dead. It's up to us now, and the Maker has given us a way to survive."

Sable's eyes widened with horrible revelation. "He's talking about shades, isn't he?" she asked the real Tallyn.

"Yes."

A thousand questions flooded her mind, but before she could ask a single one, Tallyn tipped his head toward the men and said, "*Watch*."

"This power you're using... it is not of the Maker," the younger Tallyn said, with conviction and warning. "You must tread carefully, Ventus. Azir warned us—"

Ventus grabbed the younger Tallyn's robe and jerked him close. "Azir got himself *killed*. His methods *failed* the Maker, and now *your* ideas are infecting and dividing what remains of us. Consider which side you're on, Tallyn. Do you understand?"

A younger Tallyn stilled, his expression tight.

The real Tallyn watched, his eye ablaze with old fury.

"I understand," said a younger Tallyn.

Ventus released him and stormed off without another word. A younger Tallyn stood like stone, watching Ventus retreat.

"After Azir died," the real Tallyn said before Sable could ask, "I began questioning his interpretation of the Maker's will and our purpose here, and so when Ventus continued along that path, I began challenging his methods."

"I didn't realize the Maker's will was debatable," Sable said with acid.

He looked at her. "You're angry with the Maker?"

"I don't believe in gods."

"Don't condemn the Maker for the actions of his followers."

Sable grunted. "Now you sound like Tolya."

"There are always extremes, Sable. Since the beginning, mankind has put his own twist on the Maker's will, as Ventus did and does still. It's what men do. We are masters at manipulating truth to suit our desires. But don't condemn the Maker for the sins of man."

Sable didn't get the chance to argue. Her lungs pinched and the world blurred, but this time, when the world righted itself, Sable was ready on balanced feet.

They were standing inside a beautiful mausoleum. A dozen men were gathered—including the younger Tallyn—all in fervent discussion.

"It has to be tonight," said one, pale and inked like everyone else. At first glance, Sable took him for a Silent, but his expression was warm and too human.

"We have to get past the shades," someone else said.

"Let me handle them," the young Tallyn said.

"Can you handle so many at once?"

"I will," a young Tallyn said with resolve. "But you'll have to move..."

His words trailed as the walls caught flame. It was a strange sort of fire, white and unnatural, and it began melting the stones. Men yelled, and some held up inked palms and spoke a language Sable didn't know, trying to put out the flames with power Sable didn't understand. Others tried the door, only to find it barred.

And the flames grew.

And grew.

One stretched right through Sable, and she gasped instinctively but felt no warmth.

"My concern was shared by more than just myself," Tallyn continued behind her. "We'd gathered to combat Ventus, but we were betrayed." A pause. "I alone survived."

His face turned a little toward her, illuminating the horrible scars.

Scars from fire.

Men screamed, devoured by white flame, and Sable landed back in Tallyn's sitting room. The screaming faded to a crackle, and the flames condensed to the stove, innocent and orange. But his memories were stamped upon her mind forever.

"After my betrayal," Tallyn continued quietly, "Ventus cut out the others' tongues, lest anyone rise to question him again. We were all bound through our ink. It's how Azir created us, but most of my binds melted, severing my... tie to them. So there was a blessing from it all."

Sable sat quiet, processing everything she'd seen and heard, and it was a lot to process. She supposed Ventus—and Tallyn's—tie to the Liagé shouldn't have surprised her, considering Ventus's faith in the Sol Velorian god, and his supernatural power. As far as she understood, only those of Sol Velorian blood could be born with the Maker's divine power, and though Ventus possessed it, he'd always persisted he wasn't Liagé. Technically, he'd told the truth. His former self had been carved away by Liagé glyphs, and the power they'd infused into his body had turned him into a monster.

It made sense now why the shades had answered to Ventus. He had created them. Which meant he was also the reason the rest of them had needed nightglass.

To fear a thing only gives it power over you, Tallyn had said. And shades had given Ventus and his Silent total power over The Wilds.

Her brow puckered with thought. "I thought I killed him.

Ventus. I cut a major artery in his neck, and Jos stabbed him through the heart." She nodded at Jos. "But then... I watched his skin knit together, and he summoned the shades with his blood. We ran away as fast as we could, so I don't know if he survived or not."

"You're right to be concerned," Tallyn said. "Ventus was created *shiva*." Seeing the question in Sable's eyes, he said, "The Liagé word for Restorer. Restorers are difficult to kill, because they have the unique ability to heal themselves."

"Even after a knife wound to the heart?"

"Even after a knife wound to the heart." He nodded. His one eye glittered. "He's still alive, Sable. Though fate and I have severed every tie possible to Ventus, I can still feel him through the Shah."

Sable cursed her luck, and then her breath caught as a thought struck her. "Then he can still feel *you*."

"Yes."

"Which means... he can find *me*."

Tallyn shook his head. "No, he can *feel* me. He can't *find* me."

"Why not?"

He grinned. The effect—though intended in earnest—was chilling. "I *was* Azir's first for a reason."

Sable regarded him. "Why haven't you tried fighting him back, then?"

"I'm just one man," he replied, "and though my connection to them was severed in the flames, so was much of my connection to the Shah. And you've never truly witnessed the breadth of Ventus's power. With the others, I stood a chance. Alone, I'd certainly die. Especially now. I'm not... what I was." A pause. "Skanden is no longer safe for you. Ventus won't stop searching for you."

Sable wrapped her arms around her legs and threaded her fingers together. "I know."

"But what's even more disconcerting," he said, stopping her thoughts, "is the chakran that followed you here."

Sable's gaze snapped to Tallyn. "Chakran...?"

Tallyn didn't answer immediately. "There are two types of spirits in this world that pass on to the afterlife. The spirits of those with the Shah—the Liagé—and those without. A chakran is the spirit of a Liagé."

Sable remembered the inky darkness that'd followed her in the forest, and a chill shuddered down her spine. "And you believe one is following *me*."

"I found you because that chakran set off the old wards of the mausoleum. Those wards... well, you saw them. They're in ruins. They haven't stirred since the day Ventus destroyed them, and so when I saw their light, I came at once." His eye searched her, and in it, she saw a hint of fear. "I smelled the chakran the moment I stepped outside. The odor is... very distinct."

Sable frowned, remembering the stench and trying to understand. "But where did this... Liagé spirit come from?"

Tallyn inhaled deeply. "It's extremely difficult to summon a Liagé spirit. Their powers..." Tallyn considered his words. Not to hide the truth, but to explain it in a way that Sable would understand. "When Liagé die, their powers bleed back into the fabric of creation. Like rain, filling streams and rivers and lakes. Redistributed, if you will, to give power to the next Liagé, and the next, and so on. For someone to draw the spirit of one from death—a chakran—one must pull from those streams and rivers and lakes. Only a zindev has power to bring the dead to life, but even so, that depth of power is extremely rare."

"Necromancy," Sable said for clarification. She knew the word from one of Tolya's oldest books.

"Of a sort, yes."

Sable hadn't really believed necromancers were real—just exaggerated tales meant to frighten children. "And what does a... chakran do?" she asked with growing unease.

Tallyn leaned forward, elbows resting upon his knees. "A normal spirit might possess a body for a short time, to do its master's bidding, but it leaves a body mostly intact when it departs. A chakran consumes a person's soul. There's nothing left of the person inside."

Sable didn't ask the question that dangled at the end of her tongue: *Why me?*

What in the burning wards would a chakran want with *her*? But she couldn't ask that question. Not without inviting a slew of other questions that she absolutely could not answer.

Misreading her, Tallyn said, "Not to worry. The old power in the mausoleum should've destroyed it, if not severely weakened it, and once you make it over the Rotte Strait and into the Provinces, it shouldn't bother you again."

Sable thought back on her first experience with the chakran, that night in Skanden, and she wondered how many ward abuses it could withstand.

"Could this... zindev just send another one?" Sable asked.

Tallyn scratched his nose. "It isn't likely. In summoning a Liagé spirit, the zindev is in essence stealing from future Liagé. It is a perversion of power. It's more likely that he, or she, would see this chakran through until the end rather than risk drawing another one forth."

And then, abruptly, Tallyn sat up. "Who is our friend here?"

It took Sable a second to follow, and then she glanced back at Jos. Sleep dulled his hard edges, and he looked almost peaceful. "We're not friends."

"No?" Tallyn asked surprised, studying her. "For not being friends, you're quite determined to save him."

Sable shrugged. "I'm a healer."

It wasn't difficult to see that Tallyn wasn't satisfied with her answer.

"His name is Jos," she continued to fill the bloated silence.

"He's from Southbridge. He says his father is dying, and he's offered me a large sum to heal him."

Tallyn sat quiet. "You haven't accepted it yet."

"No."

"Why not?" When Sable didn't answer, Tallyn said, "You don't trust him."

She exhaled slowly and drummed her fingers. "I don't know. I *do* believe his father's dying, and I don't think he means me harm."

"*And* this supposed large sum would help set you on your feet," Tallyn suggested.

Sable pressed her lips together and nodded.

"You *could* stay here."

She met his gaze.

"I understand your predicament, as an Istraan," Tallyn continued. "I can't offer you much of a life here, and you wouldn't be able to leave this house, but I *can* offer you safety from Ventus *and* this zindev, should he attempt to send anything else after you. It is the very least I can do for Tolya."

His offer humbled her. "Tallyn... You've already done more—"

"Don't give me an answer now," he said. "It's something for you to consider before our handsome Provincial awakens. A decision made out of desperation is never a good decision. I merely want you to have an alternative when the time comes."

Sable's gaze flickered to Jos.

Tallyn stood and gestured to the mug. "Finish it. It'll help replenish your strength. There's an extra blanket in the hutch if you need one. You're welcome to stay until your friend is able to travel. You'll be safe here." He started to go.

"Tallyn."

He stopped and looked back.

"I was with her when she passed," Sable said. "I did everything I could for her, but..."

It wasn't enough. It was *never* enough.

Understanding shone in Tallyn's eye. "I know, child. I also know that she loved you as her own."

The words squeezed around Sable's brittle heart, and her eyes burned.

He bowed his head. "Goodnight." And he left.

Sable wiped her eyes, snagged the blanket from the hutch, and had barely curled upon the floor beside Jos when exhaustion took her.

18

Grag Beryn was a man of the Blackwood; he'd been born to it. Those who knew him often remarked how he'd been birthed from the very trees, skin rough as bark, eyes emerald as leaves, hair black as the woods themselves, despite the years he'd seen. His voice was like woodsmoke, strong and peppered, and it traveled without bounds. If there was game to be had in these woods, Grag knew where to look and how to find it, and he'd never been afraid.

Until now.

His woods had changed. There was a subtle shift in the air, an off and unfamiliar scent to the changing wind, and the trees were quiet as they had never been. They watched, but they did not give. These trees that had long been his friends—his provider—were suddenly keeping secrets.

"Find something, Grag?" Fyrok called from a dozen paces away.

Fyrok, like Grag, was a hunter, and he was the youngest of Grag's crew. Grag used to hunt with Fyrok's father, but when his father had come down with a nasty infection that devoured his organs, Fyrok had taken his place. Still, at only seventeen, Fyrok was a better hunter than some of Grag's seasoned men. Fyrok hadn't closed the gates of thought that men sealed shut over time. And, like Grag, he had a hunter's intuition.

Grag rubbed dark earth between his fingertips, then sighed and glanced around. "Nothin'," he said with a huff, standing. They'd been out here for two days, and they hadn't come across a single buck. Grag hadn't even found tracks, though he'd discovered a set of turkey prints, but a rutting turkey wasn't going to keep the people of Skyhold fed for winter.

"Don't worry, Grag," Keffyn said. "They're probably all scared of the new smell." He cuffed Fyrok on the shoulder.

Fyrok rolled his eyes.

"Scared or not," Dev said, glancing back at them, "Hagan's gonna want a pretty treasure when we return."

"He's your king now, so best start using his title before he makes *you* that pretty treasure," Keffyn replied.

"If only he could be so lucky." Dev smirked.

Keffyn snorted and kept walking.

"From what I hear, our king gets lucky plenty," Rosin chimed in, then uncorked his flask and took a long swig.

"It's unfortunate his powers of seduction don't lure Stovich to stand down," Klaus added from the back.

"Stovich ain't gonna do scat," Keffyn said. "Man's all talk."

"Man also owns most of the agriculture," Rosin commented.

"Yeah, and who staffs his slaves?" Keffyn asked rhetorically.

"Speaking of Stovich, you hear what happened in Reichen?" Dev asked, all seriousness.

"Careful, Dev," Grag warned.

"What?" Dev defended with a shrug. "The way these rumors've spread, it's practically public knowledge."

"Except it's not."

"The five hells are you talking about?" Klaus demanded, looking from Grag to Dev.

Dev had everyone's attention now.

Despite the gravity in Grag's eyes, Dev pushed on, "All the townsfolk were found dead. Men, women, and children… left in a heap on the temple steps."

"*What*?" Rosin gasped.

"I think you're full of scat," Keffyn remarked.

"Swear to the gods," Dev said.

"And the Scabs?" Rosin asked.

"Gone. Like they vanished."

"Well, this just gets better and better," Klaus murmured sardonically.

"If that's true," Rosin said, "no wonder Stovich's been clawing at Hagan's back for reinforcements."

"*If* that's true," Keffyn added.

"And you know what else I heard…" Dev dipped his head conspiratorially. "The bodies… their eyes were missing. Like they'd been ripped from their sockets."

Rosin made a gagging sound.

"No…" Klaus shook his head with disbelief.

"That's what I heard." Dev held up a surrendering hand.

"That's the creepiest piece of scat I've ever—" Keffyn started.

"What is it, Grag?"

All eyes looked to Grag, who'd crouched, parting the grasses as he stared at a thick trail of mutilation.

"What in the…" Klaus started, and he followed after Grag.

The others followed, too, Dev's macabre story forgotten.

Blood stained the earth and grasses in a crimson trail, littered with flecks of skin and hair, and—Grag stepped around the tree—muscle and intestines. So terrible was the carnage, Grag wouldn't have known the poor creature had he not spotted the wolf's mutilated paw.

"Lina's Mercy," Keffyn whispered behind him, crouching low. "What did this?"

Corinth was famous for its wolf population. Wolves roamed these woods in packs, though they rarely brought Grag and his men any trouble. As long as Grag minded his own business, they minded theirs. But they'd yet to see any wolves on this hunt.

Grag frowned and searched the trees for answers. "I don't know."

The men stared at the grotesque canvas of death.

Fyrok crouched nearby, touched the blood, then wiped it on grass. "A gray wouldn't do this, would it?" His question was for Grag.

Grays—bears indigenous to these parts—didn't travel this far from the mountains, and he'd never seen a gray act in this way. "No," Grag said. No creature indigenous to this world would do this.

A stiff wind pushed the trees, and the pine needles rustled, sounding like rain. Grag glanced up and scanned the thick boughs.

What are you hiding?

JERIC HAD NEVER KNOWN pain like this.

From his toes to his fingernails, an immeasurable force pulled him apart. His bones were like cord, pulled taut enough to snap. Fire scorched his veins, and when he opened his mouth to scream, water rushed in.

No, not water. Blood.

The taste of it filled him, drowned him as it slid down his throat and into his belly, yet repulsed as he was by the taste, he wanted more. Thirsted for more. Needed more.

His stomach clawed for it, demanded it. *Yearned* for it. A savage creature raged inside of him, caged only by the thin shell of his will—a will he clung to with hopeless desperation. He could not let it break. He didn't know why, only that he could not.

And then he saw faces. So many faces, floating before him like a mirage, fading from one to another. All people he had killed, lives he had stolen. So many lives, and he remembered every one.

He hadn't expected to remember.

He shouldn't remember. They meant nothing to him.

Their blood flooded him, and their dying screams played like a terrible symphony in his mind, screeching and discordant.

Red.

Red.

Red... Beautiful, intoxicating *red.*

He gulped it in like a starved man, reveling in the symphony that'd seemed so terrible before. It was not terrible now. It was a masterpiece.

The glorious rise and falls of their cries, the raw pulse of distant screaming. It was the anthem of a hunter—his anthem—and he would have more. He would engorge himself with it.

A firm voice cut through the chaos. A woman's voice. He only caught one word, but it seemed important, and like the faces, he didn't understand.

His bones stretched farther, and new pain pricked at the fringes of his awareness. The monster inside of him ravaged his will. Cracks splintered his resolve, and the monster poured through the holes, flooding him with insanity, consuming him with bloodlust. It needed to feed. *He* needed to feed. He needed blood, and he would have the woman's first. How sweet it would be.

Jos.

There was that word again. Why did he know it? Why did it matter?

Red.

Red.

Red.

A sharp crack reverberated through him, bold and thunderous and bright.

Lightning.

It pierced the red and broke it apart, like a sun bursting through clouds. In that moment, in the spaces between red, he saw hazel eyes.

Her eyes. Angry and demanding and clear.

Brilliant.

He suddenly remembered that Jos was the name he'd been called as a boy, by his mother. A wave of heat engulfed him; something inside of him shattered. And he felt himself falling... falling...

Then...

Nothing.

A whisper. Warmth and then...

More nothing.

Light flickered far away, but it dissolved even as he turned toward it. The darkness stretched, cold and infinite.

Lonely.

He had never felt such loneliness before.

Murmurs aroused the silence. He felt a brush of warmth, followed by gentle touch and a song—a beautiful song. The notes wrapped around him, lending him strength, lighting a path and coaxing him forth. This time, he grabbed hold. He clung to the notes, refusing to let them go, gripping until his fingertips bled, and they carried him onward. Song seeped into his skin like rays of sunlight; the light turned blinding. And then he opened his eyes.

19

Sable knelt beside Jos and checked his stitches. Three black lines were all that remained of the horror that'd almost taken his life. She wondered if they'd remain black for the rest of his days. Regardless, it was a small price to pay.

Jos had been sleeping solidly for the past four days, though Tallyn assured her Jos *would* wake. After that first night, Tallyn had pulled a straw pallet from beneath his bed and spread it before the fire, and together, they'd lifted Jos onto it. Sable had been surprised that a recluse like Tallyn would keep one, but when she voiced as much, he explained that he'd always kept it for Tolya.

Even in this, the old woman seemed to be looking out for her.

Tallyn's home proved to be a sanctuary, exempt from the cruel laws of nature that pervaded over The Wilds. Not even shades encroached upon his land, though their distant howls echoed throughout the night. Tallyn's power seemed a convenience—one that allowed a person to hide from the world—and Sable almost envied him for it.

Tallyn remained a steady and quiet presence, as if he'd said all he meant to say that first night and had decided to give Sable space to sort through it all. And it was a lot to sort through. She still didn't know what to do. She couldn't go back to Skanden, and according to Tallyn, who'd ventured into Craven to purchase clothing and supplies for them, Ventus was very much alive and searching every town in The Wilds for her. If she chose to stay with Tallyn, she might be *safe*, but she'd be a prisoner. It would be no different than her life in Skanden, but she was so tired of that life, of hiding. Of survival.

She wanted to *live*.

Which meant she'd have to leave The Wilds altogether. But this left her with the same questions as before: Where would she go? Istraa? Would they even let her return? And how would she get there? She had *nothing*. What little items of value she owned were still at Tolya's, and she didn't dare go back there. She thought of Jos's offer, but she couldn't think on that offer without also remembering the harsh words he'd spoken.

She sighed and regarded Jos. He didn't look so frightening now. Sleep stripped years from his life, making him appear almost youthful, and, somehow—painfully—even more handsome. That first night at Tallyn's, sleep had tormented him. Sable had woken to his thrashing and cries, and the only thing that'd calmed him back to sleep was her singing. She'd pressed her palm to his cheek, but she hadn't sung the lullaby she'd sung to Jedd. It hadn't felt right for Jos, and so she'd let her heart guide the notes until Jos's body relaxed and he drifted back to sleep. Every night she'd done this, though each night he'd responded faster. It also meant she'd had to arrange her bedding on the hard floor beside him.

She'd cut away his tunic and left his chest bare in order to have easier access to his wound, and she'd thrown the scraps of fabric into the fire. Sometimes when she looked at him, the sight of him filled her with wonder. She'd seen many bodies over the years, all shapes and sizes, but she'd never seen anyone built like Jos.

His body was a weapon, his torso a trained landscape of hard rises and sharp creases. There was no waste, no excess. Even his shape was a discipline. He bore a handful of scars, but the one beneath his left pectoral often drew her attention. It was a flat bubble of silvery skin. A knife wound, she imagined, that'd come precariously close to his heart. She wondered who'd made it, and thought that, perhaps, this trouble with the shade wasn't the first time Jos had tempted death.

A tattoo of a sword ornamented his left bicep. It encircled the rounded muscle, hilt to tip, and the hand guard had been artistically drawn to resemble a wolf's head. Sable wondered why this symbol was important to him. She wondered what all of his markings meant, for each told a story about a life that remained a mystery to her, and it made her think: had the scars made the man, or had the man caused the scars?

She dipped her fingers in a salve she'd made with lavender and gently wiped it over the stitches. She'd done this three times a day for the past four days to help the skin heal, and so far, it seemed to be working. A few days more, and she'd remove the stitches. She glanced at the scar beneath his chest, dipped her fingers in the salve, and rubbed some of it there as well.

A prickle of awareness tickled her mind. She stopped humming and glanced up to find Jos watching her.

She had a feeling he'd been watching her for a while.

He didn't speak, didn't move. He merely looked at her, eyes deep and shifting like the seas, his expression unreadable. The words he'd spoken stood between them like giants, and Sable drew her fingers from his chest and glanced away.

His hand came to rest upon her shoulder.

She looked at his hand, at him.

"Thank you," he said.

The words fell out in a pained whisper, wrapped in apology, and as she held his gaze, she saw that the man who had closed his eyes on this world wasn't the same as the man who had woken. Jos had been a storm, raging and deadly, ripping the world apart with his power, but *this* Jos stood like a survivor in the aftermath, in quiet surveillance of all that had transpired, his body ripped open, soul laid bare, looking at her with nothing but gratitude.

She placed her hand over his, surprised by his warmth. "You're welcome," she said quietly.

The silence breathed, their gazes held, and Sable felt something thaw between them. Jos pulled his hand away and glanced down at himself, at the shade wound. A crease formed between his brows.

"I'm doing everything I can to help them fade," she said, "but you might have those lines permanently."

His fingers trailed over the stitches, but he held his thoughts close. Still, they draped a heavy blanket of solemnity over him.

"You should eat," Sable said, standing. She walked to the stove, spooned leftover stew into a bowl, and snagged a hunk of bread.

Jos was sitting up when she returned, though the exertion had cost him some of his color. He crossed his legs, rest his elbows on his knees, and pressed his fingers to his temples.

"Here," she said.

He glanced up. His eyes focused on her a second later.

She held out the bowl and bread. "Try to eat."

Jos's gaze shifted to the bowl, but he said nothing, did nothing. Sable didn't take offense; he hadn't meant any. He was a man come back to life, having a difficult time accepting the gift he'd been given. Having a difficult time *believing* it. She placed the bowl beside him on the floor and sat opposite him. His gaze flickered to her. He dropped his hands and let them dangle.

"How long have I been asleep?" Jos asked quietly, clearing the rust from his throat.

"Four days."

The blue in his eyes deepened. He looked to the fire. "We're in Craven?"

"Just outside of it."

He glanced back, curious.

Now wasn't the time to share Tallyn's story. Jos had plenty of other details to sort through, and Tallyn's past was a difficult thing to digest even when one was in a strong frame of mind.

"This house belongs to an old friend of Tolya's," Sable continued carefully. "His name is Tallyn. We're lucky he found us. He had a curative I've never seen." She held his gaze a moment more. Her eyes kept wanting to drift lower, to his bare and muscled chest, so she looked pointedly at the fire.

Flames crackled; a log popped.

"You were right," Jos said. "About Gerald. I should've listened to you."

"Probably," she said with a dash of spice. "*But*. I live here. I have the advantage—I guess you could say—of seeing what it does to people. I can't fault you for doubting."

"But you fault me for my words."

She looked back at him.

Conviction filled his eyes and made them shine. "As you should. I was wrong. I shouldn't have spoken to you like that. I..." A pause. He cleared his throat. "I'm sorry."

Those last two words came out rusted and unfamiliar. But also genuine.

Sable held his gaze a long moment, then nodded curtly and looked back to the flames. She bent one leg and wrapped her arms around her knee, though she felt Jos's eyes on her every movement. At last, he reached for his bowl and dabbed at the soup with his bread. For a few moments, they sat in a companionable silence while he ate.

"How far are we from Craven?" Jos asked, setting the bowl down.

"About an hour," Sable replied. "Miraculously, it hasn't

snowed since we arrived, so the roads are still clear. Otherwise, we'd be trapped here for winter." She wondered if Tallyn's power had something to do with this, too.

"Two days from Craven to White Rock?" Jos asked.

"Yes, and about that... traveling from here will be a challenge. Ventus is searching for us."

He looked straight at her, eyes sharp as knives. "I *killed* him. With *your* help."

Sable considered her next words. "How much do you know about the Shah?"

His head cocked to the side. "More than I would like."

She'd assumed the subject would make him uncomfortable—it made most Provincials uncomfortable—but for Jos, she sensed that discomfort ran far deeper than most. She proceeded with caution. "Ventus has the ability to heal himself."

"From a knife to the *heart*?" Jos asked, incredulous.

"I know," Sable said, with empathy and a sigh. "I wouldn't have believed it myself if Tallyn hadn't seen him riding out of Craven with two Silent."

Jos stared at her. "Ventus is Liagé." It was a question, a statement, and a threat.

"No..." Sable hesitated. "Ventus is... something else. He's always done little things. Tricks with fire, shows of illusion. Never anything like summoning shades or *healing fatal wounds*. Whatever he is, he's alive, and there's a *very* large bounty on our heads."

Jos didn't speak immediately. He looked like he was still battling fatigue while building his thoughts. "I'm assuming this... Tallyn told you this?"

"Yes." Sable tucked a clump of hair behind her ear. "He and his Silent are searching every village, and the guards have been alerted."

Jos leaned back on his hands and inhaled deeply. After a long moment, he said, "All my coin was on that horse."

"I *might* be able to help there," Sable said. She'd given this a good bit of thought while Jos had been sleeping. "At least until we reach the Provinces."

Jos looked intrigued.

"I'm one of two healers in The Wilds. I've earned a few favors over the years." She winked.

He raised a brow. "And how do these *favors* compete with a *very* large bounty?"

"That's why I said *might*."

Amusement brightened his eyes. Just then, the front door opened and Tallyn stepped through, bringing winter with him.

Jos went completely still.

The door closed, a breath passed, and Jos was on his feet rushing Tallyn with a poker from the fire.

"Jos, wait!" Sable shouted, bolting after him.

His speed never ceased to amaze her.

Jos shoved Tallyn against the door, one hand gripping Tallyn's shoulder while the other pressed the tip of the fire poker to Tallyn's neck. Tallyn's hands opened in surrender, and the cloth bag he'd been holding fell to the floor.

"Jos, he's not what you think!" Sable gripped Jos's arm.

His gaze whipped to her, lethal and deadly, every muscle flexed to kill.

"*Please*," she urged, giving his arm a good squeeze. "This is Tallyn. *He's* the reason you're alive."

Jos's eyes narrowed, his muscles coiled. His gaze shot back to Tallyn, who, to Sable's surprise, didn't appear frightened in the slightest. He merely regarded Jos with curiosity and something else Sable couldn't place.

"He's a Silent," Jos hissed the word.

"*Was*," Sable corrected.

Jos didn't relent. The poker pushed against Tallyn's neck, creasing skin.

"Jos." Sable repeated, digging her nails into his bicep.

"*Trust me.*"

The moment held, tense and uncertain. Jos blinked hard, as if blinking away haze. His jaw clenched, unclenched, and his gaze darted from Sable to the Silent. And then—finally—he lowered the poker.

He gave Sable a hard look, then stalked away and tossed the poker on the hearth, where it clattered. He gripped the mantle, his back to them, and his tight shoulders expanded with a slow, deep breath.

Sable felt as though something very important had just happened.

"Have I come at a bad time?"

At the sound of Tallyn's voice, Jos glared over his shoulders, first at Tallyn, then Sable.

"Yes, he can talk," Sable said.

Jos rolled his eyes back to the fire.

Sable approached Jos, explaining what Tallyn had shared about his past. She explained how Tallyn had found them at the ruins, and when she finished, Jos stood quiet, hands squeezing the mantel, eyes fixed on the flames. Sable and Tallyn exchanged an uncertain glance.

Tallyn interrupted the silence. "I have news that might interest Jos." When Jos didn't respond, he continued, "A giant of a fellow, who goes by the name of Braddok, is lodging in White Rock."

At this, Jos's head whipped around, and his gaze pinned on Tallyn.

Any other man would've flinched beneath that stare. Tallyn simply continued. "Sable asked me to inquire whether any Provincials had wandered into White Rock recently." As Tallyn said this, Jos's gaze slid to Sable. "I discovered six," Tallyn continued, "but out of those, I assumed the gentleman with the strongest disposition to be the man you're hoping to find." A pause. "I see I assumed correctly."

Jos's composure faltered. It was the briefest of moments, but Sable noticed.

"Is he all right?" Jos asked sharply, despite the emotion swelling in his eyes.

"As far as I can tell," Tallyn continued. "I only inquired briefly so as not to draw unwanted attention to your friend, *however*, I understand that he's staying at Gaventry Inn. My contact spotted him at the tavern. Apparently, he likes ale."

Jos grunted and turned back to the hearth. He released the mantel and dragged a hand over his face.

Thank you, Sable mouthed to Tallyn.

Tallyn looked only at Jos as he nodded, then picked up the cloth bag he'd dropped and presented it to Sable.

"Clothes," he said to her unasked question.

"Thank you." She hesitated, then added, "Jos and I should be ready to leave tomorrow morning." She hadn't told him she'd decided to leave with Jos, and, honestly, she hadn't made up her mind till right then.

Tallyn regarded her a quiet moment, and by the look in his eyes, Sable thought he'd probably expected her answer, but he tucked his personal opinions out of sight.

"Of course. And if you don't mind, I'm going to retire for the evening. I have some tasks that require my attention." He dipped his head. "Goodnight."

"Night."

Tallyn cast one last glance at Jos and disappeared into his room. The moment Tallyn's door closed, Jos turned around to face Sable squarely.

"You told him about Brad." His tone wasn't scolding, but it wasn't quite friendly either.

"I did," she admitted. "I wanted to make sure he wasn't in trouble. Death is a difficult thing to carry, and you're carrying enough of it."

Jos just stared at her.

Sable walked toward him and held out the bag.

He glanced down at it.

"Tallyn purchased a new tunic for you," Sable said.

"What's wrong with the one I have?" He glanced about the room, looking for it.

"I used it to start a fire."

His gaze shot back to hers, and he regarded her as if she were made of pieces he couldn't comprehend.

"I had to cut it off," she explained, gesturing at his wound. "It's a token better left behind, anyway." She strode to a small door in the back of the room and opened it.

"Where are you going?" Jos asked after her.

"To ready your bath. You smell terrible."

SABLE WAS SITTING before the fire when Jos called her name from the washroom.

She'd left the door ajar, anticipating that he might need her help. She took a deep breath and stood, then walked to the washroom and pushed the door in.

Jos sat in the wooden basin, arms resting upon the rim. The water was high enough to conceal anything private; she'd made sure of it. A small voice ridiculed her caution. She'd seen lots of a naked bodies, and she'd already been naked with him.

But this felt... different.

Upon her entry, Jos dropped his arms from the basin and sat forward. Water sloshed around him. "I need you to..." His brow furrowed, he looked at her. "Would you cut my hair? Please."

She hadn't expected his question, and she suspected there was more to the cutting than the tangles.

"Sure," Sable said, stepping into the room.

Jos presented a dagger, hilt first.

She eyed it, then him. "Do they just sprout from your body?"

A smile grazed his lips, and he pressed the dagger closer.

Sable took it from his hands, set it on the stool, then moved behind him and touched his hair. He stiffened at the contact, then—slowly—relaxed as Sable combed her fingers through the tangles.

"All of it?" she asked.

"Yes."

She grabbed the dagger and systematically began cutting his hair, letting the wet clumps fall at her feet. Jos sat still and quiet, his eyes closed while she worked. It surprised her that Jos would entrust her with something that made him so vulnerable, but then, if she'd intended to kill him, she'd already had plenty of opportunities.

Once she'd cut away the bulk of it, she slowed her pace, meticulously trimming the hair close to his scalp. The top she left a little longer, blending it into the sides. He had such beautiful hair, she couldn't bring herself to sheer it off completely. Still, she had to admit that the short hair fit him.

"Where do you learn these pieces?" he asked quietly. His eyes had opened a sliver.

Sable paused, confused, and then she realized she'd been singing quietly. She abruptly pressed her lips together and focused on trimming Jos's hair.

"I didn't mean to stop you." His dark lashes brushed his cheekbone, as if he were trying to see her in his periphery. "I hear musicians often, and I've never heard the pieces you sing." He hesitated. "You sang to me while I slept."

She couldn't tell if he was asking or thanking her. "Yes, well, your nightmares kept me awake, and it was the only thing that calmed you down."

His shoulders expanded with breath, and he unfolded his hands upon the tub's rim.

"All right." She set the dagger on the stool. "Is that enough?"

Jos ran his hands over the top and sides. "Yes. Thank you."

"I'll be back with a broom." She left and returned to find Jos standing beside the tub, wrapped only in a towel.

Her cheeks warmed at the sight of him, so she set to work at once, sweeping up his hair. But just as she began, Jos wrapped a firm hand around the broom, stopping her. Her eyes met his.

"Let me do this," he said quietly.

The heat of him warmed the space between them, and the scents of lavender and soap filled her head.

Sable abruptly let go of the broom and hurried out of the washroom. A few seconds later, Jos resumed sweeping the washroom floor.

He eventually emerged, fully dressed (thank the wards), and carrying a cloth bundle full of what Sable assumed was his hair. He crouched beside her, whispered something beneath his breath, and tossed the bundle on the flames. The cloth sizzled, consumed by fire, and the scent of burnt hair tinged the air. He abruptly stood and scooped her blanket off of the floor.

"What are you doing?" she asked.

"You'll sleep on the pallet tonight." He sat on the wooden chair.

His words caught her off guard. "Jos, I'm fine on the—"

"*Take it.*" He cast her a sharp glance. "I know you haven't slept."

"You can't sleep in that chair."

"I've been sleeping for four days. I don't need any more sleep." He stretched his legs and arranged the blanket over them.

She could see by his expression that there would be no arguing with him, and honestly, a night on the soft pallet sounded blissful. Her spine ached from Tallyn's unforgiving floor. She crawled to the pallet where Jos had spent the past four days. His gaze followed her there, and once he was satisfied she intended to stay put, he looked back to the fire. The flames reflected in his eyes, and they were the last thing Sable remembered before falling asleep.

20

Snowflakes drifted lazily from a gray sky, dusting the horse's mane and Sable's cloak, but she wasn't cold. Jos sat before her upon the horse they shared, and his broad shoulders blocked much of the intermittent wind. They'd purchased the horse in Craven, thanks to Tallyn's unexpected and generous donation. Of course, Sable had mostly hidden outside of the city while Jos conducted business within. His short hair disguised him, as well as the stubble now shadowing his face, though his height still garnered a few second glances.

They trotted steadily toward Riverwood with good weather, stopping only to hide Sable when they heard other travelers approaching, which wasn't often. Most travelers had gone to Skanden for Belfast or hunkered down for the impending winter, and Sable silently praised their good fortune. It was almost as if some greater power held the weather at bay, helping her escape.

"Do shades only attack humans?" Jos asked while they rode.

"Not always, but they prefer humans," Sable answered, swaying with him. "They can't make more of themselves out of rabbits."

Jos glanced back enough that she could see his profile. "You have rabbits? And here I thought all you grew in The Wilds were demons."

Sable grinned. "The animals have learned to survive like we have, but if they're caught out at night, the shades get 'em. It's never a pleasant sight."

"What do you mean?"

"Shades tear their victims to pieces. Flesh, blood, intestines... everywhere." She shuddered, picturing the carnage she'd found during a recent outing. "Sometimes I'll come across the mess while scavenging for herbs."

Jos swayed with the horse, quiet, and Sable swayed with him.

"What about Gerald?" he asked.

He wanted to know why the shades hadn't ripped *him* to shreds.

"I'm not sure," she answered. "Shades will leave victims whole in order to make more of themselves. But..."

"A Silent got to Gerald before those shades arrived," Jos answered for her.

"Yes," she said, then added, "I wouldn't be surprised if Ventus found Gerald dying and healed him just enough to then change him. To get back at you for killing his Silent. It's something he would do."

A bluebird zipped passed, singing a bright and cheerful melody, then perched upon a mound of snow. As Sable regarded it, she realized it wasn't a mound of snow, but a roadside cairn, mostly buried. Bits of gray stone peeked through, and the tip of a red banner lashed at the wind.

She'd been searching for it for the past thirty minutes.

"There," Sable said, pointing to the marker.

A second later, Jos spotted it. "A village marker?"

"Yes. They're a mile outside of every village, and someone's usually tasked with keeping them visible."

"That *someone* isn't doing their job very well."

"This is a land of criminals," Sable said. "By definition, they don't follow rules."

"Point taken," he said with a smile to his voice.

A few miles later, the great Riverwood wall came into view, and Jos slowed their horse to a complete stop. "You're going to climb *that*."

They'd discussed their plans while traveling. Jos would proceed through the main gate, survey the situation, and clear the path for Sable while she climbed the wall's eastern corner and slipped into the village, unseen. Of course, Jos hadn't seen the wall when he'd agreed to the plan, and now that he was looking at the impressive palisade, he was clearly having second thoughts.

"Have a little faith," Sable said dryly.

"Don't confuse faith with folly," he said. "I'll find another way. Wait for me over… Sable?"

Sable slid off the horse and landed in the snow. "You have twenty minutes before I start climbing." Before the sun slept and the shades emerged.

"Good?" she asked.

His blue eyes pierced from within the shadows of his cowl, but she couldn't read the expression there. He looked back to the wall, and a slow cloud of breath rose from his lips.

Sable started walking away.

"Sable."

She glanced back.

His jaw squared, and his eyes flashed. "Be careful."

She raised a brow. "Judging by our short and, if I might add, very exciting history together, I'd say *you* are the liability here."

A grin quirked at the edge of his lips, brightening his eyes. He turned his head away from her and urged the horse onward. He didn't glance back again.

Sable watched him go, then moved silently through the forest toward the village. The only potential hitch in their plans, as far as she was concerned, were the guards. One watch tower sat over the main gate, and two smaller posts guarded the eastern and western edges. The eastern post had a vantage for Sable's climb, and this was where Jos came into play.

Sable pressed herself to the wall and waited. The forest was a palette of white and gray, untouched and serene, and the cold air shocked her bones, now that she didn't have Jos's body to block the wind, which grew stronger with the evening. She waited a few minutes more, until howls echoed from deeper in the woods.

Time to go. Jos had better be ready.

Sable faced the wall and climbed. She moved like a spider, clinging to the creases between snow-dusted stumps. Her boots slipped a few times from the snow and ice, but she caught herself, moving steadily up, higher and higher, finding knobs and cracks and holes, until finally, she reached the crest. There, she perched, listening, but the falling snow muted the world. She peered over the edge.

The walkway lay empty and quiet.

She threw one leg over the wall, then the other, careful not to knock over the stone wards, then slid silently onto the walkway and stopped in a crouch.

"Aren't you full of surprises?" said a smooth, deep voice.

Sable whipped her head around.

A few paces away, Jos waited like an assassin in the shadows—cowl drawn, leaning back against the wall, arms folded lazily over his chest.

Sable stood and dusted herself. "I didn't see you there."

"Obviously." He peered over the wall, taking in its full height, and then looked back at Sable, quiet.

Sable surveyed the empty street below. "Where's the horse?"

Jos didn't answer immediately. "The groomsman is keeping him for the night."

Sable nodded and rubbed her hands together. They were

numb from climbing, and her joints ached with cold. "And the guards?"

"Mostly concerned with their game of Spades. However, some of our eastern friends required a bit more... creativity."

Sable's eyes narrowed. "What did you do to them?"

He flashed his teeth.

She took a step toward him. "Jos, you promised—"

"*Relax*, my little altruist. They're alive. But we might want to hurry before they wake." His gaze skirted the streets below.

Satisfied he'd kept his word, Sable slipped a dagger from the folds of her cloak and held it out to him, hilt first.

Jos stilled. Sable approached and stopped an arm's length away, dangling his own dagger before him. He plucked it from her hands and eyed it, then her, his gaze as sharp as the knife in his hands.

"When?" he asked.

Sable only smiled.

His eyes narrowed. "I might have needed this."

"But you didn't." She winked, strode past him, and stopped at the ladder. From her vantage point, Riverwood was a collection of squat gables and chimneys, each twisting and bending, forcing their way through the crowd. Snow dusted the rooftops, piling in corners and on ledges, though the streets were mostly slush. She waited for a passerby to round a corner before climbing down.

"Are you sure about this?" Jos asked.

He wanted to know if she trusted Gavet, the smuggler—the man they were going to see. The one who owed her a favor.

She glanced up at him. "I wasn't sure about *you*."

His expression tightened.

She continued her descent. Jos's cloak whirled as he turned onto the ladder and climbed down after her. The two of them reached Gavet's storefront with little consequence, ducking only twice as guards wandered past. Sable led Jos through a side alley to Gavet's backdoor, but he settled into the shadows, angling himself to keep watch.

Sable rapped three quick times, waited, then rapped twice more.

No answer.

She glanced back. Even knowing where Jos stood, she could hardly see him.

She turned back to the door and rapped again. She was about to knock a third time when someone shuffled inside. A rectangular slat in the door slid open but closed before Sable could get a proper look. A lock clicked, and the door creaked open.

"Hi, Gavet," Sable said with a smile.

Gavet was in his early thirties, standing a few inches taller than Sable and built just a few meals thicker. He had a head full of rich, curly, dark hair and a face that was prettier than it was handsome, which he often used to his advantage. Many people mistakenly assumed that whatever was given to the body was stolen from the mind, and vice versa, and those clients never saw the double-edged deal until it stabbed them on both sides. Gavet had never employed those tactics on Tolya or Sable, however. A smart man didn't play games with his health, and Gavet was a smart man who also happened to suffer from a chronic ulcer.

Gavet took her in from head to toe, and his eyes narrowed. "All of The Wilds is looking for you," he said, glancing furtively behind her.

This was not a good start.

"I need a place to stay," she said seriously. "Just for the night. I can pay. I've also brought enough medicine to get you through winter." Thanks to Tallyn, who'd helped her collect proper ingredients to increase her bargaining power, just in case.

"Can you pay five hundred crowns?" Gavet asked sharply.

Maker's mercy. The bounty had increased since Tallyn's

report, but before she could respond, Gavet asked, "Who's that?" He gazed past her, at Jos, who'd emerged from the shadows.

"A friend."

"He's the one helping you, isn't he?"

"Gavet, I wouldn't be here if I had any other choice," Sable said tightly, hiding her desperation. "You know that. I've never asked you for anything before. One night, and we'll be gone. I swear."

Gavet scrutinized her. He had the upper hand, and he took pleasure in holding it there.

A whistle blew in the distance, sharp and piercing, jolting the sleepy evening awake. Shouts sounded nearby. Whatever Jos had done had just been discovered.

"*Please*, Gavet," Sable said through her teeth. "Just this once."

Gavet considered her, his face a blank. "Leash your dog," he snapped, jerking his chin toward Jos, who went impossibly still. "I don't trust him."

Gavet opened the door, not once removing his gaze from Jos. Sable too cast a meaningful glance at Jos, silently urging him to behave, before ducking inside. Jos checked the alley, then followed, and Gavet closed the door behind them.

They were standing in Gavet's kitchen. A fire burned in the small hearth, and hanging over it steamed a pot of mouth-watering aromas. Sable hoped Gavet had made extra.

"Care to tell me what's going on?" Gavet asked. His gaze drifted to Jos, who moved silently about the room, checking behind tapestries and around shelves. "If you break anything, you'll pay for it in fingers," he snapped at Jos.

Jos ignored him. He opened a cabinet, pulled out a flask, and shook it.

Gavet's face turned red. "I said—"

"Calm down, Gavet," Sable interrupted. "He's practically harmless." She waved a dismissive hand at Jos.

Jos's sharp gaze landed on her.

Sable smiled at him, then turned back to Gavet, who folded his arms with a snort.

"Tolya's gone," she said, forcing the words out. They were still hard to chew.

Gavet's gaze steadied on hers. If he felt anything, he didn't show it. "When?"

"Six days ago." Out of the corner of her eye, she noticed Jos resume searching the room.

Gavet processed this new information, his brow furrowed. "Where have *you* been for six days?"

"Hiding," she said, not willing to share more. "But I can't stay in The Wilds."

"Not with a bounty like that, you can't," he added sarcastically. "But do tell: Why is Ventus pursuing The Wilds' best, and now *only,* healer?"

"You tell me," she cut back. "Why is there a bounty on my head?" According to Tallyn, Ventus had publicly accused her of stealing, and he'd accused Jos of killing his Silent, though Ventus hadn't listed Jos by name. Jos was an "unknown accomplice." But Gavet always knew more, and Sable was very interested in hearing what the smuggler had heard.

Gavet pursed his lips and folded his arms with a huff. "Well, there's the obvious." He waved a hand at her. "He claims you stole from him, you're a fugitive on the run, and that he"—he jerked his chin toward Jos—"killed a Silent during your escape."

Sable laughed. "The Lord of Thieves. Offended when his thieves steal."

"If you stole from Ventus, you're an idiot."

"I didn't steal from Ventus." She picked up an ivory statue of Beléna, the Istraan goddess of beauty, and felt an unexpected twinge of sadness. She set it back on the mantel. "I stole from Velik."

"The *butcher*?" Gavet clucked his tongue. "Gods, I wish I'd known this sooner. I could've used a pair of deft hands on a few recent jobs. And Velik of all people. I'll be damned—though he deserves it." Gavet scratched his trimmed beard. "Trying to get back at him for something he did?" His eyes flickered over her face, brightening as his mind drew conclusions. "Or was it something he said? I know he hates your kind. But I've always taken you for someone with iron skin." His eyes matched his tone, both of them goading.

"Even iron breaks under stress," she said sharply.

Gavet watched her, his smile predatory. "Are you broken, Sable?"

She smiled back, all teeth. "Aren't we all broken just a little?"

In her periphery, she noticed that Jos had stopped to listen.

"I can't argue that," Gavet said, then tilted his head, studying her. "You know, it really *is* unfortunate I didn't know about your thieving habit sooner. I would've enjoyed working with you. You always say such interesting things."

Sable didn't respond. The word interesting meant too many things to people like Gavet.

"So... who's your friend?" Gavet nodded toward Jos, who now leaned back against a wall, watching them. "Is it true you actually killed a Silent?"

Jos gave no answer.

"Gavet, meet Jos, my current employer. Jos, this is Gavet, the most arrogant smuggler you'll ever meet. Assuming that wasn't already obvious."

"And also the best," Gavet added, fingers splayed theatrically over his chest. He looked over Jos, then back at Sable with a knowing look in his eyes. "What sort of employment?"

Sable leveled an irritated look on Gavet. "The same sort of employment I'm usually hired for. Did you want your medicine or not?"

Gavet rolled his eyes. "You're no fun."

"There's a bounty on my head. I don't have time for fun."

"On the contrary, it might do you some good. You've always

taken yourself far too seriously." Gavet smirked. "Pity, such a pretty thing like you, and a gorgeous man like that..." His eyes warmed on Jos. "Unless, of course, you entertain *other* preferences."

A shadow passed over Jos's already dark face.

"No..." Gavet cocked his head, reconsidering. "It's not that..."

"By the wards, Gavet," Sable snapped, annoyed. "You're as bad as the tavern ladies."

"Worse." Gavet winked, then strode to the steaming kettle. "Does your friend talk? Or does he also employ you to be his mouthpiece?"

"Your business is with Sable, not me," Jos said quietly, dangerously.

Gavet smiled. "Ah. A Provincial. Southbridge, is it? I do a lot of business with folk from there, though your accent is a bit harsher than most. Spend a good deal of time in Corinth?"

Jos's lips pressed together, and he didn't speak again.

"Beautiful country, Southbridge," Gavet continued, pulling bowls from the shelf. Three, to Sable's relief. "But too close to Corinth for my tastes, and dangerous for an Istraan. There be *wolves* near."

He, of course, meant the Wolf of Corinth, King Tommad's younger son, the second prince, who was responsible for slaughtering hundreds—maybe even thousands—of Sol Velorian refugees. He'd shown equal animosity toward any Istraan caught protecting them, and the people of Corinth revered him for it. Sable despised him.

Gavet handed Sable a bowl and a slice of bread he'd snatched from a plate. Warmth seeped into her palms, and she inhaled deeply the scents of rosemary, fennel, and caltis. Bits of potato floated in the broth. Gavet grabbed a bowl and bread for himself, then took a seat, leaving Jos's portion at the table.

"How'd you get past the guards?" Gavet asked, dipping the bread in the broth.

Sable joined him at the table. "I climbed the wall."

Gavet froze, bread hovering over the bowl, and he glanced up in surprise. He looked to Jos, who hadn't moved from the wall. "Him too?"

Jos didn't answer. Sable didn't doubt he'd said all he meant to say to this man.

"He went through the main gate," she answered for him, then added, with bite, "He's not as recognizable as I am."

Gavet waggled his brows at that, then bit into his soggy bread. "Well, you can't go back that way now."

"Obviously, but what other way is there?" she asked.

Gavet smiled wickedly. "I'm a smuggler. There's always another way, as long as one knows where to look."

21

After dinner, Gavet led them into his cellar, where they were to sleep for the night. It was cozy, as far as cellars went, cramped with his life's collection of goods—all items he'd smuggled over the years, just waiting for the right buyer. Sable spotted pieces from all over the Provinces and beyond: Istraan throwing stars; a lantern made of thick bubbled glass, framed in rope and metal, meant to endure the strong gusts native to The Fingers; a wooden oud, its body painted in beautiful swirls of fire, with pearlescent knobs and lustrous black strings. Sable had never seen such a beautiful instrument before. Unable to help herself, she strummed a few chords, earning herself a curious look from Jos and a glare from the greedy smuggler.

Regretfully, she stepped away from the oud then spotted an Istraan silk draped over a stool, dyed the purple of a desert sunrise. She approached, and rubbed the silk between her fingers with a nostalgic pang. It was even softer than she remembered.

"You'll be safe down here," Gavet said, pulling blankets out of a chest made of rose-colored wood Sable had never seen. "I've got some clients making deliveries in the middle of the night. It's better if they don't see you." He set the blankets on top of a gilded table. "Need anything else? A drink, perhaps?"

Gavet sounded as if he thought they needed one.

Jos didn't answer. He'd taken to checking the cellar in the same way he'd checked the kitchen.

"No, this is perfect. Thanks," Sable said.

"Here's a pot if either of you need to relieve yourself in the night, and don't slip anything into your pockets, little thief." He winked at Sable. "This might be a mess, but I know every item in it and where it rests." Gavet's eyes trailed Jos as he spoke. He seemed to catch himself, then looked back to Sable. "Make sure your employer doesn't take anything, either. At least, nothing that belongs to *me*."

Sable gave him a look.

He smiled, all mischief. "I'll leave this for you." He set the lantern on a shelf filled with trinkets and oddities, cast one last glance at Jos, then climbed up the ladder and closed the hatch.

"There had to be a better option than *that*," Jos said sharply.

"There wasn't." Sable snatched one of the blankets Gavet had left. "I told you. This is a land of criminals. We work with what we've got."

"I don't trust him."

"I never said I *did*. Besides, I didn't trust *you*, and here we are."

He regarded her as she stepped around items. "That's different."

"You're right." She glanced sideways at him. "Being with you is far more dangerous. You've almost gotten me killed—twice—and now I'm the most wanted woman in all The Wilds."

"Most women would envy you for that title."

She gave him a flat look. "Funny."

He smiled, all teeth, then picked up an Istraan star and ran his finger along one of the arched edges. "How is it you know him?"

Sable chose a spot to sleep and started moving items out of the way. "Gavet's been a patient of mine for years."

"What does he suffer from?"

"It's not really your business."

A pause. "Did you ever visit him in the middle of the night?"

Sable stopped arranging her blanket and glared at him. "It's not like that."

"I know it's not. *Clearly*, you're not his type." A dark smile curled his lips. He set the star down. "I'm asking why he expects deliveries in the middle of the night. Don't people here travel by day?"

"Yes, but that doesn't mean they conduct business strictly during the day."

Jos frowned, unconvinced.

Sable moved a small crate to the base of a standing mirror, but her reflection gave her pause. Tolya had never owned a mirror. Most people in The Wilds couldn't afford one. She couldn't remember the last time she'd seen her reflection so clearly—the palace, perhaps? —and the woman staring back surprised her. As a child, Sable's features had always been too big for her face, but her adult face held them well. As if it'd finally earned them.

Such a pretty thing like you, Gavet had said.

Her dark hair fell a little past her chin now, and though her skin hadn't seen the sun in years, it'd retained its coppery hue as if Istraa refused to let her go. She searched her reflection for pieces of Ricón or her papa, but she couldn't find them there. She'd never known her mother, and she found herself wondering if she resembled her, and if they shared the same hazel eyes, for they certainly hadn't come from her papa.

At the mirror's edge, Sable spotted Jos slinging his cloak over a chair. He lifted the edge of his tunic and ran his fingertips over the stitches.

"We should probably take those out," Sable said.

Jos caught her gaze in the mirror. He looked wary, but she couldn't be sure. He was still difficult to read.

"Come on," she said, gesturing for him to sit on her blanket.

With some apprehension, he did as she'd asked. He pulled his tunic over his head and propped himself back upon his elbows, and Sable knelt beside him. She cut the knot and tugged out the first stitch.

"Gods*damnit*." Jos hissed. "A little warning?"

"That *was* your warning."

He looked at her through half-lidded eyes.

She gave him a look. "It's better if I don't warn you. That way you're relaxed." A snip, a tug.

He hissed again and glanced sharply away from her, grumbling something she couldn't hear. His muscles tightened with expectation.

"Jos."

He looked at her a second later. His expression hovered between leeriness and aggravation.

"How'd you get that?" She nodded toward the scar beneath his heart.

His gaze slid to the scar as if suddenly remembering it was there, and then his brow furrowed. "It's... not a story for now."

She pulled another stitch. He hissed and shut his eyes.

"Right now is a *perfect* time," she said. "It'll keep you distracted."

But Jos didn't offer any more, and he kept his eyes shut until she yanked out the very last stitch.

"There. See?" Sable gathered the threads. "That wasn't so bad, was it?"

He opened his eyes an annoyed sliver.

Sable smiled, all innocence. "The good news is you're healing beautifully, if I do say so myself."

He grunted, sitting up. "The bad news?"

"It's not necessarily *bad*, but I still think you'll have those stripes permanently."

Jos glanced down at the lines. "That should make for some interesting conversations," he mused.

"Just keep your clothes on and..." Her voice trailed as she realized what he'd meant. She held up a hand. "Never mind. It's none of my business."

An imperceptible grin touched his lips before he pulled his shirt back over his head. "Thanks." He jumped to a stand, grabbed a blanket, and walked away to arrange his own bed—directly beneath the hatch.

Sable lay down, hands tucked behind her head, and stared up at the ceiling. She thought of how much life she'd missed, hidden away in Skanden, like all the items buried down here in Gavet's cellar. How many *experiences* she'd missed—experiences so common and natural to someone so handsome as Jos.

"Look what I found," Jos said suddenly, crouched so close she startled.

She glared at him.

He smirked, dropped a round, wooden board on her blankets, and set the lantern on the floor beside them.

Sable looked at the board and sat up straight. "*Hokstra*...?"

It was an Istraan strategy game—a very difficult strategy game, in which one conquered the stars. Ricón had taught her how to play after catching her in the rafters time and time again, spying on him and his friends as they'd played it. She hadn't seen the game since leaving Istraa, and not even the palace had owned a set this beautiful. Where had Gavet found it?

Jos admired the pieces as he took them out of a small drawer embedded in the game board, polished ivory or obsidian, each a representation of an Istraan saint, warrior, or god.

"You know how to play?" Sable asked in surprise.

"I know the basics."

"Who taught you?"

"No one. I saw it played once."

"*Once*? Jos, men spend their entire lives mastering this."

He arranged the ivory pieces upon one side and the obsidian pieces upon the other, both armies standing opposite the gilded sun at the center.

"No, Nián goes over there." Sable pointed to the appropriate star. Jos moved it accordingly. "And Asiam... no... no... *yes*. No, Saredd stands on Asiam's other side... no... Oh, just let me do it."

Jos sat back, triumphant.

Sable folded her legs, tucked her hair behind her ears, and set up the pieces. It'd been years since she'd done it, but as she held them, touched them, the memories returned. The saints, the warriors, their god, where they stood and how they moved.

"There," she said once she finished. She glanced up to find Jos watching her.

His gaze dropped to the board, and he turned the obsidian side toward himself. "Your move."

Sable raised a teasing brow. "Hoping you'll remember how to play by watching me?"

"Something like that." He lay on his side, propped himself upon an elbow, and stretched his long legs.

Sable eyed him, then moved.

Jos surveyed the landscape like a scout, looking for advantage, studying his enemy for weaknesses. His forehead creased with decision, and he moved. It wasn't a traditional move, but then, he wasn't a traditional player.

"Don't go easy on me," Jos said.

"Don't flatter yourself," Sable said, then took her next turn, cornering two of his most important pieces.

Jos frowned. "That's a rutting good move."

"I know."

His gaze cut through her.

She beamed.

His eyes narrowed, and his attention fell back to the board.

"Quiet," he said.

Sable realized she'd started humming. So she hummed a little louder.

His gaze shot up, but he didn't look annoyed. In fact, a spark lit his eyes, and he made his next move, evaded capture, and scooped up her ivory Beléna.

Sable stopped humming. "Basics, huh?"

"I'm a fast learner."

"You're also a liar."

He chuckled. The sound resonated through his chest more than his mouth, and it warmed through Sable. "Your turn."

Back and forth they worked—in silence—each of them focused on the board before them, moving pieces, staking claims, each pressing forward to conquer the sun. Sable marveled at the way his mind worked, how he capitalized on the unexpected, catching her off guard more than once. She adjusted her tactics, anticipating his stealthier approach, and a few times she caught him watching her. She thought he looked a little impressed.

Jos's fingers brushed two saints before settling on his Saredd, but rather than move it, he said, "You were caught smuggling Scabs, weren't you?"

Sable stopped drumming her fingers and glanced up. The intensity in his gaze pinned her in place.

"That's why you're here, isn't it, Sable?" he continued, rolling Saredd absently between his fingers. "Is Sable even your real name? It's not an Istraan name."

"Stop trying to distract me from the game. *Your* move." She nodded to the piece in his hand.

Jos's smile was predatory—a challenge accepted. "You hate The Wilds. You miss the desert. I see it in your eyes every time you're reminded of it." His gaze flickered pointedly to the purple Istraan silk she'd touched earlier. He'd been paying attention. "And music... it pours out of you. It's like you're constantly moving to a song only you hear, but you don't perform, though I sense you easily could. Instead, you keep to the shadows so no one sees you, and you walk on your toes so no one hears you, but not because you're shy." He cocked his head to the side. He was a tracker, following clues, gathering them up faster and faster with that sharp mind of his.

"You don't want to draw attention to yourself," he continued. "It's how you've survived as an Istraan all these years—alone, as a woman. It's why you keep your hair short, to help hide your heritage, but you don't cut it completely, as you should. Your heart is in Istraa, but you won't return, which tells me you were forced to leave. That's not a surprise. Everyone in this godsdamn place was forced here one way or another. Most of them are criminals. You said so yourself. You even claim to be a thief, but I don't buy that. I've known thieves. Many of them. You don't have it in you."

He was goading her, trying to get under her skin. Trying to pull out the truth.

Sable stared straight back, her expression stone. "*It's your move.*"

He threw his Saredd across the room, and Sable jumped. Obsidian struck stone and clattered to the floor. Black rimmed Jos's irises, and the blue within stormed.

He wasn't playing anymore.

He knew the truth—somehow—and he was taunting her with details, trapping her inside of them until she confessed. Sable calculated how many paces it would take to reach the ladder. In her periphery, she found the Istraan star.

"No, you're not a thief. You're too compassionate," he said, daring her to deny it. "You saved my life *twice* when you had no reason to trust me. You would help a Scab if they needed it, and you did. You were caught, so you fled." He paused, letting his verdict sink in, so certain he was right. A hunter, closing in for the kill. "Tell me I'm wrong."

By. The. Wards.

Sable was speechless.

No one had ever seen her so clearly, and even though he hadn't guessed the complete truth, he'd guessed enough to leave her stunned, and also largely relieved. He didn't know. She wondered how long he'd been mulling this over, trying to figure her out.

He leaned closer still, over the gameboard. His hot breath feathered across her face, and he smelled of pine and earth.

"Tell me"—his eyes moved back and forth between both of hers, his gaze penetrating—"I'm wrong."

Maker's Mercy, he was beautiful.

Her gaze slid over the strong lines of his jaw, the fullness of his mouth, and rather than argue his points as she probably should have, she leaned forward and kissed him.

His lips were soft, and the scruff around his mouth scratched her face a little, but then she grew increasingly aware of the fact that he wasn't kissing her back.

He'd gone rigid.

Jos gripped her shoulders and shoved her back. His eyes were so dark they looked black, and a dangerous shadow fell over him.

Sable opened her mouth to speak, but words evaded her. She felt... confused, and embarrassed, and also a little angry, and his fingertips were digging into her shoulders. She shook her head a fraction, trying to shake sense into it. Trying to quiet the strange and sudden ringing in her ears. "I'm... I don't..." She cleared her throat; her cheeks burned. "I shouldn't have—"

Jos grabbed her chin and kissed her hard.

Sable's apology died on her lips.

He squeezed her chin and kissed her again, and again, stealing her breath, her confusion and anger. Stealing away every other thought until all that remained was *him*. His mouth was fever-hot, and his tongue tasted sweet as it slipped into her mouth and pushed against hers, insistent and demanding.

Emboldened, Sable kissed him back.

Her tongue pushed against his in a dance of power, and Jos groaned. The sound was almost pained. Still holding her face, he climbed onto his knees and tried scooting closer, but his knees bumped the Hokstra board. With a growl, he shoved the game aside. Pieces flew everywhere, gods clattered to the floor, and Jos drew her in his arms, closing the last threads of space between them.

His hands clawed through her hair as his mouth covered hers completely, ravenous. The force of his kiss pressed her back into a crate. Something rattled, knocked off balance. Sable didn't know what. Didn't care. He slid her from the crate and lowered her onto the blanket, his knees between her legs. He tugged his tunic up and over his head and tossed it behind him, but just as he lowered himself on top of her, Sable hooked her leg around his and rolled him onto his back.

He looked up at her with surprise, and then his eyes narrowed, burning with a desire that made her pulse race out of control. She had never been with anyone before, and even though she and Jos had already been naked together, this felt completely different. He hadn't looked at her then—really looked at her, as he did now—and his attention both excited and terrified her.

He reached up, grabbed a fistful of her hair, and dragged her mouth firmly down to his. Some of her hair spilled over his face, but he buried himself in it, breathing in deeply as he kissed her through it. A little thrill moved through her body and, instinctively, she squeezed her legs, pinching his thighs between hers. He groaned against her mouth, and in one fluid motion, he flipped her onto her back again, dumping her onto the blanket. His boot knocked the small table, a vase toppled and shattered, and a collection of marbles spilled upon the floor.

They froze. Marbles rolled.

Sable laughed, but Jos smothered it with his lips, as if he wanted to catch the sound. Devour it. He sank on top of her, and her laugh quickly turned into a soft moan. His body burned hot as a brazier through her thin tunic, and she ran her palms over his back, marveling at the smoothness of his skin and the hardness of his muscles, shifting as he touched her, kissed her. He was like the desert, his breath a sultry night, his hands the blazing sun, and everywhere he touched, his fingers set fire to her skin.

His lips moved down her neck and teased along her collarbone, and a little gasp caught in Sable's throat. He dug his fingers into her hips, pulled them firmly against his, and Sable felt suddenly and inexplicably impatient. She grabbed his face, dragged his mouth back to hers, and kissed him hard.

He growled against her mouth just as someone pounded on the hatch above.

"What's going on down there?" Gavet called through the hatch, his tone suspicious.

He must've heard the vase explode.

Sable pulled her mouth from Jos's, her heart speeding out of control. "Nothing!" she called out, trying to sound calm, which was almost impossible when Jos started kissing down her neck again. "Jos tripped over a crate!"

Jos nipped her ear and tugged at her shirt.

"Remind your *employer* to be more careful," Gavet said with irritation. "I have contacts in Southbridge. If he breaks anything, I'll recover the expense one way or another."

Gavet's tread thumped on and faded to silence.

Sable turned back to Jos, but he'd gone still. He hovered there, one elbow beside her, his other hand at her waist, his expression unreadable.

"Jos…?" She leaned in to kiss him, but he turned his head away from her.

She pulled back, hiding the sharp pang she felt.

"Gods, what am I doing?" he murmured. His gaze slid around her face, bewildered, and he pushed himself off of her.

Cold air chilled her skin where his lips had been.

He sat back on his heels, his broad back to her, unmoving. Lantern light gilded his pale skin.

"I don't understand," Sable said, wondering what in the wards she'd done wrong.

The quiet stretched, awkward and brittle at the edges. Jos raked a hand through his hair, but his fingertips searched for length that was no longer there.

"Is it because I'm Istraan?"

"Get some sleep," he said. His voice was deep and raw. "It's late."

Without a glance in her direction, he jumped to his feet. He grabbed his shirt from where it'd caught on the oud, strode to the foot of the ladder, and lay down upon his blanket.

"Really…?" Sable said sharply. "That's it? You're going to just—"

"*Goodnight*, Sable."

Sable clenched her teeth. She adjusted her shirt while trying to calm her still-racing heart.

"Oh, and Jos…" she said. "You're wrong." She turned off the lantern and lay down.

But he didn't answer.

JERIC LAY flat on his back, staring into the darkness while flicking his thumb over the edge of his dagger.

Sleep wouldn't come. He told himself it was the hunter in him, the part that never shut off, the part that always listened, always watched. He shoved his dagger beneath his makeshift pillow and turned on his side, his back to her. He couldn't see her, but he felt her there like a campfire blazing in the night.

And his body still ached.

He dragged a hand over his face. Tomorrow, he would get Braddok. Tomorrow, they'd ride out of this rutting hellshole and take her straight to Skyhold, where he would hand her over to his brother and be done with it.

Jeric gritted his teeth and shut his eyes. The sweet taste of her lingered on his tongue.

Godsdamnit.

22

"You hear about King Tommad?" Alv whispered.

Silas scanned the cards spread on the small table, lit dimly by the lantern.

"He's dead."

Silas paused and glanced up, doubtful.

"I swear it," Alv continued, glancing furtively about them. As if someone would hear them down here, in the skal mine. "Tessa says he's been sick for months and just passed. Says Prince Hagan is waiting for the Wolf to return before he makes an official announcement. Doesn't want no trouble from the jarls. Especially Stovich. I hear he's been a thorn ever since what happened in Reichen."

Silas raised a bushy brow. "She knows an awful lot about Prince Hagan's intentions."

Alv folded his arms at the insinuation. "Say what you—"

Something clattered deeper in the mine, where the Scabs slept. Then... quiet.

They exchanged a glance.

Eventually, Alv shrugged and was moving to play his card when a child laughed. This time, Silas stood.

"Maybe one of 'em's sleepwalking," Alv suggested.

"Then I'll chain them to the rutting wall," Silas growled. "Be right back."

Alv nodded.

Silas grabbed a torch from the wall and walked deeper into the mine. Alv watched his silhouette grow dim until he turned a corner. With a sigh, Alv sat forward in his chair, thumbed through his cards, and looked at the spread. He frowned. Silas was going to win. Again.

He glanced down the mine, then reached over and picked up Silas's hand. He switched a few cards, set them back down exactly as Silas had left them, then reclined back in his chair and waited.

And waited.

Alv tapped his foot and stared at the shadows. He hated guarding the mines. It was like staring at a mouth that was always open, always hungry. His superiors said this wasn't a demotion, but everyone knew better. The mines were where they sent the guards who'd caused trouble in the commander's ranks, and Alv and Silas had caused their share. Corinth was spread thin enough, guarding the border and fighting the resurgence of rebel Scab groups; it couldn't afford to discharge them. So they put them here, in the deep and dark, guarding over Scabs who mined for skal. Not that Alv could complain. Those Scab women provided a constant source of entertainment.

Alv frowned at the shadows. Where was Silas?

And then he heard a whisper.

Alv froze. "Silas?" he called out.

Nothing.

He pulled his dagger free. "Silas, that you?"

No answer.

"Don't be playing tricks on me..."

Alv watched the shadows. A stiff wind ripped through the mine, and his lantern flickered out, plunging him into total darkness.

Alv cursed, tucked his blade beneath his arm, and fiddled with the lantern, trying to bring it back to life. Glass rattled, and his fingers shook with fear and desperation. He needed to stay calm. There was nothing else down here—nothing that he or Silas hadn't let pass through the opening. Silas was playing tricks on him again. "Silas, godsdamnit! I'll..."

He'd just struck the flint when he heard the faintest hiss. Something cold brushed his neck.

Alv jumped, dropped the flint, and knocked the lantern off the table. It crashed to the floor as ice-cold fingers wrapped around his neck, his arms, pulling him under, and Alv screamed.

SABLE SAT UP WITH A START, and a single note rang in her mind.

Do not fear the path ahead, the voice said again, *I will be with you.*

The cellar was dark, the world asleep. No light shone through the floorboards above, and when she looked in Jos's direction, all was quiet. She was starting to lie down again when a strong arm wrapped around her, pulling her back against an even stronger body, and a hand clamped over her mouth.

Sable started.

"It's just me," Jos whispered in her ear.

She relaxed a little, but she immediately knew something was wrong. He peeled his hand away and released her.

"What is it?" she whispered.

"We've been discovered."

Sable looked at the darkness above. She couldn't hear anything unusual, but then, Jos had senses she didn't understand.

Jos shifted against her and pushed something into her palm. "Here."

It was a knife. Sable shoved it into her belt. "Is Ventus here?" she whispered.

"I don't know, but there are guards upstairs. There could be more outside."

She didn't doubt him, but that would mean Gavet had betrayed them.

A floorboard creaked above, and Sable felt a rush of fury. "That godsdamn, spineless piece of scat."

"I think I'm starting to wear off on you," Jos said dryly.

"I'll kill him."

"In a few minutes, you might just get your chance." His shoulder brushed hers. "Wait here."

"You're going to handle the guards. By yourself."

"I mean it, Sable," he said firmly.

There was no point in arguing with him, so she didn't.

He moved away from her. Ladder rungs creaked beneath his solid weight, and he pounded on the hatch. Meanwhile, Sable felt her way forward in the darkness. He could give all the orders he wanted. She didn't have to obey them.

"Gavet," Jos called. When Gavet didn't answer, Jos pounded again, harder this time. "*Gavet.*"

A shuffle and a scrape, and, finally, footfalls thudded overhead. "Yes...?" Gavet's irritation was muffled through the hatch. "Gods above, do you have any idea what time it—"

"Open the hatch. Sable's not breathing."

Silence.

It was a smart move. *She* was the prize, after all, and if anything were to propel Gavet to open that hatch, it would be for fear that his prize had been compromised.

"What do you mean, *not* breathing?" Gavet asked.

"I mean she's not breathing," Jos growled. "She had a reaction to one of her sleeping draughts, I think. I need something to stop the swelling."

Sable frowned. He was an excellent liar, and then she wondered if this should concern her.

Wood scraped against wood, the hatch opened, and dim light shone down, partially blocked by Gavet's silhouette.

Sable ducked deeper into the shadows of the cellar.

"Where is—" Gavet started.

Jos grabbed him by the collar and slammed his head against Gavet's. Gavet's head lolled to the side, and Jos shoved his limp body out of the way. Shouts sounded above, boots thudded and metal scraped, but Jos had already pressed his hands on either side of the opening and hoisted himself through, kicking in the knees of a guard on his way out.

By the wards, he moved fast.

Above, men grunted and bodies crashed. Sable scrambled up the ladder and peered through the opening just as a guard swung a chair. She ducked, chair legs whirred over her head, and she scrambled onto the floor and made a dash for the guard's legs. He yelped in surprise, then kicked at her. She jerked Jos's dagger from her belt and stabbed it through the guard's boot. He screamed and whirled the chair around, but Sable jerked the dagger free and rolled away.

Right into Jos's boots.

He glared down at her, eyes ablaze.

She shoved off of him and threw herself onto another guard's back. The guard whirled, trying to throw her off, but she wrapped her limbs around his neck and squeezed. He choked, grabbing at her arms, but she held on like a desert snake, constricting. He rammed her into a wall, slamming her back into plaster. She winced. A picture fell and crashed to the floor, but she didn't let go. Finally, the man gasped and slumped to the floor, unconscious.

Sable climbed off of him just as someone came at her with a sword.

Jos interceded with his sword and the entire weight of his body. The guard cried out, barely able to fend off the force that was Jos. He was incredible to watch, really. Like the eye of a storm, beautiful and untouched, spinning the world around him into chaos and destruction.

Another guard bolted through that destruction, making an escape for the door, but Jos threw one of his blades and caught the guard between the shoulders. The guard jerked and fell on his face, while Jos returned to fight the first guard. He didn't see the guard coming up behind him.

Sable jumped to her feet, snatched the Beléna statue from Gavet's mantel, and slammed it over the guard's head. He grunted and toppled to the floor. Sable didn't know if he was dead.

Jos glanced back, and his gaze found hers, furious.

Still looking only at her, he jerked his dagger from the chest of the guard he'd been fighting. That guard slumped to the floor behind him, forgotten.

"Gods*damnit*, Sable!"

Sable set the statue back on the mantle. It looked strangely out of place, like a tree left standing after the rest of the forest had burnt to the ground.

Jos took a furious step toward her, his face tinged red from exertion and anger. "I told you to wait."

"And...?"

His jaw clenched. "I'm trying to *protect* you."

"Are you?" she challenged.

His lips pressed in a line, trapping words behind them.

Sable tossed his bloodied dagger at him. He plucked it from the air without taking his eyes off of her. She turned away from him in search of Gavet and spotted him coughing on his breath, propping himself on his forearms. She made her way for him.

"Sable..." Jos warned behind her.

Sable ignored him and shoved her boot between Gavet's shoulder blades, pinning him to the floor. Gavet grunted, straining to breathe, arms splayed. "Sable..." he started.

"You spineless piece of scat," Sable growled. She gave him a good hard shove, then pulled her boot away.

"I had no choice..." He struggled to push himself upon all fours. "They knew you were here, and if I didn't..."

She grabbed him by the collar and yanked him to his knees. "When will he be here?" she demanded.

"I don't—"

She jerked him harder. "*Don't* lie to me, Gavet."

His expression strained; his throat bobbed as he swallowed. His eyes flickered to Jos, then settled back on Sable. "I... sent a pigeon as soon as you arrived. He was in White Rock."

Which meant Ventus would be here any moment.

Sable was so angry, her fists trembled. "After *everything* I've done for you... you would betray me like this."

"I didn't have a choice!" Gavet said through his pain. "You know the power he holds. He would've destroyed my business—"

Sable let go of his collar and punched him square in the face. He cried out and toppled back against the wall.

"Curse you and your business, you rutting coward." She spat at him, and he flinched. "Shame on me for thinking I could ever compete with your pocketbook."

"Sable... *please*..."

Sable plucked the dagger off his belt and shoved it through hers. "I won't forget this, Gavet."

She left him there and maneuvered over bodies, around broken chairs, and past Jos. She strode down the hallway, opened the back door, and stepped out into the bitter night. There, in the darkness of Gavet's back porch, she stopped. The night was too quiet, and an unnatural mist had fallen over everything.

Ventus was here.

She sensed Jos behind her, but she didn't look back. "He's already here," she whispered.

A beat. "You're certain?"

"Yes." Sable stared absently ahead, watching her breath depart in a cloud. "You should go. It's me he really wants, and you can bet your merciless gods he'll have more than two Silent with him this time. *Go*. Find your friend. Get out of here while there's time."

Jos grabbed her shoulders and turned her around to face him. His eyes glittered in the night. "This isn't just your fight anymore, Sable. He killed one of mine."

"You won't win this fight, Jos," she snapped. "If it's revenge you want, then *live*."

He studied her; his expression warred.

"Go," she urged, shoving him away from her.

There you are, little sulaziér.

23

Ventus's guards filed into the alley. Two knelt behind barrels, crossbows aimed, and the rest fanned out, blocking their exit. Gavet's back door creaked open, and four more guards appeared in the doorframe. One carried a torch. Sable blinked away the sudden brightness, then noticed one of the four held a crossbow aimed at Jos.

They were trapped.

She glanced back down the alley as a shadow melted from the darkness. A Silent. And another, until Sable counted four of them. *Four.*

Ventus appeared behind his Silent, his robed silhouette a stain upon the night.

Beside her, Jos stood impossibly still, sword already drawn.

Come with me willingly, sulaziér, and his death will be quick.

"It's me you want," she growled, and she stepped into the alley, arms out. "Let him go."

He killed one of my Silent.

"And *you* Changed his man. I'd say you're even now."

Jos's face angled toward her, his body tense. He could only hear one side of the conversation, and he didn't like it.

Ah. You figured it out. I knew you were special. I wonder if your Provincial knows just how special you are. Perhaps we should give him a little display? Break the walls around your power and show him what you truly are?

Sable was wondering what power he was referring to when her temples wrenched. The pain was a punch to her skull. She gasped, her knees gave, and she fell upon all fours. Ventus squeezed harder. Her lungs clamped down, her breath strained, and something deep inside of her tingled. It was the same sensation she'd felt all those years ago when she'd played her flute.

But she was not holding her flute.

Heat pushed against her ribs. There, the pressure began building and building, like a kettle about to boil over.

Ventus squeezed even harder.

Something inside of her gave, like fissures cracking through glass. Expanding. The warmth pushed more intensely now, against the fractures, and Sable fisted her hands, squeezing her abs, physically trying to hold herself together. But the pressure surged and the fissures spread, breaking her apart, and Sable yelled through clenched teeth.

"Enough," Jos's command cut through the agony.

The pressure relented; the glass, miraculously, held. The warmth receded, simmering deep, and Sable had no idea what Ventus had just done to her.

She glanced up. Three of the guards at Gavet's back door had dropped. The fourth stood stone still, torch raised as Jos held his sword to the guard's throat. In Jos's other hand was a crossbow, which he'd aimed straight at Ventus.

In the ambient light, Ventus smiled.

Suddenly, Jos gasped and dropped to his knees. The crossbow clattered to the ground, and his sword scraped against the cobblestones. Jos heaved for breath, forcing himself to his feet, but his knees gave out and he collapsed again.

A strong hand gripped Sable by the hair, and she yelped as

the guard who'd just been Jos's prisoner yanked her back. Jos yelled through his teeth, hands fisted upon the cobblestones, and his body convulsed, over and over again, each time more violent than the one before.

Ventus was going to kill him.

Sable bucked hard, smashing her head against her captor's nose. The guard cried out and staggered back, stumbling off of Gavet's porch. Sable snatched the torch from the ground and pulled a candle from her boot—*don sar*, they called it in Istraa. Night star. She'd known what it was the moment she'd spotted it in Gavet's cellar. Ricón used to collect them before he'd learned to make them himself. The explosions were always so colorful.

She touched fuse to torch, and the fuse sparked.

"Here's a display, you rutting monster," Sable snarled, then pointed the candle at the barrels of ale that Ventus's Silent and guards stood behind.

Ventus growled and squeezed her skull tight, but he was too late. The *don sar* shot from Sable's hands, and Sable dove at Jos. Like a comet, the *don sar* blazed through the alley, straight at the barrels. Sparks flew, spewing stars.

The guards didn't register what was happening until the explosive hit.

Sable landed on top of Jos as a great *boom*! shook the night.

Light. Heat. Smoke.

Sable's ears rang, and she staggered to her feet, pulling Jos with her. "Hurry!" she yelled at Jos, then coughed.

Jos swayed a little, gazing at the flames in disbelief.

"Come on!" She pulled him back through Gavet's house, and the two of them sprinted through the mess they'd left, pushing their way to Gavet's front door and out onto a dark and empty street.

Shouts echoed behind them, and the night seemed a little brighter.

"This way!" she hissed.

She bolted down the street, making sure Jos followed, then turned down another alley.

"The five hells did you get that?" he asked as they ran.

"Gavet's." Sable made a sharp right, down another alley.

"I take it back. You do have it in you."

Sable would've laughed if she weren't breathing so hard.

"The stable's that way." Jos pointed. In contrast to her, he was barely winded.

"Heading there. Back way."

They rounded a corner and ran right into a handful of village guards. One opened his mouth to speak, but Jos silenced him with an elbow. The man staggered back, and Jos punched through two more. A fourth moved in with his sword, but Jos knocked it out of his hands and caught it with his other.

The man's lips parted. "The hell are *you*?"

Jos flashed his teeth, whirled, and stabbed the man through with his own sword.

Not for the first time, Sable was glad she wasn't on the other side of that blade.

They sprinted on. Faces peered through windows, trying to see the cause of the commotion. Some opened doors, looked out, and promptly closed them again.

"This way!" a voice yelled somewhere behind them.

Sable shoved Jos down a narrow alley. She could just see the stables through the slim crack between walls. They reached the end, waited a breath, checked the street, then bolted for the stables and pushed through the doors.

A groomsman stumbled toward them, delirious with sleep. "What are you—"

Jos shoved him into a pile of hay. "Third one on the left," he said to Sable.

Sable found the horse happily sucking water from his trough.

"No time to saddle," Jos said, but Sable was already jumping on the horse's bare back. He climbed on behind her, gave the horse a swift kick, and they exploded out of the stable.

Guards flooded into the street.

Jos charged through them with a yell, whirling his sword while Sable kicked at hands and faces, knocking them back whenever she could. They galloped down the road much too fast, heading for a gate that was closed.

Behind them, the sound of galloping horses erupted. Jos cursed, urging their horse faster. Through the din, a soft click snagged Sable's attention—a whisper, a warning—and she ducked, pulling Jos with her just as bolt whizzed passed. It struck stone instead, ricocheting into the night.

"We need to open the gate," Jos growled.

"Hold them off, and I can—"

Half a dozen village guards rushed out from the shadows, spreading in front of the gate to block their exit.

Jos cursed.

A furious yell rose about the rest, and a behemoth of a man flew out of nowhere, barreling through the guards like an avalanche. Men cried out and dropped to the ground. The man whirled around, and Sable glimpsed ruddy hair. It was the man who'd been with Jos during her failed rescue attempt, Braddok.

Jos jerked their horse to a halt and leapt from the saddle, "Godsdamnit, Brad! Where have you been?" he yelled as he charged fearlessly into the melee.

"Waiting for your pretty arse, as usual!" Braddok yelled back, slamming his forehead into a guard. The guard's eyes rolled back and he collapsed, crossbow sliding out of his hands.

Sable jumped off the horse, scrambled forward, and snatched the crossbow from the ground just as a dark figure landed in a crouch before her. It hissed through a mouth of black teeth and inked skin, and Sable took an involuntary step back.

Two more Silent appeared near the gate. And the fourth landed before Jos.

The Silent encircled them, corralling them and pressing closer. The few remaining guards hurried out of the way to watch the certain bloodbath. Braddok wiped a hand across his sweaty brow and spat bloodied saliva on the ground. "Godsdamnit. I'm really sick of these things."

The Silent standing before Jos hissed, then closed in. Jos blocked fast, stopping the Silent before it could slice open his throat. The Silent stepped back, and the two circled each other. Predator to predator.

The guards watched. Even Sable held her breath.

And then Jos took the offensive. He attacked in a storm of strikes, pressing the Silent back, farther and farther. Guards jumped out of the way. Jos grabbed one and used him as a shield. The Silent didn't slow, didn't stop or care. The Silent stabbed, nightglass pierced armor, and Jos's human shield sagged, dead. Jos shoved him aside.

A second Silent joined in.

Braddok charged into the third, knocking it to the ground, but the Silent near Sable leapt into the air with supernatural strength and landed on top of Braddok, nightglass in hand.

Sable raised the crossbow. She'd never shot one before, but it couldn't be that difficult. She aimed, waited for a clean shot, then fired. String snapped, air whirred, and the bolt landed in the Silent's shoulder.

It wailed and whirled on her, then came at her in a rush. She ripped another bolt from the bow, set it, and fired again. It struck the Silent's thigh, but it did not slow.

Metal flashed.

The Silent collapsed with forward momentum, but its head dropped to the ground and rolled a few paces away. Jos stood behind it, sword dripping crimson.

And Ventus roared with fury.

A shock of pain punched through Sable, and she collapsed.

In her periphery, Jos and Braddok dropped too. Ventus held all three of them captive with his power.

He whirled into a shapeless form of night and shadow, and reappeared before her. Sharp nails dug into her chin, and he dragged her to her feet. His black eyes bored into hers, and he smelled of blood and steel and ice. *You will pay for this.*

Sable reached for Gavet's dagger, which was still in her belt, but an invisible force jerked it free and sent it soaring. It clattered onto the cobblestones, well out of reach. Ventus grabbed her wrist and whipped her around to face Jos and Braddok, who both heaved on all fours, features twisted in agony.

One Silent approached Jos. It grabbed him by the collar and yanked him to his knees. Jos yelled through his teeth, the veins in his temple bulging. He couldn't fight back—not with Ventus's power holding him captive. The Silent pressed a nightglass blade to Jos's neck. Behind them, Braddok lay in debilitating prostration.

"Let them go!" Sable yelled. "I'll go with you… I won't fight, I swear!"

I will make clothing from his skin, and you will wear it. You will always remember what happens to those who oppose me.

The Silent began to carve. Slowly. A bloom of bright red stained Jos's neck.

Right behind Jos, there was a sudden twist of wool, followed by a soft crack. The Silent that'd been carving Jos's neck crumpled in a heap of robes, its head bent at an impossible angle by the hands of the newcomer now standing behind it.

Jos fell forward and caught himself on the cobblestones with a gasp. The intruder looked up. Golden light flickered across a face made cruel by thick scars.

"Hello, Ventus."

It was Tallyn.

24

It took Sable a moment to recognize Tallyn, for the man standing before them was not the Tallyn who had saved her life. Fury made his hideous face cruel, inhuman, and there was nothing kind in his gaze now, nothing warm—only hatred. A strange mist clung to his robes, obscuring his lines. It seeped out of him, making him look almost ethereal—a spirit of the night, materialized. Even the lanterns dimmed and quivered, their flames cowering in Tallyn's presence, which was far more robust than Sable had known it to be, as if he'd never quite expanded himself before her. His power unfolded his frailty, filled in the cracks and hollows, and transformed this broken man into something magnificent and terrible—like Death, finally come to take what was owed him.

And Sable was afraid.

She hadn't seen this side of Tallyn. If he'd shown her even a hint of this, she never would've trusted him. Seeing him like this, she believed that Tallyn had been Azir's first.

The two remaining Silent hissed, moving protectively toward Ventus, and Ventus's guards stepped back in fear. Jos climbed to his feet beside Tallyn, wary as he regarded his unexpected savior.

Braddok also lumbered to a stand, but he held near the guards, ready to intercede should they decide to attack.

"Tallyn." Ventus turned the one word into two, his expression a twist of loathing and disgust. "Look at you. You wear your treachery well."

Tallyn said something to Jos that Sable could not hear.

Jos's eyes narrowed.

"Kill them," Ventus snarled. "But Tallyn is *mine*."

The guards near Braddok raised weapons and took a small step.

Braddok smacked the flat of his blade against his palm and smiled. Uncertain glances passed between the guards, and the one in front charged. Braddok ducked, and, in a maneuver surprisingly fast for one his size, he rolled the guard over his back. Another guard moved in, but Braddok spun and whacked the guard's back with his sword, and the guard tripped on the cobblestones. Three more charged him, but Braddok ran his sword through one, grabbed the heads of the other two, and smashed them together. He pulled his sword from the first and flashed a smile at the remaining guards.

"Come on, ladies," he goaded. "Don't wet your panties."

With a yell, the rest of the guards swarmed Braddok, but this time, Jos stepped into the fray. Tallyn, however, did not. His gaze remained fixed on Ventus while chaos erupted behind him.

Sable jerked against Ventus's hold, trying to get away, but he squeezed so hard, his nails broke skin.

"You cannot win this, *vindaré*," Ventus said.

"I am not here to win, *Aiaon*," Tallyn replied in a voice dark as night. "That privilege belongs to the Maker. We can only hope to be of service to Him in the life He grants us."

Ventus growled. "Always such pretty words."

"Perhaps that is why the Maker spared my tongue."

The two Silent hissed.

It struck Sable that Ventus wasn't speaking inside Tallyn's head. Perhaps he could not.

"Hand over the girl, and I will spare them," Tallyn said simply.

"*You*? What can you do, Tallyn?" Ventus said the name like a curse. "You are deformed. An abomination. Your very existence is an insult to the Maker."

"That was always your failing, Ventus. The idea that you alone knew what the Maker expected from us. You twisted His words to write your laws. You used His power to establish your own. You destroyed Him to take his place."

"And what are you doing?" Ventus snarled. "Attempting to destroy me in order to take mine?"

The two Silent rushed Tallyn, but he lunged aside faster than humanly possible and delivered punches Sable didn't see coming until the Silent flew back. They arced through the air, then slammed into a second-story wall with a force that would've shattered the bones of a normal person. The Silent bounced to the ground but quickly jumped to their feet—one tilted its head and popped its neck. They hissed and leapt into the air, toward Tallyn. Tallyn threw off the first as the second landed on his back, choke-holding him.

Watching Jos fight the Silent had been impressive, but this... this was like watching a fight between gods.

Ventus began dragging Sable away from the battle.

"Let me go!" Sable demanded, grabbing at his wrist, clawing and scratching until it bled, but even as the cuts formed, his skin knit together.

Tallyn growled and slammed a Silent against a brick wall. Part of the wall collapsed and brick rained down upon the cobblestones.

Climb, Ventus said, shoving Sable at a saddled stolik.

Sable punched at him, but Ventus knocked her fist aside and

struck her jaw so hard, she fell to the ground. She struggled upon all fours and flexed her jaw. She tasted blood.

Climb.

He grabbed her by the hair, jerked her up, and a glimmer caught her eye.

Gavet's dagger. It lay on the cobblestones just a few paces away.

Sable stood, making an impressive show of unsteadiness, then lunged for the dagger. Ventus's power seared through her at once, and she landed in an agonizing coil. With a determined growl, she uncurled her body and dragged herself toward the blade. But Ventus wasn't deterred that easily.

An invisible force flopped her onto her back, knocking the wind from her lungs. Her head whipped back, striking stone, and she cried out in pain.

But she'd collected her treasure.

Climb, sulaziér.

Sable wheezed, struggling to fill her lungs with air, and the pain in her head squeezed tight. Dots marked her vision, and the world blurred. She staggered to her feet, swaying and unsteady, but slowly made her way back to Ventus. Once she reached his stolik, she feinted to climb into the saddle, but at the last second, she whirled on Ventus and plunged Gavet's dagger into his chest.

He hissed, black teeth bared in rage, but he did not fall. His hand clamped around her wrist, nails carving into her skin as he held her firmly before him. She tried to break free, but his grip was too firm. And then he jerked the dagger from his chest and rammed it into her side.

Sable gaped in shock as Ventus pulled the bloodied blade free. Pressure swelled where he'd struck, swift and hot, and she pressed her fingers over the wound. Blood oozed between her fingers, and a new pain throbbed somewhere deep.

"*Ventus.*"

Ventus looked back.

Tallyn stood a dozen paces away, hands and face painted in blood. Exhaustion bent his stance and strained his features, but both Silent lay on the ground behind him, dead.

Ventus snarled with all the rage of hell. He forgot Sable and dematerialized, rushing Tallyn in a whirl of screams and shadow.

"Tallyn..." Sable tried to yell, but the word came out in a whisper, cut short by a pained gasp.

A split second before Ventus struck, Tallyn dissolved into the mist, and when Ventus materialized, Tallyn reappeared behind him, swaying a little upon unsteady feet.

"Go, Sable!" Tallyn demanded as an invisible force launched him into the air. He collided with a wagon; wood exploded. Tallyn climbed to his knees and pushed bloodied palms out, lips moving fast with silent command. Scraps of wood and nails rose all around him, as if lifted by strings. They trembled in suspension as Tallyn's power waned. Nails and wood fragments rotated midair, pointing at Ventus, and with a determined snarl, Tallyn snapped his palms forward. The fragments shot forth in a deadly wall of spikes.

Ventus pressed two bloodied palms forward, chanting commands of his own.

The shards froze a few feet away, suspended. Nails and wood quivered, caught between opposing forces. Tallyn and Ventus yelled commands through their teeth, louder and louder, and then the air pulsed.

Wood exploded, nails fired like arrows in all directions, first-story windows shattered. Sable ducked behind the horse while glass, metal, and wood pieces rained down.

"Get out of here!" Tallyn yelled at her.

Sable blinked, her mind suddenly hazy. The world tilted. She started forward, tripped on a stone, then caught herself on a lamppost. She staggered forward again, but her body swayed and she fell. This time, a pair of arms caught her.

"You're bleeding," Jos said.

"I'm... fine."

Jos peeled her hand from her waist and cursed. "Brad!"

Braddok yelled as he threw off three guards. He glanced back, caught Jos's gaze, then began a retreat.

"We need... to help Tallyn," she said.

"We need to get you out of here," he said through his teeth. He picked her up as though she weighed nothing and set her on Ventus's stolik, then mounted behind her, wrapped an arm around her waist, and gave the stolik a swift kick.

Sable struggled to sit up and opened her mouth to say something about the gate, but then they were galloping through it and into the night. Tallyn must've opened it when he'd arrived.

"Stay with me," Jos demanded, holding her tight. Another set of hooves galloped behind them.

"White Rock—"

"We're not going to White Rock," he cut her off. "Tallyn has a boat waiting for us at Hiddensee."

Hiddensee was a port about an hour from Riverwood. She just needed to hold on till then.

Suddenly, the night erupted with howling. Jos cursed again.

"Jos!" Braddok yelled behind them.

"I know!" Jos urged their stolik faster.

Sable held tight to the stolik's mane, and Jos rode with all the fury of a tempest. Her body felt too cold. She knew she'd lost too much blood, but they couldn't stop yet. The shades would catch up to them.

She shut her eyes, and the sounds of the stolik's tread thundered through her chest. It was a steady drum, a rolling percussive beat, and she willed it faster, silently urging the tempo to fly.

Strangely, the tempo obeyed. The percussion raced, pounding through her with impossible speed, and the shades' howling faded away.

"Hold on!" Jos yelled, clenching her tight.

It was only when the tempo slowed that Sable opened her

eyes. She was surprised to see lantern light ahead, illuminating docks and sparkling black water. Hiddensee. By the wards, she must've passed out.

"Gods above," Braddok said, catching his breath. "I ain't never seen a horse run like that..."

His voice trailed as a man's stocky silhouette appeared in a halo of buttery light up ahead.

Jos slowed their stolik to a stop. "I'm looking for Survak," he called.

The man didn't move. He regarded them lazily as pipe smoke floated around his head. In Sable's periphery, shadows moved.

"Tallyn sent me," Jos added.

The silhouette pulled the pipe from his lips and exhaled a cloud of smoke. "You are?" It was a deep voice, rough around the edges, as salty as the sea.

"Jos. This is Sable. And Braddok."

The silhouette turned in the light, revealing a sea-weathered face. The man was middle-aged, with short silvery hair and a command in his stance that challenged Jos's own. "Survak," he said.

Howling sounded in the distance, and the stolik snorted and shifted in place.

Survak's eyes narrowed on the night, and then he jerked his chin toward one of the docks. "Follow me. And hurry. The horses can come too, so long as you can get 'em aboard."

A galley bobbed at the end of the dock, black against the night, its masts stabbing upward like spears.

Jos dismounted and turned for Sable, but she was already sliding out of the saddle. Her boots landed, and she swayed. Jos put an arm around her waist to steady her.

She waved him off. "I'll..." *...handle the horses*, she'd meant to say, but the edges of her vision darkened, and she collapsed.

25

Jeric caught Sable in his arms.

"What's wrong with her?" Braddok asked.

"She's lost too much blood."

Survak gave a sharp whistle. Four crewmen appeared on deck.

"Help them with the horses," he ordered the crew. To Jeric, he said, "Follow me."

Jeric exchanged a glance with Braddok.

"I'll stay with the horses," Braddok said.

Jeric carried Sable on deck and followed Survak. Members of the crew glanced over, but no one said a word. Survak made his way to a small door near the quarterdeck, opened it, and motioned for Jeric to follow.

"She'll be out of the way in here," Survak said.

It was a small room, large enough for a cot and a nightstand. Survak lit a lantern and hung it from a hook in the ceiling as Jeric lay Sable upon the cot. Dark red blood soaked her shirt. Jeric peeled the bloodied fabric away and sucked air through his teeth. The two men exchanged a glance.

Survak dug through the drawers of the nightstand, grabbed a small satchel, and tossed it to Jeric.

"Medicinal supplies," Survak said. "They're meager, but it's better than nothing."

Jeric ravaged the satchel. Some cloth, a flask of—he uncorked it and took a whiff. Mytvinn. Strong stuff. He tossed it, and the cloth, on the bed and kept digging. Tweezers. A small blade. "Do you have needle and thread?"

"On deck. For the sails."

"I need it."

Survak didn't ask why. He ducked out of the small cabin and returned a few moments later with a couple of needles and a spool of thread. Jeric grabbed a needle that wasn't rusted and used the lantern flame to burn and sanitize the end. The boat lurched with sudden movement, and he pressed his palm to the wall to steady himself.

"I've got to go," Survak said. "Let me know if you need anything."

Jeric jerked his chin and tried threading the needle. He needed smaller rutting fingers. Seconds later, the door creaked open, and Braddok stepped inside.

"Horses are secured, but they're not too happy. That stolik pissed all over the deck." He stopped behind Jeric. "Godsdamnit, that's deep." Then, with a cock of his brow, "You know what you're doing?"

"No, but you know that's never stopped me before." Jeric poured the mytvinn over her wound. Sable winced, and her head turned to the side, features tight with pain. Jeric steadied his hand against her waist and said, "Try to hold still." He pierced the needle through her skin. She hissed, teeth clenched and body tensed, but she held still. Even in pain, she was a fighter.

Braddok stood quiet, watching Jeric work. It was strange, stitching skin, but not so different than mending leather, which he had done plenty. He moved quickly but carefully, one hand steady at her waist, pausing when the ship rocked. He finished, tied a knot, and cut the string with his teeth, then rinsed the wound once more with mytvinn. He glanced up to find Braddok watching him, but Braddok didn't say a word.

Suddenly, the ship lurched so hard that Jeric fell against the cot. The lantern swayed, the ship creaked, and Jeric's stomach rolled unpleasantly.

Braddok eyed him. "You okay?"

Jeric's mouth watered, his skin felt hot, and he tugged at his collar. "Watch her."

Braddok nodded.

Jeric ducked out of the cabin and into the cold night air. The sails above had opened in full, and the crew sat on deck, rowing long oars in masterful synchronization. Those nearest eyed Jeric as he strode to the rail and vomited into the sea.

"The cabin'll do it to ya quick," Survak said a moment later.

Jeric spat into the black water and wiped his mouth against his sleeve.

"Here." Survak pulled a small water skin from his cloak.

Jeric didn't take it.

"It's just water."

"There are two people I trust in this world. You're not one of them."

Survak tipped the water skin toward Jeric. "Smart man." He uncorked the skin, took a long sip, then handed it to Jeric.

This time, Jeric took it and downed a long draught. He rinsed the acid from his mouth, then held the water skin back to Survak.

"Hold on to it. We've still got some time before we beach."

"Which is where?"

Survak leaned his arms against the railing. "The Black Cliffs."

Jeric frowned. "Stykken patrols those." And Stykken, ruler of The Fingers, did not like Jeric's family. The disfavor reached far back, over borderlines which Corinth currently owned—lines rich in skal ore. If they were caught, Stykken would recognize him.

"Aye. As he's patrolled them for twenty years," Survak said. "I know his blind spots. Besides, there's not a ship in all the Provinces that can outrun The Lady." Survak patted the railing like an adoring father.

"The Lady...?"

Survak grinned, then turned and leaned back against the rail. He brought his pipe to his mouth and exhaled, but the wind snatched his breath away. "You can't see her now, but she's beautiful. Graceful as a swan—all the proper manners of a lady. But don't let her beauty fool you. She's cunning. Designed for stealth and speed. A huntress." He paused. Smoke curled over his lips. "You wouldn't know anything about being a hunter, would you?"

The water skin stilled at Jeric's lips.

Survak took a slow pull from his pipe. "I know who you are."

Jeric lowered the water skin. "And who's that?"

"I've been around a long time, boy." Survak didn't use the term *boy* in a demeaning way, but rather as an older man addressing a younger man. "I've seen a lot of faces. There are some faces a person never forgets."

Jeric's eyes narrowed.

"I knew you the moment you stepped on that dock," Survak continued, glancing furtively over his shoulder at the men rowing below. "I don't doubt Tallyn knew it too, but he didn't say a word. Sly bastard. Knows me well. Never would've agreed to this if he had."

Jeric stood stone-still, watching Survak, wondering how this would unfold.

"But I'm a man of my word," Survak continued. "I told Tallyn I'd help, and I intend to. But watch yourself. Make yourself small. Don't snarl, don't bite. My men'll catch scent of a wet dog real quick, and you won't win that fight."

"Is that a threat?" Jeric said lowly.

"It's a promise." Survak looked straight at him. "Wolves are land animals. My men breathe the sea. You don't have the advantage here."

"There a problem?" Braddok asked suddenly, appearing before the two men.

Survak leaned off the railing and stood tall upon steady sea legs. "Just giving the rules of the ship." He exhaled a long breath of smoke and cast a weighted glance at Jeric. "I trust you'll pass them along."

Jeric didn't respond. Survak glanced between the two men, touched his temple in an informal salute, and left them to themselves.

"She's sleeping," Braddok said before Jeric could ask. "Comfortable, too, by the looks of it." He leaned his forearms upon the railing and cast a quick glance after Survak. "What in the five hells was that about?"

Jeric leaned against the rail, took a swig from the water skin, and wiped his lips on his sleeve. "He knows."

Braddok tensed. "How in the rutting—"

"His men don't know," Jeric cut him off. "He said he'd get us safely to shore."

"You believe him?"

"Oddly, yes," Jeric said, pushing the cork back into the skin. "Anyway, I don't see that we have a choice."

The sails whipped in the stiff breeze, and the ship rocked. Waves swelled and rolled, and the wind pushed white caps into the water's surface. The men stood quiet, gazing out into the darkness. Jeric had always found Braddok's presence companionable and easy, but right then, it only served as a reminder of the man who wasn't there.

He combed a hand through his short hair.

"It's not your fault, you know," Braddok said quietly. "He would've come even if you'd said no."

Jeric squeezed the rail.

"We're honored to—"

"To what, Brad?" Jeric snapped. "Serve my godsdamn brother? It's no risk to him. He only risks *my* men." Jeric caught himself, and quieted his voice. "*I* killed him."

"You didn't—" Braddok started.

"*I killed him.*" Jeric enunciated each word, careful to keep his voice low. "He turned into a godsdamn shade, Brad, and I had to kill him." He didn't say Sable had done it. He'd never lied to Braddok before, and he wasn't sure why he felt the need to hide this small detail now, but it didn't matter. Jeric had brought Gerald here. He might as well have driven the blade through his chest. He should have, but he hadn't believed Sable when she'd warned him. He hadn't believed her until he'd felt the power of the corruption for himself, and he would've suffered the same fate had it not been for her relentless care.

Braddok frowned. "But I saw that Silent run him through."

"We..." Jeric caught himself. "Sable believes Ventus turned him."

"Turned him?"

Jeric shared what Sable had explained about shades and her theory concerning Ventus's powers. Once he finished, Braddok stood, silent.

"I saw them," Braddok finally said. "Came out of the shadows all of a sudden, but they weren't interested in me. They ran right off."

"You're welcome for that," Jeric said darkly. "They chased us right into the Kjürda. Nearly died of hypothermia."

A wave crashed, spraying them both. "What happened?" Braddok asked.

Jeric quickly—and quietly—explained his journey with Sable, his infection, and what had transpired, though he left out a few details. When he got to the part about Gavet's betrayal, Braddok interrupted.

"Sorry I wasn't there sooner. I was in White Rock, like we

talked about. Figured I wouldn't be any use to you dead. But I'd leave during the day, searching for your royal ass."

"Careful," Jeric warned, checking over their shoulder.

"Then I got your message."

Jeric looked at Braddok. "Message?"

"Yeah, saying you'd be in Riverwood." A pause. "You didn't have it sent?"

"No... Tallyn must've."

"Well, I got his note, then," Braddok continued with a shrug. "By then the sun was setting. Thought I'd wait till morning, but then I saw those godsdamn Silent take off. I knew something was going on, so I followed. Figured if they were gonna face the night, I rutting well could."

Jeric swayed with the boat. His stomach rolled again, but the fresh air held the nausea at bay.

"I shut his eyes," Braddok whispered, threading his fingers together. "Said a prayer. Best prayer I've ever said, and that bastard wasn't even alive to hear it."

Jeric stared at a horizon he couldn't see. Wind howled, snapping the sails. "I'm sorry, Brad," he said. "I won't let Hagan use you like this again."

Braddok snorted. "You're such a cocky bastard."

Jeric glanced over at his friend.

"No one uses me." Braddok flashed a smile full of teeth. "I'm here because I decided to be here. At *your* side. Say that again, and I'll lay you flat."

Jeric allowed a small smile.

They stopped talking while a few members of Survak's crew moved behind them, adjusted a sail, and returned to the main deck.

"So what now?" Braddok whispered once the men had walked on. "You think she can do what your brother claims?"

Jeric tapped his thumbs upon the water skin. "We'll find out soon enough."

"Have you told her the truth?"

"No."

Braddok turned around and leaned back against the rail, studying Jeric. "You don't want to tell her."

It was a question and an accusation.

Jeric stopped tapping his thumbs. "It hasn't been the right time. We discussed this."

"That's not what I said."

"What you said is nonsensical," Jeric said tersely.

Braddok's eyes narrowed a little. "So when?"

"When we get close."

"She'll find out eventually."

"I know that," Jeric snapped, feeling an unexpected surge of irritation. "But we need to wait till we're out of The Wilds. We've been gone three weeks. We've no idea what's happening in the Provinces. Until we do, it's better to keep pretenses."

"Better for who?"

Jeric stared hard at his friend. "If you have something to say, Brad, say it."

Braddok regarded him a long moment. His eyes narrowed, and he unfolded his arms and pushed off the railing. "I don't think I need to. *Wolf*." He whispered the last word, but it hit harder than all the rest, and then he walked away.

HAGAN STOOD before the statue of Aryn, gazing at its chiseled perfection. Aryn, the conqueror. It was after Aryn's example that Hagan had decided how to rule, not his poor excuse of a father's.

He felt a familiar presence behind him, but he didn't turn. "You found something," Hagan said quietly.

"I did, your grace," Rasmin replied.

Hagan's gaze skirted the great chamber. Two lesser priests stood below, near the altar where a handful of citizens knelt in prayer. A half-dozen Corinthian soldiers guarded the temple's entrance. He'd asked Commander Anaton to station some of his men there after the terrifying event in the courtyard, and he was satisfied the commander had complied, despite his shortage of resources. Below, one of the priests chanted. The deep sound reverberated through the temple's vast spaces.

"Shall we?" Hagan glanced back at Rasmin.

Rasmin inclined his head.

The two of them strolled beneath the arches of the temple's perimeter, footfalls silent amidst the low chanting.

"Any news concerning my brother?" Hagan asked.

"He's en route with the woman," Rasmin said quietly. "His journey is not a simple one. I'm sure he has good reason for his delay."

"My jarls are quick to bite with him gone. Stovich, especially."

"And they'll bite fatally if Prince Jeric doesn't return with her."

Hagan stopped and faced Rasmin square. "I am risking my throne for this, Head Inquisitor."

Rasmin leveled a weighted look on his king. "If I may, sire, you are risking your throne if you don't acquire her."

Hagan's eyes narrowed. "You have new information for me."

Rasmin tipped his head, and the two resumed walking.

"I returned to the coordinates on the map," Rasmin continued.

"And?"

"I found… a tree."

"I should hope you found many of them, Head Inquisitor," Hagan sneered. "You were in a forest."

"This is a sacred place, your grace. A burial site."

Hagan's attention piqued. "What sort of burial site?"

Rasmin gazed furtively about them. "Mubarék's resting place."

Hagan had not expected this. "Saád was killed in Baraga. We have at least a dozen witnesses…"

"I'm not talking about his great-grandson."

Both quieted as a lesser priest strode past them, lighting candles.

Hagan looked skeptically at the Head Inquisitor. "You're certain?"

Rasmin nodded. "Someone drew forth Azir's spirit," he said quietly. "Azir *lives*."

Hagan was taken aback. "That's impossible."

"*Improbable*," Rasmin corrected. "Need I remind you that all things are possible with the Shah? The Liagé work in probability."

"Spare me the semantics, Head Inquisitor."

"The Liagé called it *zindev*," Rasmin continued. "Necromancy—the art of bringing life back from the dead."

Hagan regarded him a long moment. "A tree told you he was brought back to life?"

"The traces of power I found at the site are irrefutably the work of a *zindev*. I've never seen their like, and I've studied the old Liagé texts ad nauseam. It requires immense power to draw forth the spirit of a Liagé, as this *zindev* has done. The act itself is frowned upon, even by their own kind."

Hagan gazed at the altar below. "What does this mean for us?"

A pause. "I fear that this necromancer is working with the rebel legion, and has resurrected Azir to fight against you."

Hagan frowned. "Even if you're right, what could Azir possibly do in spirit form?"

"He won't remain in spirit form, Your Grace. He'll find a body to occupy, but he was a very powerful Liagé in his day. He would be a grave danger to you in any form."

Hagan's lips pursed. "Do you have any idea who this necromancer could be?"

Rasmin's eyes shone like ink. "No. Even so, in all my years here, no prisoner has exhibited this depth of power."

"And you believe this necromancer is working with the legion?" Hagan asked.

"I'm certain of it, considering how the bodies were found at Reichen and Dunsten, and seeing how close they've come to you *here*, I advise that until we capture this necromancer and find the legion, we hold off your coronation—"

Hagan slammed his fist against a column.

The Head Inquisitor's lips pressed together.

"No," Hagan said firmly. "We proceed as planned."

"Sire, the zindev alone is far too powerful, and until we find him—"

"*Then. Find. Him.*" Hagan leaned close, eyes aflame. "That is your job, is it not, *Head* Inquisitor?"

Rasmin made no reply, but his eyes shaded.

"Rumors about what happened in those villages are spreading through Corinth like wildfire," Hagan hissed. "And now my hunters fear the rutting woods."

Rasmin looked curious.

Hagan smiled tightly. "Perhaps you should speak with Grag Beryn. Let him tell you what he found. It's only a matter of time before word of this necromancer's actions on *my* life reach Stovich, if it hasn't already. To cancel the coronation will be seen as weakness."

The Head Inquisitor did not answer immediately. "I understand, Your Grace, but my concern is and has always been for your safety—"

"Then find this necromancer and the godsdamned legion, and deliver their heads on pikes," Hagan snarled. "Post them outside my gates for all to see. Let the people know what happens to those who threaten my throne."

Rasmin's gaze fell in deference. "Yes, Your Grace."

26

Sable opened her eyes to a dimly lit and very tiny cabin. After a moment of gentle rocking, she recalled that she was on a boat, but she had no recollection of how she'd come to be lying in a cot, buried somewhat comfortably beneath a pile of woolen blankets. She tried to sit, but a sharp pain pierced her side.

"Careful," said a low voice.

She lay back down and glanced in the direction of the voice.

Jos sat on the floor a few paces away, leaning against the wall opposite, his long legs crossed before him and his sword laying across his knees. His head was tipped back against the wall, and his eyes were open a sliver, watching her.

She wondered how long he'd been sitting there.

"Did we... lose him?" she managed. It hurt to talk, to breathe.

"Yes," Jos said a second later. "For now."

The cot rocked her, and the planked walls creaked. A hanging lantern swayed, throwing light and shadows about the cabin.

"How are you feeling?" Jos asked quietly. There was concern in his voice, but also restraint.

"Lucky," she replied, then slowly pushed back the blankets.

Her tunic was stained red, but her wound had been neatly dressed. She glanced up and met Jos's gaze.

"I cleaned it the best I could," he said. "I'm afraid my stitches aren't as neat as yours, but they should hold. Still, you should go easy on them. I have no idea how deeply his knife penetrated."

Sable touched the wrapping gently, grateful and also humbled that Jos had done so much for her while she'd been unconscious. She pressed on the space over the wound, just a little, to get a feel for its depth. "He didn't cut anything vital, at least." Which was nothing short of a miracle. Still, it would take weeks for this to heal, and just as long to regain her strength. The wound was deep, and she'd lost a lot of blood. She glanced at Jos, who looked steadily back, his expression inscrutable.

"Thank you," she said.

He held her gaze. He nodded a moment later.

Something about him had changed. It was difficult to pinpoint what, exactly, or why, but she'd expected him to be... easier, once they caught up with his friend. From the moment Tallyn had given them news of Braddok's survival, Jos had seemed lighter, almost conversational—for him, anyway—but a shadow of heaviness clung to him now.

"Are you feeling all right?" she asked, noting he looked a little pale.

He frowned. "You have a hole in your side. How I feel is inconsequential."

Sable squinted in the low light and realized, perhaps, that there could be a very practical reason for his solemnity. "You're *green*, Jos."

"Boats don't agree with me."

"There's not much that does." She'd meant it as a joke, but she was so tired, it came out honest.

A grin quirked at his lips, but it didn't lighten his mood.

A new thought struck her. "Is your friend okay?"

"He's fine, Sable." His lips parted as if to add more, but then his brow furrowed, and he closed his lips again.

She studied him, but a wave of dizziness hit her, and she closed her eyes while it passed.

"You need rest," he said, making a sudden decision. Wood creaked.

Sable opened her eyes as Jos stood and sheathed his sword. She couldn't argue with him. Already, her consciousness fought her, pulling her under. "Where... are we headed?"

"The Black Cliffs."

"Doesn't... Stykken patrol them?" she asked, straining against another shock of pain. Maker's Mercy, she could use some Maiden's Breath right about now, but she doubted she'd find any on this boat.

"Survak assured me he'll get us through without issue," Jos said. His eyes warmed a little. "But right now, you need rest. You lost a lot of blood, Sable."

Sable closed her eyes and didn't argue. She couldn't. Her consciousness had slipped away.

She didn't see Jos approach her cot. She didn't feel the blankets move as he adjusted them over her shoulders, covering her, nor did she hear him whisper in the softest voice, "Forgive me."

As INSTRUCTED, and also because she couldn't help it, Sable kept to the bed, lulled in and out of consciousness by the soporific lullabies of groaning wood and crashing waves and thunderous skies. It was as if nature itself colluded, forcing her to rest. A couple of times, Jos was there forcing her to drink water, but she mostly slept. She dreamed often, and it was always the same, of heat and sunlight and storms, a powerful voice calling her name —her true name. The melody inside of her sang louder than before, and it did not quiet. It was a constant and unwavering pitch amidst the natural world around her, and Sable wondered at what Ventus had done, what he had broken. He'd spoken of her supposed power again, and she'd felt something inside of her crack. What it meant, she had no idea, but as her sleepiness waned, her thoughts moved down the trail of her current circumstances.

She was sailing away from The Wilds—a land that'd harbored and hidden her for ten years. The significance was not lost on her, and she hadn't expected to feel a twinge of sadness. The home that'd sheltered her all those years no longer existed, and neither did the woman who'd built it. It was time for Sable to move on, as she'd so often dreamed. But, as Sable was beginning to realize, dreams were dangerous. Dreams were shiny and perfect things, tantalizingly seductive with their promises. They professed they were better than now, more beautiful than here, forever stealing one's ability to simply *be*.

And Sable had been content, in a way, though her dreams wouldn't allow her to see it. Her time in The Wilds wasn't the sort of life she would've chosen for herself, but she'd had *life*, which was more than some could say. Now that she was heading for Provincial shores, what would she do? She had no crowns or anything to her name, and Jos was her most promising sponsor. He'd also proven to be an invaluable bodyguard, despite the recent... complication. She still wasn't sure what to make of what'd happened in Gavet's cellar, just as she couldn't explain Jos's behavior now.

Regardless, it was dangerous for a young woman—especially an Istraan—to travel alone, and on top of that, she was injured. So she decided to stay the course for now, follow Jos to Southbridge, and take him up on his offer—assuming it still stood. Once there, she could decide what to do.

And maybe, just maybe, she'd contact Ricón.

She was sitting up and taking a sip of water when Jos opened the cabin door, followed by a gust of cold and salty air. Seeing her awake, he stopped in the threshold. His hair was dark from rain, and his eyes were a startling shade of blue. The fresh air seemed to be doing him some good. He wasn't green anymore.

"Good, you're awake," he said, snatching a cloak from a hook on the wall. "We're near The Cliffs."

"Maker's Mercy, already?" she said, more to herself. The Cliffs were at least six hours from The Wilds by boat, and she'd slept away the entire journey. She corked the water skin, threw back her blankets, and slid her feet out of the cot. Her boots, she noticed, had been set neatly on the floor beside her.

"Can you walk?" Jos asked, approaching steadily, cloak in hand.

"I think so..." Slowly, gingerly, she leaned over to slip on her boots, but the stitches pulled.

Jos noticed. "Let me do that."

He handed her the cloak and knelt before her, bringing the scent of rain with him. He grabbed one boot and opened the laces, slipped it onto her foot and tied it, then repeated the process with her other boot. Sable watched him while he worked, admiring the precision of his movements and the strength in his hands, and when he finished, he looked up. Their gazes met, and her heart drummed a little faster. He blinked and looked away, standing as he opened her cloak. She slid into it, and then he took a step back as if to put distance between them.

Sable gripped the edge of the nightstand and, very carefully, pulled herself to her feet. There she waited, finding her balance, then met Jos's inquiring gaze and nodded once. He strode to the door and held it open, but his eyes tracked her every step, ready to catch her should she fall.

She didn't.

She slipped past him, ducked beneath the lintel, and stepped out onto the deck. Cold, salty air ripped through her cloak, cutting her to the bone, and rain drizzled all around. The sky overhead was dark with clouds, and thunder rumbled in the distance.

Like the storm from her dream. And she was heading toward it.

A few nearby crew members glanced up from where they sat, hunched over oars. One whispered to another. A third smiled broadly at Sable, but when they spotted Jos right behind her, they all abruptly turned their attention back to rowing.

"I see you've been busy making friends," Sable said wryly, glancing back at Jos.

He eyed her sideways, though his eyes warmed with amusement as he nodded toward the helm.

She spotted Braddok leaning against the rail, speaking with a middle-aged man with silvery hair, drawing smoke from an impressively long pipe. Sable vaguely recognized him as the gentleman from the docks, Survak.

He wasn't a small man by any means, but Braddok dwarfed him. He dwarfed everyone. Braddok glanced over at her, then Jos, and she got the impression that he didn't care for her, or trust her with his friend. Not that she could blame him. He'd lost one friend because of her, and he'd almost lost another.

She spotted the horses on deck, harnessed to a rope-and-leather contraption. Straw had been laid out beneath them, though Ventus's stolik kept clawing at it and pushing it aside. He looked particularly irritated.

"Ah, there she is," Survak said as she approached, pulling the pipe from his mouth and angling himself to face her and Jos.

Sable stopped before him, steadying herself upon the railing. "We owe you our lives—"

"Tallyn's the one who conned me into this," he said, but in good humor. "And from what your friends tell me, it seems you three are very fortunate to be here. Especially *you*." He shoved the pipe back in his mouth, and his gaze drifted to Jos.

Something passed between the men, and Jos snagged her gaze before looking to the horizon, where a dark wall stretched.

The Black Cliffs of Voiar.

Notorious for their currents and jagged faces and hidden rocks, most captains avoided them. Too many had sidled close, puncturing their hulls along the sharp rocks nestled just beneath the water's swirling surface.

"I thought sailors generally avoided The Cliffs," Sable said, pushing hair out of her eyes.

Beside her, Jos gave Survak a look that suggested he'd voiced this very same concern while Sable had been sleeping.

"Which is precisely why I use it," Survak answered. "What one man fears, another man exploits."

Jos's eyes narrowed on the sea, and Sable thought he'd probably received this same response.

"There's a grotto hidden behind a waterfall in The Cliffs," Survak explained. "I use it sometimes. Stykken doesn't know about it."

Brom Stykken ruled The Fingers. Sable had met him once, when he'd sailed to a port near Trier to conduct business with her papa. Brackish man. Rough as the sea, skin like worn leather, and eyes like a shark.

"How do *you* know what Stykken does or doesn't know?" Braddok asked, folding his thick arms over his chest.

"I know he doesn't know about this. If he did, it'd be guarded. These shores are his most coveted mistress, and he'll be damned before he shares them."

Within the hour, the galley anchored and the crew lowered a dinghy into a patch of relatively calm water. Just ahead, nestled into a small cove amidst the cliffs, Sable spotted a thin sheet of water plunging over a crack in the wall.

Jos and a few of Survak's men untied the agitated horses from their harnesses.

"They won't fit in the dinghy," Sable said.

"No, they won't," Survak said. "They'll have to swim."

Which meant someone would have to swim with them. Sable looked to the small cove amidst the cliffs. Though the current wasn't as turbulent there, the water still swirled in palettes of blues and whites.

"Sorry, lass, but I can't draw The Lady any closer to those cliffs."

In the end, it was decided that Jos would swim with the horses. Sable couldn't, because of her wound, and the horses seemed to prefer Jos. Also, Jos and Braddok both agreed that Jos was the better swimmer, though Braddok didn't look too happy about the decision.

Sable climbed into the dinghy with Braddok's help, and once they began floating away, Sable called out, "Survak!"

She meant to ask after Tallyn, to make sure that Survak would check on him.

Survak peered over the railing, and her words caught. Seeing him now, she had the strangest sensation they'd met before. It was another time, when a man much younger than he transported a girl much younger than she from farther down this shore to the opposite.

A grin touched Survak's lips, he winked, and then he vanished behind The Lady's rail.

SURVAK WATCHED the dinghy float away, and said a quick and silent prayer to the Maker. He hadn't a clue what the Maker was doing, pairing her with the Wolf, but he wouldn't interfere. There was something at work that neither he nor Tallyn understood, but the Maker never asked for understanding. Only faithfulness.

And he would be faithful. As Tallyn had been faithful.

Still, he would pray for her safety.

27

Hagan stormed into the council room, and all heads glanced up. Hersir was there, seated near one end of the table, Astrid beside him. Hagan hadn't spoken with the Lead Stryker since Jeric's departure, when Hagan had made it abundantly clear what would happen should Hersir proceed with Jeric's induction. Hersir had heeded Hagan's warning, and he'd kept a safe distance ever since. Until, on Hagan's orders, Commander Anaton had demanded the employment of Hersir's Strykers to investigate the legion, which had brought Hersir out of his private command center and into the public far more often than he preferred.

On Hersir's other side sat Godfrey, master of coin and questionable things. Godfrey came from a line of men who consistently held the position as one of Skyhold's wealthiest patrons. Godfrey's fortune permitted him an active roll in Skyhold's transactions, both locally and internationally, though Godfrey's primary interests lay in Corinthian arms.

Next to Godfrey sat Commander Anaton, angled at the door, positioning himself to be the first line of defense, should anyone be foolish enough to attack. On Anaton's other side sat Hagan's most powerful jarl, and arguably the most disruptive: Jarl Stovich.

He was furious about what'd happened in Reichen and Dunsten—both towns under his jurisdiction. He'd been the loudest voice against King Tommad's rulings, and now he was the loudest voice against Hagan's. Taming him usually required a few swift lashes of humility that only the Wolf could deliver. It helped that Stovich's daughter thought herself in love with Jeric, who—clever Wolf that he was—rarely discouraged her.

But the Wolf wasn't here.

Stovich's dark eyes followed as Hagan took a seat beside Astrid. The chair immediately on his right—Jeric's chair—remained empty. Yet for Hagan, Jeric's absence filled the seat more than his presence ever did.

"Where's Rasmin?" Astrid asked.

"The Head Inquisitor had business that took him away." Hagan looked at Commander Anaton. "Report."

The commander sat up straight. "Thirty Scabs have taken Fallows Pass."

"Are they part of the legion?" Hagan asked, hoping that this news would bring them closer to uncovering the legion's whereabouts.

"I don't know," the commander replied. "They could be just another insurgent faction. I won't know for certain until I can detain one for questioning. I've sent reinforcements, but I need more men."

Hagan frowned. They'd already squeezed Corinth dry, and he didn't dare send more of his own guards in light of recent events. Hagan looked to the jarl. "Stovich."

Jarl Stovich leaned back slowly; his chair creaked. "I don't have men to spare, Your Grace." His tone was full of implication.

"What about the border?"

"Then Stovichshold would be undefended against Davros."

"Davros isn't our enemy right now."

Stovich's eyes narrowed. "Who *is* our enemy now? Have we even determined that yet?"

"If this group *is* working with the legion," Commander Anaton said tightly, "this could be the opportunity we've been waiting for. It would be foolish not to sieze it."

Astrid folded her hands on the table, and her gaze slid from the commander to Stovich.

Jarl Stovich sat forward. "I've already lost too many people to your father's negligence, and you've done *nothing* to replenish my losses. I *will not* sacrifice more."

"Careful, Stovich," Astrid said quietly, but potently. "Despite your personal opinions, Hagan *is* your king now."

Stovich bristled but relented with a frown.

"How many can you spare?" Commander Anaton asked, matter-of-fact.

Stovich simmered, drumming stumpy fingers upon the table. "Twenty-five. No more."

"Is that enough, Commander?" Hagan asked.

Stovich grunted.

"Maybe. At very least, it will slow them down until we acquire more men," the commander said.

"I'll find you more men," Godfrey said. Godfrey knew a lot of people. The man spun better webs than a spider.

Commander Anaton nodded sharply.

"Have my brother's men turned up anything of consequence?" Hagan asked the commander, drawing Astrid's direct scrutiny. The others looked surprised, as well.

"Stanis sent word once they reached Reichen," Commander Anaton replied, "but I haven't heard from him since."

"You sent the Wolf's men to Reichen?" Stovich asked, eyes narrowed.

Hagan eyed him sideways. "I did."

Stovich glowered. "You did that knowing full well that I was on my way here—"

"I will do whatever's necessary to protect Corinth," Hagan said tightly. "Especially when those I've entrusted with guardianship over my people fail."

Stovich's expression darkened.

"Have Stanis report to me directly when he returns," Hagan said to the commander.

Commander Anaton nodded. "There is another issue that requires your attention, Your Grace."

Hagan waited, feeling a twinge of unease.

The commander continued, "Jarl Rodin reported that Yllis mine has gone dark. According to his letter, his guards left to relieve the night watch and arrived to an empty mine. The Scabs were gone, and the night watch was found dead, just like the people in Reichen and Dunsten." Just like the inquisitor in the square, he had not said, but everyone heard it anyway.

Uncertain glances flitted across the table.

Gods, where was his godsdamned brother?

Hagan looked sharply at Hersir. "Have you learned anything about the necromancer, as I asked?"

"What necromancer?" Astrid interrupted, just as sharply.

Hagan looked at his sister. "The Head Inquisitor and I believe a necromancer—someone with power over the dead—has somehow escaped his notice, and he's working with the legion."

Murmurs erupted, and doubtful glances bounced across the table.

"You can't be serious, brother," Astrid said wryly.

Hagan's eyes flashed, and Astrid's gaze fell to the table. He then looked to the others, his expression severe, daring them to challenge his words. "We believe a necromancer is to blame for the particular way the bodies were found."

Stovich sat forward. "Did you conclude this before or *after* one of the inquisitors tried to kill you?"

Hagan ignored him, though his blood ran hot. "Hersir...?"

All eyes turned to Hersir, and Hersir shook his head a fraction. "No. And if I may..." He paused, his expression hardened. "Your inquisitors are better suited for *inquisition*. My Strykers are designed to *strike*. They'd be better utilized elsewhere, like reinforcing the Fallows and getting to the bottom of our legion problem." He nodded to the commander.

It was little wonder his brother admired Hersir. They shared a similarity of disposition. A calm that was also severe, as if the world were an irritation—an incompetence—and they alone knew how to get anything properly done. Being that they, as individuals, managed to accomplish what usually required the might of an army, Hagan usually let the arrogance go.

Not today.

"They are perfectly utilized here," Hagan said.

"I'm not suggesting we send all of them," Hersir persisted. "I'll keep some here to watch for the necromancer, and the rest can aid the commander in locating the legion."

"I agree," Astrid said, before Hagan could argue. "We have powerful resources here that would do well on our border, rather than waste them sniffing old Shah tales. O*ne* Stryker can do the work of *fifty*." Here, she looked sharply at Jarl Stovich, who shifted irritably in his chair.

"We have a godsdamned Scab necromancer *in this city*," Hagan argued.

"We have hundreds of Scabs in this city," Astrid said, her tone acerbic.

Hagan slammed a fist on the table, and she jumped. "Skyhold takes priority. I'll not spare any more—"

"Your Grace," said a new voice.

Hagan glanced up, fuming.

Galast, one of his personal guards and overseer of skalsmithing, stood in the threshold. In Hagan's fury, he hadn't even heard the door open.

"I'm sorry to interrupt, but there's a matter that requires your immediate attention."

A beat. "Well?" Hagan snapped.

Galast's gaze flickered uneasily to Godfrey. "Perhaps we can speak in private—"

"Out with it, godsdamnit!"

Galast stepped inside and closed the door behind him. "The armory, sire. Everything... every weapon and shield and piece of armor we've stored... all of it's gone."

IT'D BEEN four days since Sable had stepped foot on Provincial soil, though she hadn't spent much of that time actually stepping *on* it. The stolik did all the walking, much to her chagrin. The wound in her side remained tender enough to keep her properly saddled. Sometimes Jos rode with her, but mostly he walked beside the horse, guiding it through The Fingers' challenging terrain.

The Fingers was named for its shape, how its narrow and rocky ridges stretched into the sea like the fingers of an opened hand. Their villages, it was said, had been built into the sides of the rock, clinging to cliffs like barnacles, stubbornly weathering storms the Eastern Sea lashed upon its coasts. Sable had never been to the villages herself, but she'd met people from there. They were hard, gruff of speech and manner, as if the salty air had fermented them into something strong and unsavory. The Fingers remained the Five Provinces' first defense against the distant lands beyond the Eastern Sea, but those lands hadn't beached their shores in generations. The people of The Fingers mostly kept to themselves now, and they expected the rest of the Provinces to keep to itself too.

Sable would've liked to visit the infamous villages, but that would have to wait. The Fingers were too close to The Wilds, and Jos had already spent enough time away from his dying father.

They moved steadily south along The Fingers' western

border—the palm, it was called, from which the fingers stretched. It wasn't smooth like an opened palm, but resembled a cupped palm, all bumps and ridges and deep, long creases. It didn't provide much in the way of food, either. They'd already finished what little Survak had spared them. The rest was up to their wily devices. Jos caught a few rodents with his bare hands, using those unparalleled senses and stealth that often left Sable silently awed. For herself, she constructed a small sling out of rope Survak had given them, surprising both Jos and Braddok when she successfully slung a rock and killed a rabbit.

Braddok had snorted, impressed, then looked annoyed that Sable had impressed him.

"Where did you learn to do that?" Jos asked, looking at her with surprise.

Ricón had taught her how to use a sling so she could help him hunt the palace grounds for snakes. Of course, she couldn't say this, so she shrugged and said nothing at all.

There was an easier path, a little farther west and nearer the great plains of Davros, but Jos didn't want to be seen. Sable couldn't find a reason to disagree. They still didn't know Ventus's fate, or Tallyn's for that matter, and if Ventus *had* survived, she didn't think he'd stop at The Crossing this time. With that thought in mind, Sable endured their rough trek, hoping Tallyn had survived, and also hoping the flute had abandoned her for good.

From dawn till dusk they rode, stopping only to give the horses a break or to replenish their water skins. At night, they found shelter behind the lee of a rock, always open to the night sky. That first night, when the sun dipped below the horizon, habit shocked her nerves into fright, but eventually she found peace sleeping beneath a night full of stars. This sky shared some of Istraa's stars, though oriented differently, and there were also new stars Sable didn't know. There was a whole world she didn't know, and as they traveled, she thought more and more on all that she'd missed, locked away in Skanden for so many years. With Jos's reward, discovering that world might be possible. Maybe she wouldn't settle in Istraa after all. Maybe she wouldn't settle anywhere.

Eventually, the rocks relented, sloping into gentler stretches of land. Trees huddled in the land's broad crevices, and the grass grew again as they made a slow ascent out of The Fingers' tundra and into the high desert of Corinth's boundary. Jagged, snow-capped peaks marked the southern horizon. It'd been years since Sable had seen those mountains. The Gray's Teeth Mountains, they called them, named after the enormous gray bears indigenous to those parts. She'd always loved the Baraga Mountains of Istraa, with their gentle slopes and broad backs, like giant tortoises sleeping on the sands. Unlike the Baragas, Corinth's mountains rose sharply, like stone teeth, as if Corinth were a monster trying to swallow the world.

"When did you plan to turn west?" Sable asked as those stone teeth began swallowing the sun. She blinked in the breeze, trying to wet her eyes. The air was much drier here, and the skin on her knuckles and lips cracked. She'd expected Jos to change course sometime today, but he had not.

Jos's face turned toward the setting sun, and sunlight gilded his hair. "Let's camp there." He gestured toward a crop of boulders crowning a small hill.

Braddok gave Jos a long look, then nudged his horse toward the hill.

"You didn't answer my question," Sable said.

"Tomorrow," he said. It was a word thrown to placate her. He urged their horse after Braddok.

"Jos."

He glanced back. Sometimes, when she looked at him, she remembered their kiss. And sometimes, when he looked at her, she thought he remembered it too, though that night seemed a distant thing now. It angered her how easily he'd put it behind him. She would've confronted him on it, but she wasn't comfortable discussing it in front of his friend.

"Tomorrow," Jos said at last, and his gaze moved to the mountains. "There's something we need to discuss first."

Sable felt a prick of unease. "Which is...?"

A muscle worked in his jaw. He didn't meet her gaze. "We'll talk after we've eaten."

Sable studied him a moment, then slid from the horse.

"It's not far," Sable said at a sharp glance from Jos. "And I need to move my legs."

He nodded a fraction, and together, they walked their horse to where Braddok stood, unsaddling his. He glanced over at them and frowned. Braddok hadn't been outright rude to Sable, but she felt his disapproval all the same. It didn't bother her, really. She interpreted his disapproval more as a sign of loyalty to his friend than as a personal slight against her.

Wings flapped and an owl landed on the rock beside her, regarding her with an intense yellow-eyed stare. She'd spotted the owl earlier, floating in the distance. She remembered only because it'd surprised her to see it, out in the open and during the day. It also explained why they hadn't spotted any rodents.

The owl wore a rich coat of black and white, and its thick black brows ended in tufts like two horns. Its long talons curled like tiny daggers and could easily mangle a man's face.

"Go on," Sable whispered to it. "We won't catch any dinner with you around." She batted a hand at the owl. The owl hooted and took flight.

"And we certainly won't catch dinner if you warn the food away," Jos mused behind her.

"Predators make for bad meat."

"Bad meat is better than no meat."

She cocked a brow at him. "I take it you haven't eaten owl."

A small smile shadowed his lips as he watched the retreating bird, then cast Sable a sideways glance and said, "Actually, I have," before turning away.

Sable found herself looking after him as he dug through the horse's saddlebags. Braddok glanced up from the fire he was building and snagged her gaze, and Sable turned her attention back to the task at hand. She gathered what kindling she could find, added them to Braddok's small pile, and perched on the rock where the owl had landed. She checked her bandage and carefully unwound the wrapping from her waist. Jos's stitches held, and the cut was knitting itself together well, despite the constant jolting. The skin around the cut was still tinged pink, but faintly. She would've liked to apply cannis to soothe the inflammation, but that would require going into a town.

Sable rewrapped the wound, adjusted her shirt, and glanced up to find Jos watching her. He looked back to the kindling and struck flint to steel. She wondered what he meant to discuss. She pulled her sling from her pocket, tucked her hair behind her ears, and glanced around for dinner prospects.

"Here." Jos approached, handing her the water skin.

She grabbed it, uncorked the spout, and took a sip.

"We're not far from Stovichshold," Braddok said suddenly.

Jos leveled a hard look on his friend.

Braddok stared resolutely back. "It might be worth—"

"Brad."

Braddok's lips pressed together. His gaze flickered to Sable, and he sighed and picked up his flask of akavit.

"What's in Stovichshold?" she asked, looking from Braddok to Jos.

Jos stared only at Braddok, features tight with irritation. Clearly, this was a matter not meant for Sable's ears. At last, Braddok set down the flask and picked up his scabbard.

"I'm going hunting," Braddok said gruffly.

Jos gave no response, but then Braddok didn't linger to hear one.

Jos looked after his friend a moment, then stepped around the fire and picked up Braddok's flask. He uncorked it, took a whiff, and, to Sable's surprise, drained the contents.

She set down her water skin. "Out with it, Jos."

He didn't look at her, didn't speak. He stared at the flames with determination in his eyes, as if sorting through his words, deciding how best to say them, but also wishing he didn't have to.

"Jos." She took a liberty she hadn't taken since Braddok's arrival—speaking to Jos with the quiet familiarity they'd shared at Tallyn's and later at Gavet's, speaking directly to the man hidden deep inside, the one with whom she'd made herself vulnerable.

It worked. Jos glanced up.

She couldn't read the expression there, but a deep note inside of her wavered with unease.

"Sable, I..." His resolve faltered; his jaw clamped shut. He looked back to the fire, as if he couldn't look at her and say whatever it was he needed to say.

Sable waited, and a dark cloud of trepidation bloomed inside of her. A major chord turned minor, its intervals diminished.

"We're not heading to Southbri—" Jos's words cut short. His gaze fixed on a point behind her.

Too fast, he leapt past her, colliding with a shadow she only just noticed as Jos and the other figure tumbled to the ground. Grunts sounded, but Jos quickly took the advantage, pinning the intruder's thick neck to the ground with his bare hands. It was another man, near Jos's age, with hair like wheat, worn long on top but shaved on the sides, and a full beard added grit to an imposing face.

In the same instant both men stalled, gazing wildly at the other, and Sable realized that Jos recognized the man as surely as the man recognized Jos.

"Stanis...?" Jos gasped, bewildered. His hands relented, and the man's grimace stretched into a wide grin.

"I'll be damned," Stanis replied in strong Corinthian.

The accent arrested Sable.

Jos didn't notice. He jumped to his feet and extended a hand, which Stanis took, and Jos jerked him to his feet.

"Are you alone?" Jos asked.

"Chez and Aksel are here too, somewhere. Bastards." Stanis smirked, glancing behind him. "Looks like they found Brad."

Sable followed his gaze to where three figures ambled up their small hill. Braddok, and two other men he clearly knew well, drew three horses behind them.

"We were just heading back from Stovich's, when I thought I saw..." Stanis's eyes had been sliding back toward Jos but hooked on Sable and stopped there, sinking deep. "What do we have here?" he drawled, taking a step toward Sable.

Jos moved fast, placing himself between them.

Stanis looked surprised, and he regarded his friend with curiosity and then a smirk. "Got a little Scablicker gift for your brother, Wolf?"

Jos went rigid.

Time stilled, teetering on the edge of a blade.

Suddenly, Stanis was background—a colorless sky—his lewd words no more than a distant howl, save one: *Wolf*.

Sable slipped from her perch. She stared intensely at Jos, and her heart drummed faster with each passing second. "What did he just call you?"

Jos stood too still. Slowly, his face angled back, and his eyes fastened on hers. And Sable knew. Living in a land of thieves, she had seen that look a thousand times. Jos was a man caught, trapped by his lies.

Braddok and the other two men arrived. One chuckled about something his companion had said, but Braddok elbowed him in the ribs, and they fell silent. They stopped at the camp's edge, glancing between Jos and Stanis and Sable.

But Sable only had eyes for Jos.

"Who are you?" Sable's words filled the camp, carved an edge.

A muscle worked in Jos's jaw, but he didn't answer.

She thought of his skill, his speed, and his senses. She thought of his authority and the lethal shadow that hovered over him—a shadow, up until now, she'd stopped seeing.

She thought of his tattoo, the wolf hilt, and his tapestry of scars.

"*Who are you*?" she demanded, fearing his answer as much as needing to hear it.

He turned to face her fully, not once pulling his eyes from hers. "I am Jeric Oberyn Sal Angevin," he said lowly, and in a perfect Corinthian accent. "Son of King Tommad Angevin the third. The youngest prince and the Wolf of Corinth."

Sable stared at him, paralyzed. Each word was a fist, striking her mercilessly.

Jeric Oberyn Sal.

Jos.

King Tommad's youngest son, second heir to the throne. The Wolf of Corinth. The greatest threat to the Provinces this generation had ever known. The man responsible for slaughtering hundreds, or possibly thousands—including many of her own people. And he stood not three paces from her, surrounded by what could only be his infamous pack.

Maker's Mercy.

She took an involuntary step back, fingers pressed to her temples. "You're the *Wolf*," she said with revelation. With revulsion.

Jos stood silent, but his eyes stormed.

No, not Jos.

The Wolf.

By the wards... How could she have been so stupid? How had she not seen...

A new horror struck her. Did he know *her* truth? Was that the reason he'd sought her out? Or was his father—Corinth's king—

truly ill, and by some cruel twist of fate, he'd stumbled upon her? Sable didn't believe in fate, but as her mind raced frantically through the details, she didn't think he knew *her* truth. Otherwise, he wouldn't have tried so hard to discern her past in Gavet's cellar.

Otherwise, he wouldn't have kissed her.

The memory made her suddenly and inexplicably angry. "You..." Her voice trembled with fury, and her hands curled into fists at her sides. "I can't believe I *kissed* you!"

The Wolf flinched.

Stanis laughed.

Braddok folded his arms and looked on at the Wolf as if he'd suspected something awry all along and was glad to finally have evidence. The two men beside Braddok grunted in surprise, then quieted at a harsh look from Braddok.

The Wolf took a step toward her, his expression severe. "Sable—"

"You *lied* to me!" The words trembled out in a fury.

"Yes," he hissed. "I lied to you. But only about who I was!"

Sable slapped him across the face.

The sound cracked the night; the Wolf's head snapped to the side.

"You little bitch..." Stanis took a furious step toward her, but the Wolf thrust out an arm. Stanis stopped in his tracks, simmering in restraint.

The Wolf's gaze snapped back to Sable, his eyes ablaze, and his left cheek blushed an angry red where she'd struck him. "I came to you because I need your help"—he ground each word through his teeth—"*as a healer*. I didn't tell you the truth because you never would have come."

"And why do you think that is?" Sable snarled.

"Think what you want of me." His voice was low and unsteady. "I don't care. But I *will* see you safely home, as promised. That, I swear."

"What good is your word?" Sable spat.

His eyes narrowed. "I don't see that you have any other choice, Sable."

"I never had a choice, did I?"

His silence was answer enough.

She looked at him with loathing and betrayal. "You rutting monster. I should've left you in the Kjürda."

Fury shadowed his face and sharpened the lines.

"Stay away from me," she warned, slowly backing away from him.

"I still need your help, Sable," the Wolf continued, eyes fixed on her as he took a step closer. "It's *your* choice how that will go."

Sable took another step back. She didn't know what to do, only that she could *not* go with the Wolf to Corinth. Whatever the Wolf's reasons, his inquisitors would discover her truth soon enough.

So Sable did the only thing she could think of.

She kicked the Wolf in the groin, and she ran.

28

Sable sprinted down the hill, her boots slapping the hard earth. She had no idea where she was going, only that she had to get away. Far away. Behind her, the Wolf yelled at his men to hold back, then called after her, but she didn't stop. Her eyes trained on the shadows, arms pumping as she ran for a large copse of trees they'd passed earlier. The shadows could hide her as they'd so often done. Then she could slip away. It was her only hope now.

How could she have been so stupid? Her eyes burned, but she told herself she would not cry.

She would not.

She wiped her nose as she ran, but behind her, the Wolf's pounding tread drew nearer.

"Sable, wait!" the Wolf yelled.

Her stitches pulled tight, and fire seared her side, but she urged herself forward until—finally—she reached the trees. She dodged right, then maneuvered through the shadows as quickly and quietly as possible. She heard the Wolf enter the forest after her, and then...

Silence.

Sable pressed her back to the nearest tree and held her breath. A breeze pushed through, and the leaves whispered. She wished they'd tell her where the Wolf was hiding. She scanned the shadows, waiting for what felt like an eternity, and a twig snapped to her left—far enough she thought it safe to move. Sable peeled herself from the tree and tiptoed in the opposite direction, ears pinned on the forest, and a force slammed into her, knocking her to the ground.

"Sable, *stop*," the Wolf growled, wrapping strong arms around her and holding her tight. "I'm not going to hurt you!"

"Then let... me... go!"

He did not. So she slammed her head back into his face.

He cursed, and his grip loosened. She slipped out of his arms, climbed to her feet, and stumbled right into someone else's arms.

"Gotcha," Stanis snarled, pinning her arms to her sides.

Sable bucked. Stanis cursed, then whirled her around and punched her. Pain exploded in her jaw, and the force sent her reeling. She tripped over her feet and tumbled to the ground.

A grunt sounded behind her, and she glanced back to see two silhouettes, one clutching the other.

"Hit her again," the Wolf said, his voice darker than she'd ever heard it, "and you walk home alone." The Wolf released Stanis with a jerk. "I told you to stay back."

Stanis only grunted in reply.

Another pair of hands grabbed Sable and hoisted her to her feet. She fought, albeit weakly. The grip was too strong, and her shirt clung to her, damp with what could only be blood. The wound in her side had opened. She glanced up to see the Wolf's silhouette looming before her.

She spat at him.

Braddok jerked her back. The Wolf didn't say a word. He simply stood there, his silhouette black against the night, and then he stormed off, toward camp. Braddok shoved her after him, and Sable knew that she had just lost her one and only chance at escape.

JERIC REACHED camp ahead of the others, where Chez and Aksel waited.

They looked to their alpha for answers, but Jeric couldn't bring himself to speak. He crouched beside the fire and warmed his trembling hands. They did not tremble from cold.

"One of you find Stanis," Jeric said.

Chez grabbed his scabbard and jogged off. Aksel lingered, quiet, watching his alpha with reserve. A few minutes later, Braddok returned with Sable.

Jeric didn't look up.

Braddok led Sable toward the fire, opposite Jeric. "Some rope, Aks?"

Aksel rummaged through a saddlebag and tossed a bundle at Braddok.

Jeric looked up and met Sable's gaze across the flames. He didn't know which burned hotter.

He didn't know why it angered him.

Braddok cut the rope, using once piece to secure Sable's ankles and another to secure her wrists. She did not fight him.

Jeric almost wished she would.

"You might wanna check her, Wolf," Braddok said. "Her shirt's soaked through."

Jeric noticed the dark stain then.

He jumped to his feet and approached. Sable wouldn't look at him. He crouched beside her and peeled back her shirt. She didn't move, didn't flinch. She was like stone, her gaze fixed on nothing. He unwound the wrapping and cursed. The thread had ripped through her skin, and the wound bled freely. He glanced up to find her glaring at him. As if he were the one who had given her this.

Perhaps he was.

"Brad," Jeric said tightly. "I need akavit."

Braddok got up, scooped his flask off the ground, and shook it. His brow wrinkled as if he didn't understand why it was empty but also wouldn't have been surprised if he'd finished it without knowing. He stalked to the horses and found another flask, which he tossed at Jeric.

Jeric caught it and uncorked the lid, and Sable looked sharply away as he poured akavit over the wound. She sucked air through her teeth and shut her eyes. The stitches needed to be replaced, but they didn't have the right supplies. Instead, he used a clean dressing from the saddlebags and wrapped it around Sable's waist. She stiffened at his touch but didn't say a word, her eyes fixed decidedly away from him.

"Sable..." he started.

Her gaze speared through him, cutting his words short. In her eyes was the loathing he'd seen from so many: hating him for who he was, what he was, and what he had done—for everything he represented. It'd never bothered him before; he'd taken pride in it.

It bothered him now.

Chez returned with Stanis, and Jeric stood. Chez winked, joining Aksel by the fire, hand open and demanding some of the hardtack Aksel was currently chewing. Jeric regarded Stanis, but Stanis wouldn't return his gaze. Stanis had always been the wildest of them, but lately, his behavior had been volatile—belligerent, even, as if drunk off of the blood they had collectively spilled.

Stanis took a seat at the rim of firelight, his back to Jeric.

"Where's Gerald?" Chez asked.

Jeric and Braddok exchanged a long look.

Chez's gaze darted from Jeric to Braddok, then leaned forward with a sigh. Stanis looked over then. Jeric sensed Sable's full attention, too, though she didn't look over.

"How?" Chez asked.

"A knife to the heart," Jeric answered. He let the words sit, not wanting to divulge more. He only hoped Sable would allow him this.

Gerald's fate was a risk they all took, every single day. He wasn't the first man they'd lost, but he'd been one of the best, in skill and character.

"That true?" Stanis asked sharply, eyes narrowed on Braddok.

"Is what true?" Braddok barked back.

Stanis's eyes flickered suspiciously to Jeric. "Where've you been, Wolf? You leave suddenly. Didn't say a godsdamn word—"

"He doesn't have to tell you scat," Braddok cut him off.

Stanis threw down his scabbard and stood. "I think we have a right to know why Gerald died for some godsdamned Scablicker."

His words filled the camp, and before Braddok could make a stand against them, Jeric said, "Gerald didn't die because of *her*. He died because of *me*. Because I failed. Over and over again. I failed to stand for you."

"Wolf, we know who holds your strings—" Braddok started.

"And I'm cutting them," Jeric said sharply. "I am joining the Strykers."

Silence fell.

Chez broke it with a hammer. "*What*?"

When Jeric didn't deny it, Chez and Aksel looked to Braddok, hoping *he* would deny it, but Braddok looked solemnly back with a shrug. He'd known for some time. Stanis regarded Jeric with an expression Jeric couldn't read.

Aksel sat forward. "Hagan will never allow it."

"He is," Jeric said.

Aksel looked bewildered.

"Hersir's performing the ceremony when I return."

"But *why*?" Aksel asked.

Jeric looked from man to man, his gaze settling on Braddok. "Because I won't risk your lives for my brother's whims. Not anymore. I'll serve Corinth, but on my own, without your blood on my hands."

Jeric's words settled and took root.

Chez dragged a hand over his face. "Gods above. The hells am I gonna do now?"

"Join me on king's guard," Braddok said with a wink.

"No, thanks," Chez replied dryly. "I prefer to see a bit more action."

"Which is why I said to join me on king's guard." Braddok waggled his brows.

Chez snorted.

"Godsdamnit, Wolf," Aksel grumbled with a sigh, resting his forearms upon bent knees. "I feel like my life's about to become excruciatingly boring."

"Good," Jeric replied. "Boring means alive."

Aksel rolled his eyes and chucked the last remnants of hard-tack on the fire.

Jeric glanced at Sable, who looked immediately away from him.

"What are you three doing out here, anyway?" Braddok asked.

"We were coming back from Stovichshold. Your brother asked us to check on..." Chez's gaze flitted to Sable before answering quietly, "...things."

Hagan had gone behind his back and used his men. Jeric gritted his teeth. "Why?"

"We—"

"*—shouldn't* talk about it here," Stanis cut him off. He tipped his head toward Sable.

"She's not a threat," Jeric said.

"She's a Scablicker," Stanis growled. "That's reason enough, though I expected you'd know that, *Wolf*. We still don't even know why she's here."

"If I say she's not a threat," Jeric said dangerously, "she's not a threat."

Stanis's cheeks turned crimson.

Jeric nodded for Chez to continue.

"There's been an... incident," Chez continued, casting a quick glance in Sable's direction.

"What sort of incident?" Jeric asked.

"Right after you left, Reichen was attacked."

Jeric's eyes narrowed, and he remembered the map. "Attacked how?"

"Not sure. All the Scabs are gone, cattle too. But the people were found dead in a pile on the temple steps."

"Gods..." Braddok sat forward.

"All of them?" Jeric asked, sitting upright.

Chez nodded. "And that's not even the worst of it. We didn't see the bodies in Reichen. Anaton had them burned, but we *did* see them at Dunsten."

Jeric and Braddok exchanged a glance.

"Nastiest thing I've ever seen. Skin was chalk white and translucent. You could see the veins through it, but they were black as ink, and their eyes..." Chez hesitated. "They were gone. Nothing left but empty black pits."

"The five hells...?" Braddok said.

"Swear to the gods."

Jeric frowned.

"People are spooked," Aksel said. "Stovich is pissed."

"Of course he is." Braddok grunted. "Surprised he's not storming Skyhold."

"He is," Aksel said. "He'd left for Skyhold just before we arrived."

Jeric met Sable's gaze across the fire. Despite her anger, he could tell that this news concerned her. He would've asked if she'd seen anything like it in The Wilds, but he didn't think she had. He also didn't want to draw any more attention to her.

"Did you find anything at the sites?" Braddok asked.

Chez shook his head. "Nothing, other than bodies."

"Any idea where the Scabs went?"

"No. It's like they just vanished."

Jeric leaned back on his hands. "Leads on the people behind this?"

"There are rumors..." Aksel said, tossing a twig on the flames. "We keep hearing about a legion."

"Legion," Jeric repeated.

"Yeah. We don't know anything definitive, but we think it's a group of Scab rebels. The guards keep hearing rumors in the mines."

"What are the rumors?"

Aksel shrugged. "The Scabs think this legion is going to set them free."

"We are Legion, Legion is we... soon we'll be free!" Chez mocked. At a sideways glance from Jeric, he said, "That's what they keep saying, anyway. No matter how many times they're beaten."

Over the years, there had been a handful of times when Scab slaves had attempted to rise up against their masters. But this... Jeric had never heard of anything like this before, and it disturbed him. He turned his men's words over and over as he watched the fire. All this time, they'd been concerned about Kormand, Brevera's ruler, attacking their borders, when there was a threat already within.

"What are you thinking over there, Wolf?" Braddok asked.

Jeric didn't answer immediately. "I think we need to hurry home."

"And so what Asorai created, mankind, in its constant quest for power and knowledge, defiles. Man takes the precious gifts The Maker has given, twists them to suit their own selfish desires and their own selfish ends, letting darkness into the world. And the darkness grows, feeding off of lies and deceit, obscuring the light, the truth, giving rise to evil. The people cry out to The Maker, furious that He should abandon them, when they never truly wanted Him near in the first place."

— Excerpt from Il Tonté, As recorded in the Eighth Verse by Juvia, the Liagé First High Sceptor.

29

The next few days dragged mercilessly. A vicious storm escorted them south, unleashing torrents of rain so strong they were often forced to find shelter and wait. For Sable, the sky above mirrored the storm raging within.

She blamed herself for not seeing who the Wolf really was. She should have. But the stories had painted a predator, all snarls and death and destruction. They had failed to show the Wolf as a man—a vulnerable, warm-blooded, and beautiful man—and therein lay the problem. Sable had come to know the man, and she had a difficult time reconciling the two as one.

She shared the Wolf's horse, which only made it worse, and the silence between them became a living and breathing thing. She wanted to hate him. She tried to, but then she'd remember the moment he woke from Tallyn's, and all the moments that followed, and where the hatred should have been, her chest squeezed instead, aching from the loss of something that was never real to begin with.

On the third day, the rain relented, and Chez, Aksel, and Stanis ventured off to hunt. Braddok took the horses to a nearby and very swollen stream, and the Wolf stayed with Sable. It was a habit he'd made, as if trusting no one else to make sure she didn't run. Which, Sable thought, was wise, because she would have.

Sable wandered down the stream's edge to a calmer sort of inlet, and there she crouched to dip her bound hands into the cool water. She cupped her fingers and brought what little she could to her lips. Soon after, she sensed the Wolf standing behind her. She didn't turn, but dipped her hands back into the stream instead.

"Have I killed someone you love?" he asked suddenly.

Sable wondered how long he'd been wanting to ask her this question. She plunged her hands deeper into the water, letting the cool soothe her chafed wrists. The Wolf crouched beside her, grabbed her chin, and turned her face toward his, forcing her to look at him.

The blue in his eyes was so deep it looked violet.

"I'm trying to understand," he said tightly.

"What's there to understand?"

"Why this hatred?" he growled. His patience waned. "I understand your anger. I expected it. But this..." His eyes flickered over her face. "It's still *me*, Sable... I am not your enemy. I don't understand why you're treating me like one."

Sable lifted her bound hands between them. "And this is how you treat your *friends*?"

"That isn't *my* choice," he said, releasing her chin. "I'd leave you free if I didn't think you'd run."

"Then I'm not really free, am I?"

His brow hardened. "You still haven't answered my question."

"My answer doesn't matter," she said through her teeth.

He leaned back a little, eyes searching, still not comprehending.

"If you *had* killed someone I loved," she continued, "would it change anything? Would you tell me you were sorry? Would you mean it? Because if you're going to question your actions on *one* life, you'd better question your actions on every single one of them."

He leaned close; his eyes stormed. "What would you know of my fight? You've been hiding in The Wilds with your head in the godsdamned snow. Everything I've done is for the protection of my people, just as you steal to protect—"

"That's different—"

"Is it?" he cut her off. His hot breath mixed with hers. "You think you're better because you're a *healer*? We both deal in the currency of fate, Sable."

Her eyes narrowed. "Don't you dare compare my actions to yours. You've slaughtered hundreds of innocent people—"

"*Innocent*?" His teeth flashed. "Is it innocent when Scabs send their children to poison our wells? Is it innocent when they burn our buildings with our people trapped inside? Was it innocent when they took *my mother* and delivered her heart in a box? Or does none of that matter because it's Corinthian blood?"

Sable's mouth clamped shut. She hadn't heard any of that before, and she would've called him a liar except for the part about his mother. There was no lie in that. Her heart squeezed a little, thinking on what that must have done to him.

"There are always two sides, Sable," the Wolf said lowly. "Don't dismiss mine simply because it complicates yours."

They glared at each other, a battle of wills. At last, Sable turned her face away.

He didn't speak to her again.

EVENTUALLY, the six of them began a steep descent into the Valley of Kings. Sable had never traveled this deep within Corinth, and looking at it now, she understood why it inspired so many songs. It plucked a string deep inside of her, and a bass note breathed in her ears, warmed by the wind and flourished by the chimes of distant birds, her heart the timpani that gave it pulse. Again, Sable wondered how something so beautiful could be the source of so much pain.

A lake basked in the densely forested valley below, glittering like sapphires. Behind it stretched imposing walls of granite, their jagged snowcaps tinged pink from the setting sun. And nestled right up against those mountains, like a dragon protecting its hoard, stood a magnificent fortress.

Skyhold.

According to the verses, the Liagé had constructed the fortress and presented it as a gift to the Corinthian people—a symbolic link to the Maker. It'd been a promise of peace and prosperity, that though their gods clashed, Corinth and Sol Velor would live in harmony. Now, the fortress proved a mark of defiance, repurposed to physically block the Sol Velorian god from ever stepping foot on this world again.

A city sprawled at its feet, encircled by an enormous black wall. Sable had never seen so many buildings in all her life, not even in Trier. They huddled like a crowd of nobility, with boastful towers of pride, each posturing to stand grander and taller than the one beside it. There was more wealth in this city than all of Corinth.

"Go on," the Wolf said to his men as they stood at the valley's edge. "We'll catch up."

Braddok eyed Sable, then nodded at the Wolf and galloped off with the rest of the pack.

Sable was wondering what the Wolf intended when he suddenly shifted against her and cut her bindings free. The ropes slid from her wrists and dropped to the ground.

"You're a guest here, Sable," he said. "And despite what you think, I'll hold to my promise. I *will* see you safely wherever it is you want to go after this."

"Don't act like you're doing me a favor," she snapped, holding up her freed hands. "You waited till I couldn't run." Well, she *could* run, but she wouldn't make it far. Not this deep within Corinth.

The Wolf's arm tightened around her waist, pulling her closer, and his breath warmed her ear. "It isn't wise to alienate the one friend you have in this land."

"*Friend*?" She laughed darkly. "I don't have friends." The memory of Gavet's betrayal hovered over her.

The Wolf held her tight, his body tense against hers. At last, he leaned back, threw her cowl over her head, and adjusted her cloak around her shoulders. "Then at least stay hidden," he said tightly. He gave their horse a swift kick and galloped furiously after his men.

And the great fortress approached.

They were a few dozen yards from the gate when Sable spotted the crosses. From a distance, she hadn't noticed them for the enormous black statues standing on either side of the gate—statues of Corinthian gods that were still under construction, thanks to dozens of Scab slaves currently working them. But as they neared, she realized that what she'd initially dismissed as spindly black trees weren't trees at all.

They were wooden beams of crucifixion.

Bodies hung from stakes like some macabre garden, men and women alike—even a child. Crows perched on heads of patchy black hair, pecking at the slow disintegration, stealing whatever they could while leaving white flecks of disgrace upon the freshly tilled soil below. Most of the bodies were Sol Velorian. The rest, death made too difficult to distinguish.

A crow laughed cruelly, sawing through the quiet, and as they rode past the bodies, she smelled the rot. The putrid stench of decomposition. Her stomach turned, and she glared back at the Wolf.

"And you wonder why I hate you," she snarled.

The Wolf's arm flexed around her, and he looked sternly

ahead at the approaching gate, where his men waited, speaking with a few guards.

They tore through the wide open gate. Sable expected the Wolf to slow once inside the city, but he only pushed harder, navigating the streets on instinct and leaving his men in the dust. People jumped aside; guards scrambled to clear a path. The Wolf powered through them all, holding Sable close, physically shielding her from curious eyes. And there were many. So many.

Up, up, up they galloped, winding through a maze of tight and winding cobblestone, while buildings crowded in like an angry mob. Banners and clothing lines were strung between cantilevered upper stories, blocking the sky, and a haze of sweat and livestock and smoke tainted the air.

The Wolf turned onto a wide and sloping street. The cramped city fell behind, and the street leveled at an enormous drawbridge suspended by thick chains. Below stretched a canyon of rock and forest. Above loomed the great fortress, spires puncturing the clouds. Their stolik thundered over the wooden planks and passed more guards, through a pair of broad and open doors, and into a large courtyard, where a young man shoveled hay.

The Wolf dismounted before their stolik came to a full stop. No sooner had his boots touched the ground than the young man called out, "Prince Jeric!"

The title caught Sable off guard. Of course, he was the prince of Corinth. She knew this. But since the day she'd learned the truth about him, she'd thought of him as the Wolf, the hunter, the killer. His men addressed him as Wolf.

She'd almost forgotten he was, first and foremost, a *prince*.

The Wolf Prince turned around as the young man set down his shovel and jogged toward them. The man had curly, straw-colored hair, prominent bones, and an eager smile that made him seem younger than he probably was.

"Farvyn, your grace," the young man stuttered in a pinched voice, bending in a bow before the Wolf, though his pale gaze kept shifting curiously to Sable. "Remember me? I was the messenger who found you and your pack—"

"I remember," the Wolf snapped.

The young man—Farvyn—stood tall and grinned. He was missing one of his canines. Judging by the rest of his teeth, it'd probably rotted out of his head. "Moved me to the stables after that. Figured I'd be more help here, I wager, though I enjoyed..." His voice trailed at a dark look from the Wolf, and Farvyn's expression faltered. He cleared his throat. "I'll take him for you..." Farvyn reached for the horse.

The Wolf turned his body just so, making it clear that Farvyn would not be taking anything anywhere.

"Where's Dom?" the Wolf asked.

"Below, gettin' fresh feed. All this rain keeps rotting it."

Just then, Braddok and the others trotted into the courtyard. Braddok flashed the Wolf an irritated look.

"I'll take it from here," the Wolf said to Farvyn. "Go help my men."

Farvyn hesitated, then remembered himself. "'Course, your grace." He scurried off to help Braddok and the rest of the Wolf's pack.

The Wolf held out a hand to Sable.

It isn't wise to alienate the one friend you have in this land.

Sable pressed her lips together and, reluctantly, took his hand. He helped her out of the saddle, and, truth be told, she was glad for his support. Her side ached, and even with the Wolf's aid, her balance was unsteady.

"Wait here," he said, then escorted the stolik through a small archway. He returned a minute later, just as Braddok approached.

The two men glanced briefly over at Farvyn, then exchanged a long look.

"I'll go on with them." Braddok gestured toward Chez, Aksel, and Stanis, who chattered a few paces away, giving Farvyn instructions and more than a little harassment.

The Wolf clasped Braddok's shoulder. "I'll find you after."

"If you're lucky." Braddok winked.

The Wolf grinned.

Braddok cast one last glance at Sable, then started after the others.

The Wolf turned to face her. Looking at him now, Sable felt as though a gulf stood between them.

"We need to find my brother first," the Wolf said. His lips parted as if he wanted to say more, but he closed them and extended an elbow instead.

Sable didn't reach for it.

"Sable," he warned, his tone strained.

She looked away from him and took his elbow.

He led her across the courtyard, pushed open the doors at the far end, and led her into a great hall. There, her eyes wandered from impossibly high arches to blazing hearths so tall and so wide, a half-dozen Braddok-sized men could have stood abreast within. Tables stretched along the length of the room, empty except for burning candelabras. Two tiered, wrought-iron chandeliers hung from the ceiling, and the floor was a mosaic of black-and-white patterns, coated in gloss so thick it looked wet. At the end of the hall stood a magnificent chair.

Corinth's throne. It was all black—glossier, even, than the tiles—with a wide seat and broad back as though it'd been built for a giant. Embedded into the back of the chair was a wolf's head, and the throne's legs ended in feet, balanced upon black claws.

A courier rushed past, then stopped to bow to his prince.

The Wolf walked faster, pulling Sable after him. She sensed he didn't want anyone to get a good look at her.

A few other men stood about—one in blue robes so dark they looked black, the others dressed in rich wool and leathers of the Corinthian style. They chatted quietly, then stopped when they spotted their prince and his veiled guest. Before they could say a word, the Wolf led her to a small door between two of the great hearths, where a guard stood, armed in black-and-silver plates. He nodded at the Wolf and stepped aside, opening the door. Beyond was a long and narrow stone stairway, lit dimly by burning sconces.

"Is it always so dark here?" Sable asked.

The Wolf gazed up the stairs. "Yes." And then he led her forward.

He slowed a little on the stairs, for her benefit. It hurt to draw a full breath, and the exertion—and altitude—was quickly wearing her down. The stairs leveled into another hall, littered intermittently with openings to other, smaller corridors, but the Wolf didn't veer. A few more men guarded this hall, bowing their heads to the Wolf Prince as he passed, though their eyes followed.

The Wolf stopped before a pair of guarded double doors at the end of the hall. Beyond, Sable heard the faint murmur of voices.

The Wolf tipped his head toward her. "Don't speak unless I say," he said too quietly for the guards to hear. "Even if you're asked directly. I will speak for you. Do you understand?"

A thousand responses crowded for voice, but all that came out was a curt, "Yes."

His eyes flickered over her face, and then he stood tall and released her arm. "Stay behind me," he murmured. He took a deep breath, pushed the door in, and stepped through. Sable followed.

The chatter inside died.

The space beyond was of moderate size, built to hold the large table at its center, which was currently occupied by a dozen men, who—judging by the heavy and awkward silence—had been discussing something of great importance before the Wolf had interrupted them.

"Just as I suspected," the Wolf said without ceremony. His

deep voice filled every corner, charged the silence. "I'm gone for a month, a legion has breached our borders, and you're all sitting around the table having a chat."

Glances crossed in uncomfortable silence.

"So you've heard," said a man's voice, but Sable could not see who'd spoken. The Wolf's broad shoulders blocked her view.

"You lost an entire legion of Scabs," the Wolf said. "That sort of news travels fast."

Postures shifted and shrank, and a chair creaked as its occupant stood. A note rang inside Sable's head like a chime, sudden and insistent, and now she could finally see the man who had spoken.

He had hair like fire and eyes of steel, and, Sable noted with some surprise, the Wolf's strong square jaw. He also shared the Wolf's height and authority, though his physique lacked the Wolf's sharp discipline, and where the Wolf carried an edge of deadliness, this man carried only cruelty. It was in his eyes. Like a snake, he stared without blinking, his thoughts twisting behind a cold veneer, always searching for the perfect moment to strike.

"Brother, how good of you to join us," the man said in a cloying voice, and confirmed Sable's suspicions.

This was none other than Prince Hagan Angevin, heir to Corinth's throne, and the Wolf's older brother. Sable had always believed the Wolf to be the Provinces' greatest threat. Now, looking at his brother, she wasn't so sure. There was something about him that set her on edge.

Prince Hagan's gaze drifted to Sable, and the note in her head rang louder.

The others noticed her then and strained to see the person within the cloak, and Sable was glad for her cowl.

"A word, Hagan," the Wolf said sharply. It was not a request.

Prince Hagan smiled. It was a cruel smile, one that delighted only in pain.

"Of course." He turned to address his council. "Leave us."

Chairs screeched, and the council exited the room. One man, dressed smartly in armor, clasped the Wolf on the shoulder and cast Sable an inquiring glance as he left. The rest filed out, save a woman and an elderly man dressed in heavy robes. Sable was struck by the woman's uncanny resemblance to the Wolf. They shared the same storming blue eyes and burnished hair, though hers fell in rivulets to her waist. She was as beautiful as the Wolf was handsome.

"Go on, Astrid," Prince Hagan said quietly but firmly.

"If you don't mind, I'd like to hear what Jeric has to say," she replied in a voice that didn't care at all whether or not the prince minded.

"I do mind."

Her expression darkened, but Prince Hagan's resolve did not waver. Something passed between brother and sister, and finally, in a furious gather of fabric, the princess stood and strode for the door. She stopped before Sable with harsh appraisal.

There was something... off about the Angevin princess that Sable couldn't place. Her eyes narrowed.

The princess sneered, then left, slamming the door behind her.

The note in Sable's head quieted.

The robed man lingered, and Sable realized she'd been wrong to call him elderly. To do so would diminish the strength of his being, and there was nothing frail about this man. He was old in the way Tolya had been old, as though he'd survived years beyond that which was permitted. There was no hair upon his head, and the rest of his body was hidden beneath an exquisite robe the same midnight blue as that of the man in the hall, but his was trimmed in silver. His eyes were dark and fathomless, as if he saw the past and present and future in one glance.

Wary, Sable looked away from him.

"He stays," Prince Hagan said, nodding at the robed man.

The Wolf bristled with restraint. "You sent my men to Stovich's."

"*Your* men?" Prince Hagan scoffed. "You've set your sights on being a Stryker. I didn't think you'd mind."

The Wolf took a step forward. It was a subtle push of power. "You had no right to do that."

Prince Hagan picked up a decanter and filled his glass. "On the contrary, I had every right."

The Wolf cocked his head to the side. It was a sharp motion, as if catching a new scent, one he didn't like or trust. "Where's father?"

Prince Hagan picked up his glass, admired the craftsmanship. The back of Sable's neck prickled with unease.

"Hagan."

Prince Hagan downed the glass and slammed it on the table. He looked at his brother, all humor erased. "He's gone, Jeric."

A deadly quiet settled in the room. It swelled and roiled, filling the cracks.

Corinth's king was dead.

Which meant Prince Hagan was now king. There was no further use for Sable here. Or was there?

Her gaze flitted to the robed man, who was watching her intensely. She glanced away again.

The Wolf's eyes narrowed on his brother, his features sharpened. "When?"

"Soon after you left."

The Wolf's hand flexed—a habitual tick, Sable realized, as if holding himself back from instinct. From grabbing his sword. "You knew he wouldn't last, and you sent me anyway."

Hagan refilled his glass. "Come, Jeric. We haven't had a father in years. Don't pretend you're upset."

The Wolf took another step. He was fury contained in ropes of experience, pulled tight enough to snap. "I lost a good man because of this, Hagan."

"You have lost many. But your errand wasn't for naught, despite what you may think." Here, he picked up his glass and tilted it toward Sable. "Are you going to introduce me to our guest?"

Sable watched him, and her unease intensified.

"There's no need," the Wolf said lowly. He turned to Sable and reached for her arm.

"*No need*?" Hagan said. "You bring me Sar Branón's bastard daughter, and you expect to take her away without first giving us a proper introduction?"

The moment stood outside of time, frozen in bewildering suspension, and his words trapped her like a spell.

Sar Branón's bastard daughter...

By the wards.

It wasn't possible. Not even the Wolf had figured it out. So how in all the stars had Prince Hagan learned the truth?

The Wolf's gaze whipped back to his brother. "What in the five hells are you talking about?"

But Hagan only had eyes for Sable. "Fascinating. All this time, and he never discovered the truth about you."

Sable felt the Wolf's scrutiny on her then, but she didn't turn to look. She couldn't, and confidently wear the lies she had always worn—the very lies that would save her now. The Wolf had warned her not to speak, but he hadn't anticipated this. And Sable had to defend herself; she was the only one who could.

"You're mistaking me for someone else, Your Grace," she said with impressive calm, despite her pounding heart. "My name is Sable. I'm just a healer."

"Sable." Hagan cocked his head, eyes unblinking. "Curious name for an Istraan, isn't it?"

"I'm from Skanden, so I don't find it curious at all."

Hagan took an easy step forward. "It's a nice little story, surina. You're quite convincing. Even my *Wolf* brother failed to sniff you out."

The Wolf turned to her. "What is he talking about?"

Still, Sable looked only at Hagan. "I am not the sar's bastard, Your Grace," she said firmly, though the words felt like rocks in her mouth. "Whoever convinced you of this is greatly misinformed. His bastard died. Years ago."

Hagan's eyes flickered to the robed man, who then approached Sable.

"*Tell me what is going on*," the Wolf demanded.

"Go ahead, Head Inquisitor," Hagan said to the robed man, who stopped before Sable.

Head Inquisitor.

Maker's Mercy.

The Head Inquisitor drew an object from his robes: a flute.

Her little bone flute.

The sight of it here, in the Head Inquisitor's hands, took Sable by so much surprise, she momentarily forgot her composure.

The Wolf noticed, and he fell impossibly still.

Hagan smiled. "There, you see? I thought the flute might rekindle your memory."

"What is that?" the Wolf asked, his voice dangerously low.

"Why don't you ask Sable?" Hagan said her name with irony.

Without meaning to, her gaze met the Wolf's.

In that moment, all of her lies collapsed. Walls she had carefully erected and hidden behind—walls and supports that had given her safety and purpose—all of them crumbled like sand and left her standing on a solid rock of truth.

The Wolf's eyes shifted like the seas before a storm, and his expression darkened as all of the lies she had told, and all of the details she had hidden, suddenly fell into place.

"You... are the *sar's bastard*?" His words were arrows, and they sank deep.

She opened her mouth to deny it, but the lies would not come —could not come. The Head Inquisitor held the flute closer to her. Instinctively, Sable flinched back, but too late. The flute touched her shoulder and the etched glyphs pulsed to life, glowing with silvery moonlight.

Illuminating the truth before them all.

The Wolf hissed and stepped away, as if she'd burned him.

"She's also Liagé," Prince Hagan interjected.

"*No*," Sable persisted, glaring at Hagan. "The power has nothing to do with *me*. The flute's an old Liagé relic, and somehow it—"

"Illuminates only at your touch?" Hagan finished instead, his sarcasm thick. "Did it illuminate that night as well, when you played Sar Branón's entire court to sleep? Or when you killed the little surina with your music? I've always wondered: Were you trying to elevate your standing, *bastard*?"

Sable's heart pounded hard and fast, with fear and memory, and her nerves hummed with flight. "If I'd known what it was, I never would have—"

"But you did, and it killed Surina Sorai," Hagan said, cutting her off. "Instead of executing you as Sar Branón should have, he smuggled you into The Wilds and let you live while the rest of us believed you dead. Fortunately, or, perhaps, unfortunately for you, I never believe what I'm told."

"And what is it you're hoping to achieve? Are you trying to elevate *your* standing by showing the Provinces I'm alive?" Sable snapped, throwing his words back at him. "Sar Branón hasn't sent for me in ten years. He won't care that I'm here now."

The words stung more than she'd anticipated, and they came out in a fury.

Hagan regarded her, his expression inscrutable. "Perhaps. Perhaps not." His gaze flickered to the Head Inquisitor. "She's yours."

"You can't..." Sable started.

Pale hands grabbed her arms from behind. Her gaze whirled to the pair of robed men holding her, their cheeks scarred grotesquely.

Inquisitors.

"Let me go!" Sable yelled, kicking and punching at the inquisitors, but they held tight.

The Wolf watched, unmoving.

"I can't, surina," Hagan said, regarding her like a snake. "You are far too valuable."

The Head Inquisitor stood before them, watching with undue calm as Sable bucked like a wild animal. Something tore in her side, and a cool cloth covered her mouth. A faintly familiar sour scent filled her nose, coating her tongue, and her world went black.

30

It was only when Rasmin's inquisitors began dragging Sable away that Jeric snapped out of his stupor. He rushed for the opened door and pressed his palms to the frame, blocking the inquisitors' exit.

Hagan gave him an annoyed look. "Move, Jeric."

Jeric did not move. "What do you want with her?" His eyes darted from the Head Inquisitor to Hagan, demanding an answer.

"That is not your concern," Hagan said.

Jeric seethed, barely able to draw a full breath, his body was so tight. "You lied to me," he said through his teeth.

Hagan frowned. "Did I?"

Jeric slammed his fist against the doorframe, and the door rattled upon its hinges. One of the inquisitors flinched.

"Gods*damnit*, Hagan!" Jeric snarled. "Did you send me to retrieve the sar's bastard?"

Hagan held his gaze and said simply, "Yes."

Jeric's blood ran hot; his body trembled at the edge of self control. "How could you—"

"We need unity, Jeric," Hagan cut him off. "Now more than

ever. That should come as no surprise to you. *You're* the one bringing reports of how vastly I'm opposed." Hagan's expression turned severe. "Father was weak. He let Corinth grow weak, and he left a mess in my hands. An inquisitor tried to kill me while you were away."

Jeric's eyes narrowed to slits.

Hagan smiled derisively. "You didn't know? There is, apparently, a necromancer who's evaded Rasmin's notice."

The word stopped Jeric's thoughts short. Tallyn had spoken of a necromancer—one who'd sent the chakran after *her*. Were they the same?

"Where is this necromancer now?" Jeric asked sharply.

"I don't have a rutting clue. Do you think I'd be telling you this if I knew the answer? And now, his power is infecting our godsdamned woods!"

"What in Aryn's name are you talking about?"

Hagan's steely eyes flashed. "There's a new hunter in our woods, it would seem. One more dangerous than you. It has Grag and his men spooked. It slaughters our wolves and rips them to shreds, leaving nothing behind but a smear of blood and intestines."

Jeric stilled. It sounded too familiar.

He caught the Head Inquisitor's dark gaze.

"And that's not our only problem," Hagan continued. "The legion you so rudely mentioned before my council has made off with Murcare's *entire* supply of arms."

Jeric looked darkly at Hagan. "Honestly, Hagan. I don't think you could've made a greater mess if you'd tried."

Hagan regarded Jeric, unamused. "I am not the only Angevin tasked with guarding the Corinthian people."

"Don't you dare put this on me—"

"I'm not." Hagan's gaze flickered over Jeric with decades-old bitterness. "You just delivered our victory."

Jeric looked sharply at Hagan. "You're going to force Sar Branón to intercede."

This time, the Head Inquisitor spoke up. "Not exactly. We're going to use the bastard for her power."

"You're… *what*?"

"I will use whatever means necessary to protect Corinth," Hagan said. "There is a legion attacking our villages—a legion we can't find—and we believe it's working with the necromancer. Right now, the only way I see to fight this necromancer is with a Liagé of my own."

Liagé.

Gods. All this time. Sable.

Sar Branón's bastard, and a godsdamned Liagé. He wanted to refute it, but he'd seen her face. He'd seen her terror at Hagan's words.

He remembered her music.

"You think a godsdamned flute is going to save you?" Jeric snarled. He was a red sky before a storm.

"Look around you, *Wolf*," Hagan hissed, arms spread toward the walls. "We are *failing*. Our enemies move right beneath our noses, stealing from us while leaving shameless displays on our doorstep. Riling the people and making us look weak. It's time we fight fire with fire."

Jeric approached Hagan with slow steps and gripped Hagan's collar, jerking him close. "How *dare* you. I've spent my entire life purging Corinth of sorcery, and you would turn around and use it for gain. After everything they've done."

The loss of their mother hovered over them like a feral beast.

Hagan's eyes hardened, steely and cold. "I rule Corinth now, Jeric, and if I *dare* to use a Liagé to protect my throne, by the gods, who are you to question me?"

Jeric glared at his brother.

His brother glared back.

His godsdamned *king*.

"Do it," Hagan growled. "I know you want to. *Hit me*. Strike me down."

Gods, how he wanted to.

Jeric's knuckles blanched, his body trembled with a lifetime of fury, and the edges of his vision burned red.

Red.

Red.

Red. Furious, destructive red.

His eyes squeezed; his nostrils flared.

It was exactly what Hagan wanted. What he always wanted: to unravel him, to control him, as he controlled everyone else.

Jeric shoved Hagan off with a snarl.

Hagan caught himself and adjusted his collar.

Jeric took one step forward and loomed over him. "*Never* use me like that again."

Hagan's eyes narrowed as he righted himself. "I am your king, brother. I will use you however I please."

The brothers stared at one another, two players at a furious impasse, held back only by witness and law. At last, Jeric spun around and started for the door, his cloak lapping powerfully at his knees. His gaze skirted Rasmin and the inquisitors. Their prisoner.

He gritted his teeth and clenched his fists. Gods, it hurt to look at her.

He met Rasmin's keen gaze, and without another word, Jeric stormed through the door and down the hall.

RASMIN WATCHED the Wolf Prince kick over a candelabra. It toppled and clattered upon the stone floor, startling the guards, who then scrambled to pick it up. Once the Wolf disappeared around a corner, Rasmin turned back to find Hagan staring after him also. Hagan's gaze snagged Rasmin's before he looked thoughtfully down at the woman.

Rasmin did not trust the look lingering there.

"We must hurry," Rasmin said. "Before she wakes."

"Yes, of course," the king said distractedly, then his gaze sharpened. "You're certain about her?"

Rasmin looked down upon the head of rich dark hair before him. The woman who would save his people, as was promised. "As certain as I have ever been, your grace."

31

D*o not fear, I will be with you…*

Sable startled awake to darkness, and the echo faded.

Do not fear…

The air smelled musty and old, the shadows too dark. She felt around blindly, trying to get some idea of her surroundings, and soon discovered she lay on a narrow bed that'd been shoved against a cold wall of stone.

She slid out of her bed and carefully felt her way forward. After three small and hesitant steps, she reached a door of solid wood. She searched for a handle but found none, so she pushed. The door didn't budge.

She made a fist and pounded. "Hello?" she called out in a raw voice.

No answer.

She coughed on a tickle and pounded harder. "Is anyone there?"

Still nothing.

She banged the door with both fists until her palms ached,

then kicked it, realizing—too late—her boots had been removed. She hissed a stream of curses as her big toe throbbed.

"Argh!" she yelled, punching the door one last time before sliding to the ground and leaning her head back. If someone so much as whispered on the other side of the door, she was going to hear it.

A tremor moved through her body, followed by a sharp wave of dizziness, and Sable closed her eyes. Whatever substance the inquisitors had used still lingered in her system. She tasted lemon and—she licked her lips—an earthy essence, tinged with veroot.

Nightdew. A strong soporific. Simple to make, but the ingredients were difficult to obtain.

Sable didn't remember falling asleep again, but a metallic jangling startled her awake. Voices murmured faintly beyond the door, and Sable cursed her negligence as she stumbled to her feet. Dizziness hit her again, and she braced herself against the wall just as the door cracked open. Light spilled in, and she blinked against the sudden brightness, shielding her eyes with her hand.

A silhouette stood in the threshold, head bent beneath the low lintel. The figure spotted her standing there and said sharply, "Have a seat, Surina Imari."

King Hagan gestured to her bed, stepped into the room, and set the lantern on the floor.

Sable blinked at him. The nightdew made her slow. "Where… am I?"

"Safely tucked away where no one can find you." King Hagan frowned over her, and it was then, in the lantern light, that she noticed her clothing had been replaced with a modest brown and shapeless dress. Still, she felt exposed beneath his scrutiny, stripped bare and vulnerable, without anywhere to hide.

Sable gathered what little strength she had left and stood tall. She would not wilt before this snake. "If you're hoping to ransom me, you're out of luck. I told you: Sar Branón hasn't sent for me in ten years. He won't risk Istraa for me now."

King Hagan studied her with cold and unblinking eyes. "I'm not concerned with Sar Branón. At least, not yet. What I need, only *you* can provide."

He paused, letting his words sit and fester. And how they festered.

"And what's that?" Sable asked, showing none of the fear pumping through her veins.

He took a step closer, and every muscle in her body tensed. She knew too well of his reputation, how he took what he wanted, when he wanted it. She drew solace in the fact that her door stood open, but even if her screams were heard, would anyone come?

Would anyone care?

His eyes caressed her face, and he reached out and touched her hair. Sable snapped her head away. He smiled, amused, but dropped his hand. "I see why my brother liked you."

"Really?" she bit back. "I guess you weren't paying attention earlier."

"You don't know Jeric as I do."

She didn't want to discuss the Wolf. Especially not with him. "What do you want?" she snarled.

He considered her, then said, "It's simple, really. I need you to play for me."

Sable blinked. "Play."

Hagan withdrew the flute from his robes.

"Where did you get that?" she demanded.

"It doesn't matter. What *matters* is that the two of you become reacquainted."

He held it out to her. This time, the glyphs sprang to life even without her contact.

She didn't take it.

He roughly grabbed her hand, forced it open, and shoved the

flute into her palm. At her contact, the glyphs flared bright. He curled her fingers firmly around it, and he did not let go.

"You will learn," he said, gaze fastened on hers. Madness writhed within. "You will learn to harness your power, and you will use it to help me."

Sable glared straight back. "I don't know what you're talking about."

He squeezed her hand around the flute so hard it hurt. "Don't play me for a fool, surina."

"I'm not *playing* at anything. I tried telling you before: *I* don't have power. It's the *flute*! Find someone else! Last time I played it, it killed someone I loved. Is that what you want? You want someone to kill your adversaries with music?"

"Not *someone*. *You*," he said. "And I don't want you to kill them. I want you to make them *mine*."

Sable was taken aback. "What... are you talking about?"

"It's not the flute, Imari," he said lowly. "It's *you*. The flute illuminated for *you* because *you* have the power—power over the soul. With your music, you can bend anyone to your will."

She stared at him, nonplussed. "Who told you this nonsense?"

"I did," said a new voice.

The Head Inquisitor stepped into the room, all robes and shadows, a specter in the lantern light. He exchanged a look with King Hagan, and then Hagan released her hand and took a small step away from her.

Sable looked between the men, bewildered. "I don't know where you got the notion that *I* have this ability, but the *flute* has the power. Not me."

"No, Imari," the Head Inquisitor said. "This flute only has power in the hands of a Liagé—the *right* Liagé. It merely amplifies what's already inside of you."

"I'm not Liagé! My papa is the sar of Istraa—"

"And your mother?"

Sable's thoughts stuttered to a halt. She remembered Ventus, what he had broken, what he had said.

"The Shah leaves traces. Someone has spent a great deal of energy erasing yours."

And then she thought of Tolya.

"They know what you are."

Not who. *What.*

Had she been wrong all these years? Was... *she* the monster?

"I saw you at the palace that day," the Head Inquisitor said, breaking through her spiraling thoughts.

"That's..." *...impossible*, Sable meant to say, but as she thought back on that day, she couldn't remember much more than Sorai. Her papa had invited guests. Dozens of guests—many of whom her young mind had blurred. Had the Head Inquisitor's face been one of them? She thought she'd remember a face like his —*eyes* like his—but then, she'd been so nervous about performing, and she'd spent most of the evening alone on the palace rooftops...

"You were only nine, I believe," he continued. "A sprightly little thing, always climbing on the rooftops. Always walking in a dance to a melody only you seemed able to hear. Your *kunari* — Vana, wasn't it?—wandered the palace searching for you. I couldn't decide if I wanted her to find you or not. You were quite entertaining to watch. And then there was your older brother, Ricón, who knew very well where you were but pretended to be as dumbfounded as the lot of them."

Sable trembled, unable to speak against him. His words were a battlefield, a torment to endure, yet impossible to look away from. And they brought pain. So much pain.

And now, so many questions.

"I watched you play," he continued, taking a step closer. "I knew the moment you began that something was different. That *you* were different. When you played, I watched the Shah take you as I had seen it take so many others. I watched it touch everyone present, though they were unaware—so captivated, they were, by your music. It was then I knew what you were."

Sable saw her little sister lying dead on the travertine floor, and her throat squeezed with old pain.

"You had no control over your power then," he continued evenly. "But you *can* learn to control it, and I can help you do that."

Her thoughts spun in a frenzy. Partially because the memories overwhelmed her with emotion, and partially because his claims were too great to digest. And also because the nightdew still flowed in her veins, making it difficult to focus.

"A legion of Scabs is attacking our villages and stealing our arms—a legion we can't seem to find—and we believe they are being aided by a necromancer," the Head Inquisitor said.

Necromancer. The word burned through Sable's mental haze like a brazier.

Tallyn had mentioned a necromancer. Were they the same, the necromancer aiding this legion and the one who'd sent a chakran after her? She'd wondered what a necromancer could want with a bastard Istraan, but if she truly was what the Head Inquisitor claimed...

"The power this necromancer has exhibited is nothing like I've ever seen," the Head Inquisitor continued. "We don't have the power to fight him, but *you* do. Because you have power over souls—living *and* dead."

She squeezed the little flute in her hands. A flute, apparently, with power only *she* could wield. "You... want me to learn how to use this... *power*"—she looked straight at the king—"to bend your enemy to your will."

"Yes," King Hagan answered.

"You *must*, surina," the Head Inquisitor interjected. "Your power stirs within you. You feel it." His voice urged her to acknowledge his words.

Sable was too aware of the fissures Ventus had created, the

power humming behind the cracks, and the melodies now ringing incessantly in her head.

Music... it pours out of you, the Wolf had said. *It's like you're constantly moving to a song only you hear...*

They know what you are.

...*what* you are.

What.

Sable stared at the little flute in her hands and swallowed hard. Suddenly, she saw her papa, the fear in his eyes as he sent her away with three of his very best Saredd.

Fear. Not anger, not disappointment. But fear, because he'd realized what she was: Liagé.

By the wards. It hadn't been the flute at all. It'd been... *her*.

Her breath came too quick, her pulse too rapid. A drum gone out of control.

"You can't suppress your gift forever," the Head Inquisitor continued. "Trust me in this. I've watched it take many. It's better that you learn to control it before it consumes you."

Sable glanced up and finally found her voice. "For as long as I've lived," Sable said, her words low and uneven, "you've murdered people for the Shah. And now you want me to use mine. To help you."

Hagan's expression darkened. "It's not a choice, surina."

Sable chucked her flute across the room. It struck the wall and bounced on her bed, then clattered to the ground. "You rutting hypocrite." She spat on the floor at his feet. "I'd rather—"

Hagan struck her across the face. The force of it knocked her to the ground, but before she could right herself, Hagan grabbed her arm and hoisted her to her knees. Behind him, the Head Inquisitor stood still and silent, eyes narrowed.

"You will do *whatever* I ask, when I ask it," the king snarled, so close his spittle landed on her nose. "Or you will suffer."

"I've already suffered," Sable growled. "*All my life*, I've suffered. Kill me, I don't care. You'd be doing me a favor."

He glared at her, and the madness roared. It called on him to act, to *hurt*, but necessity diffused his urge. He released her arm with a shove and barked out a name she didn't recognize. Two Corinthian guards entered, dragging a woman between them.

No, a girl, probably no older than nine or ten. A Sol Velorian slave girl.

Her small frame showed severe malnourishment, her cheeks too hollow, eyes too deep, and her black hair was stringy and matted. She stood on unsteady legs, despite the two guards holding her up.

"Suffering means different things to different people," Hagan said sharply.

"What are you doing?" Sable demanded, standing and wiping the blood from her lip.

Hagan eyed the girl. "She was born here. Her mother was a Scab. Her father... most likely one of my guards, but it's impossible to know which one." He gave Sable a vicious smile, and for the second time in Sable's life, she knew what it was to want a man to suffer.

He stopped before the girl, grabbed a clump of her hair, and forced her to look up at him. There were no tears. Sable expected this little girl's tears had been beaten out of her a long time ago.

King Hagan slit the girl's throat.

Sable gasped. She lurched forward as the girl toppled to the ground, wide-eyed, while her blood spurted on the ground.

"You..." Sable hiccuped on shock. Her hands curled into fists, and she lunged for Hagan, but a guard shoved her back against the wall. Everything inside of her squeezed. Demanding justice. "She was just a *child*!"

"She was a halfbreed and a bastard," Hagan replied simply, handing his bloodied dagger to the other guard. "I've done her a favor."

"You rutting—" Sable started, but the king pushed the guard aside, gripped her chin, and ground her skull against rock, forcing her to look at him. She hated every angle of his face. She hated the icy blue of his eyes, and the superior curve of his brow.

She hated that this *thing* was the Wolf's brother.

"I will kill one," he continued sweetly, "every single day you don't cooperate. Do you understand?"

Sable's teeth ground in fury.

"*Do you understand*, Imari?"

Sable's gaze fell to the girl whose only crime had been existing. "Yes." The word fell like a curse.

Hagan wiped the blood from his hand across Sable's cheek. "Good," he said, then he let go.

Sable sagged against the wall and used her dress to wipe the blood from her face.

"Clean this up," Hagan ordered his guards. He glanced back at Sable. "I'll see you tomorrow. I hope you make the right choice, surina." And then he ducked through the door.

The Head Inquisitor lingered, eyes fixed on the girl, and then his gaze found Sable's. She couldn't read the look there. Without another word, he turned and left. The guards picked up the girl's body and dragged it after them, leaving a smear of blood behind. The door latched closed; locks clicked into place. Sable stared at the bloodstain. Fury churned within her, but then her fury morphed into something else entirely, and Sable slumped to the ground and cried.

32

Sable didn't know how much time had passed. She'd fallen asleep to her tears and woken in an awkward position upon the stone floor. Her jaw ached where Hagan had struck her, and when she touched it, the skin felt tender. The lantern still burned on the floor, but she'd rather the darkness so it could hide the bloodstain.

She spotted a cup and a plate of bread near the door, and her stomach growled. How long had it been since she'd eaten? But eating now felt like a betrayal to the girl who'd lost her life upon the floor.

Sable sat up. Her head spun, but that wasn't from nightdew. This weariness was from a basic lack of nutrition, exacerbated by her recent loss of blood. Her body was starved and severely dehydrated.

She crawled to the plate, grabbed the stale bread, and leaned back against the wall as she took a bite. She picked up the cup with a shaky hand, sniffed it, then washed down her bite with water. Her eyes fell to the stain. Over and over again, she saw the knife, the blood. She picked up her cup and started tilting it over the bloodstain to rinse it clean, but stopped.

She shouldn't forget the sort of man she was dealing with. She set the cup down.

The girl had been born here. This shouldn't have surprised Sable. After all, Corinth was notorious for its harsh treatment of Sol Velorian slaves, and that didn't limit itself to construction and household chores. The girl had lived a miserable life, and maybe now she could be free of it, of them. For that, Sable even envied her.

Sable turned the bread over in her hands and squeezed. It exploded; crumbs flew everywhere.

Why should death *ever* mean freedom? Why did some get to determine a person's value, or who was cursed or who was blessed?

Yes, the Sol Velorians and their Liagé had almost succeeded in taking over the Provinces, but were there not extremes in every people? Hagan was an extreme. Did that make all Corinthians monsters?

She thought of the Wolf.

He'd acted under his sense of right, his sense of justice, according to his people and his gods. And he had been... well, not kind, exactly, but he'd eventually treated her with respect. And she... she'd trusted him with her life, before she'd discovered who he was. The Wolf was a predator, but he was no monster. Men like Hagan and Ventus were monsters, because they didn't possess the compassion that made one human.

She was not like them.

Sable pushed herself upon shaky legs. She stood there for a moment, gazing at her flute, which glowed dimly, and then she stepped forward. Step after step. Over the cold stone, across the stain of blood.

The stain of one whose blood wasn't so different from her own.

A halfbreed and a bastard.

Sable didn't know her mother, but now she wondered more

than ever. Her papa would know. Little Imari never would've demanded an answer, but Sable was not little Imari. And if she wanted the chance at getting answers, that meant she had to return. She had to *live*.

A man imprisoned is also alive. But that does not mean he lives.

Tallyn had not been born Liagé, yet, by no design of his own, he'd been given power and had used it to *help*. To fight a battle against an evil that Sable was only beginning to see and understand.

No, birth did not make man a monster. Choices did.

She picked up her bone flute and sat on the edge of her bed, turning the flute over in her hands, watching the glyphs pulse with her touch. One symbol she recognized, with some surprise. It'd been etched onto one of Skanden's wards. What it meant, she had no idea, and she wondered at the complexity of it. The *power* inherent to each stroke. An entire language had been lost with the Liagé. An entire people. A land, a god. Because the world had been afraid. *She* had been afraid right along with them.

And now she wondered at their god—not Ventus's version. But Tolya's, and Tallyn's.

The Maker.

Sable trailed her fingers over the glyphs. "I can't believe you're evil. You gave us wards, which protected Skanden for years."

And wouldn't it benefit her to know her power? Before it took her as the Head Inquisitor had claimed would happen? He hadn't lied about that part. She could feel the power there, slowly building behind the cracks and fissures, ready to explode out of her.

But.

But.

Did she dare attempt to channel that power?

She saw little Sorai lying on the floor, forever frozen in youth because Sable had stolen her future. Sable squeezed the flute. She'd give anything to go back in time and trade places with her

—give Sorai *her* life. Why had Sorai been taken and Sable left behind?

And…

What would Sorai think of Sable now, if she could watch from the heavens? Would she accuse her of wasting her life—something so precious? Would she blame Sable for spending all of these years hiding away like a coward, trying to atone for her sin with herbs and poultices? With petty thievery?

Sable shut her eyes. Her next inhale trembled.

Keys jangled at the door.

Sable opened her eyes just as the door opened. King Hagan entered her chamber, followed by two guards and a young Sol Velorian man with wiry limbs and clothing covered in a black, soot-like substance. A mineworker.

Maker's Mercy. Had a day passed already?

"Well?" Hagan asked without preamble.

There was no time to think. This man's life hinged on her cooperation. Sable fumbled awkwardly with the flute. Hagan watched her with those sterile and unblinking eyes, and Sable lifted the flute to her lips.

The motion felt… false. Like being told to kiss a stranger before an audience and convince them of love. Her fingers twitched over the openings, unsure. They'd once held the object with such care and confidence, doting over holes they'd intimately known. But now they were just holes, and her fingers wandered a foreign landscape. Even her ears betrayed her, failing to hear melody. Failing to give her fingers direction.

The seconds stretched into a minute, and her arms trembled. Sable drew in a breath and formed her lips above the mouthpiece, though her jaw ached where Hagan had struck her. Her fingers found purchase, but the exhale would not come. It lodged in her chest, unwilling to release itself. Unwilling to commit.

Sable gulped down her breath and pulled the flute away.

Hagan's eyes narrowed. "I see."

"I'm trying," she said. "It's just... I haven't played in years. It'll take time."

He turned back to one of his guards and jerked his chin.

The guard pulled a knife.

"No, please... *wait.*" Sable lifted the flute back to her lips.

Before she could inhale, the guard sliced the Sol Velorian's throat open.

Sable turned her face away, flute clutched tightly in her hands as the guards dragged the body away. Her anger became a living thing inside of her—one with teeth.

"You monster," she snarled. By the wards, she would kill him.

King Hagan touched her cheek and turned her head to face him. His palms were clammy and soft, unlike his brother's warm and callused ones. And then he kissed her.

Sable squirmed, revolted, but he held firm and shoved her to the wall. So she bit down on his lip hard enough to break skin. He hissed, pulled back, and slapped her.

Her face snapped to the side, and her cheek burned.

"Don't *ever* do that again." His eyes scathed over her once, and then he left the room, slamming the door after him.

33

Jeric raised his sword with a yell and swung. It hit the tree hard and sank into the bark. The force of it rattled up his arm, jarring his bones. He gritted his teeth, jerked the sword free, and hacked again and again, chunks of bark flying. When he could no longer grip the sword, he threw it aside and struck the tree with his fist, over and over, until his knuckles bled, and then he growled and started kicking it.

"Jeric..." said his mother's voice.

His body ached, but he didn't stop. He would not stop until he had nothing left.

"Jeric," she said quietly, grabbing his arm.

He threw her off, but she did not reprimand him. That wasn't why she'd come. She knew the pain he felt—had often felt—and she'd come to bring him back.

But he didn't know if he could come back from this. It was too much. Hagan had done many awful things to him over the years, but this trumped them all. It was only when Jeric sagged back against the tree that his mother approached. She didn't speak as she drew him into her arms, and now he was too exhausted to push her away.

His sobs broke against her chest. His hands curled into fists, pressed against her back, and she held him, let him rage, let him grieve. Only when he finished did she unwrap her arms from him to grab his shoulders and hold him steadily before her.

She was crying too.

"Don't let him break you," she said firmly. "He sees what I see, and it threatens him."

Jeric gritted his teeth again and looked away.

She touched his cheek, turning him back. Her eyes moved between both of his—eyes he'd inherited from her. "He is my flesh and blood, and for that, some part of me will always care for the infant the gods entrusted to me. But hear me, Jos..." She looked fiercely into his eyes as she spoke the nickname she had given him. "I know he's a monster. Eventually, all of Corinth will know it too. There's too much Angevin in him. But you... you are *mine*, Jos, and you have to be smarter." She squeezed his shoulders. "You have to be cunning. Resourceful. Do not show him your heart, because he will use it to control you. People like Hagan... they feed off of others' pain. Do not feed him yours."

Jeric trembled in her grip. "I hate him."

Deep sadness filled her eyes—one that had more to do with her monstrous son than Jeric's hatred of him.

"I know, darling." She squeezed his shoulders one last time and let go. She tucked a lock of blonde hair behind her ear that'd loosed from her braid and glanced around. "Where is he?" she asked quietly.

Jeric wiped his face on his sleeve. He nodded for her to follow and led her to the sack he'd dumped upon the riverbank. The cloth had turned completely red. Jeric didn't know the wolf's body had so much blood.

His mother crouched beside the sack and pulled it back just enough. Her face paled, and her eyes hardened with anger as she closed the sack again. "I'll help you bury him."

"I forgot to bring—" Jeric started.

"I brought shovels," his mother said, anticipating his words. She stood and started for the horse she'd left beside a tree.

A twig snapped nearby, and Jeric looked.

He sensed it before it happened: the snap of string, the whir of flight. In those few seconds of premonition he would never be able to explain, he cried out to his mother. But he was too late.

An arrow sank into her back. Her body jerked from impact and she cried out, staggering against the horse. Another arrow hit, then another. Jeric ran to her as she collapsed to the ground with three arrows sticking out of her back. A Scab appeared between the trees, his arrow aimed at Jeric.

Something inside of him snapped.

At the last second, he dove. The arrow whizzed past. He rolled fast, grabbed his sword as he lunged to his feet, then rose up behind the Scab and shoved his sword through the Scab's belly.

Somewhere in his mind, he knew this wasn't right. That wasn't exactly how it'd happened.

The Scab fell, and more appeared in his place. Jeric fought them all. His mother faded away, and the scene shifted from forest to field to canyon. The sun was high. Sometimes the moon. Scab after Scab. First warriors, then villagers, then their flocks. Their children. Then the Istraans who harbored them. It was a steep slope slick with blood, and he was tumbling down it too fast to stop himself.

And then he saw *her*. The Istraan.

The Liagé.

She grabbed his ankle and held him fast—suspended between light and the infinite abyss spreading at his feet, calling out his name. If it swallowed him, he knew he'd never emerge. But she gripped him tight, her song holding him firm, her eyes demanding he stop. Demanding he toss his sword into the pit so that he could climb out and live. For a split second, her face morphed into his mother's, and then it became *hers* again.

But he couldn't let go of his sword. *Her* people had done this to him, made him this. *She* shared their blood, their curse.

He raised Lorath to her throat, and her song silenced.

What have you become, my darling Jos? his mother's voice echoed grievously in his mind.

And then he was gazing down upon his own face—a face slowly being cocooned in darkness. His teeth stretched into canines, his eyes yellowed, roving and crazed, and he snapped powerful jaws at the blade. Jeric then slipped in the blood, lost grip of her hand, and tumbled into the darkness.

Jeric woke with a start, covered in sweat, and a sharp pain pulsed in his side. He lifted the edge of his tunic where Gerald had clawed him. The scars had healed into three clean, black lines, but they ached. They'd ached ever since he'd left Skyhold. He didn't know what it meant, and he'd abandoned the one person who might.

He pushed his tunic back into place. A bird chirped above as night's shadows brightened with predawn light. Jorvysk—a fellow Stryker—slept just a few feet away, his back to Jeric, and the horses stood beside the tree where they'd left them. Jeric's stolik snorted softly.

What have you become, my darling Jos?

He jumped to his feet, gathered his things, and arranged them in the stolik's saddlebags. Jorvysk stirred a few minutes later.

"You're eager this morning," Jorvysk said with an undignified yawn.

Jeric filled his flask at a nearby stream while Jorvysk collected his things. Jorvysk had been a Stryker for two years, which, in Jorvysk's opinion, made him an expert in... everything. Jeric wasn't sure how much more he could take.

"I'm not comfortable sending you alone right now," Hersir had said, shortly after Jeric had taken his vows. "You know what's happening out there in those woods."

"I also know what's happening inside Skyhold's walls," Jeric had said. "Don't you think I'd be better served here, keeping an eye on the city?"

"What you think no longer matters," Hersir had said sternly. "You're *my Stryker*, and if I ask you to investigate the Blackwood, you'll investigate. Do you understand?"

Jeric held Hersir's gaze. Jeric's smile stretched, delayed. "I understand."

Yes, he understood. He was a spoke on Hersir's wheel now. Jorvysk's company had been an unwanted addition, and as they rode on, Jeric found himself wondering if he'd simply traded one tyrant for another. At least this tyrant had a conscience.

Hagan had attended the induction ceremony. Jeric had spotted Astrid there, as well, but both she and Hagan had slipped out of the hall immediately after Jeric's vows, and neither lingered to offer congratulations. Not that he'd expected it, and oddly enough, he hadn't felt like being congratulated.

What have you become, my darling Jos?

Jeric absently turned the Stryker ring on his finger—the one Hersir had given him after he'd taken his vows—then urged his stolik onward.

"Hey!" Jorvysk called after him, saddling up and trotting after him. "Everything okay?" he asked, once he'd caught up.

Jeric's eyes narrowed on the road ahead. "Fine."

"No need to be nervous," Jorvysk said, misinterpreting Jeric's mood, as he consistently did. "We'll find what's hunting the wolves."

Jeric didn't answer.

"Grag and his men... they spook easily. Grag thinks he's got some connection to these woods." Jorvysk sighed and glanced at the rustling leaves above. "Think the man smokes to much grass. Makes him paranoid."

Jeric cocked a brow, and Jorvysk winked.

"If I had my bets," Jorvysk continued, "I'd say some Scabs probably caught a wolf and ripped the poor bastard to shreds just to scare us. Ain't no creature in this world that could mutilate an animal like that."

Jeric didn't agree, but he didn't offer enlightenment. People like Jorvysk didn't want a discussion. They already knew everything.

"Scabs always hunt in packs," Jorvysk continued. "You rarely find one in the woods alone. Sometimes they'll use one as a lure, but there's always at least a half dozen out there hiding. You'll wanna check your back first. They like to come up behind, slit your throat."

Jeric glared at the sky.

"I came up on a pack of 'em this one time. Leader was taking a piss when I got him in the back." Jorvysk chuckled to himself. "Shot down the rest of 'em before they even knew I was there. They had a woman with 'em too. She was a rare treat." He laughed again, but this time there was an edge to the laughter.

Jeric glanced darkly back at Jorvysk.

Jorvysk bristled. "Don't look at me like that, Wolf. You steal from them too. We just steal different things."

Jeric looked back at the road.

"How many have you actually killed?" Jorvysk asked conspiratorially, as if expecting the rumors to far exceed the actual count.

Jeric didn't respond.

"I've got one hundred and seventy, give or take a dozen. Hard to count anymore." He snickered. "Come on, Wolf. How many of the bastards have you got? Fifty? A *hundred*?"

What have you become, my darling Jos?

Jeric stopped his horse and looked around. The wind stirred his hair. "One thousand, two hundred and sixty-three."

The words fell out of him, unbidden, in slow confession.

One *thousand*, two hundred and sixty-three.

Gods, he even knew the exact number.

If you're going to question your actions on one life, you'd better question your actions on every single one of them, she had said.

Jorvysk's vaunting expression stalled, and he stopped his horse beside Jeric. "That's your pack combined, right? Because even that would be—"

"No." Jeric said, eyes fixed on the road, unseeing. "That's just me."

Jorvysk gaped at him. "You're rutting serious?"

Jeric gave him an annoyed look, then kicked his horse into a trot before Jorvysk could say another word.

Jorvysk didn't talk as much after that, thank the gods. The two of them tracked their way through the Blackwood until they reached the steep, rocky terrain at the foot of the Gray's Teeth Mountains.

Gray territory.

The men exchanged a glance. What few clues they'd found—blood or animal hair and entrails—had led them here.

"Guess we're going up," Jorvysk said.

The trees grew thinner as they climbed, and a bitter wind nipped at them. The narrow path climbed, switching back and forth to ease the steep incline, and they stopped often to give their horses rest. The thin air proved a strain on all of them, but Jeric kept his attention pinned to their surroundings.

"Awfully quiet up here," Jorvysk said warily, glancing about them.

Jeric filled his water skin in a small stream and took a long draught.

Jorvysk folded his arms and leaned back against a boulder, watching Jeric. He'd been doing that a lot, ever since Jeric had admitted his death toll.

Jeric refilled the skin.

"Who's Sable?"

Jeric froze; water bubbled over his hand. He glanced up and caught Jorvysk's gaze.

"You call out her name at night," Jorvysk said.

Jeric stood and capped his water skin.

"Who is she?" When Jeric didn't answer, Jorvysk said, "A lover?"

"None of your godsdamned business," Jeric said, shoving his skin in his belt as he strode for the horse.

Jorvysk pushed himself off the rock and followed. "She dead?"

Jeric leapt in the saddle and looked hard at Jorvysk. "I said, it's none of your godsdamned business."

Jorvysk regarded him a long moment, then climbed into the saddle, and the two of them continued up the mountain. The farther they climbed, the greater Jeric's unease. They should've spotted evidence of grays by now.

It wasn't long before the front pillars of a bridge came into view, dusted with fresh snow. The pillars bent toward one another, joining at the apex and forming an archway large enough for a god. Realization widened Jeric's eyes.

"Is that..." Jorvysk started.

"Kerr's Summit."

Kerr's Summit had been built by the Sol Velor as a gift for the people of Corinth, though they'd originally named it *Vandi e'Sancta Mai.* Gateway to the Holy Land. That was well before the Sol Velor's Liagé had betrayed them. Jeric's great-grandfather, Kerr Angevin, had renamed the bridge after himself.

Apparently, pride was an inherited trait in his family.

The bridge spanned a deep crevice in the mountains where snowmelt rushed into the River Dienn—a river named after the Corinthian goddess of water and rain. The only other passable point along these mountains lay three days in either direction. The bridge provided access to one of the Gray's Teeth's shallower passes, which led straight to Corinth's former capital: Sanvik. But Sanvik belonged to Brevera now, and as people ceased using the pass, eventually the bridge was abandoned to nature and the grays. Time and weather stained the white stone black in various places, and moss crept over its grand archway and supports, slowly reclaiming it.

"I'll be damned," Jorvysk said eloquently. "Thought that thing crumbled ages ago."

Jeric stopped his horse at the foot of the bridge. He could just make out remnants of old wards etched into the stone, faded with time. The river roared beneath, drowning out all else, and to his right, the Dienn careened over a cliff, disappearing into a cloud of mist. Even from here, Jeric felt its spray.

He understood why it'd originally been called Gateway to the Holy Land. Up here, on top of the world with such beauty all around, one felt as though they stood at Aryn's gates. Of course, Aryn wasn't the god the Sol Velorians had had in mind when they'd named it.

What have you become, my darling Jos?

Jeric leapt out of the saddle, and his boots landed with a crunch. Jorvysk watched from his saddle as Jeric stepped onto the bridge and stopped before a pillar. He held out his hand, fingertips hovering over a faded ward. He took a slow breath and pressed his palm against it. Grit and cold pushed against his skin. He frowned, not sure what he'd expected—*if* he'd expected—then pulled his hand away and glanced ahead. Across the bridge, nestled at the base of the mountain peaks, stood a small cluster of buildings dusted in snow. They'd once been an outpost where guards lived and merchants traded, but that'd been a very long time ago.

"Looks abandoned," Jorvysk said.

"It does look that way," Jeric said, then grabbed his stolik's reins and led him onto the bridge.

"What are you doing?" Jorvysk asked.

"Investigating."

Jorvysk dismounted with a grunt and followed, or tried to. His horse jerked and pulled, and Jorvysk cursed to the heavens. In the end, Jorvysk was forced to secure his horse at the bridge and cross alone.

Once across, Jeric loosely hooked his stolik to an old post and looked around. Their answer was here. He couldn't say how or why he knew it, but he did. He patted his stolik, then left him to search the grounds.

"Wonder how long it's been since anyone's seen this?" Jorvysk asked.

"Not as long as you might expect." Jeric dusted snow from a charred log.

Jorvysk frowned at the evidence. "Think the Scabs have been hiding here?"

"Seems likely." Jeric stood and drew his sword.

"Then where are they now?"

"Good question."

With a slight motion, the two split up to search the buildings. Jeric found nothing of consequence until he reached the old bunker. A ladder of beds lined two walls, and a dark hearth stood between them. It was a skeleton of a home, its flesh and blood having been stripped away over the years, leaving only bones behind. Jeric moved to the hearth and pressed his fingertips into the ash.

They were still slightly warm.

He investigated the bed frames and rubbed his fingers over the wood. Dust coated the creases, but not the faces. A glint of metal caught his eye, wedged between one of the planks and the wall. He reached in and pulled a dagger free.

A Corinthian dagger, made of skal. He wondered if it was part of Murcare's stolen inventory.

He shoved it in his belt and dropped in a plank to search under the bed. There, he found a hunk of half-eaten bread and a small, empty vial. He grabbed the vial and sat back on his heels.

What in the...?

It was the vial he'd uncovered during his last hunt with his pack. The one he'd left with Rasmin.

The cork was gone, the contents emptied, though the rancid residue remained. Jeric scanned the room again, senses on high alert, and then his eyes narrowed on the broken window.

Boards creaked beneath his weight as he approached. He noticed the deep grooves in the floor and walls around the window, as if something had been trapped inside and clawed its way out. Jagged shards of glass were all that remained of the window, and a black substance stained some of its edges. Jeric bent his head closer, careful not to touch the shards, and noted a tiny patch of leathery black skin frozen to the glass.

That wasn't the soft, silvery fur of a gray. The wound in Jeric's side ached.

He was suddenly glad he'd demanded Rasmin give him one of the nightglass blades he'd confiscated months ago while hunting with his pack.

A shadow fell over the room, and Jeric looked to the sky. Bruised and swollen clouds collided above, and the wind pushed stronger, smelling of rain. He'd forgotten how quickly the sky changed in these mountains. With one last glance about him, he slipped the vial into his pants and stormed out of the bunker.

"We need to go," Jeric said, approaching Jorvysk, who was arranging wood for a fire.

Jorvysk glanced up. His brow wrinkled in confusion.

"I know what's killing the wolves." And judging by the grays' continued absence, it was probably near.

Jorvysk arched a doubtful brow. "Oh? And what's that?"

"You wouldn't believe me if I told you." Jeric tossed the skal dagger at Jorvysk, who barely caught it.

"The hells?" Jorvysk looked from Jeric to the blade. "Where'd you find this?"

"In there." Jeric jerked a thumb toward the bunker. He didn't show Jorvysk the vial. "Let's go." He had questions for the Head Inquisitor that could not wait.

And he needed more nightglass.

Jorvysk's expression soured as he stood. "You're a right bastard, you know that? You think I don't know what you're doing?"

Jeric didn't know or care what Jorvysk thought he was doing, and he strode for his stolik.

Jorvysk grabbed his arm.

Jeric glared at him. "Let go of my godsdamned arm before I break yours."

Jorvysk's confidence wavered, and suddenly, Jeric's scars burned. He glanced past Jorvysk just as a massive dark shape emerged from behind the bunker.

Jorvysk released Jeric's arm. "What the...?"

The shade bolted for them with impossible speed and lunged in a snarl of claws and fangs. Jeric shoved Jorvysk, and the two of them leapt apart as the shade landed between them.

"The hells is that!" Jorvysk yelled, scrambling to his feet.

The shade's yellow eyes fixed on Jeric, and it snarled, taking a step toward him. Jorvysk threw his new skal dagger, but it bounced off the shade's hide. Because skal wasn't the right material.

It took another predatory step toward Jeric, peeling back its lips, showing off wide rows of needlelike teeth. Its pupil contracted, focusing, as if it recognized Jeric. As if it knew what Jeric had almost become—what still lived within those three little lines—and Jeric's scars flared hot.

Jorvysk ran at the shade, but it swung a powerful arm, launching Jorvysk into the air. He screamed, collided with the ground, and rolled over with a moan. The shade turned on Jeric.

What have you become, my darling Jos?

Suddenly, the shade bore his face—his eyes—as it stalked steadily toward him. Ready to finish the job Gerald, the changling, had started. To make Jeric's outward appearance finally reflect the violence within.

I am not that man, whispered a voice inside his head.

The shade took another step, but rather than move away, Jeric drew the nightglass blade and took a step forward. The shade growled, eyes narrowed. Jeric took another step, holding the nightglass steady. He feinted to the side, flicked his wrist and threw hard.

But not fast enough.

The shade leapt into the air, and the nightglass soared beneath it, out of reach. Jeric cursed, and the shade charged him. He reached desperately for his sword, Lorath, but before the shade could make contact, the stolik barreled into it, knocking it off course. It shrieked, stumbling over itself, and skidded across the frozen ground, knocking Jeric's nightglass blade even farther away.

Jeric seized the opportunity.

"Jorvysk!" he yelled, mounting the stolik at a sprint. The blade was forfeit. The stolik took off with Jeric, and they galloped straight at Jorvysk. Jeric lowered his hand, Jorvysk gripped his wrist—all animosity between them forgotten—and Jeric swung Jorvysk behind him just as the shade righted itself.

The stolik galloped on, hooves thundering over the great stone bridge, and the shade barreled after them. Jeric found himself looking hopefully to the wards, but the shade bounded across the bridge, undeterred. The wards were too faded, too gone.

Jeric wished he knew what they meant. How to use them.

He looked ahead, where Jorvysk had left his horse, but he was nowhere to be seen. Behind him, Jorvysk cursed. And the shade was gaining on them fast.

Jeric made a hard right, following the canyon, looking for a place to jump. Shades couldn't swim in The Wilds; he hoped they couldn't swim here. Water was the only reliable weapon he had left.

At last, Jeric found what he was looking for.

"Go," he said to the stolik. "Don't look back." To Jorvysk, he said, "On my count..."

Jorvysk didn't need to ask to know what Jeric intended. Jeric was already standing in the saddle, attention fixed on a lip of rock jutting over the raging Dienn.

"Are you rutting *mad*?"

"One..."

"We'll never make that!"

The shade swiped, the stolik swerved.

"Two..." Jeric steadied himself, releasing the reins.

"The water's too shallow!"

"Three!" Jeric gave the stolik's neck a good shove, urging him onward before grabbing Jorvysk's tunic and jerking him off of the horse.

They fell.

The shade shrieked.

Jorvysk screamed, flailing, smacking Jeric in the face on the way down. Down into darkness as the cold consumed them.

34

Jeric emerged with a gasp. Water frothed around him, carrying him away and dragging him down, but he kicked hard, intent on the nearest bank. Somewhere between the swiftly moving current and his own strength, he made it to a rock and grabbed hold, steadying himself against a river that kept trying to steal his anchor. He glanced back. Jorvysk's head bobbed desperately above the water, arms flailing for purchase.

Jeric was struck by a split second of irony, of another time, another place. With a resigned growl, he let go of his refuge and dove back into the water. A little later, he and Jorvysk were clambering up a rock, drenched, and choking on the Dienn. Jorvysk rolled onto his back, arms folded protectively over his stomach, eyes closed. Jeric gave him a quick once-over, just to be sure the shade hadn't nicked him, and then he glanced back at the river.

Amidst the white swirls, he spotted a large black shape lodged between two currents, its head submerged. Jeric watched it a moment, then stripped off his cloak and sword, removed his belt, which he then wrapped around his arm, and dove back into the river.

Water roared in his ears as he swam, hand over hand, pushing against the current. Swimming was much easier without his cloak and sword, but his body dragged with fatigue.

Perhaps this hadn't been his best idea.

He reached the shade, grabbed a limb and pulled. It didn't budge. He pulled again, harder this time, and the body came with it. Its skull was completely bashed in on one side—dead.

Good, that made this easier.

Jeric worked fast, wrapping the belt around the shade's ankle. Water pulled him under, but he fought on, kicking his head above water as he worked, and once the belt was secured, he swam back toward Jorvysk, dragging the dead shade after him.

Jorvysk knelt on the rock's edge and stretched out his hand. Jeric kicked hard, reached up and clasped Jorvysk's wrist, then handed him the end of the belt. Jorvysk looked incredulous.

"Take it," Jeric demanded.

Jorvysk hesitated.

"It's dead."

Jorvysk looked from Jeric to the shade's bobbing form, then reluctantly took the belt. Jeric climbed on top of the rock and took the belt from Jorvysk.

"What do you plan to do with it?" Jorvysk asked as Jeric moved, dragging the shade's form around the rock, out of the brunt of the current.

"They need to see what we're up against." Without it, he could never prove Rasmin's guilt, either.

"No way in hells we can carry that thing home, let alone haul it out of the gorge."

"We're not hauling the whole thing." Jeric pulled on the belt, dragging the shade up, feet first. "Grab its legs, but watch out for the claws. They're poisoned."

Jorvysk didn't move.

Jeric gave him a withering look. "It's not going to attack you. It's dead."

Jorvysk still didn't move.

Jeric grunted. "Here." He handed Jorvysk the end of his belt, which Jorvysk took, but the weight caught him off guard. He lurched forward, caught himself, and adjusted his grip. Once Jeric was confident Jorvysk wouldn't slip or let go, he grabbed the shade by the ankles and pulled.

And pulled.

He gritted his teeth, straining—even with Jorvysk's help—and with a final heave and a curse, Jeric dragged the rest of it onto their rock.

Jorvysk sighed and dropped the belt. "Gods... thing's heavy as a godsdamned house."

Jeric stood there a moment, catching his breath, marveling at the creature: its athletic build, the oversized bones and striated muscle, as if it'd been created for speed and power. Its inky black skin was hard as armor, and excepting the few wiry tuffs at its feet, it was hairless.

Jeric found it difficult believing this had once been a man—that this monster had once smiled and spoken and walked upon two legs. Now, its spine bowed unnaturally, grotesquely, and all four legs were equal in length, ending in bony pads of long, deadly claws.

He thought of Gerald. He was glad they'd found him before he'd become this, or Jeric never would've known his friend.

"You think the legion brought this here?" Jorvysk asked quietly.

Jeric regarded the creature. Tallyn had said the first shades were created, and Jeric suspected that whatever had been in the vial had done just that. Had Rasmin created the shades? Was he working with the legion?

Was he the *leader* of the legion? Had the necromancer been one of Rasmin's prisoners? And had Rasmin helped the necromancer escape?

Round and round these questions turned, but Jeric could not

settle on an answer. Because it didn't make sense. Rasmin held one of the most powerful positions in Corinth; why in the gods would he jeopardize that, siding with the very people he'd spent his life torturing?

"I have no idea," Jeric answered at last.

He crouched and lifted one of the shade's feet, careful not to prick himself. He squeezed the foot padding, and a black substance oozed out of a small hole at the nail's tip.

Jorvysk's gaze sharpened on Jeric. "How'd you know about the poison?"

Jeric didn't answer. He set down the claw and moved to the creature's skull, which was as large as a horse's head and shaped like some gruesome cross between man and hound. Its forehead protruded, but Jeric couldn't tell if that was natural or warped from injury. Its jaw was over-formed, jutting obstinately forward, giving it an exaggerated overbite, and the hinges swelled with knots of muscle. Its flat nose sloped sharply into its wide-set and vacant yellow eyes, and its large ears tapered into a point, the pinna opened to heighten sound. Every inch was optimized for the hunt—the kill.

Jeric grabbed his blade, held the edge to the shade's neck, and began sawing. It was like trying to cut through steel. After a few minutes of sawing, the leathery skin tore open; black blood bubbled. It took Jeric a good half hour of sweat and muscle, but the shade's head eventually dislodged. Jeric grabbed it by the ears and set it upon the rock so that its dead yellow eyes stared at Jorvysk.

Jorvysk's eyes narrowed. "Mind turning that away from me?"

Jeric moved to one of the shade's feet and began sawing it off too. He worked with extreme caution, careful not to nick himself with poison.

"I think the head's enough," Jorvysk remarked with some irritation.

"Probably."

"Then what are you doing?"

Jeric jerked the foot free and set it beside the head. "This is for someone else."

"Who?"

Someone who understood what it was. Someone who knew how to study it. Someone he'd left in the bowels of his home with his rutting brother.

When Jeric didn't answer, Jorvysk said, "You think our healers can replicate it?"

"No. Hopefully, they can use this to develop an antidote."

Jorvysk looked confused. "We already killed it. It won't be terrorizing the Blackwood anymore."

For a fleeting moment, Jeric remembered his own ignorance, and he felt annoyed for Sable.

"If there's one shade, there will be more." He knelt beside the shade's body and gave it a good shove. It tumbled over the rock and into the water, bobbing in the froth before the current dragged it under.

"How the hells do you know any of this?" Jorvysk demanded.

Jeric picked up his bloodied sword and crouched at the rock's edge to rinse it off. "Because I've encountered them before. In The Wilds."

A beat. "You were in The Wilds?" When Jeric didn't respond, Jorvysk asked, "What in the gods' names were you doin' up there?"

Jeric wiped his blade on his cloak, which lay in a soggy heap beside him.

"You better stop ignoring my questions, Wolf."

At Jorvysk's tone, Jeric glanced back.

Jorvysk's eyes flashed. "You aren't my superior anymore. We're equals. And if you don't start acting like it, I'll make sure you regret your oath."

Jeric sheathed his blade and stood, towering over Jorvysk,

who scowled up at him. Jeric flashed a smile, all teeth. "I'll try to do better."

Jorvysk's scowl deepened. Jeric turned away and wrapped the evidence in his cloak, tying it up with a knot. He scanned the banks and looked for a good spot to climb out of the gorge. He found one, secured the bundle through his belt, and motioned for Jorvysk to follow.

Thunder rumbled, and the clouds unleashed their torrents, making the climb slick, but they eventually made it out, sopping wet and freezing. It was nothing like the chill Jeric had felt in The Wilds, after almost drowning in the Kjürda. Jorvysk wanted to find shelter until the storm passed, but Jeric pressed on, intent on finding his stolik. And he did, just a few miles farther down from where they'd launched into the Dienn.

"I'll be damned..." Jorvysk said when he spotted the glorious mammal. "Thought the horses would be halfway to Brevera by now."

"Yours might be," Jeric said, to which Jorvysk grunted. Jeric rubbed his hand over the stolik, checking for harm, and the stolik's tail swished. It was then and only then that Jeric agreed to stop for the night.

They found shelter amidst a huddle of trees and built a small fire, and Jorvysk killed a squirrel, which the men ate. It was mostly bone, and the meat was tough, but it did the job. When Jeric finished, he leaned back against a tree trunk, stretched his legs, and watched the flames, occupied with his thoughts, which were rudely interrupted by Jorvysk's chewing.

"You're awful quiet," Jorvysk said, swallowing a bite.

Jeric picked up his flask and took a long sip of water.

"At least we found what's been terrorizing the wolves," Jorvysk said, wiping his lips on his sleeve. "Hagan can put that bastard's head on a pike outside the walls, beside the Scabs. Fitting if you ask me. Let it be a warning."

At the word bastard, Jeric thought of *her*.

A bastard. Surviving all those years in The Wilds because of something she couldn't help or control. And she'd become a healer. She'd spent her life helping others, when the world had scorned her. She'd helped him, when he'd scorned her too.

"So." Jorvysk sipped his water, then wiped his lips clean. "What made a *prince* decide to join the Strykers, anyway?"

Jeric glanced over.

Jorvysk tore a bite of squirrel from the stick. "Not like you needed glory." He spat grease through his teeth at the fire. Flames sizzled and hissed. "You really kill that many men?"

It hadn't just been men.

What have you become, my darling Jos?

Jeric watched the flames dance. "Yes."

"I don't believe you."

Jeric didn't argue.

"So what's in it for you?" Jorvysk continued. "You're a rutting Angevin. You have everything in the world." He made a wide arc with his flask. "You can go wherever you want, take whatever you want. There's not a woman alive who won't lift her skirts for the pretty Wolf Prince." He winked jealously at Jeric, then took a swig. "You get bored? Needed some new scenery? A new thrill?"

Jeric tilted his head back against the tree with half-lidded eyes.

"Come on," Jorvysk urged. "What happened?"

It was time to throw Jorvysk a bone before he turned rabid. The man had intervals of acceptable silence, and Jeric had pushed this one to its limits. "Nothing happened."

Jorvysk laughed and tossed the greasy stick on the flames. "All of us have a reason, Wolf. Something that led us here. Something we were running from. We join the Strykers so they can't touch us. We join the Strykers so we can still have a purpose and hope Aryn honors us in the afterlife. So I wanna know: What is the Wolf Prince of Corinth running from?"

Jeric closed his eyes completely. He would not answer this. But also…

He wasn't sure of the answer anymore.

"Is it Sable?"

Jeric opened his eyes to slits. "If you say that name—" He heard a sound in the trees. He bolted upright and grabbed his sword, eyes and ears trained on the forest.

Jorvysk looked around, confused. "Hear something…" His words trailed at a sharp look from Jeric, and he drew his sword instead.

Jeric crept out of their camp and moved deeper into the trees. The rain stopped, and the world beyond their campfire was almost too dark to see.

But not completely.

Jeric heard a quick breath and a rustle. "I know you're there. Show yourself," he commanded, taking a step.

Silence.

Jorvysk, who'd followed Jeric's lead, rounded the tree from the other side.

"Gotcha," Jorvysk growled, surprising the eavesdropper, and the person cried out.

It was a woman's cry.

Jorvysk dragged her into the light of their camp, and Jeric followed.

"Sil vai me!" she yelled. *Let me go.* She kicked against Jorvysk's pull, but he shoved her to the ground. Before she could get up, he pushed her down with his boot, holding her there.

"There more of you?" he barked.

"Noi—"

"Don't lie to me, Scab."

"Noi!" she cried out, straining to breathe. "Juss me," she said in common tongue, but with a thick accent.

Jeric believed her. He didn't sense anyone else near.

"I think you're lying." Jorvsyk crouched, grabbed a fistful of her hair, and jerked her head back, holding a dagger to her neck.

"Jorvysk." Jeric's tone warned as he stepped closer.

Jorvysk ignored him.

"I swear to gott..." the woman said. "I'm alone. Pliss—"

"And what's a Scab doing all the way out here, alone?"

She winced in pain, her jaw locked.

It could have been *her*, out here all alone.

"I'll take it from here," Jeric said.

It wasn't a request.

Jorvysk glanced up at Jeric, eyes narrowed. "This isn't your game anymore, Wolf. You'd better figure out which side you're on."

"She's alone," Jeric said lowly. "She's harmless."

"*She's a Scab.*" Jorvysk glared at Jeric, and then looked back at the woman. "You'd better talk, before I cut up that pretty face of yours."

"I saw your fire... and... I was cold..."

"Where'd you come from?"

"Davikan."

Davikan was a skal mine located a few hours' ride northeast from where they were. Jarl Rodin oversaw its operation, and he managed the Scab slaves who mined the ore, but Jeric had always used the term *managed* loosely. Rodin's working conditions were so poor, even Hagan sent men to improve them. They couldn't properly mine ore if Rodin kept letting all the slaves die.

"You escaped?" Jeric asked, wary, especially after what they'd learned about the Yllis mine.

"Yes... with two others," she said, "but they were caught... *fava*..."

Jorvysk gave her hair a hard pull. A tear rolled down her cheek. "I swear! I only wanted out of the mine..."

Jeric came to a stand before her.

She looked up at him, dark eyes wide with fear. And then the face morphed into *hers*.

He blinked, and the Scab's face returned. "Where are you going?" Jeric asked.

"Istraa."

"You're not on your way to join the legion?" Jorvysk asked sharply.

"I have no interest in war—"

"So you've heard about the legion."

"Juss rumors." When Jorvysk pulled her hair tighter, she added, "They say… the legion will set us free."

"Who are they? Scabs like you? Who's leading them?"

"I donn know, I swear! I do not wish to fight. I juss want to live!"

"Unfortunately, the two come hand in hand." Jorvysk sneered. And then he whipped her onto her back and straddled her.

Jeric went rigid. "What are you doing?"

"Teaching you a few things, Wolf," Jorvysk said, then ripped the woman's shirt open.

She cried out, writhing, trying to free herself. "Fava… Fava…"

Please… please…

Jeric suddenly felt tight—his body too confining.

He shouldn't care. Hagan took this liberty countless times—he knew that. And she was a Scab. She wasn't human. She wasn't natural. It had always been his reason for allowing it.

His excuse.

Jorvysk shoved up her skirts, and Jeric looked away.

"Don't worry, Wolf, I'll save some for you," Jorvysk jeered.

The woman screamed, and Jeric heard a slap. The screaming turned into sobs. Jeric thought of Hagan. He thought of every Sol Velorian his brother had raped and killed.

You steal from them too. We just steal different things.

Suddenly, he saw *her*. It was *her* body trapped beneath

Jorvysk's, *her* dark hair splayed in the dirt. Those were *her* sobs and *her* pleas. *Her* tears and *her* voice.

What have you become, my darling Jos?

"Might as well lie back and enjoy it," Jorvysk sneered, grunting as he adjusted himself. "It's gonna take me a while to—"

White-hot anger exploded through Jeric, and he tackled Jorvysk.

Jorvysk cried out in surprise, pants around his knees, and both men tumbled to the ground. They untangled, and Jorvysk staggered upon all fours, looking furiously at Jeric. "You rutting Scablick—"

Jeric punched him in the jaw before he could finish the word.

Jorvysk fell back and rolled away before Jeric could strike him, then climbed to his feet and threw a punch at Jeric. It was slow, sloppy, and he tripped on his pants. Jeric grabbed Jorvysk's arm, pulled him in, and rammed his knee into Jorvysk's swollen groin. Jorvysk cursed and lunged forward, barreling his head into Jeric's chest and shoving Jeric against a tree. Jeric grunted, then grabbed two fistfuls of Jorvysk's hair, pulled his head level, and slammed his forehead against Jorvysk's. Jorvysk staggered back, unbalanced, and hastily pulled up his pants just as Jeric ran at him.

Jorvysk raised his arms to ward off Jeric's blows, but Jeric did not stop. Not even as Jorvysk fell to the ground and begged him to. Not even as Jorvysk's arms fell away, and his body went slack.

Finally, Jeric sagged back, staring at Jorvysk's body. Jorvysk stared vacantly at the night, blood streamed down his nose, out of his mouth, and his jaw hung at an odd angle.

Jeric stood up, staggered back, and swallowed. He held up his hands and looked down at them. His knuckles were swollen, cracked and bleeding, and his hands were covered in blood.

Corinthian blood.

He glanced up.

The woman huddled at the fire's edge, gaping at him and trembling as she held her shirt together.

"Go," Jeric said quietly. His voice cracked. "Run south. Stick to the feet of the Gray's Teeth. Don't stop until you reach The Spine. Do you understand?"

She stared at him, bewildered. Terrified and also confused.

He pulled a small pouch from his pants and tossed it at the woman. It landed at her feet with a jangle, but she didn't move.

"Take it," he said.

She stared at him, paralyzed with fear and disbelief. She took the pouch, hesitated, and glanced up at him.

He looked steadily back. "*Go.*"

She climbed to her feet, held her clothes close, and ran off into the woods.

The rain fell.

Suddenly, the ground tilted beneath Jeric's feet. He stumbled forward. One step. Two. He staggered past Jorvysk's dead body, stopped beside a tree, and pressed his palm to the bark, steadying himself. The world spun in a blur of memories—of faces and blood and horror. All of the things he had done. All of the lives he had marginalized and stolen.

And all of the things he had done simply because he had permitted them.

What have you become, my darling Jos?

Pressure built in his chest—too tight. Blood rushed in his ears, his breaths panted, and he vomited, over and over again, until he had nothing left to give, and then he fell to his knees and screamed.

"Of all classes of the Shah, there is none equal to the Sulaziér. While all others act upon the physical world, the Sulaziér acts upon the spiritual. It is said to be the voice of Asorai himself, for it holds power over the living and the dead, and Asorai, in His infinite wisdom, will not give each generation more than one."

— The Shah, A collection of teachings according to Moltoné, Liagé Second High Sceptor.

35

Sable did not know how long she lay on the bed, staring at the ceiling. She felt numb, body and soul. Even the melodies inside of her had fallen silent.

She turned her head to the side and watched the lantern burn, its flame flickering dimly. She could set fire to her bed. End her life here and now, on *her* terms. But then she thought of Tolya.

Tolya, who'd given so much so that Sable might live. Tolya, whose dying words urged her onward still. And then she thought of Tallyn and Survak, who'd also risked their lives—possibly even given them—for hers. What a way to repay them.

She looked back to the ceiling. And then she sat up.

The Head Inquisitor believed in her power so much so that he'd convinced Hagan to send *the Wolf of Corinth* to retrieve her. If she had this kind of power—command over the living and the dead— shouldn't she be able to use that same power to escape?

Sable set the flute in her lap and turned it over. The glyphs pulsed in her hand.

They could be wrong about her. But...

But.

They could be right, and if they were, she might have a chance at freeing herself. She might even be able to free the Scab slaves and their tortured Liagé. Then, perhaps, Sorai could forgive her. Perhaps... she could learn to forgive herself.

Sable closed her eyes and held the flute, reacquainting herself with its shape. Her flute was an old friend, and like any old friend, it would take time to catch up on the life they had missed.

She lifted the flute to her lips. For a moment, she simply held it there, settling into position, letting her body uncoil. Her fingertips grazed cautiously over the holes, remembering them by name, by feel—silently calling out to them, one by one.

She settled on three and covered them with a bit of pressure, but not so much pressure that she couldn't pull back. The memory of what'd happened the last time she'd played loomed over her like a starved and feral beast.

Sable took a deep, steadying breath and exhaled to calm her racing heart. Her next exhale, she released through the mouthpiece.

An A whispered, soft and uncertain. It trembled with fear and apprehension, as if it'd forgotten what it was, or what it'd been created to do. It looked around, wondering where it should go next, and without clear direction, it faded into silence.

Sable pulled the flute away from her lips and released the rest of her breath.

The glyphs shone faintly, but the pressure within her slept.

With a bit more confidence, she flexed her bruised jaw and tried again. The A sang out, stronger this time—purer than her voice had ever been. It breathed, standing upon shaking legs, filling the little chamber with sound, and when Sable reached the end of her breath, the A reached a decided finish.

Sable let out a little puff of relief. "There, that wasn't so bad," she said to her flute.

She adjusted her fingers, inhaled again, and released a B. It warbled at first, as the A had done, but then, as if drawing confidence from its predecessor, it filled steadily out, boastful and proud, and Sable slid into a C sharp. Up the scale she played, one note sliding into the next, each stronger than the one before, until she'd gone up and down the scale and landed powerfully on the tonic.

Still, the pressure slept.

Thus emboldened, Sable continued. She moved through the scales, major and minor. Her fingers were stiff, lacking the clarity they'd once possessed, and the endurance. She'd gone through all of the scales only twice before her mouth needed a break, and her spittle started flying everywhere, but then her gaze drifted to the blood stain upon the floor, and she kept playing.

Scales soon turned into song.

The attempts were awkward at first. They tested her as she tested them, slowly discovering the correct patterns for the songs now crowding her head. Her jaw ached, and her spittle kept flying, but she pushed on. She stumbled through basic pieces she'd played as a child, which seemed to come easiest, and when she'd gone through all she could remember, she gave her mouth a short break before starting over again. She played at a laboring pace, forcing each finger into obedience, forcing her lungs to fill and her mouth to hold form. She'd played halfway through the pieces a second time when the pressure inside of her stirred.

It was a subtlety, a whisper against the invisible walls inside—the ones Ventus had cracked. She felt them then, the places where they were weak. The places the pressure slipped through.

Her next note hitched, the glyphs flared bright, and she stopped. She had no idea how this... *power* was supposed to work, or how to channel it. The Head Inquisitor had offered guidance, but she didn't want anything to do with him. Besides, if she were going to get out of here, she needed to learn to control it for herself. Without his twisted influence. Determined, Sable lifted the flute to her lips, closed her eyes, and tried again.

The pressure increased.

She held her note steady, the cracks and fissures inside of her strained like a skein too full of water. Her lungs constricted, her jaw cramped, and Sable ended her note. For a moment, she stood there, panting, her chest too tight, hands on fire. She inhaled deeply, but it didn't fill her lungs as much as it should have, and then she tried again.

The pressure surged like wildfire, and white light flared. Sable bent forward, contracting her belly, physically trying to hold herself together, but the pressure escaped through the cracks, spilled through her chest, warm and tingling, and shot her arms all the way to her fingertips.

And then...

She was in the desert, soaring over the dunes. Faster and faster, whirling and tumbling with the savage wind. It ripped across the golden sea, to where rocky sentinels stood like tables. It tore through them, over them, and dark clouds collided above. Lightning flashed, and a great drum of thunder rolled through her body like a command from the heavens. Something inside of her shattered.

Heat followed—a shock so hot, so consuming, she was certain her bones would melt.

Be strong, Imari. Do not fear, said the voice from before—the one that drew song from her soul. *For as surely as the sun rises, I will stand with you. You are my chosen, and through you, I will make a great nation. If only you have the courage.*

Sable opened her eyes and found herself staring up into the Head Inquisitor's face.

She blinked, confused and also a little delirious as she glanced around, coming to the quick realization that she was lying on the floor. Her head throbbed, and she closed her eyes. She felt like she'd been run over by a wagon.

"Is she going to be all right?" asked a voice Sable distractedly pinned as Hagan's.

A cool hand rested upon her forehead. "I believe so, but she needs rest, your grace." The hand pulled away.

Hagan made no reply. At least, none that she could hear.

Sable forced her eyes open and started to sit.

"Careful..." The Head Inquisitor placed a hand on her back to help.

She was too exhausted and pained to argue.

The Head Inquisitor crouched beside her, his face inscrutable, while Hagan stood behind him frowning. Just outside of her door were two guards holding an older slave between them. Today's consequence of her failure.

"What's the last thing you remember?" the Head Inquisitor asked.

Her stomach rolled, and she turned onto her side and dry heaved.

The Head Inquisitor looked on at her a long moment, but she couldn't read the expression there.

"Well?" Hagan demanded.

The Head Inquisitor glanced back at his king. "I would like some time alone with her, Your Grace."

Hagan's features hardened.

"She's trying as best she can," the Head Inquisitor continued, undeterred. "Allow me to employ my expertise here. If she refuses to cooperate, I will let you know."

Hagan regarded the Head Inquisitor, and a silent exchange passed between men. "See that you do," Hagan said at last, then snapped his fingers and left. His guards—and the slave—trailed after him.

Sable was too pained and exhausted to feel any relief.

"Here," the Head Inquisitor said, holding out a cup. "It's water. Drink. You need it. I'll fetch you some food as well."

She grabbed the cup with a trembling hand and took a slow sip.

"Describe what happened before you blacked out," he said.

Sable licked her lips and closed her eyes with a sigh.

"I can't help you if you don't tell me what happened."

She opened her eyes a sliver. "You mean you can't help *you*."

He crouched before her, his dark robes pooling upon the stone. He smelled strongly of incense. "Imari."

This close, Sable noted the dark splotches pillowing the skin beneath his eyes.

"I'm trying to *help* you," he said quietly. "In order to do that, I need your cooperation."

She glared at him. "You're the Head Inquisitor. Getting Liagé to cooperate is your specialty, isn't it?"

He stared back, his face a blank.

Sable set the cup down and stood. She wobbled a little and held on to the bed for support. The Head Inquisitor didn't move to help her; he simply watched with that inscrutable way of his.

Sable eased herself onto the bed with a sigh. A muscle in her neck pulled, and when she tried to stretch it, she found she couldn't turn her head all the way to the left.

The Head Inquisitor stood. "You're done for the day. We'll try again tomorrow."

Sable adjusted herself on the bed and winced from the pain in her side. "No, I'll try again *now*. Unlike you, I care when Sol Velorians die."

"No one will die, Imari. That, I swear."

"Your word means nothing," she snapped. "Nor do the gods upon whom you swear."

He regarded her in silence, then glanced away and bowed his head. "Goodnight, Surina Imari."

He snatched the flute from her nightstand, and its glyphs faded completely.

"Wait—" Sable started, but he was already gone, locking the door behind him. Sable stared at the door, and she was still staring at it when sleep overwhelmed her.

"Surina Imari...?"

She opened her eyes to the voice.

The Head Inquisitor stood over her with a plate of fruit and bread, which he set at the end of her bed. "How are you feeling this morning?"

Morning.

She had slept the day and night through.

Maker's mercy...

Sable pushed herself up to a sitting position, and her head spun. She closed her eyes, giving herself a moment, and then opened her eyes again.

The Head Inquisitor studied her with those omniscient black eyes.

She glanced at the ripe fruit and fresh bread, then back at him. "Why?" she asked.

His head cocked to the side in question.

"Why are you feeding me?" She gestured at the plate. "Why do you care if I rest? Am I some pig you're fattening up for the slaughter?"

He didn't answer immediately. "Your questions have complicated answers."

"Try me."

He didn't respond. He *was* the inquisitor, after all. He'd built his life on *inquisition*, not disclosure.

Her stomach growled. She suddenly felt too famished for pride, and she wolfed down some of the fruit and the bread, not caring that the Head Inquisitor watched her. Once she finished, he set the flute on her lap, and the glyphs pulsed to life.

"Try again. This time, I'm going to watch."

Sable eyed him. "You *do* remember what happened the last time I played before an audience."

He arched a brow. "Yes, and I should think it proper motivation for you now."

Sable frowned. "You're not concerned?"

"That you'll put me to sleep? That you'll kill me where I stand? If you run out these doors, you'll fall into the hands of a dozen guards who'll take you straight to their king, after they have a bit of fun with you first. No, I'm not concerned."

Sable scowled.

He gestured at her flute.

"My playing could still kill you," she said.

The universe expanded in his eyes. "It seems more likely it'll kill *you* first. Pick up your flute, surina."

They stared at one another. Sable, with fire; the Head Inquisitor, with the vastness and patience of the universe. But Sable's little flame was no match for eternity.

Sable set the empty plate on the bed and picked up the flute.

"Play exactly what you were playing when it happened," he said.

Sable slid her legs out of the bed and stood. Her balance swayed once, and she lifted the flute to her lips. Still, she hesitated. Her head throbbed, and she wasn't eager for a repeat of yesterday's pain.

The Head Inquisitor waited.

With a resigned sigh, Sable shut her eyes and exhaled into the flute. The note came slow and wary, and the pressure inside of her pulsed faintly.

The Head Inquisitor remained silent.

So Sable played on, warming through scales before moving into pieces. She played a lullaby first, one Vana used to sing to her. Then she played her papa's favorite anthem, but as she slid through those last few boisterous measures, the pressure warmed through her chest and the glyphs shone bright.

"Stop," the Head Inquisitor said sharply.

Sable stopped and opened her eyes, straining to stand upright from the tension now pulling within. Like strings, all tied to a central point in her belly, contracting.

He studied her, his expression granite. "Describe what you feel."

Her forehead wrinkled. "It's... hard to describe."

"Try," he said simply.

"You're the *expert*." She tossed his own word back at him. "Why don't *you* explain what I'm feeling."

If her disrespect bothered him, he didn't show it. He didn't show anything.

He folded his arms. "Yes. It's true I have decades of experience with the Shah and its Liagé, but I've never encountered one with your... particular ability. Forgive me for wanting to hear *your* interpretation."

"I forgive you for nothing."

He regarded her. "Fair. I can't expect forgiveness from one who can't even forgive herself."

Sable pressed her lips together and glanced away.

Still, he waited.

"It... starts out as a pressure," Sable said at last. "Deep in my gut."

"Is the pressure always there?"

Sable chewed on her bottom lip. "No. I never noticed it before. Not until..." Until Ventus had begun *something* in her that the voice in her dream had shattered completely.

Not that she'd admit any of that.

"Not until *what*?" the Head Inquisitor prodded.

She looked into the depths of his eyes. She wondered at all they had seen. "Not until I escaped The Wilds."

He looked at her as though he didn't believe she were telling him the whole truth, but he didn't press her further. "But it's there now."

"Yes."

"Always?"

She exhaled a slow breath. “Yes.”

The Head Inquisitor nodded once, as if jotting down a mental note. “Did Prince Jeric catch wind of this?”

At the Wolf’s name, her gaze faltered, and her chest tightened unexpectedly. “No.”

The Head Inquisitor was quiet for so long, Sable glanced back at him. And then he nodded at the flute, tucking his thoughts safely away. “Again.”

She stood there, expecting him to ask more—say more—but he didn’t. Her lips parted, giving room for a dozen questions she couldn’t voice. Like, where was the Wolf now? And loudest of all…

Did he really loathe her so much that he could abandon her to *this*?

“Surina.”

Sable glanced up.

The Head Inquisitor’s black eyes shone. “We can’t choose how we are created. We can only choose what we do with it.”

“What of *your* choice?” she snapped.

His veneer did not crack. “Choice is past. *Choose* is present.” He tilted his head to the flute. “Now play.”

Sable considered his cryptic words, then picked up her flute and played.

It was a piece Ricón had adored, of battles and loss and love. He’d always been a bit of a romantic, and she suddenly wondered if adulthood had stolen that from him. Her fingers stumbled over the notes, but she soon found her rhythm, and the pressure inside of her surged.

She peeked at the Head Inquisitor, whose face looked ghostly in the pale light of her flute, but he made no move to stop her, so she pushed through the melody, through victory and sorrow. The notes squeezed out of tight lungs as warmth spread through her chest and down her arms, and the glyphs burned bright, so bright.

Still, the Head Inquisitor did not stop her.

Sable pulled the flute away, panting and sweating, struggling to catch her breath.

"Why did you stop?" he demanded.

She looked sharply at him. "Because this is exactly what happened yesterday."

"Good. Play through it."

She gaped at him.

"Hold down your power," he said as if the solution were obvious, "And finish the piece."

"Just *how* am I supposed to do that?"

"To embrace the Shah isn't to deny it," he said, "nor should you give it dominion over you. Let it breathe, give it life. Let it flow, but give it anchor. Otherwise, it'll drift beyond your control."

"And how many had to die so that you could learn that vague bit of nonsense?"

The universe darkened in his eyes, all stars gone. "Finish the piece."

She glared at him. "You're not helping me at all."

"Neither will just standing there. *Play*."

"But how am I supposed to anchor it? *To what*, exactly?"

"Preferably upon something immovable. Most anchor it to their identity—their name. Since you won't even answer to yours"—he gave her a pointed look—"find something else that roots you. Something unshakeable. Something—or someone—foundational to who you are."

Sable's gaze swiveled to her flute.

Someone foundational to who you are.

Tolya came to mind. Without Tolya, Sable wouldn't have survived The Wilds all those years. Without Tolya, Sable would not have *wanted* to survive.

"And then what?" Sable asked.

"When you feel the Shah begin to stir, think only on that foundation. Focus on it. Let nothing else enter your mind. Force the Shah to that anchor, let it wrap tightly around it, and when you're certain the bond is secure, then, and only then, can you carry it wherever you want it to go. Otherwise, it will pull *you* down and drown you in it."

Sable frowned at the Head Inquisitor.

"It will make more sense when you try," he said.

She eyed him. "And you know from experience?"

"*Again.*"

Sable grunted but did as instructed, and the pressure surged.

Think only on that foundation... let nothing else enter your mind.

She thought of Tolya. She pictured her face, her wild hair, the sound of her voice, her eyes, demanding and impatient. She held the note longer, let it breathe, to give Tolya a moment to take hold of it. The warmth spread through her chest like strings and pulled tight, making it difficult to breathe.

Force the Shah to that anchor; let it wrap tightly around it.

Sable pushed against the restraints and forced out another note. It squeaked out of her, strangled with twine, but she held and held, spittle flying everywhere while she focused on Tolya's wrinkled face and stubborn eyes.

Take it, Sable thought with desperation. *Why won't you take it?*

The Head Inquisitor's face was the next thing she saw, hovering over her and frowning.

Sable groaned and closed her eyes. "How long have I been lying here?"

"A while." He set a plate of fresh bread and hard cheese beside her head, which, she suddenly realized, lay atop the pillow on her bed.

Sable shut her eyes against a throbbing headache, but then her stomach rolled again and her last meal came up with it.

The Head Inquisitor waited while she emptied her stomach onto the floor, and once she finished, he presented her with a rag and water. He helped her sit, and then she wiped her face and took a slow sip of water while he set the food where she couldn't immediately smell it.

"Is this normal?" she rasped, then swished her mouth with more water.

"I don't know. If you'll recall, I've never dealt with your particular brand of power before."

She looked scathingly at him.

"Go on," he said. "Drink some more."

She did as instructed, then leaned back against the wall with a wince.

"Where does it hurt?" he asked.

"Where doesn't it?" She laughed darkly, then grunted against a particularly sharp pain in her side. She closed her eyes while the sensation passed.

"What did you focus on?" he asked.

She opened her eyes.

He waited.

"A person," she said sharply.

"Who?"

"Just... someone."

He considered her. "And is he or she immovably foundational to who you are?"

Sable pressed her lips together. "Yes."

He sat quietly, then said, "Finish that cup, and let's try again."

And so it was, day after day. Sable played through pieces, imagining Tolya's face, but each and every time Tolya merely stared at her with those stubborn eyes, and Sable would wake hours later, on the floor, or, if the Head Inquisitor was feeling generous, on the bed. He advised her to find another anchor, and so she eventually tried that too. She remembered Ricón, his laughing eyes, his conspiratorial smile, but he wouldn't take hold either, rejecting her as everyone else had done, abandoning her to The Wilds. She tried Sorai next, then her papa, and her other brother, Kai, and when those didn't work, she tried the Smetts and Ivar. She even tried her stepmother, Sura Anja, but none of them took the cursed rope she'd offered.

"I can't..." Sable groaned one painful afternoon, clutching her stomach as she lay upon the stone floor. Everything ached. Her pain was a constant pulse now, as if the ropes inside had wrapped around her too many times and were slowly squeezing her to death. "I can't... do this..."

"You *must*," the Head Inquisitor insisted, crouching beside her. "You're not focusing hard enough."

Her mouth tasted like bile. "I'm focusing... as hard as I can..." She swallowed hard, struggling to sit. Her body trembled with weakness. Every day, the Shah stole a little more of her. It would take until she had nothing left. "I can't play anymore."

The Head Inquisitor grabbed her shoulders and looked hard at her. "You have to, Imari."

"Thank you, Head Inquisitor," said a new voice. "I'll take it from here."

Hagan stepped into her chamber and closed the door behind him. There were no guards with him—no Sol Velorian slave, either—but this brought her little comfort.

"She needs more time, Your Grace," the Head Inquisitor said in an angry tone that surprised her.

Hagan took one step closer, but his presence filled her small prison. "You've had three weeks with her, and we're no closer than we were before."

Three... *weeks*? Sable thought, astonished.

The Head Inquisitor stood tall. "Her power is unique—"

"Leave," Hagan cut him off, and when the Head Inquisitor did not move, he added, "I will not ask you again, Head Inquisitor."

The universe swelled and trembled in the Head Inquisitor's eyes, but at last, he bowed his head.

"Of course, Your Grace," the Head Inquisitor said stiffly. His robes rippled as he strode from the chamber and closed the door behind him.

Sable looked at Corinth's new king. Hagan could do whatever he wanted to her, and she would be powerless to fight him. She had nothing left.

His gaze moved over her, and his frown deepened, creasing the edges of his mouth. "You look terrible."

Cutting retorts clawed behind her lips, but she lacked the strength to voice them.

He took two steps and crouched before her. He gripped her chin, forcing her to look at him. He looked as though he were waiting for something, and when she simply sat there, staring numbly up at him, he grunted. "Aren't you disappointing."

She said nothing, showed nothing.

"What must I do to get your cooperation? I need your power, Imari. I need it *now*." His eyes narrowed. "What is the problem?"

She didn't answer.

He squeezed her chin harder.

"I don't..." She winced, but not against his grip. The invisible ropes squeezed around her lungs, making it difficult to breathe. "I don't know."

He squeezed her chin so hard her eyes watered. "I suggest you figure it out."

"I'm... trying..."

"*Try harder.*"

"I can't—"

He slapped her across the face.

The clap echoed in the small chamber, and the force of it knocked her on her side. Her cheek burned, but before she could right herself, Hagan dropped on all fours over her, hemming her in. Sable froze, his face a handbreadth from hers.

"You godsdamned Scab," he spat, his spittle landing on her nose. His hot breath smelled of pipesmoke and pepper as it brushed over her face, and his eyes writhed with madness.

He grabbed her hair and jerked her head back, exposing her neck. "You think the gods set you apart, but you're weak. Just like the rest of your kind. You will never be more than *this*." He gave her hair a hard pull, and she gasped in pain. "A *tool*, meant for someone better than you. Stronger than you. You are *mine*, Imari, and if you don't do what I ask, I will make you suffer for the rest of your pathetic life. I will give you children, and I will take them away. They will scorn you, as you deserve to be scorned. They will hate what you are, and through them, I will destroy the last of your kind. Then, and only then, I will let you die." He licked her neck, then kissed her jaw softly. "Do you understand?"

Sable shut her eyes tight, forcing out the feel of his cold, wet lips against her skin. "Yes," she whispered.

He let go with a shove, and she slumped against the bed. Hagan stood over her a moment, then left, slamming the door in his wake.

Yes, she thought. *The Wolf does despise me that much.*

36

"Your Grace..." one of the guards stuttered, stepping forward to intercept Jeric.

Jeric ignored him.

"Prince Jeric... His Majesty has asked—"

Jeric stalked past the startled guards, pushing through the doors and into the council chamber.

The chatter within died.

The council gaped at the Wolf Prince, who strode forward in a storm of wool and steel, his boots thundering upon stone.

Jeric's gaze swept the table of familiar faces, his eyes cutting like a scythe. There were more jarls than usual, as Jeric had expected. Hagan's coronation, and the Day of Reckoning feast that followed, would take place tomorrow evening. Most of Corinth's jarls were already in town, posturing to sniff their new king's stinking arse.

Jeric's gaze dropped on Hagan like a gavel, and Hagan's steely blue eyes narrowed. He tipped his head and smiled his most vicious. "Brother."

Jeric stopped at the table's edge and stood before his brother.

He opened the sack he'd brought and dumped his gift upon the table.

There was a collective gasp as the shade head landed on the Provincial map. It rolled over territories, smearing black blood over boundaries, and knocked over the carefully positioned figurines. Gazes darted across the table, uncertain. Beside Hagan, Astrid paled.

"I found the problem with the *wolves*," Jeric said darkly.

Hagan stared at Jeric; their gazes warred.

"What is *that*?" Hagan gestured at the gruesome sight.

"A shade," Jeric replied. Jarl Vysr frowned. Commander Anaton leaned over the head and examined it. "A creature found in The Wilds. It hunts humans—uses them to create more shades. It's not easily killed with steel or skal; its skin's like armor. We've never seen it here because it can't pass over The Crossing, and, fortunately for us, shades don't swim."

"Then what in the five hells is it doing *here*?" Jarl Stovich demanded.

Jeric looked straight at the Head Inquisitor. "Perhaps *you* want to answer that, Head Inquisitor?"

The Head Inquisitor gazed levelly at him, giving away nothing. "Your implication is misplaced, Your Grace. I'm as disturbed by its presence here as anyone."

Jeric tossed the vial at him. It landed with a plink and rolled into the inquisitor's hands. He gazed down upon it, his features tightening.

Astrid strained her neck to see around Hagan.

"I found that at Kerr's Summit," Jeric said.

"The Summit...?" Jarl Vysr said with surprise.

"What is it?" Hersir asked.

"A vial I obtained from a pack of Sol Velorians while hunting with my men. However. It was left with the Head Inquisitor for inspection."

The Head Inquisitor looked steadily at Jeric. "I never received this vial, Your Grace."

Jeric flashed his teeth. "Convenient."

"Why are we upset about a vial?" Stovich glanced from Jeric to the Head Inquisitor, impatient.

"Because I believe its contents made that." Jeric nodded at the head.

The Head Inquisitor picked up the vial, brought it to his nose, and sniffed. His eyes found Jeric, and Jeric's certainty wavered. Jeric had never been able to read the Head Inquisitor. For that reason alone, he'd never trusted the man, but this cracked even the Head Inquisitor's granite veneer.

"Are there more?" Astrid asked. Unlike everyone else, Astrid didn't seem to fear this monster. Jeric envied her strong constitution, which, he'd always assumed, sprouted from her staunch faith in the gods.

"I don't know," Jeric answered tightly. "But in my experience, if there's one, there are more."

"Where's Jorvysk?" Hersir asked.

Jeric looked over, forcing himself to hold the Lead Stryker's gaze. "He's gone."

It was as if Hersir heard the words but did not understand them. Could not fathom them. Jeric could see that he wanted details, but those details would have to wait.

Jeric pulled the Stryker ring from his finger and tossed it across the table. It swiveled as it rolled, then came to a stop before Hersir.

"You can have that back," Jeric said, then addressed the others. He couldn't bear to stand in that room another moment. "If you'll excuse me, I'm tired from cleaning up after your gods-damned messes."

Hagan's face darkened.

Jeric turned on his heels and left, slamming the door after himself.

LATER THAT EVENING, Jeric knelt before the statue of Lorath, head bowed and sword flat across his knees. He'd spent countless hours here, in this private garden, praying Lorath would bring the Sol Velor to justice—through him. That he'd be an instrument for their destruction, to bring his mother justice and Corinth honor. But now...

He did not know what to pray.

He did not know what to feel.

He did not know what he believed.

He picked up his sword and turned it over in his hands. His father had given him this when he'd come of age. It was made of the finest Corinthian skal, forged specifically for his style, his build. Hagan had been jealous. He could see Hagan's face even now, twisted with envy for the subtle preference their father showed Jeric. Not that King Tommad had loved Jeric more. It wasn't about Jeric at all but Meira, his deceased wife and the mother of his children. Every so often, King Tommad had surprised Jeric with something special, like this sword. In those rare moments, King Tommad had looked upon Jeric and remembered his wife, wanting to pay penance for his neglect.

His father had never been the same after her death. When she'd died, Jeric had lost both parents.

Jeric had named his sword after the god he understood most—Lorath. The god of justice, of vengeance and blood, of action and cunning. It'd seemed right that this instrument, given to him in light of his mother's death, should also be used in avenging her.

Now, he wondered if the name only insulted her memory.

What have you become, my darling Jos?

The air shifted. He sensed another presence at the edge of the small garden. The person waited a few seconds before approaching with heavy steps. Jeric didn't need to look to know it was Braddok.

Braddok stopped beside him, quiet, gazing at the statue of Lorath. "Heard you were back," he said at last, breaking the silence. He sounded a little offended.

Jeric didn't reply.

"Also heard you made a scene before the council."

"Hardly." Jeric sheathed his sword. "As usual, your sources exaggerate."

"You dropped a godsdamned shade head in the middle of the rutting table."

Jeric glanced up. Braddok's expression made him grin despite his mood, and he stood. The two clasped shoulders.

"Might I ask who's sharing such delicate information with a mere member of the king's guard?"

"Delicate, my arse." Braddok grunted. "You pulled that little stunt on purpose."

"I've missed you, Brad."

"Missed you too, Wolf. Things are boring when you're not around." Braddok winked.

Jeric smirked.

"I also heard you handed back your Stryker ring," Braddok said, eyeing him.

Jeric snatched his cloak from where he'd draped it over a stool.

"Is that even allowed?" Braddok asked.

"I don't care."

A pause. "Wanna tell me what happened?"

"No."

Braddok watched Jeric shrug into his cloak.

"So? Where've you been?" Jeric asked, changing the subject.

"At the Barrel," Braddok said at last, resigned to Jeric's silence on the matter. He was a good friend in that way. "Like any good king's guard."

Jeric chuckled. "Then you ought to be..." Jeric's words trailed as he sensed another presence.

He glanced back. Hagan stood at the garden's edge.

"Er, yeah. I'll be at the Barrel with the pack." Braddok gave Jeric a knowing glance. "You should join us... when you're done," he added with a cursory glance at Hagan.

"I just may," Jeric said.

Braddok gave Hagan a proper salute, crossed the garden, and disappeared through the doors.

Hagan took a step, as if entering a sparring ring.

"You left quite an impression today," Hagan said.

Hagan's ability to wrap threats in a package of silver and roses had always impressed Jeric.

Jeric smiled tightly. "I usually do. I *am* the pretty one, remember?"

Hagan stopped before Jeric, his steely grays colder than a winter sky. "Never humiliate me before my council again."

Jeric stared straight back. "Don't pin your failures on me."

Hagan took a small step closer, body coiled and tight.

Jeric rested a hand on the hilt of his sword, never breaking Hagan's gaze. "Don't start a game you can't win, Hagan."

Hagan's nostril's flared. "Whose side are you on, brother?"

Why was everyone asking him that question lately?

"The same side I've always been," Jeric growled. "Corinth's."

But even as he said the words, he wasn't so certain anymore.

"And I am Corinth's *king*," Hagan continued, his tone menacing. "Either you're on *my* side, or you're a traitor to the crown. Don't think for one moment that shared blood will keep your *pretty* head from my little garden beyond the wall."

Jeric flashed his canines. "You'll have to catch me first."

He shouldn't have said it, and he regretted the words as soon as they fell out of his mouth.

Hagan's eyes shifted. It had always been so, like some other consciousness taking over, twisting madly, sick with pleasure, and Jeric wondered what darts Hagan would throw at him now.

"Yes... so quick—so skilled with your blade," Hagan snarled. "Infamous for your skill in hunting Scabs and Liagé, yet you failed to recognize the Liagé right beneath your nose. I'm surprised at you, Wolf. Have your senses dulled?" He cocked his head to the side, eyes narrowed. "Or were you... distracted?"

Jeric watched his brother carefully, his expression impassive.

"You spent weeks with her, and yet you don't ask about her," Hagan said.

Jeric's eyes narrowed. "Why would I? She's Liagé."

Hagan regarded him. "Well, since you won't ask, I'll tell you." He paused for effect, then bent his head closer to Jeric. "I've decided to marry her. She is the daughter of the sar, after all."

Jeric's blood ran hot, a liquid inferno scorching his veins. His senses heightened, and everything focused on the life standing before him. The precious seconds before a kill. "What did you say?" Jeric asked darkly.

"I think you know very well what I said." Hagan paused. "You don't approve?"

Blood rushed to Jeric's ears. "The people will never accept her," he said. It wasn't his real reason.

"When the people understand what this alliance means for Corinth, they will. United with Istraa, we'll be undefeatable. And she'll give me strong sons," Hagan added with a smile that crawled into Jeric's mind. "I can tell by the way she fights when I touch her."

Jeric punched Hagan square in the face.

Hagan staggered back, but before he could regain his balance, Jeric hoisted him up by the collar, holding him close. He was a knife's edge from killing his brother, whose bottom lip was bleeding and already beginning to swell.

"Ah, there it is." Hagan grimaced. "I knew you felt—"

Jeric shook him hard, silencing him. "If you've so much as *breathed* on her—"

A click sounded to his left, then his right. In Jeric's periphery, archers took position upon the second-level walk.

Gods*damn*it.

Hagan had planned this. He'd expected Jeric's reaction and brought backup.

"I'd advise putting me down before one of them fires," Hagan said through his teeth.

Jeric seethed, arms shaking. His rage was an avalanche, wild and deadly, but if he gave in to it, Hagan's archers would surely end his life, and *she* would suffer for it.

With a defeated growl, he released Hagan.

Hagan stumbled back and wiped his bloodied lip on the back of his hand.

Jeric's skin was too tight, his rage leashed by a thread. He had to get out of there. He stalked past Hagan and stormed for the doors.

"Where are you going?" Hagan demanded after him.

"To get a drink," Jeric snarled.

Hagan didn't try to stop him.

Jeric spotted Astrid lingering in the shadows of the second-story corridor, watching them. Their gazes met, and she promptly turned and left. Jeric wondered how much she'd seen, how much she'd heard.

Not that it mattered.

He'd made a decision, and he didn't have much time.

37

Sable lay on her bed with the flute pulsing beside her, but she couldn't bring herself to play it. Her body was too weary, teetering on the edge of awareness, and she feared one more lapse into unconsciousness would be a lapse from which she'd never recover.

The Head Inquisitor had come to visit her shortly after Hagan. He hadn't asked what'd transpired, but his instructions had held an urgency they hadn't before.

"It will go easier for you if you figure this out," he'd said. "This... obstacle, between you and your control over the Shah. You *must* break it down, Imari."

"You think I'm not trying?" Sable had answered, having difficulty breathing. Her lungs contracted with ropes that would not loosen, and pushing against them caused her great pain.

He'd considered her. "I know you are."

He hadn't said another word, hadn't offered any new ideas. He had simply left the plate of food and started for the door. There, he'd paused. "His Majesty will be quite preoccupied over these next few days, celebrating his coronation and the Day of Reckoning. Take the time to rest." And then he'd left.

Sable had fallen asleep afterward, and she'd woken to a small cache of herbs, which had been tied neatly upon her plate. Minsing, lavender, and veroot. All responsible for promoting sleep and suppressing pain, but not in very large quantities. The Head Inquisitor probably didn't trust her with more.

With a resigned sigh, she'd plucked the leaves and added them to her water. She'd finished the glass and fallen asleep not long after, then woken to the brightly burning lantern. Her flute lay beside her, its symbols glowing faintly.

You must *break it down, Imari.*

He was right, but she couldn't bring herself to move, or care. Her body was a rock, heavy and unresponsive. And her mind...

The Head Inquisitor had been right not to give her a larger dosage.

By the wards, she was tired. So tired. Of hiding. Of fighting.

Of existing.

She wanted to close her eyes on the world, fall asleep and never wake up again.

Do not fear... The voice echoed in her mind. A sun piercing clouds. *You are my chosen, and through you, I will make a great nation. If only you have the courage.*

"Courage," she grumbled. "Courage for what? Making a nation through that monster's rutting seed?"

Of course, there was no answer.

Sable glared at the ceiling—at the voice that kept speaking ambiguously in her dreams, telling her not to fear.

Sable picked up her flute and held it like a weapon. "Who *are* you?"

Still, no answer.

"What do you want from me?" she cried in anguish. Her throat clamped down, and a hot tear leaked over her cheek, but suddenly, she couldn't stop her words. A lifetime of anger and bitterness and pain broke through her chest. "You tell me not to be afraid—that you'll be with me—then *where are you*? Where have you *ever* been? Is this my punishment for her death? *I was a child*. I didn't mean for it to happen, but it did, and I carry that with me every ruttting day of my life. So *what else do you want from me*? Haven't I suffered enough?"

Again, no answer.

Sable screamed and chucked her flute across the room. It slammed against the chamber wall with a tinny echo and clattered to the floor. She slumped forward with her head in her hands, and the tears came.

They came in a flood. Deep, wrenching sobs that tore her apart from the inside. A lifetime of pain, of regret and suffering and loneliness. Such loneliness. Her shoulders trembled with it, and her body contracted, unable to draw breath as her sorrow spilled out of her. She was breaking apart, and she didn't have the strength to hold herself together anymore.

She didn't *want* to hold herself together anymore. She'd lost all reason to.

And so she cried. She cried until she had nothing left, until the tears no longer came. Until her consciousness drifted and took the pain with it.

Imari... said the voice, like embers on a cold night.

Sable's head lolled to the side. A single note hummed in the depths of her soul, low and mourning, and her chest reverberated like a plucked string.

Imari.

"Leave me alone..." she replied weakly.

It is time, Imari.

Keys jangled outside her door.

She didn't open her eyes. She no longer cared. The door opened, and the pressure shifted in the room as a body entered. A creak of leather, and the door closed.

Still, Sable didn't open her eyes. It didn't matter. She didn't matter. If only she'd died in her sleep.

The silence stretched. And stretched.

A throat cleared.

Sable cracked her eyes open.

The sight of Braddok startled her at first—his enormous silhouette squeezed into her small chamber. He hunched forward a little, holding himself as compact as possible, as if he wasn't sure where to put the bulk of himself. He watched her with steady eyes, and she had the impression he'd entered with a very specific kind of resolve, but the sight of her had stopped him short. She wondered how terrible she looked, and what three weeks down here had done to her that would cause a man like Braddok to hold back.

Braddok looked... presentable. Clean and tidy in a way that didn't quite fit him, like a wild bear dressed in king's robes. He'd undoubtedly readied himself for the feast he was supposed to be attending.

Except he was *here*.

His eyes fixed on her cheek, where Hagan had struck her, and his brow furrowed.

"Don't you have a coronation?" Sable said roughly, wiping her eyes and pushing herself to sit up.

A beat. "Aye," he said, then tossed a bundle at her.

It landed on her bed. She didn't turn to look.

"Put that on," he said. When she didn't move, he ducked his head lower, and his voice dropped to a whisper. "You're getting out of here."

She stared at him, the words foreign. A moment later, they unfolded like new blooms, lurid and aromatic, tilting toward the sun. Drinking in light—desperate for it—but also afraid that it was nothing more than some cruel illusion.

Braddok frowned. "Did you hear me?" he said again, more fervently, and with growing concern. "I'm getting you out of here."

The clouds broke apart, and Sable looked at him, uncertain. "And going where?"

"I don't know," he said gruffly. "Wherever you rutting want to go. That's *your* business. I'm just here to help you get out. The Wolf would've come himself, but he can't miss the coronation. Not without raising questions."

Sable's heart skipped a beat. Warmth spread through her body, bright and unfiltered, and a bass note breathed deep inside of her.

The Wolf was setting her free.

"The Wolf sent you." She repeated it because she couldn't digest the words. She repeated it because she wanted to hear Braddok say it again.

"Aye," Braddok said, "and if you don't hurry, everyone at the temple will return, and we'll never get your arse outta here."

Sable turned her head to look at the bundle Braddok had tossed upon her bed. A cloak, about her size and made of expensive wool, and a pair of pants and a tunic. Sable pulled a sheathed dagger from the pile, then looked at Braddok, who shrugged and said nothing.

Why now, after all this time?

"Well?" Braddok said. "You coming or not?"

Go, Imari...

Sable staggered to her feet. Braddok's arms tensed outward, ready to catch her. She stood there a moment, testing her balance, and then, when Braddok looked certain she wouldn't fall, he turned decidedly around, giving her privacy. With careful and unsteady hands, Sable took off the simple brown—and now filthy—dress and put on the clean clothes. Her fingers fumbled weakly with the fabric, but even as she put them on, new strength thawed her stiff and frozen bones.

Hope's greatest power was replenishing the strength that despair had stolen.

She slipped into the cloak, secured the dagger at her waist, then turned to face Braddok. Her eyes felt like cotton.

He looked over her once, and his gaze settled on her bare feet. "Don't you have shoes?"

"I did."

His lips pinched together, hidden within that ruddy beard of his, and then he faced the door, listening a moment before opening it. A dimly lit hall stretched beyond, quiet and empty.

"Where are my guards?" Sable asked.

"Drinking, I'd wager. I gave them the night off. There *are* some perks to everyone knowing you're the Wolf's favorite."

He seemed pretty proud of this role.

"Won't they report you?" Sable asked.

"Better not. Or I've plenty of stories to share with His Majesty," Braddok said with a wink, then glanced down the hall. "Hall's clear. Let's go." He stepped aside to give her room.

Sable cast one last glance about her prison, and her eyes settled on the flute. The glyphs shone softly in the lantern light. She considered leaving it, but then she thought of every other time she'd tried leaving it behind, and so she picked it up and tucked it away into the folds of her cloak. She joined Braddok in the hall, and he closed the door after them.

Sable hadn't seen much of Skyhold beyond her prison; she'd been unconscious when they'd dragged her there. A few narrow corridors branched from the winding one they walked, their depths swallowed by darkness, and everything smelled cold and wet and old.

"Where are we?" Sable whispered.

"Beneath the castle," Braddok answered. "It used to be an old dungeon, but the Angevins keep their catch beneath the temple now. Except for you, it seems. This is mostly used for storage." He stopped before one dark opening, examined it, then grabbed one of the lanterns and led them into the mouth. This hall was narrower than the first, and Sable caught whiff of something foul. Her nose wrinkled.

Braddok noticed. "There's an entrance to the sewers down here. Not many know about it."

Ah. "And you know about it because...?"

"Because the Wolf and I used to steal cakes from the kitchens and hide down here."

The simple and very human confession made Sable grin.

"Ah, here we are." Braddok stopped in a crouch and set the lantern down beside a grate in the floor. It'd completely rusted with time, so she was surprised when Braddok lifted it silently and with little effort. He glanced back, noting her puzzlement. "We might have snuck out once or twice," he added with a smirk.

Perhaps she and the Wolf Prince had more in common than she'd realized.

"Now, listen," Braddok said, all seriousness. "The sewers beneath Skyhold are a rutting maze. King Tommad tried to improve them, but it ended in a mess of old and new lines. If you keep to the main artery, you'll get out just fine." Braddok bent forward, reached beneath the lip of the opening, and tugged. A rope loosed, and its end plunged into the darkness below. "The main artery isn't always obvious. It's part of the original construction. Much of it's crumbling, but you'll know it by the writing on the walls. *Apparently*, the Liagé even blessed their own scat."

Sable peered down the dark hole, catching strong whiffs of human waste. "Where does it end?"

"Near a mile outside the city," Braddok said, sitting back on his heels. "Where the Fallow joins the Miur. You'll find a horse waiting for you there, tied between the Kissing Rocks. And here." He tossed a cloth pouch at her.

She barely caught it and almost dropped it for the weight. Coins jangled. A lot of them.

"The Wolf asked me to give that to you," Braddok said. "Said it's the amount you agreed upon, plus extra for your troubles."

Sable's heart grew too large for her chest. She tucked the

coins into her cloak as Braddok set a pair of large boots before her.

"Can't have you walking through that muck barefooted," Braddok said, matter-of-factly, and also barefoot. "I've got plenty to spare."

Sable took them gingerly. "Thank you," she whispered.

He nodded once and glanced down the hole. "You'd better get going."

Sable slipped her feet into Braddok's enormous boots. They were still warm, and she suddenly realized how cold she'd been. Of course, his boots had been made for a giant, but she wrapped the strings around the heel twice, so they wouldn't slip off. She patted herself once, making sure the dagger and coin were secure, then lowered herself into the hole, supporting herself upon the first rung of a roped ladder.

Braddok held out the lantern, which she took.

"Don't drop it," he said.

"Can you get back?"

Braddok snorted. "Please. I could navigate these halls in my sleep. In fact, I think I might have once or twice..." He glanced furtively around, then looked seriously back at her. "Be careful. The sewers aren't a place for a princess."

Sable grinned up at him. "I'm a thief, remember? The shadows are old friends of mine."

Braddok grinned back.

The moment held, expanded. It was a silent truce, one of mutual respect.

"Thank you," Sable said quietly. "Tell the Wolf..." She stopped, uncertain of what to say. Of what she felt. None of it was right. None of it was enough, and all of it was complicated.

Braddok seemed to sense as much and said quietly, "I'll tell him."

She nodded once, then slowly descended the rope ladder, and Braddok closed the grate after her.

Sable's boots landed on damp earth. She held up the lantern and looked around while trying not to gag on the stench. The tunnel had been roughly hewn, glistening with condensation and dark with mildew, which made it difficult to tell if the dark splotches were stains or old Liagé writing. She held the lantern high, searching for symbols—anything that might give her direction—and then, in her periphery, she caught a shimmer. She held the lantern toward it as she approached the opposite wall, and the shimmer held. It was a symbol—one she couldn't read—but its origins were unmistakable.

It was fitting, she thought, that the writing that'd protected her all those years in Skanden would guide her now.

I am with you...

With a quick glance to the ceiling above, Sable continued on through the muck and horrible stench. Plugging her nose did little to dull the smell, so she gave herself over to simply taking quicker and shallower breaths.

But by the wards, it smelled awful.

Soft earth gave way to wet earth, and before long, she was ankle deep in sludge and waste. She found that if she kept to the perimeter, the waste was shallower, though it still leaked into Braddok's boots. She tried not to think about it, and she was glad she didn't have any open wounds on her feet.

The symbols were a constant guide, leading her down the tunnel, deeper in rock, and they kept her from turning down the dozens of tunnels that branched from the one she walked—a couple of which smelled inviting. Still, she heeded Braddok's warning, and she did not veer.

Water droplets plunk-plunk-plunked in the distance. Somewhere, a rat screeched, and something skittered past, but Sable walked steadily on. She wondered which part of the city lay above her, and then she thought of the Wolf. Not once—in three weeks—had he come to see her after leaving her with his monster of a brother, and now he was letting her go. Why? She wondered if she'd ever get the opportunity to ask him. She wanted to ask him.

She wanted to ask him a lot of things.

A noise from up ahead stopped her in her tracks. She held the lantern forward, eyes strained on the shadows ahead, but she couldn't see anything. In both directions, the tunnel vanished in darkness.

Water dripped in the distance.

Then...

Silence.

Braddok hadn't said a word about people dwelling in the sewers, but plenty of people had lived in Trier's sewers, though her papa had stationed guards to keep them out.

She pulled the Wolf's dagger free of its sheath, thankful he'd given it, and took a slow step, then another.

Hello, little sulaziér.

Sable spun around.

And Ventus smiled.

"Man walks a road that seems right to him, but only death awaits him."

— Excerpt from Il Tonté, As recorded in the Seventh Verse by Juvia, the Liagé First High Sceptor.

38

Rasmin stood before the altar, gazing upon the great statue of Aryn. Hagan had been publicly declared king. Rasmin himself had placed the crown upon his head.

"Is there anything else, Head Inquisitor?"

Vysryn was the only inquisitor who remained. The rest had returned to their private chambers beneath the temple.

"That will be all this evening," Rasmin said, gazing only at the statue.

He felt Vysryn depart, followed by a distant click as the heavy door to the Temple's underbelly closed.

And then Rasmin sighed.

Too late. He was too late. Perhaps, as he had so often worried, he'd distanced himself so far outside of the Maker's good graces that his prayers would forever go unheard.

Perhaps he'd doomed the woman to death instead.

He pressed his palm to the ivory. It was so cold, so hard and unforgiving, like the gods they represented—gods of a kingdom he'd served for three generations, searching for her.

And he had failed her.

Rasmin closed his eyes, and then he felt it. A subtle shift, a shudder to the air. It touched him like water rippling out from a source, and he smelled a faint metallic tinge.

The Shah.

He opened his eyes, lowered his hand, and scanned the hall behind him. A few hours ago, this hall had been filled with people from all over Corinth, gathered to witness Hagan's coronation. Now, shadows were the only guests, teasing and taunting as they danced upon the columns, the statues, obscuring the depths of the great dome above. Rasmin placed a hand on his waist, where he kept a nightglass dagger hidden within his robes.

Some habits were impossible to break.

"Rasyamin."

Rasmin froze.

It was a voice he'd not heard in a very long time, and a name he had not been called in even longer. He looked to the sound as a figure melted from the shadows. The figure wore all black, his face whiter than death, and his black eyes shone with triumph.

It was a face Rasmin knew well, for he had created it. A *very* long time ago.

"Time has not been kind to you," Ventus said, smiling cruelly.

Rasmin's eyes narrowed. "How long have you been here?"

Ventus's eyes glittered, and he took a step closer, admiring the statue of Sela—goddess of the harvest—beside him. "I had always wondered how you'd survived, Rasya. *If* you'd survived. I didn't think it possible, but now..." He looked back at Rasmin with condemnation. "I understand."

These were not Ventus's words. This was not Ventus's way. It wasn't Ventus's nickname for him. That nickname had been designed by another...

A dozen pieces clicked into place.

The tree. The chakran.

The necromancer.

"Azir." The word fell out of Rasmin's lips as a whisper.

It was Azir's smile, cruel and arrogant and darkly amused, on another man's face.

"Fitting, isn't it?" Azir said with Ventus's voice. "That I should come back and possess the body of the Liagé *you* created. It's almost as though you created it for me, in anticipation of this day. *My* Day of Reckoning. You always had a keen mind for understanding the prophecies, my brilliant Rasya."

Each word was barbed, like weeds, digging deeper, wrapping tight and strangling.

"And you always had a way of understanding them in whichever way suited your interests," Rasmin replied.

Azir's eyes flashed. He took a step and opened his hands. Rasmin noticed fresh ink markings upon his palms and around his fingers. "And what are you doing here, Rasya? Suiting Corinth's interest? For you're certainly not suiting the interests of our people."

Rasmin's expression tightened. "The interests of *our people*? You led tens of thousands of us to our deaths, laid waste to our homeland, and you accuse *me* of not suiting the interests of our people?"

"And I have paid for those mistakes," Azir hissed darkly. "For one hundred and forty-two *years* I have paid, shackled between worlds. You should know, Rasya. You're the one who orchestrated it."

"And I would do it again."

"You would fail." Azir took a step. "Thanks to your alta-Liagé"—he gestured at his hideous form—"I now have a power I did not possess before."

Rasmin watched him.

"It's a funny thing, your *blasphemous* creations." He said the words in mockery, as those in the past had called it when Rasmin had first displayed his creations to the people: the alta-Liagé. The ones Rasmin had made when the Maker had not provided enough.

"So many loathed you for this," Azir continued. "That you could take something so pure—given us by the Maker—and manufacture it to serve us. They would never be true Liagé, they said, and as it turns out, they were right. For I would never be able to break the Shah's bounds in my old body, but this..." He stroked his robes, admiring himself. "This does not follow natural law. This body can bend and manipulate it in ways I never could've dreamed." Azir looked back at Rasmin, eyes like an abyss. "I suppose I should thank you."

The air shuddered; the candles flickered. Shadows danced upon Azir's face, and for the first time in a very long time, Rasmin felt a prickling of fear.

"What do you plan to do?" Rasmin asked lowly. "Remind the Provinces why they should fear us? Slaughter those who stand against you until there is no one left but the Sol Velorians?"

Azir did not look away. "The Provinces *should* fear us, and they will pay for what they've done to our people. *You* will pay for your hand in it as well, but I am not the Maker. Only He can decide your judgment."

It struck Rasmin, then, that none of his inquisitors had come to check on him.

"How did you get inside the temple, Azra?" Rasmin asked, using the old name for Azir. The one he, and all of Azir's inner circle, had called him. The one that meant Redeemer. Perhaps Rasmin should've asked him this question first.

Perhaps he should have done a lot of things.

Azir's smile sent a tingling at the base of his neck.

Rasmin's fingers twitched with old memories. He no longer wore the ink on conspicuous places, and he didn't know if what he wore beneath his robes would be enough. It'd been a very long time since he'd maximized their potential, and even then, Azir had been the most skilled Saredii—guardian—of their time. That was *before* he'd harnessed the power of the thing he now possessed.

"And now, you will die with your Corinthian gods," Azir said, then crouched low, placing both palms flat against the polished black tiles. And the great Temple of Aryn shook.

Rasmin stumbled, catching himself upon the altar. Azir chanted, eyes rolled back showing only whites and teeth clenched with strain. The tile split beneath his hands, cracks branching outward, ripping through floor, climbing columns and statues like ravenous vines.

"Azir!" Rasmin shouted, stumbling his way forward. Chunks of ceiling crashed to the floor and exploded beside him. "Stop! You'll destroy us both!"

But Azir did not stop; his chants filled the spaces, ripping the very fabric of the temple apart. Lorath's stone sword fell, and Rasmin dodged as it exploded on the place he had been standing. It caught his ankle, and he yelled, trying to pull himself free. He couldn't change forms thus bound. Beside him, Aryn's marble head cracked and slid from its body, smashed through the altar, and with a final, violent rumble, the ceiling came crashing down.

JERIC GLANCED across the great hall and met Braddok's gaze.

It was done.

He felt a tightening in his chest where relief should have been.

Braddok found his place at a table beside the rest of Jeric's pack. Men with whom he'd fought and laughed. Men who shared his purpose—to rid the world of the accursed, of those who would try to destroy them.

Of those like Sable—like Imari. But Imari had not been like them. She'd spent her life *helping* others. *Not* destroying. *He* had done that.

"Your grace?" Jarl Stovich asked beside him, impatient for a response.

Jeric thumbed his mug of akavit. Astrid had requested their best brew this evening, overseeing its preparation in honor of Hagan's coronation. To show the jarls that Corinth would prosper as it never had beneath the heavy chains their father had wrapped around its heels.

Jeric picked up the mug and downed a sip, feeling it burn on the way down. "You'll have to discuss matters of betrothals with my brother," Jeric said, setting the mug back on the table. "He wears the crown, if you hadn't noticed."

"Yes, but *you* keep it shining. Everyone knows that. He is many things, but he's no fool. He listens to you."

Jeric drummed his fingers upon his glass, absently eyeing the crowd against a backdrop of chatter and lute music.

Music made him think of her.

"It's not a bargain you should refuse," Jarl Stovich continued. "I have one thousand men. Good fighters, all of them. Loyal to me. And you need them if you expect to secure Corinth and find this legion."

"You've been given an entire *hold*, Stovich," Jeric remarked dryly. "That should be payment enough for one thousand men, and you've failed to secure *that*."

He hated banquets. The posturing and subterfuge. Gods, it was all so rutting predictable. He downed another drink.

"You know it's not so simple," Stovich said with bitter bite. "My men had no heart for your father, and they've even less for *him*." He jerked a chin at the new king.

"Careful, Stovich." Jeric flashed his teeth. "He is king now."

Stovich stared straight back. "And you know as well as I that title doesn't birth affection."

"Perhaps their leader should persuade them otherwise," Jeric said darkly.

"Perhaps their king should give them reason to." Stovich eyed the Wolf Prince and leaned closer. "Show them that when our people are *murdered*, you won't wait for it to happen again before you come to their aid. That you'll work tirelessly to catch the one behind it and bring him to justice. Show them that you won't let them freeze and starve when the winter is deep and the days are short."

All of these things, Jeric's father had allowed over the years of his reign, with this legion being their most recent affliction. All of these things, Hagan would now face, for all rulers carried with them the failings of their predecessors. They either rose above it, or the weight of it buried them deep. Jeric honestly didn't know which of these Hagan would be. Hagan wasn't strong—this was where Jeric had always come into play—but he was cunning. Would that be enough?

Would Jeric help Hagan be enough?

"I am offering you Kyrinne," Stovich continued. "There isn't a man in all of Corinth who won't envy you. She'll give you strong sons." Stovich nodded in the direction of his oldest daughter, the Lady Kyrinne Brion, beloved jewel of Stovichshold.

Jarl Stovich had always wanted a closer position to the crown. He loved his daughter too much to fate her to a life with Hagan, but he loved power too much to avoid the crown completely. Hence his proposition to Jeric.

Lady Kyrinne sat at a table with other eligible daughters of Corinth—all of whom had been proposed to King Tommad as options for the two princes. Sensing their attention, Lady Kyrinne glanced over. She smiled at Jeric, as she so often did. She'd always given Jeric special attention, which he'd encouraged on more than one occasion. A few of the ladies beside her glanced over, then whispered and smiled together behind hands. No one could deny that Lady Kyrinne was beautiful, with her long, honey-colored hair, bright blue eyes, and enticing figure. A figure so full and voluptuous because it had never wanted. Hair long and shining because it had never starved. Eyes bright because they had never known horror or hardship.

She was, Jeric thought, like the jewels in Hagan's crown. Glittering and beautiful, fawned over and coveted.

Empty.

He didn't want a jewel. He wanted a sword. He wanted an equal.

He took another swig just as someone clanged a glass. Jeric, and the rest of the room, looked toward the sound. To Jeric's surprise, Astrid stood, glass in hand, smiling at the crowd and their brother.

"A toast!" Her voice rang out clear and true.

People grabbed their glasses, all eyes intent on the princess of Corinth. The musician sat back, resting his lute upon his knee. Braddok snagged Jeric's gaze and shrugged as both men looked to the Angevin princess. She rarely spoke up like this, but it was a rare occasion.

"To my brother, Hagan," she continued, looking from Hagan to the crowd. "I won't deny that the past few years have been somewhat... tumultuous with our neighbors, friendly though they are."

This earned her a few chuckles.

"We move forward into uncertain times," she continued to the room. "Corinth is fractured. Even now, many of you sit beside the very men and women you've conspired against, but celebrations bring out the best in us." She smiled, all teeth. "Or perhaps that's just the akavit."

A few less laughs this time. Some bristled.

Jeric watched her. Astrid knew better than to poke a sleeping bear.

"But," Astrid continued, "I believe we can come together. I believe Corinth can be the power it once was. A power that actually held weight in this world. One that made the people tremble, and one that"—she looked at each and every face— "had dominion over all others."

The room listened, intrigued.

Jeric sat forward with gnawing concern.

Astrid looked to Hagan, whose expression boasted with pride and affection.

"To His Majesty, King Hagan," Astrid continued, gaze steady on Hagan. "May the gods guide you as you lead the good people of Corinth through the times ahead. That they would grant you wisdom so that you may be the leader they all deserve. And that by the gods, may you claim the victory *you* deserve."

Hagan's smile stretched and adored. The people cheered, toasted and drank.

Jeric did not.

He studied his sister, running her words over and over in his mind, for they would not settle. Like sand, they slipped through his fingers, piling on the ground to bury truth beneath them.

"For this special day," Astrid continued, "I have a gift for you, brother, and if you'll allow it, I'd like the guards to bring it here for all to see."

Hagan sat forward, his interest piqued. "What is it?"

"It's a surprise. One—I might add—I went to great personal risk in finding, but... worthy for this Corinthian king."

"Please," Hagan said, swollen with ego. He was always one for grand displays. "By all means."

Jeric glanced at Braddok, who, like the others, only regarded the exchange with intrigue. And why shouldn't they? Why shouldn't a sister dote upon her brother at his coronation?

Astrid bowed, all grace and humility, then clapped her hands once. The sound cut through the silence, the doors to the hall opened, and Corinthian guards marched in. Jeric counted ten, carrying a long platform between them, its weight shared upon their shoulders. Atop the platform was a large and shining black crate made of skal, designed in solid black sheets, so that whatever lay inside couldn't see the world beyond.

Or, so that the world beyond could not see the thing within.

His skin tingled with warning, and Jeric chided himself. This was *Astrid*. The woman spent more time at the temple than the inquisitors.

In perfect unison, the guards heaved the platform upon the floor, before Hagan's table. The guards stood back at attention, clicked heels together, and saluted their new Corinthian King.

"You *have* been busy," Hagan said to Astrid, sitting forward as he admired the skal crate.

She clasped her hands together again, and the front wall of the crate fell open.

Jeric froze.

Silvery markings decorated the inside of the door—markings like the ones on Skanden's wards and on the bridge at Kerr's Summit. The old Liagé language.

A form melted from the shadows within, then another, stepping onto the warded skal ramp and into the light.

Jeric was on his feet at once.

Shades. Three of them.

A woman screamed; the crowd gasped in horror. Jarls reached for weapons that were not there, because—on Astrid's insistence—all had been forced to leave arms at the door for the new king's safety. All, that was, but the guards.

The ten guards who'd carried the platform drew swords and crossbows, bolts fixed on the crowd. One aimed at Jeric, and Jeric glanced across the hall to find Braddok in a similar predicament. Some of the guests tried the doors, only to find them barred from the outside.

One guard fixed a bolt on Hagan's face, and he raised his arms. "*Astrid*! What is the meaning of this?"

Jeric slowly and steadily reached for the blade he'd tucked into his vest, but a point dug between his shoulder blades. He glanced back. Another guard held a skal sword at his back. Through the helm, Jeric noticed a pair of furious dark eyes.

Sol Velorian eyes.

Understanding dawned, dark and terrible.

"So this is where all the missing Scab slaves and skal has gone." Jeric's voice sliced the quiet. "You're working with the legion."

Astrid turned to face him. To Jeric's horror, her skin rippled as though a dozen hands slid just beneath the surface, distorting her features, and her blue eyes turned pure black. "No, Wolf. I *am* Legion."

The sound came from another world. It was not one voice; it was many. An inhuman warp of hissing and snarling and screams, and Jeric's blood turned to ice.

Astrid spread her arms, and her gown fell free, leaving her naked. Her hips protruded sharply, and her joints looked swollen against her emaciated frame. Her body was a canvas of inked glyphs—so numerous, hardly an inch of skin remained visible—that stretched and morphed from the hands pushing against her skin.

Someone screamed. Another began to weep.

And Jeric understood. All this time, they had been searching for a legion—an army. And it *was* an army—an army of demons living in the body of *one*.

In his own sister.

"Astrid... Did the necromancer do this to you?" Jeric asked, unwilling to believe it.

But Astrid did not answer. Her eyes rolled back, and a supernatural wind ripped through the hall. Candles flickered and dimmed; shadows whispered. Dark shapes seeped from her chest, rising like vapors until they filled every corner of the hall. A tide of darkness, held back by the command of one.

"What are you doing?" Hagan asked.

His voice was not so confident anymore.

Astrid's eyes rolled forward—pure black—and they fastened on Hagan.

A shade leapt. It landed on Hagan, pinning him to the floor, and Hagan screamed. Jeric lurched on reflex, but then his world spun and did not stop spinning. He gripped the table's edge for balance, and he noticed his emptied mug of akavit.

Akavit *Astrid* had chosen for the celebration.

His knuckles blanched as he gripped the table. Of all nights to drink the godsdamned akavit.

But the shade didn't attack. It simply held Hagan there, pinned to the ground, its needlelike teeth bared while its nostrils expanded and contracted, breathing him in, eyes ablaze with hunger. Its growl rumbled through the dark and silent hall, but another force held it back, reined it in.

Jarl Bek yelled and stumbled toward the nearest guard, but a shadow swept in. It passed into the jarl like a vapor, and Jarl Bek went rigid as stone. His eyes bulged, swirling black and unseeing, and his face twisted in horror with a bloodcurdling scream. And then his eyes seemed to dissolve into tendrils of blackness, become a part of it, then suck inside as the inky shadow gathered itself and poured out of his open mouth. Jarl Bek's body crumpled, his skin ashy white and stained by a web of black veins, and where his eyes had been, only empty sockets remained.

Lady Dona—the jarl's wife—screamed.

The shadow soaked itself back into Astrid's naked body. She shuddered as the spirit entered, then sighed and relaxed her shoulders, as if absorbing it had given her strength.

No one dared move.

Jeric gaped at his sister, sickened, and suddenly, the last remaining detail clicked into place. "You *are* the necromancer."

Her head tilted in a sharp and unnatural way, and she smiled. It was not her smile. It belonged to something else.

All this time, they had been searching for a necromancer and a legion, but they were one and the same. His sister, an Angevin with Corinthian blood, *somehow* possessed Liagé power, and she was using that power to steal lives—a *legion* of lives—and pull them inside of her body. Feeding off of their energy, to make herself stronger, more powerful, and then using those lives—those spirits—to do her bidding.

"Astrid…" Hagan cried out in desperation, still pinned beneath the shade. "Please…"

The shade lifted a long, gnarled finger and began carving into Hagan's cheek. Hagan cried out in pain as he squirmed and writhed in its grip. Finally, the shade gnashed its teeth, backed away, and returned to Astrid's side. Hagan stumbled to his feet, using the table for support, and Jeric spotted three red lines on each cheek. Like Corinth's inquisitors. Already, the lines were turning black.

Hagan looked painfully, furiously back at their sister as black and red trickled down his cheeks. "Why…?" The word squeezed with betrayal.

Astrid regarded him. There was nothing human in her eyes, and when she answered, her voice was a distortion of many and one. "You don't really want me to answer that *here*, do you? What will everyone think of you then?" She said a tsk-tsk-tsk, then stopped before him. "For so many years I hated myself for what you did to me."

Jeric suddenly wondered something he had never wondered before. He recalled the subtle looks, the awkward intrusions and harried exits.

How often he had caught Hagan in Astrid's chambers.

"But then I discovered the light," Astrid continued. "I discovered a purpose greater than *everything,* and I realized how *small* you are." She paused, regarding him with something like pity. Invisible hands snaked down her bare back, and the shadows whispered. "I now have the power to take from you what you love most, just as I took it from Father." Her voice deepened, layered and distorted. "The power to take away the only god you have ever truly worshipped: Your *self*." Her teeth flashed. "*You are mine*."

39

Sable lay bound and gagged upon the ground, with sewage soaking her clothes and hair. She watched three Sol Velorians dressed in Corinthian arms care for their weapons. This was the second time Ventus had caught her, but she didn't think anyone would rescue her this time. The one man who might probably assumed she was riding away on a horse by now.

She glared at the ceiling. *Really? You're going to get me out of my prison, only to deliver me to Ventus?*

Ventus hadn't lingered. He'd ordered his men to secure and watch over her, but he hadn't said more than that. Sable didn't know what he intended, or what these guards were waiting for, but whatever Ventus had in mind, clearly he couldn't be bothered with keeping watch over Sable, nor risk letting her go.

So there she was, lying in sewage, trying to figure a way out. On the bright side, if there was a bright side, the sewage wasn't as deep here as it'd been in other places. The men had taken her dagger and flute, and they spoke only to each other, keeping their voices low as they spoke in their native tongue—a language she knew, though their dialect differed from Istraas. Sable wanted to talk to them. They were supposed to be on the same side, and by some of the glances cast in her direction, she thought they wondered it too, but they wouldn't dare override Ventus's command.

How Ventus had come to be in command of an army of Sol Velorians, Sable could not figure out. How he was alive, Sable did not *want* to figure out, either, because that might mean Tallyn hadn't survived.

One of the guards leaned back against the wall and held her flute to the light of the torch, which they'd propped against the wall. His dark eyes flitted to her, curious and also patronizing.

"What's an Istraan doing with a Liagé flute?" he asked his fellow in their language, though his eyes lingered on Sable. "You a *ziér*?" A troubadour.

The taller guard, whom Sable pinned as the trio's leader, cast her a perfunctory glance. "It's not your job to care, *kushka*."

The guard holding the flute scowled at the dark glyphs. "It's got *skárit* all over it. Being caught with an object like this would get you killed up there." He nodded to the world above them.

Sable wanted to remind them of her current position, but, for obvious reasons, she said nothing.

The taller guard cast him an irritated look, then joined the third and stockier guard a few paces ahead. The two of them bent their heads together, discussing something quietly. The man with the flute regarded Sable, then pushed off the wall, shoved the flute in his pants, and approached.

She did not look away. To look away was to give him dominance.

He crouched before her, amused, then tilted his head, studying her. "What does he want with you, eh? A court musician?" His eyes searched, then became mocking. "You are a pretty thing. Perhaps I'll have you play privately, for me." He stroked her cheek with the back of his hand.

Sable jerked away and yelled into the gag. The other two guards glanced back.

"Juvé!" the tall one barked. "Leave her."

The man called Juvé smirked at Sable. He patted her cheek and returned to his place at the wall, but he didn't look away.

And then the world shook.

What in the wards...?

The men cried out in surprise, and the man called Juvé fell on his rear with a splash, cursed, then scrambled back against the wall. Chunks of rock and dirt rained down, and Sable curled into a ball.

When she thought the caves couldn't possibly bear any more, the trembling stopped. The men cursed, and Sable opened her eyes to pitch-black. She straightened her body, and her fingertips knocked against a rock. It must have fallen during the strange tremor. She felt around it, and, to her delight, her fingertips grazed a sharp edge.

One sharp enough to cut her ties.

She got to work in the darkness while the men struggled with the torch, and by the time flame bloomed, Sable had sawed through the bindings on her wrists. The tall guard looked sharply over at her, appraising her for damage. Sable only glared back. Seeming satisfied, he moved on and discussed rapidly with the others.

Sable set to work on her feet, and she cut through the rope just as the men broke apart. She tucked her ankles behind her, out of immediate sight as Juvé resumed his station across from her. His eyes taunted, but he eventually grew bored, pulled a small tuft of herbs from his tunic, rolled it, and lit it with the torch.

Heshi. It was a scent she hadn't smelled in years. Smelling it now transported her to hot desert nights, arid verandas, and rustling ferns.

"*Now*?" the tall guard growled.

"What?" Juvé cut back. "I'm tired of smelling this scat."

"He's got a point," said the stockier guard. "May I?" he asked, approaching Juvé.

The tall guard's expression soured, his eyes flickered past Sable, and then he set his attention ahead, in the direction Sable had come from—the direction Ventus and the rest of his Sol Velorian army had gone.

Juvé held out the herbs, and the stocky guard took a long pull. His eyes rolled back, his lids closed, and he exhaled a slow puff of smoke.

"Siéta, that's a good blend."

It was a *strong* blend, by the smell of it.

"Don't take all of it, *dásha*!" Juvé said, reaching for it.

The stocky guard stepped back, teasing him with it, and Juvé smacked him on the back of the head. He handed it over with a snicker, and Juvé murmured something Sable couldn't hear.

"Who's your dealer?" the stocky guard asked.

"That, my good man, is a secret. But I'll tell you what. Once we're done here, perhaps I'll—"

A rock clattered up ahead, and both men froze. The tall one strained to see in the darkness. Juvé looked at Sable, who glared straight back, daring him to blame her for the sound.

Which, of course, she had caused.

But they hadn't seen her throw the rock. They'd been too enthralled by their heshi.

"Saluté?" the tall one called down the tunnel. "Ventus?" He exchanged a look with the stocky one, who joined him to investigate.

Leaving Sable with Juvé. As she'd hoped.

Sable yelled into her gag, and Juvé looked over.

"Quiet," he hissed.

Sable yelled louder. Juvé stalked toward her, and Sable readied herself. She'd have to move quickly.

With one hand, Juvé gripped her by the tunic and jerked her up, her face inches before his.

"I said—" His eyes widened as he realized her arms were free, and Sable grabbed the heshi from his hand and shoved the burning end to his face. He shrieked in pain and let go.

"Hei!" yelled one of the other two as they spun around and sprinted toward her.

Sable kicked in Juvé's knee, and he screamed. She shoved him back and snatched her flute from his belt. The glyphs illuminated at her touch, and she shoved it inside her tunic to hide the light, then grabbed the torch and shoved the flame into the mud and sewage, plunging them all into darkness.

Someone cursed. Juvé cried out in agony.

Sable pressed herself to the wall, waiting. The shadows would hide her, as they had always done.

"Where's the torch?" the tall one growled.

"She broke my leg!" Juvé yelled.

"I'm going to break something else if you don't shut up, *kurjit*!"

Sable didn't move, didn't breathe.

A footfall squished, followed by suction. Then another. The stocky one was close. Getting closer.

She could feel his warmth, smell the heshi on his breath.

And then he was standing right before her.

In her mind, she envisioned his body, his height and his build. She didn't need light to navigate. With a quick breath and a prayer, she kicked low, striking his legs. She felt his knee give as he cried out, but before he fell, she grabbed his tunic and slammed her knee into his head.

Boots splashed as the tall man charged.

She ducked on instinct. Metal slammed against rock above her head. She rolled away and shoved the stocky man into the tall man's path. He tripped over the stocky man with a growl, and Sable navigated around, positioning herself behind him.

She heard their breathing. Two labored, one furious. Her ears pinned on the furious. It moved away from her, then closer, debating and unsure.

She waited, heart pounding, trusting the shadows to hold her and keep her safe.

And, perhaps, trusting a higher power.

"Enough of this!" he snarled impatiently. "You won't make it far. We've taken the city, and the others won't be so kind."

"You call this kindness?" Sable said, unable to help herself.

His footsteps squished closer.

"You're following a monster," she spat.

"That *monster* is going to help the legion free our people," he snapped, slowly approaching. "Perhaps you should reconsider which side you're on."

Legion. They were all working for some legion. Even Ventus. But who was leading it?

"I'm not on anyone's side," Sable said. "You're all the same. Corinthian. *Sol Velorian.* Slaughtering your way to the top. All you're proving is that you are *exactly* what everyone feared."

"They *should* fear us," he growled, closer. "After everything they've done to our people. But I wouldn't expect a little Istraan *zier* to understand."

He reached for her, but she heard him a split second before he moved. She leaned aside and jammed her elbow up. Bone crunched, and he gasped with surprise and pain, then wrapped his arms around her and slammed her into the wall. She hit with a grunt, her flute fell out of her shirt, and his large hand grabbed her neck, squeezing.

Beside her, the flute pulsed dimly in the muck.

His dark eyes widened on her. "It glows for you."

She clawed at his hands, gasping for breath. She couldn't answer, even if she wanted to.

He squeezed harder. "*Why* does it glow for you?"

She kicked him in the groin. He cried out, his grip loosened, and she slid down the wall, snatching her flute before ducking away from him. He charged her in the dim light, and at the last second, she whirled around and slammed her glowing flute against his temple.

His fight left him with a soft cry, and he collapsed with a squish and a plop.

"You might be surprised at what I understand," she spat at him.

"Niran?" one of the other two called out, squinting in the pale light of her flute.

Sable felt around the tall man's body for weapons and found two daggers, an Istraan star, and a sword. The sword she left, but the star and daggers she took, as well as the man's baldric, which she slung across her back to carry her weapons.

"*Vindaré*." Traitor.

Sable glanced back to find Juvé glaring at her.

"You betray your own people," he snarled. "You will regret this."

"I regret a lot of things, but this won't be one of them." She held up her flute and looked ahead, in the direction she needed to go to escape. Where a horse and one thousand crowns waited for her. Where she could run and hide and survive.

Sable closed her eyes, feet rooted to the spot.

It was all she had ever done. All she was doing now. Running from herself. Surviving as another. *Existing*, but never truly living.

Alone.

But it could never be how it was. She was different now. She knew the truth. And then she thought of the Wolf...

Prince Jeric.

Jos.

He was up there, facing whatever storm Ventus and the legion had unleashed.

I will be with you...

The flute warmed in her hand. She opened her eyes and ran.

40

"You killed father," Jeric hissed, clenching the table for support.

Astrid turned to face him, eyes pure black, inked skin rippling. The shadows above teased lower, whispering. Candlelight sputtered, struggling in the darkness.

It struck Jeric how different she was from Imari. Both of them had supernatural power, but they'd chosen two completely different paths.

"*Wolf*," she said like a caress. A shadow slipped by in breeze of whispers, grazing his skin, its touch like ice. "I thought certainly the greatest hunter this generation has ever known would've pieced this together a long time ago. What a disappointment you are."

Another shadow brushed past.

"I'm disappointed too," he said through his teeth.

Her head cocked to the side, sharp and unnatural.

"What do you want?" he spat. "The throne?"

She stepped toward him, and the hands roamed beneath her skin, stretching and distorting the glyphs. "You think I do this for a lump of skal?" Her voice perverted into many; her eyes flashed white. "Even the Wolf is no different. So... *small*, like the rest of them."

A shadow hissed, darkness blurred, and the wound in his side seared like a branding iron. The hall vanished, and suddenly, Jeric was drowning.

In blood.

Tumbling and choking and gasping for breath. There was no up, no down. Everything flared red.

Red.

Red.

Horrifying, murderous red.

All the blood he had shed, all the lives he had stolen. They all played in his mind—every kill, every agony. Every torment he had caused, and he felt them all. The misery he'd unleashed upon so many was now his alone to bear, and it weighed him down like an anchor, pulling him deeper.

Drowning him.

You are nothing, snarled a voice, warped and without tone.

Jeric screamed, but only blood rushed in. He clawed, but his hands found no purchase. He opened his eyes, but he could not see through the red. His lungs burned without breath, and he felt himself falling...

Falling...

Sable bolted in the direction she'd come, one hand clutching the flute for light, the other holding a dagger. She paused only to check her steps, and before long, she reached the ladder she'd climbed down. Thankfully, it was still intact.

She shoved the flute in her belt, then clenched her dagger between her teeth and climbed. The muscles in her side pulled a little where Ventus had stabbed her, but the fire of determination gave her strength and pushed her on. When she reached the grate, she stopped to listen, then pressed her palm to the cold metal and pushed.

It didn't budge.

She pressed harder; still it didn't budge. Slipping one arm through the ladder for support, she pulled the dagger from her teeth and wedged the tip in the gap around the grate. She wiggled the knife back and forth, trying to pry it open, but then the grate opened wide and golden light momentarily blinded her.

"Cou'za qué—"

Sable stabbed the dagger into the man's foot. He cried out in pain as she pulled it free, and then he reached for her. She ducked back, grabbed his arm, and used her grip on the ladder to pull him through. He fell with a cry, flailing, then landed on the soft earth below. He didn't get back up. She hoisted herself through the opening and closed the grate after her.

Silence.

A lantern burned ahead, casting gauzy light upon the tunnel walls. But, so far as she could tell, the tunnel was empty.

She crept forward, dagger in hand, ears pinned on her surroundings. She remembered Braddok's story about stealing cakes from the kitchens, so she knew there had to be an entrance to the fortress nearby. She reached the end of the corridor and peered around.

The tunnel beyond lay empty, the darkness muted with soft and flickering torchlight. A force tugged on her chest—like a plucked string—urging her forward. Trusting it, she hurried forward, turned left as the sensation grew stronger, made a few quick rights, and before long, she reached a winding stone stair.

She followed the stone stair, careful to keep her footfalls silent, and the air grew steadily warmer, fresher, until she reached a great oak door. There, she paused, listening, and opened it a crack. Two silhouettes waited ahead, their backs to her.

Sable checked her flute, which still rested securely in her belt, slid her dagger into the baldric, then slipped through the door. She crept steadily forward, keeping to the edges of the hall, eyes fixed on the Corinthian guards and hoping the mere smell of her sewage-covered body wouldn't give her away. Thankfully, they didn't hear or smell her—not until she slammed a marble bust of Aryn into the shorter one's head. He cried out and collapsed as the second one whirled on her, but she kicked him in the groin and pushed him back into a drapery. He gasped, trying to untangle himself while Sable shoved him against the window, her dagger at his throat.

His dark eyes narrowed on her, angry and confused.

One of the legion's, then, but wearing Corinthian armor, which concerned her.

"Where's Ventus?" Sable demanded.

"Who are you?" he demanded instead, his accent heavy.

She shoved the blade harder against his throat, drawing blood.

"The great hall!" he said through his teeth.

"Where's the hall?"

He grunted. "Up ahead. Second left. But you won't make it—"

Sable slammed the hilt against his temple. He collapsed in the drapery, unconscious, and Sable ran on. She had no idea what she was going to do, but she had one advantage: No one knew she was here.

She ducked into a niche and pulled off Braddok's stinking boots. Stealth would be easier without his shoes, and she felt more comfortable in bare feet besides. When she reached the second left, she paused to look. Beyond was an open room holding a pair of heavily guarded doors. Sable counted eleven guards, all dressed in Corinthian arms.

She ducked back around the wall, thinking hard. She couldn't get in through the main doors, but she'd passed doors to a garden, and she got an idea. Quickly and quietly, she retraced her steps, pushing through the doors and into the night. It was a shock of cold, dry air after the dank and drafty places she'd dwelled the past month, but it was fresh. The garden was dark, and a starlit sky twinkled above, a strange beauty despite the evil festering within Skyhold's walls. She scanned the shadows and silhouettes, tracing the outline of a pale statue until she found what she was looking for.

Three stories above, overlooking the garden, was a wide veranda with glass doors leading to what had to be the hall.

Sable bolted, testing the vines on the lattice beside it before climbing. The veranda's edge was still just out of reach, so she took a deep breath, patted her flute and her weapons to make sure they were secure, and jumped.

Her fingers caught stone, gripped tight, and started slipping.

Her finger joints strained as she held her body tight, legs close. At the last second, she whipped her hands open and lashed forward, gripping the base of the railing, securing herself.

She loosed a breath, then pressed a foot to the wall perpendicular and held position. She couldn't hear anything through the glass doors, so she pulled herself up, inch by slow inch, arms and shoulders burning, until she was high enough to peer over the veranda and through the glass doors.

To where Princess Astrid stood, naked and covered in inked glyphs. Shadows hovered thickly all around her, weaving in and out of her skin, and three shades crouched at her feet.

Sable almost lost her grip and fell.

Astrid?

Astrid was... Liagé?

Was *she* the necromancer?

It didn't make sense. Astrid was *Corinthian*. Liagé power only went to those of Sol Velorian blood. How could she possibly...

And then Sable remembered Tallyn.

Tallyn hadn't been born Liagé, but he'd been made into a crude representation of one. Someone could have given power to Astrid. But as Sable gaped at the eerie shapes seeping in and out of Astrid's naked body, she remembered the story Chez had shared—his grotesque descriptions about how the Corinthian people were found—and Sable realized another horrible truth. The necromancer did not lead a legion. The necromancer *was* a legion.

A legion of spirits.

They writhed around her body, melting from her skin but also tethered to it. As if they were trapped in this world, anchored to Astrid's body and bound to her command.

Sable wondered why Astrid needed them, but the answer dropped into her mind as if put there by someone else: Their life force increased Astrid's power. She was stealing spirits from the living, drawing them into herself, feeding off of their life to make herself stronger.

This was the storm—the torrential rain and lightning and thunder of which she'd been warned. This was why the voice had asked Sable to have courage, and as that thought took hold, a humming inside of her grew louder, drowning out all else. It was a cry from the heavens—a bass note swelling inside her body, deep and resonant—urging her to act, to intercede. Her nerves burned with it, enflamed with new purpose and light.

She had to stop this. Somehow.

Sable hoisted herself over the rail and slipped nearer the doors, keeping to the shadows while taking quick inventory of the hall. Hagan slumped upon the floor with three black lines dripping down each cheek. Shade poison. She spotted Jeric's Wolf pack amidst the guests—weaponless like everyone else, except for the guards under Astrid's command. Not that normal weapons would do anything against the power Astrid now wielded. But where was Jeric?

Sable looked back to Braddok, who stood stone-still, gazing at something Sable couldn't see because Astrid blocked her view. And then Astrid stepped aside.

Sable's heart stopped. The note inside of her blared, deafening.

Jeric was on his knees, eyes squeezed tight, fists pressed to his temples. Astrid moved around him in a circle, speaking things Sable couldn't hear. Jeric fell upon all fours, his face crimson and swiftly turning purple.

Because he couldn't breathe.

Sable threw open the doors.

Astrid's head turned back. Her black eyes fixed on Sable, and the spirits beneath Astrid's skin hissed. A cold wind ripped through the hall, and the candles sputtered out. All light left the room—save one: Sable's little flute. It shone like moonlight, dispersing the shadows and casting ethereal light over everything it touched.

"There you are, little sulaziér."

The voice chilled Sable to the bone. It wasn't human. It was a legion of sound.

"I had hoped we might work together," Astrid continued in that inhuman voice. "But I've no need for you now. My chakran's found another."

So Astrid *had* sent the chakran after her. Then who had it possessed instead?

The veranda doors slammed shut behind her, trapping her inside. Darkness reached for her in wispy fingers, as if to drown Sable in their evil tide—a tide Astrid had created.

Do not fear…

The note inside Sable split into a chord, and she raised the flute to her lips.

"You're going to play for us?" Astrid said, taunting. A face pressed against Astrid's stomach from the inside, warping the skin, and then it was gone. Behind her, Jeric collapsed. "You think a simple song can defeat *us*?"

The shadows surged in a roll of whispers. Some guests cried out and some dropped to their knees, trying to shield themselves from the encroaching black tide. Shadows grazed Sable's arms, their touch cold as ice. They hissed at her, whirling like vapors, obscuring her view of the room—her focus—and the chord inside of her pushed against the backs of her lips, demanding release.

I am with you.

Sable closed her eyes and exhaled into her flute.

The note breathed low and soft. And so very... *un*demanding.

Ice grazed her neck, but she held on, urging the sound louder as she slid into the next note. The flute warmed her hands, but the pressure inside of her slept. She thought of Sorai, her laugh and her innocent smile. The power surged. It squeezed her lungs, but Sorai turned away from her, and Sable's chest constricted.

Take it, Sable insisted.

But Sorai did not take it.

Sable's lungs burned for breath, and her consciousness began to slip. She ended her note, gasping for air. Confused. Her power was supposed to work this time.

Astrid laughed. It was a corrupted sound, distorted and evil, and then she began a chant, inked arms raised high. Astrid's head tilted back, fingers splayed to the shadows.

The shadows churned like storming clouds, whirled into a cyclone, and plunged toward Sable.

They pushed against her, trying to get inside. Sable wrapped her arms around herself, but the shadows were a hailstorm, pelting her with ice, relentlessly searching for a way in. A point of weakness.

One slipped in. Winter bloomed inside her gut and iced through her veins. Her breath stuck, the edges of her awareness dimmed, and just when she thought she would never breathe again, the pressure inside of her burst.

It flooded her in a fury of heat, searing through her chest, her limbs, her gut, melting the ice. It filled her fingertips and toes, pressing against the bounds of her body, building and building until she thought she would explode, and finally it pushed through, a needle puncturing cloth.

Light exploded from her body, filling the room—blinding. A hundred dissonant voices shrieked, glass shattered, people screamed.

The light dimmed, and Sable glanced up.

Astrid snarled and bent forward, arms clutching her chest, pained and distracted. And Sable charged.

She ran at Astrid with everything she had, colliding with a force that knocked both women to the ground. Glass shards dug into Sable's side, but the guards didn't fire; they couldn't get a clear shot. The shades didn't attack; they wouldn't risk their master. The shadows cowered, wounded and scarred from Sable's light.

It was just the distraction Jeric's men needed, and, to Sable's relief, they snatched it up. The room erupted in chaos.

Astrid hissed, clawing at Sable's face as Sable pinned her down. A guard took aim and Sable dropped, pulling Astrid into the line of fire. In her periphery, Braddok tackled the guard, then made his way to Jeric, who crawled upon all fours, heaving.

Astrid snarled and clamped her hands around Sable's wrists. Sable tried prying herself free, but Astrid's grip was iron. Desperate, Sable swung her elbow across Astrid's jaw. Astrid's grip loosened and Sable scrambled free, but an invisible force launched her into the air.

Sable cried out in surprise as she arced through the air, then smashed into a table. Candles toppled; cutlery crashed to the floor. She staggered to her feet, dizzied and confused, and looked up to find Ventus smiling cruelly back at her.

Sable's eyes widened with realization. "The chakran found *you*."

Ventus snarled, and another force sent her flying. She collided with a column, her head slammed back hard, and pain split her skull. Ventus only smiled as he steadily approached.

"Kill her," Astrid commanded.

Jeric yelled at Braddok to intercept, but shadows swooped like vultures pecking at a carcass. Astrid turned her attention back to Jeric, and Jeric dropped to his knees, gasping for breath.

An invisible force gripped Sable and flipped her on her back. She tried to get up, but she couldn't move. The force pinned her to the tiles. Ventus raised a hand, curling his fingers, and Sable's throat squeezed. A breath squeaked through her lips.

"You think yourself the Maker's chosen," he sneered. "You will never play again, little sulaziér."

The Maker's chosen...?

The edges of Sable's vision darkened, and her lungs screamed for breath. Suddenly, wings flapped overhead, and a figure materialized between her and Ventus: Rasmin, the Head Inquisitor.

Sable stared in shock as owl feathers morphed impossibly into the Head Inquisitor's cloak, which was torn in many places, and there were bruises and scratches all over Rasmin's face.

The pressure on Sable's lungs released, and she rolled over, wheezing to fill her lungs.

Ventus looked annoyed. "I forgot that bit about you, Rasya."

Rasya? Did they know each other?

"Stop this, Azir," the Head Inquisitor snarled. His expression held a fury Sable had never seen. "You will destroy us all."

Azir?

"Not today," Ventus said. "Today, you will die, once and for all." His fingers splayed before him.

Sable threw the Istraan star. It struck with a wet and sickening crunch, and blood dripped between Ventus's eyes. Ventus's eyes scathed her, and in a whirl of silver, the Head Inquisitor cut off Ventus's head.

It dropped and rolled upon the floor, but before Sable could feel a moment's relief, inky darkness seeped from Ventus's severed neck, and the air turned sour. It was the same stench she'd smelled in The Wilds. The stench of the chakran.

And as Sable watched, the chakran coalesced into the shape of a man and poured itself right into Jeric.

41

Jeric staggered forward, once. Twice. His body jerked, as if his limbs were strung to the hands of a puppeteer who'd suddenly yanked on his strings, and then he collapsed to the tiles.

"Jeric..." Sable panted, staggering to her feet.

The shadows pressed in, and people screamed. The Head Inquisitor thrust his palms to the sky and chanted words Sable had never heard. Every syllable shook with power, as if he'd gathered all the vastness from his omniscient gaze and focused it on his words.

To Sable's amazement, the shadows hissed and recoiled, trapped behind some invisible ceiling that the Head Inquisitor had created.

Astrid snarled and chanted louder, a counterargument to the Head Inquisitor's spell. Their voices battled; their commands clashed. Each word was power, and the air sizzled with it—electric. Light speared across Rasmin's barrier. The shadows screeched and roiled, but still, they could not crash through the magical barrier Rasmin was weaving. He held them back with a diffused net of power—one that sparked white like lightning each time a shadow grazed it.

Braddok and the rest of Jeric's pack tried to sneak closer to Astrid, but her shades walled them off.

Jeric's eyes opened like shutters, but behind the glass, only darkness shone. He blinked once, and the darkness dissipated, leaving blues behind.

But they did not *see.*

Sable took a hesitant step closer. "Jeric...?"

He climbed to his feet. His movements were systematic, testing each joint, flexing each muscle. He curled each finger one at a time. He turned his hand over and observed his bloodied palm as if he didn't understand why it was red.

"Jeric, *answer me*," Sable demanded.

His head swiveled toward her. His eyes locked and focused. There was nothing familiar in them.

"You will die, sulaziér," Jeric said, but it was not his voice. There was no cello, no warmth. It rasped on the edges, charred and malignant.

And Sable hated it. "Shouldn't you be dead?" she snarled at the thing inside of him. "How many rutting wards is it going to take to send you back to hell?"

Jeric's eyes narrowed. He picked up his sword and took a predatory step toward her.

Sable took a step back. Glass shards stabbed into her bare feet, but she hardly felt them. "Jeric... It's weakened! You can fight this!"

There was no recognition on his face. Nothing at all that made him human.

In the corner of her eye, she saw Braddok trying to get to them, but he was locked in battle between two Sol Velorian guards and a shade. Astrid's attention was forced on the Head Inquisitor, who stubbornly held back the roiling tide, though he'd dropped to one knee, palms still raised to the sky. He couldn't hold the shadows back much longer.

Jeric prowled toward her with a vicious snarl.

Sable stepped back but bumped into the wall. "Jos," she tried another angle, searching his eyes. Searching for *him*. "Don't let it win. You are stronger than this! Fight it!"

His eyes burned with malice, and then he stormed forward and backhanded her.

She slammed into the tiles with so much force, she skidded back a few paces. She rolled onto her stomach, wincing in pain, knowing at least two of her ribs had broken. She forced herself upon all fours just as Jeric grabbed her shirt and yanked her up, so that her feet dangled above the tiles.

"Jeric..." Sable clawed at his hands, choking on her breath. "Stop!"

He laughed. It was a cruel sound, strangled and corrupt, and then he shoved her back.

Sable went flying through the air until she slammed into the throne and bounced down the steps. Her spine popped, her ribs screamed, and she yelled as she tried to shove herself up, but her arms gave out and she collapsed.

She heard him approach, step by slow step. She gripped the steps, trying to breathe—trying to hoist herself to her knees, when something glowed at her feet. Her flute.

You must come back, Imari. They need you.

Sable blinked, and suddenly she saw the desert. Dunes gleamed gold, and a hot, angry wind kicked at the sand.

It was the scene from her dreams.

The sky bruised with terrifying clouds, blotting out the sun and casting the dunes in darkness. Rain fell in a torrent; lightning flashed.

This was the point when Sable had always awoken, when the voice would speak her name. But the voice did not speak, and the scene did not end.

This time, the sun burst through clouds like great burning arms, splitting the sky apart with its light, its fire. The clouds fled in fear, racing to the horizon until they were nowhere to be seen, leaving only light.

And then Sable saw the palace in Trier. She saw herself, as a little girl, standing upon the rooftops, face tilted toward the brilliant sun, arms opened to the sky. Waiting to be embraced and accepted.

Waiting to be forgiven.

Finally, Sable understood. She realized why her power had overwhelmed her, time and time again. Because it had never been meant for Sable.

It was meant for Imari.

It was meant for the girl who'd been born to the desert, the girl who'd climbed the palace rooftops, the girl who was wild and daring but also kind. It was meant for the girl who'd held her head high, who didn't live in fear—the girl Sable had rejected and scorned, because it'd been easier to hide from what she'd done than it was to stand and face it.

I am with you.

Sable did not know for certain whom the voice belonged to, but now she had an idea. She picked up the flute.

"You really believe you can defeat me?" Jeric sneered. "*You*? A skinny, pathetic, *weak* little girl?" His eyes flashed. "A murderer?"

Do not fear...

Sable shut her eyes and raised the flute to her lips. Imari turned her face toward her, watching from the rooftops.

Sable arranged her fingertips, trying to find the right holes. Imari remembered.

"For you, Sorai, my little desert bloom," Sable whispered. A tear leaked over her cheek.

"For you, Sorai, mi á drala," Imari echoed.

Sable breathed deep. Imari filled her lungs.

Sable exhaled, pouring every ounce of herself into the flute, letting her spirit fly away to the stars. Free.

And Imari played.

"Stop." Jeric took a step. His voice had lost its jeering.

The notes wrapped around her, through her, filling her with hope, with light. It chased away her pain, her regret and sorrow. She was all of the things she had done, but she was also none of those things.

They were her past; she'd allowed them to rule her present; they would not control her future.

"I said STOP!"

The melody lifted her up, carried her above. Weightless.

And Imari touched the sky.

The notes stitched her together, past to present, and a great calm washed over her. Every breath reached deeper than her last, each note richer, full of color and life. The notes wove through the night, touching the moon and stars before soaring back to the hall, now strengthened by the power that existed beyond herself —beyond everything.

The very same power that had spoken to her in her dreams.

And then she heard a new melody, one that mixed with her own. Every beating heart, every inhale and exhale. A patter of drums, the whispers of breath, the shrill of spirits. The hall was a symphony, pulsing and crescendoing with the sounds of humanity, tainted by evil—she heard each and every one.

The shadows shrieked, unable to bear her music. But then the symphony changed, and where her ears had heard only shrieking, her soul heard voice.

They were crying out to her—every spirit Astrid had stolen with her power. They writhed in agony, trapped in this world, a place where they should not be, tethered to her with strange black fire.

They wanted help. And Imari would help them.

Her music soothed their agony like a salve, and her notes fell like rain upon their chains of fire. The chains sizzled and charred, but still they held firm.

Astrid commanded the guards to shoot, but they did not. Could not. Imari held them all wrapped in the fabric of her music. The room was her tapestry, woven in threads of a song she composed.

And the music grew louder.

The walls shook with it, amplifying her notes like an echo chamber, and the floor quaked. Bits of plaster cracked from the walls and ceiling, falling to the floor. Finally, the spirits' chains disintegrated. One by one, Imari's notes touched them and set them free. Shadow become light; agony became peace. Each point of light morphed into a tranquil face just seconds before fading away.

Rasmin crumpled. Still, Imari did not stop playing.

Jeric collapsed before her. He writhed on the ground, and the chakran leaked from his mouth like ink, leaving Jeric motionless upon the tiles.

This spirit was not like the others—this chakran, Azir. It did not agonize; it didn't cry out for her. It yearned for *this* world, and she felt its anger like a forge. It reached for her, but the glyphs on her flute flared bright. Light sliced shadow, and the darkness screamed. It writhed and it wailed—the cry of a thousand dissonant strings. It shriveled in the light, trying to hide with nowhere to go, unable to escape the melodic chains of light Imari's flute wove tightly around it. With a final burst of power, it broke free and plunged into Hagan's body.

But Hagan's body had succumbed to shade poison. He jumped upon all fours, snarling with madness, shaking his head as if he could shake out the thing now invading his poisoned body. He yipped and he screamed, clawing at himself, and in a galloping motion, he ran at the veranda doors and jumped over the railing. The other shades followed him.

A second later, Hagan's screaming fell silent.

Astrid yelled in fury, fists pressed to her ears. More shapes melted from her body, and with each shape that fell, Astrid appeared more gaunt and frail. Imari caught each shape with her notes, punctured them with light, burned their chains, and set them free.

With a defeated roar, a thick shadow ripped itself from Astrid's body and rushed Imari in a twist of smoke. But in Imari's light, the smoke caught fire. It was a dried herb scorched in flame, edges charred and curling, until it was no more than a wisp of ash, drifting to the tiles.

Well done.

Imari ended her note, the light faded to a dim glow, and she collapsed.

42

Jeric stood before the door to Astrid's prison, gazing through the bars at his sister. Or what remained of her.

The princess sat upon a pallet the guards had laid out for her, her back erect, legs folded, and fingertips draped over her knees. They'd covered her in a simple Corinthian blue robe, but Jeric couldn't shake the memory of her naked body, flesh gaunt and pale and covered in glyphs, as shapes slithered beneath her skin. They did not slither now, but the image had seared into his mind forever.

Astrid's pale eyes stared at the wall, unseeing. She was a form without life, a face without expression, and where there had once been fire in her eyes, now there was nothing. By all accounts, the woman who had been his sister was no longer there.

"Leave us," Jeric instructed the guards.

There were ten stationed before her door and five more at the end of the hall. The door itself was warded—an artifact of another time pulled from the now crumbled inquisition chambers, though it had miraculously survived. Jeric didn't know if it would be enough, but it would have to suffice. At least until he decided what to do with her.

The guards bowed and stepped away to give him privacy but waited at the end of the hall with the others, close enough to intercede should their new king meet any trouble.

King.

He could hardly believe the mantle he'd been given. It had always been a possibility—one he'd trained for all his life. He just hadn't really expected it to happen, or so soon. Least of all, the way it'd transpired.

For generations, the Five Provinces had feared Angevin blood. Now he was all that remained. He and Astrid's empty shell.

Jeric pressed his lips together. "Astrid."

Nothing. No blink, no breath. No flicker of recognition. She sat like one of the statues in Aryn's temple—a temple that no longer stood.

"Astrid, *talk* to me," he pressed.

She did not. Would not or could not, Jeric couldn't tell. He didn't know if she was buried deep inside, or if she still possessed power as a necromancer, and he couldn't ask the one who might know—the Head Inquisitor. Rasmin had flown away that night, and no one had seen him since. Jeric still searched the sky, but he never spied an owl.

Jeric flexed his hands around the bars and leaned in close. "Let me help you, Astrid. You don't have to hide anymore."

Nothing.

And then her head swiveled toward him. The emptiness in her eyes sent a shiver down Jeric's spine, but she didn't need his fear. She needed his strength if she were to come back.

"Hagan is gone," Jeric continued. "He can't hurt you anymore. I'm sorry I didn't know. That I wasn't there for you. But I swear to the gods, Astrid... I won't let *anyone* hurt you again. Please. *Talk to me.*"

Her head cocked to the side. She blinked once. And then, she stood.

Jeric watched, wary.

She took slow steps toward him, those vacant eyes never leaving his, and she stopped an arm's length away, as if unwilling —or unable—to draw any closer to the door. Up close, the emptiness in her eyes chilled him to the core, because it wasn't human. Jeric didn't know what it was. Where *she* was. He reminded himself that the door was warded, and that Imari had ripped the legion from Astrid's body, leaving her severely weakened.

Or so he hoped.

Astrid lunged. Too fast, her fingers caught his, trapping him against the bars. Her nails dug into his flesh, and she hissed, her face contorted with madness and evil.

Jeric bared his teeth, straining to pull his hands free, but she was too strong.

Behind him, guards shouted and sprinted. And then she let go. She tipped back her head and laughed. It was a wicked sound, maniacal and crazed.

The guards reached the door, placing a barrier of skal and steel between Jeric and his sister.

Astrid looked absently at her fingernails, now pocked with flecks of Jeric's skin and blood, then she licked them clean. Without another glance in Jeric's direction, she returned to her pallet and sat down in the same position. Statuesque. Vacant.

Jeric gazed down at his hands, marked by little red crescents, and breathed deeply.

"Wolf!" called a gruff and very welcome voice behind him.

Braddok jogged down the hall with purpose, but that purpose waned as he took in the guards crowded before Astrid's door. "Everything okay down here?"

Jeric lowered his hands, hiding Astrid's claw marks. "For now."

"Good." Braddok met Jeric's gaze and nodded once. "She's awake."

Jeric froze.

Braddok grinned. "She's still a little hazy, but she seems all right. Remembered my name. Asked a ton of questions. I was planning to let you explain everything, but she's as godsdamned persistent as you—"

Jeric brushed past him.

Behind him, Braddok grumbled.

Jeric strode down the corridor, bounded up the stairs two at a time, and ran out of the dungeons. Braddok hurried after him, ducking around guards and servants, trying to keep pace with Jeric.

"Have you told him?" Jeric asked over his shoulder.

"No, I went to find you first."

"Get him," Jeric said.

"Sure you don't want me to wait a bit? Give you two some privacy?" Braddok asked with a prominent smirk.

"She is the surina of Istraa," Jeric said lowly, and with more than a little bit of irritation. "Not some godsdamned courtier."

"Yes." Braddok snorted. "Trust me. I'm more surprised than anyone that *she* ended up in your bed."

Jeric stopped so suddenly that Braddok almost bumped into him.

At the dark look on Jeric's face, Braddok held up placating hands. "All right, all right! I'm going. Can't promise I won't take a detour." He winked and retreated down the hall.

Jeric watched him go. Maybe he shouldn't have moved Imari to his private chambers. He'd wanted her there because it was the safest place in Skyhold, and he'd moved to his father's chambers, but rumors were dangerous things. Jeric sighed, turned down the hall to his chambers, and stopped at the door.

He took a deep breath, stepped inside, and closed the door behind him.

IMARI WATCHED the large and crackling fire, burning in the enormous hearth. It brought warmth to Jeric's chambers, where, according to Braddok, she'd been sleeping for the past two weeks.

Two weeks!

By the wards, she needed to stop making a habit out of unconsciousness.

Braddok explained a little of what'd transpired after she'd collapsed. He hadn't intended to, but Imari had assaulted him with questions, and as it turned out, Jeric's boulder of a friend had a heart soft as pastry dough.

And also, he was grateful that she'd saved his friend when he could not.

She learned that Hagan had jumped to his death over the veranda. The other shades had made it a little farther, bounding to the drawbridge and leaping into the canyon, where they had drowned in the river below. After a good amount of fighting, Jeric's pack and those loyal to Corinth had eventually subdued and captured Astrid's Sol Velorian soldiers. Astrid had been placed in a dungeon, as well as her followers, and they were all awaiting judgment from Jeric—who was now Corinth's king.

Imari didn't know how to feel about that.

Braddok promptly left to fetch Jeric, and so Imari forced herself to get up. It wasn't as easy as she'd anticipated. She slipped her feet from the bed onto the rug and wiggled her toes. Her power slept, though she felt it deep within, burning like the embers in the hearth, ready to rise, should she need it, but contained. A power she no longer feared.

She didn't know what to do with it, or how best to use it, but she didn't need to hide from it anymore. And maybe now it would lend her body strength where her muscles failed. So, she stood.

Her knees gave out; she cursed and grabbed the bedpost for support.

Apparently, it wasn't *that* sort of power.

"Come on," she growled at herself, using the post to steady herself. "*Walk*."

A robe had been left for her on the bed. It was a deep Corinthian blue, made of fine silk and lined with fur, and she slipped it on over her nightdress. Two of her ribs screamed when she raised her arms, but she charged on, using pain to fuel her body and wake it up. The fur slid over her skin, wrapping her in comfort, and so she pulled it closer, reveling in the sheer luxury of it. It'd been a long time since she'd worn anything half so extravagant.

Eventually, her legs cooperated with her all the way to the window, where she stood, gazing at the world beyond. The sky was winter gray, and a sharp wind rattled her window, trying to get inside. From here, she could see Skyhold's sprawling city, its impressive walls and high gables, all of them dusted with snow. Beyond that, the feet of the Gray's Teeth Mountains were visible, jagged teeth obscured by clouds, like some sleeping monster.

Imari didn't hear the door open. She didn't hear him step inside or close the door behind him, but she felt him there—felt the air shift around him. She heard his heart like a distant gong, deep and steady—a timbre that belonged only to him—and something inside of her responded to it. Like a string plucked, ringing out softly in answer to his call.

She glanced back.

Jeric stood before the door, gazing steadily back at her.

In that moment, she knew she would've done it all over again: jumped on his horse, pulled him from the Kjürda, and brought him back to humanity. She would've endured his wrath and fury and imprisonment—*risked her life* for him, without hesitation—all for the treasure of gratitude filling his eyes as he gazed upon her right then.

He'd replaced his traveling clothes with fine black leathers, trimmed to his lean and muscular build, and his sun-streaked hair had grown longer, too—long enough, now, to comb back, sharpening the strong lines of his painfully handsome face. Exertion heightened the color in his cheeks, and Imari wondered if he'd sprinted here.

"Hi." It wasn't her best response, but it was the only one that came out.

"Hi." His voice rang unsteadily; his jaw clenched and unclenched. "How are you feeling?"

"All right, I think," she replied. "You?"

"Alive, thanks to you." He took a step forward. "Imari."

He said her name like a promise, a discovery and a beginning, and she liked the sound of it on his lips, with his accent.

"Jeric," she said, then added, "Or should I call you Highness now?"

He took another step forward. His eyes pierced. "Just Jeric."

"Well, Just Jeric. I'd give you a proper curtsy, but two of my ribs are broken. So you'll have to pretend."

An imperceptible grin touched his lips, and he took another step, closer to her. "No, you wouldn't."

"You're right. I wouldn't."

He approached steadily, eyes never leaving hers, and he stopped just within reach. He might have touched her for the way her pulse responded.

"I believe this is yours." He withdrew her flute and held it between them like a truce. "I didn't trust it with anyone else."

She hesitated, then took it, and her fingertips brushed his. The glyphs pulsed to life at her touch, shimmering with moonlight. Imari worried Jeric would flinch away, but he did not. He stood there, gazing down at the object with curiosity and wonder, and the silvery light reflected in his eyes.

She was glad he didn't fear it.

"Did Rasmin give that to you?" he asked.

"No." She turned it over, trailing her fingers over the holes. There was a marking below the last hole that she'd never seen before. It was new. She wondered what it meant. "Ricón—my brother—he gave it to me as a gift when I was a child." Her brow wrinkled with memory. "Neither of us realized what it was. It didn't glow back then."

A beat. "And you kept it all this time?"

"Not on purpose," she said. "I tried getting rid of it, but it... kept finding a way back. So I hid it in the floorboards of my room. It's what Ventus found. It's the real reason he captured me that night."

By the wards, it seemed so long ago.

She felt Jeric's eyes on her as she tucked the object into the inner pocket of her robe, out of sight.

Her eyes met his. His gaze brushed over her face but hitched on her jaw, where he'd struck her while possessed. The red in his cheeks deepened, a muscle feathered in his neck, and when his gaze settled back on hers, there was a fire in them that hadn't been there before. "I will never forgive myself for how I've treated you. For bringing you here. For leaving you alone with him."

She didn't say it was all right; it wasn't. But then, he wasn't asking her to.

She clutched the robe closer, and the flute pressed against her hip. "What changed your mind?"

It was the question that'd been burning in her mind since the moment Braddok had set her free, and it was the one question Braddok hadn't been able to answer.

Jeric's brow furrowed. "I killed someone. One of my own." He scraped his bottom lip with his teeth. "He was... trying to hurt a young Sol Velorian woman. And all I could see was your face."

Imari didn't miss that he'd said Sol Velorian—not Scab.

"So I killed him." Jeric raised his hands, curled them into fists, and opened them, his expression haunted. "Every person I've killed... I remembered them all. Every single one of them. I saw what you saw. I saw what I am. What I've done."

Imari watched him, quiet, unable to believe what she was hearing, but unable to deny the raw conviction in his voice.

He lowered his hands and looked back at her. The intensity in his eyes gripped her tight, held her still. "There are two sides to this war, Imari, but it will never end if we don't stop feeding it."

Imari looked back and forth between his eyes, which were full of determination and resolve. "What are you going to do?"

"Set the Sol Velorians free."

Imari stilled, her lips parted. "All of them?"

"All of them."

If he did that, it would completely destabilize Corinth. As far as Imari was aware, Corinth relied on those Sol Velorian slaves for the bulk of their hard labor. "Can you even do that?"

"That's not a question I ask."

Imari grinned, then asked, "What about the ones who helped Astrid?"

He glanced past her, at the window. "I'm setting them free."

Imari blinked. She remembered the guards in the tunnel, and she wondered if they'd survived. "But Jeric... they hate you. They hate Corinth. Who's to say they won't try again—"

"They hate me because I have hunted them and slaughtered them," he said fiercely, looking back at her. "Relentlessly. Ruthlessly. I can't fault them for fighting back, for trying to take the freedom I've denied them. I won't forget what they tried to do, but I won't punish them for it. Not this time."

Imari marveled at the Wolf King, wondering how a man focused solely on his sense of justice had become one of incomprehensible mercy. "What about the Liagé?" she asked. Meaning: what about *her*?

Jeric heard Imari's unasked question. His eyes didn't leave hers. "They go, too."

His words settled in the slip of space between them, and Imari's chest filled with hope.

"You're not concerned about their..." She hesitated, then stood tall, accepting it. "*Our* power?"

"Oh, I am. What you have... the Shah... it terrifies me. Because I don't understand it." His gaze drilled into hers. "I am powerless against it. I thought wiping it out would make the world safer, but all it did was create Astrid." He clenched his teeth and looked back to the window, this time with regret. "I have to let it go. I have to believe there are more like *you,* who will use it for good."

Imari grabbed his fist, unfolded it, and slipped her fingers through his, holding on tight.

His hand warmed hers, and he didn't pull away.

"I'll see if Istraa can help," she said, wondering how, exactly, she would do this as the words tumbled out of her mouth. She hadn't spoken to her family in ten years. But Jeric would need all the help he could get, if he were to follow through with his plans. "Obviously, I can't make promises yet, but... I'll do everything I can to make sure you're not alone with this." She squeezed his hand tight.

He squeezed hers back and met her gaze.

And suddenly, looking up into his deep blue eyes, she remembered their kiss. When she had been Sable and he had been Jos. When neither of them were who they'd claimed to be, and if they'd known the truth, it never would've happened. Their world didn't allow for it. But it *had* happened, and Imari wasn't sure what to do with it. What she *should* do with it.

"It's so obvious now," Jeric said quietly. His gaze brushed over her face. "That you're the daughter of a sar. I don't know how I missed it before."

"Don't be too hard on yourself. Anyone looks like royalty with a bath and a fancy robe." She gestured at herself.

Jeric smiled, showing his teeth, and Imari's heart forgot a beat.

Someone knocked on the door.

Jeric took a liberal step away from her and let go of her hand.

She wanted to take it back.

"Come in," he said, as though he already knew who stood on the other side of that door.

Imari didn't have a moment to wonder. The door opened.

And Ricón stepped through.

43

Imari's heart stopped.

So often she'd dreamt of this moment, if she were ever reunited with her family. Her brother, especially. But her dreams could never fill the gaps of time—could never predict how the years would shape his appearance, his person. His ponytail fell to his waist, and there was a scar across his brow that reached precariously close to his left eye. She wondered how he'd earned it. His face was squarer now, structured by the strong bones that reminded her so much of their papa, and his muscles filled out his frame handsomely, drawing him up straighter, more commanding.

But despite all the changes—all the years that'd transformed her brother from adolescent into man—his eyes hadn't changed. They were warm and dark and loving, and pouring over with regret as they took in the sight of her.

A little squeak of air escaped her lips, and she took a step forward. "Ricón..."

His eyes glistened with emotion, and suddenly Imari was crying, unable to stop the tears. Judging by the look on his face, those years had been as hard on him as they'd been on her. And her tears fell harder.

She started for him but her legs wobbled and gave out.

Her brother was there to catch her. He wrapped his arms around her, held her tight, but not too tight. His next breath trembled, and his chest shuddered against her. He was grieving, too.

For a long time they stood there like that, the world lost in their embrace, until Ricón pulled back and held her face between his hands.

"Sano mondai..." he said. *I'm sorry.* "Sano ti mondai, mi a'fiamé..." *I'm so sorry, my little flame.* His words caught on emotion.

Imari remembered the Smetts. She remembered how she'd yearned for someone to love her so fiercely.

Ricón did.

"I never should've let them take you," Ricón said fiercely, in their language. "I should've hidden you away—anything, other than stand by like I did..."

Imari placed her hand over one of his. "You were a boy, Ricón. Don't blame yourself," she replied in their language, though she stumbled over the words, the accent. It'd been so long. Like her flute, this, too, would take time.

"Is everyone... well?" she asked, suddenly starved for any and all information concerning their family.

"Yes..."

"Papa and Kai and Vana... and Anja, they're all—"

"Yes, yes, mi a'fiamé." He smiled sadly, kissing her hands and wiping a tear from her face. "They're all fine."

"How did you get here so quickly? Trier is at least two weeks from here—even for you, *tazaviem.*" Lightning rider—an old nickname. "Did you fly?"

Ricón chuckled, then clasped her hands and backed away to look at her fully. "Sieta, look at you. You're beautiful. For a little chimp."

Imari laughed, then snorted on snot.

"And still lacking the manners befitting a surina, I see," he said, all smiles.

"And *you* still haven't answered my question," she replied, stabbing him in the chest with her finger. It was much harder than she recalled. "How'd you know I was here?"

"The Wolf sent for me," he said.

Her heart squeezed. She looked for Jeric, but he wasn't there. He'd slipped out of the room without her notice. "When?" she asked, swallowing a lump.

"Two weeks ago."

Right around the time he'd set her free.

"Does Papa know?" she asked.

"No. The letter was addressed to me. I showed no one. I didn't think Papa would let me leave if I asked." He paused and touched her face. "Not because he doesn't want you home, mi a'fiamé. He hasn't been the same since he sent you away, but it is dangerous for *me* to ride into Corinth, when Istraa is..." He stopped himself. Words crowded behind his lips, but he did not release them.

"What is happening in Istraa?" Imari asked.

His brow furrowed. "It's... complicated. I'll explain more on our journey home. But I told Papa that I was leaving to check the weak points in our border."

"You weren't concerned it was a trap?"

A mischievous smile curled his lips. "Oh, I was. But I wasn't about to ignore it... not after spending my life doubting myself for letting them take you away. So, against the wishes of Jenya and my men—"

"Jenya?" Imari asked.

"She is Saredd."

The Saredd were Trier's most esteemed warriors, and they were traditionally men.

"A *woman*?"

Ricón grinned. "*Sei*. You'll meet Jenya soon. And the others. I trust them with my life." His expression changed; his eyes searched. "The Wolf is not at all what I expected."

"He wasn't what I expected, either," Imari found herself saying.

Ricón studied her, thoughtful, and then said, "Sieta, Imari. There's so much I've missed... I want to know everything. The good. The terrible." He squeezed her hands. "And I especially want to know how in Nián you've earned the Wolf of Corinth as an ally."

The implication in his eyes warmed her cheeks. "It's... a long story."

"I'm sure," he continued, watching her intensely. "Imari... I want more than anything to bring you home. I've wanted to since the day they sent you away. But... is that what *you* want?"

She held his hands tight and gazed into his eyes. "*Yes*. I miss the desert, Ricón. I miss its heat and its rains—I miss *you* most of all. For so long I denied myself the right to desire it, because of what I did, but I've finally come to terms with that." Here, Ricón squeezed her hands. "I will not hide anymore. I want to come home."

He pressed his forehead to hers with a sigh. A decade of tension released with that one breath. "You will not face it alone, mi a' fiamé. Let's get you home."

IMARI DIDN'T SEE much of Jeric the following week. After what'd transpired during Hagan's coronation, Corinth's jarls were in a fit, claiming the Angevin line had forfeited its right to rule and challenging Jeric's position as king. This was made especially tumultuous when Jeric announced his plans. Jeric's pack didn't leave his side for a moment; they followed him everywhere as he traveled to local towns, trying to garner support from those who remained loyal to him.

Imari kept to the castle, with Ricón and his Istraan escort. They were all free to roam as they pleased, but, in light of current political tensions, Jeric advised they stay within the fortress' walls. Imari didn't mind. Her body was still weak from the power she'd exhausted, plus it gave her time to catch up with Ricón.

He'd explained what'd happened after their papa had smuggled her out of Istraa. Ricón had wanted to write, but he'd been forbidden. He'd even snuck a few letters, but they'd been discovered and promptly confiscated. Their papa had reprimanded him severely for it, warning him of what could happen to Imari should anyone connect her new identity to their family. For that reason alone, he hadn't penned another letter, but he'd never stopped thinking about her, wondering if her new life had wilted the spirit he had loved so very much.

Thankfully, he said, it had not.

Thankfully, she said, he had not seen her one month ago.

Imari visited Astrid. Jeric had mentioned his encounter with his sister, but the princess showed no improvement. She simply sat there upon her pallet, staring vacantly at the space before her. Imari asked to go inside Astrid's prison, but neither Ricón nor Jeric would have any part of that. So Imari was forced to stand behind Astrid's warded door, trying to get the Corinthian princess to respond. The whole thing left Imari uneasy. She wished Tallyn were there, or even Rasmin, just so that she might get some insight.

And then the day came for Imari to leave. She dressed in a combination of culture, with her Istraan leather pants made from a wildcat and a soft spun tunic—both items Ricón had brought. They were slightly large, but he hadn't known her size.

Her boots, Jeric had specially made for her by a local cobbler, and he gave her a beautiful fur-lined cloak of Corinthian blue that'd belonged to his mother.

"I can't take this," Imari said.

"Why not?"

"This belonged to your *mother*, Jeric."

"And she'd be proud for you to have it," he said simply. "It wasn't made to sit in a chest collecting dust." He held it closer. "Take it. I want you to have it."

Resigned, she took it from him, and he helped her put it on.

His eyes moved over her appraisingly, and he nodded, pleased.

"Horses are ready," a gruff voice spoke, and Braddok appeared. He met Ricón's gaze, and both men stood a little taller. Both were heroes in their own right. Whatever their differences, they'd respect each other on the grounds that made them great across all cultures: their loyalty, faithfulness, and skill.

What a gift it would be, Imari thought, to have men like this on the same side.

Jeric's pack stood a few paces behind Braddok. Ricón's men and Jenya—a stunningly fearsome woman—stood a few paces behind Ricón. All of them watched the exchange of nations, ready should lines be crossed.

"You have my gratitude," Ricón said to Jeric with a thick accent, then extended a hand.

Everyone watched, silent.

Jeric took a step closer. The wind tossed his hair. "You have mine, Sur Ricón." He gripped Ricón's hand firmly.

The two men shook, and the tension released. They let go, and Jeric turned to Imari.

Her heart drummed louder, and suddenly, she didn't want to leave. It was all happening so fast, and she'd barely gotten to talk to him. How could she say goodbye to him now? In front of everyone?

He stepped close. In her periphery, Ricón looked on.

"Imari." Jeric's voice was a brush through her hair, a stroke against her cheek despite the respectful distance he kept.

Without thinking, Imari moved closer and touched his face,

her palm to his cheek. His eyes locked on hers. For Imari, they were the only two people in the world.

"You are a good man, Jeric Oberyn Sal Angevin," she said quietly, and his jaw flexed a little. "And you will be an even better king. Despite how fate brought us together, I will always be grateful for you."

"For which part?" he said. "The broken ribs? Or almost dying on multiple occasions?"

She grinned. "Definitely for when I was the most wanted woman in all The Wilds."

Jeric smiled.

She lowered her hand and slipped something into his. He glanced down at the tiny pouch she'd placed there.

"Seeds from an Istraan star," Imari said. "A *real* Istraan star. If you plant them, I'm sorry to say they won't bloom in weapons. And please don't mention this to your herbalist. He still doesn't know they're missing."

Jeric looked back at her.

Maker's Mercy, she wanted to kiss him again, but she wouldn't. *Couldn't.* He was no longer Jos, and she was no longer Sable. And princesses couldn't go around casually kissing kings in front of the world. That sort of behavior started wars.

Instead, she tucked his fingers around the pouch. "In Istraa, the blooms represent rebirth and renewal, just as the sun rises each new day. I..." It seemed silly now, her reason, but she pressed on anyway. "I thought it might be something to encourage you in the uncertain days ahead. I believe in you, Jeric."

His gaze intensified, then dropped to their entwined hands.

"And... maybe it's selfish of me, but I thought it might also be something to remember me by."

He looked up again and cocked a brow. "Selfish? You're not the sort of person one forgets, and now you're trying to haunt me in flowers. I call that greedy."

She laughed, then leaned forward and kissed his cheek. He stilled at her lips; his breath hitched. She lingered there, her lips against his skin, breathing in the scent of his musk and the forest, and then, reluctantly, she pulled away.

But he didn't let go of her hand.

"I don't want to say goodbye to you," he said, his levity gone.

"You know where to find me." She winked playfully, though her heart pattered an erratic beat.

"I do." His gaze deepened, and violet warmed the blue. "I *will* see you again." He brought her hand to his lips, eyes never leaving hers as he kissed the backs of her fingertips.

She felt his kiss all the way to her toes.

He brushed his thumb across her knuckles once, strumming every string inside of her. His gaze flickered past, to where Ricón waited, watching them, and with a final squeeze, he let go of her hand.

She wanted to grab it back.

"Ready, mi a'fiamé?" Ricón called.

She inhaled deeply to calm herself, feeling flush and also... torn.

But.

It was time.

She turned away and approached Ricón, who'd saddled up and extended a hand. Imari looked to the dawn, letting the sun warm her face.

"Yes," she said, grabbing his hand and leaping in the saddle with him. "Let's go home."

TO BE CONTINUED...

ALSO BY BARBARA KLOSS

THE GODS OF MEN SERIES

Temple of Sand

THE PANDORAN NOVELS

Gaia's Secret

The Keeper's Flame

Breath of Dragons

Heir of Pendel

ACKNOWLEDGMENTS

This story had a particularly long and winding path before it reached its final destination, and that path would've been impassible had it not been for the help of some readers who are much smarter than I am.

To "my" Jenny, for brainstorming with me in those early phases, for always demanding more, for reading a million drafts and not once complaining (like ever), and also for never hesitating to let me know when I've written myself into a stinking bog. Thanks for helping me through solutions (and also for your nurse-wisdom!), for your constant support, and for believing in this story even when I tried to ruin it!

Briana (aka Alpha B) for your unwavering enthusiasm through every stage, your sage advice, and also for being Braddok's biggest advocate. He's all yours, don't worry. See! I've formally declared it, therefore it's true.

Carly, my #1.2 and romantic guru. Thanks for having strong opinions about relationships, and for demanding more out of mine! (And also for rereading the same scene so many times that you know it better than I do. I'm sorry. Is that abuse?)

My brilliant betas, Tiana, Anthony, Julie Tuovi, Kelly St.

Clare, Sylvi, Christine Arnold, and my mom. You see all the things I don't, and I'm so glad you care enough to be honest! I can't thank you enough for all your help and insight, for helping me throw the clutter away, and for making sense of the rest.

To my friend, and editor, Laura, for having the mental capacity of a computer processor. I'll never know how you hold all the details in your head at once. But even more, I'm so thankful you ask me those hard questions that have legacy answers.

My gorgeous husband, and best friend, Ben. From day one, you've been my biggest fan and support, and I can't tell you enough how much that means to me. You find the gem, even when I hand you a turd. I love you.

To all of my readers, who have been paramount in giving me the courage to keep going on those very hard days. Your love for my stories and imaginary friends is the greatest gift an author could ask for.

And also, to *my* Maker. Thank you for always finding me where I am and never giving up on me.

ABOUT THE AUTHOR

Barbara studied biochemistry at Cal Poly, San Luis Obispo, CA, and worked for years as a clinical laboratory scientist. She was lured there by mental images of colorful bubbling liquids in glass beakers. She was deceived. Always an avid reader, especially of fantasy, she began drafting her own stories, writing worlds and characters that were never beyond saving.

She currently lives in northern California with her gorgeous husband, three kids, and pup. When she's not writing, she's usually reading, trekking through the wilderness, playing the piano, or gaming—though she doesn't consider herself a gamer. She just happens to like video games. RPGs, specifically. Though now that her kids are getting older, she's finding she has to share her PS4 more than she would like.

www.barbarakloss.com
contact@barbarakloss.com

Be sure to sign up for Barbara's email newsletter:
https://www.subscribepage.com/barbarakloss

facebook.com/barbaraklossbooks
instagram.com/barbaraklossbooks
goodreads.com/barbarakloss

Printed in Great Britain
by Amazon

61125872R00267